W9-CQY-225

"Is it as beautiful as it once was? Is the sky still blue, the clouds white? Do lightning and thunder still crash from the skies?"

"I suppose. It seemed rather plain to me," she said. "Nothing but dirt and water and smelly plants."

"But what about the animals? Do hawks still wheel through the air? Do whales still spout in the sea?"

"I don't think so. They were all used up years ago. Their genes were harvested to make people into hybrids who could populate the other planets. A small sacrifice," she adds and smiles again...

"Then I'm glad I can't go back to Earth," the old sailor mutters.

from *The Sailor Who Fell From Grace With the Void*

The Berkley SHOWCASE

Vol. 5

Edited by Victoria Schochet & Melissa Singer

NEW WRITINGS IN SCIENCE FICTION AND FANTASY

BERKLEY BOOKS, NEW YORK

Waterloo Sunset excerpt copyright © 1967 Carlin Music Corp. and
Davray Music Ltd. Published in the USA by Unichappel Music Inc.
(Right Song Music Publisher) and Mondives Music, Inc.
International Copyright secured
All Rights Reserved
Used by Permission

THE BERKLEY SHOWCASE
Volume 5

A Berkley Book / published by arrangement with
the authors

PRINTING HISTORY
Berkley edition / October 1982

All rights reserved.
Introductory and biographical notes copyright © 1982
by Victoria Schochet and Melissa Ann Singer.
Born Yesterday copyright © 1982 by George Alec Effinger.
The Care and Feeding of Earthling George copyright © 1982
by Lois Wickstrom.
A Child of Earth and Hell copyright © 1982
by Jessica Amanda Salmonson.
Amana Mañana copyright © 1982 by Freff.
The Sailor Who Fell From Grace With the Void copyright © 1982
by Karl Hansen.
New Olympus copyright © 1982 by Ronald Anthony Cross.
Encroachment copyright © 1982 by Kevin O'Donnell, Jr.
The Ninth Path copyright © 1982 by Mike Conner.
Sandy Lust copyright © 1982 by Gregory Benford.
Waterloo Sunset copyright © 1982 by David Bischoff.
Tapestry copyright © 1982 by Stephen Leigh.
This book may not be reproduced in whole or in part,
by mimeograph or any other means, without permission.
For information address: Berkley Publishing Corporation,
200 Madison Avenue, New York, New York 10016.

ISBN: 0-425-05384-9

A BERKLEY BOOK ® TM 757,375
The name "BERKLEY" and the stylized "B" with design are trademarks
belonging to Berkley Publishing Corporation.
PRINTED IN THE UNITED STATES OF AMERICA

Contents

BORN YESTERDAY

by George Alec Effinger

This is a story that really needs no explanation. What it is about is as clear as can be. In a simple, straightforward, unassuming tale, Effinger makes us see the times and places when we will all feel born yesterday; those instances when we will run up against yet more of life's surprises, be they good or bad, and realize that we are forever babes in the woods, at the mercy of all that surrounds us. Poor "Mr. Frankenberg" just got an extra-heavy dose.

It was a clear, cool, beautiful night when a call came in that a suspicious-looking man was wandering along a lonely suburban road. The stars in the sky were like the dust of broken glass left behind by a smash-and-grab thief, but the two patrolmen in their car didn't notice. They drove at moderate

1

speed, no siren, no flashing blue lights, until their headlights picked out the silhouette of a very tall man staggering along the county road. He wasn't doing anything wrong, really. He wasn't doing anything suspicious, either. Just walking. Just staggering. It was only when they pulled up next to him, before Officer Kasparian behind the steering wheel could speak, that they noticed that the suspect was over seven feet tall and had a sewn-on head. Officer Block decided to call in for advice.

"Is he doing anything?" asked a sergeant at the precinct house.

"Negative," said Officer Block. "He's just standing here in the weeds. He's just staring back at us. One of his pants legs is all wet. He's probably just a drunk or something."

"He's a big mother," murmured Officer Kasparian.

"Yeah," said Block with the microphone, "he's really big. Seven foot, easy."

The sergeant was silent for a moment. "Two things," he said at last. "I want you to look real close, and answer two things. First, is he a white boy? And second, what's he wearing?"

The cops looked at each other. They didn't have the faintest idea what the sergeant was driving at. "He's white," said Block. "And he has on a dark sweater with a sport coat over that, and a pair of dark pants, one leg wet. Nothing fits, either. The jacket's almost up to his elbows. And he has these big shoes."

"Well," said the sergeant, "for a minute I thought he was one of these basketball players, but if he's a white boy that cuts it down a whole lot. And they wouldn't be caught dead dressed like that."

"Could be Bill Walton," said Kasparian.

"Naw," said Block, "I saw him on television. He has a red beard."

"What now, sergeant?"

There was more silence. "You say he has a head that's been stitched around his neck?"

"Yeah."

"Better take him over to Mercy Lutheran and get him checked out. Got it?"

"Right," said Block. "Ten-four." He put the microphone down. Both men—and the sergeant—were relieved, because once they dropped the big mother off at the hospital he was out of their hands.

Officer Kasparian got out of the patrolcar and walked slowly toward the big man. "You have a car near here, mister? You have an accident?"

The giant only stared.

"He's not really banged up like he had an accident, you know," said Block from the car. "He's just plain ugly."

"You got any identification, mister?"

"No," said the man.

"What are you doing out here this time of night?" asked Kasparian.

"I don't know," said the man.

The police officer gestured toward the rear door of the patrolcar. "I think you'd best come with us. You feeling all right? We got a call on you, but we're not going to arrest you or nothing, so don't worry. We just been told to run you by the hospital. You can call somebody there to come pick you up."

The big man said nothing. He allowed the policeman to lead him toward the rear door. The giant got in and sat down in silence. The cop slammed the door and got back in the front seat. "Wow," he said, wiping his brow and resettling his cap. "I thought we were going to be in some trouble with that guy."

Block nodded. "Big mother," he said. They drove toward Mercy Lutheran Hospital. This time they allowed themselves the flashing blue lights, but they left off the siren in case it might agitate the giant in the back seat.

Fifteen minutes later the police officers delivered the big man to the hospital, walking him up to the counter in the emergency entrance. The hospital staff was expecting them, but the nurses behind the glass partition were still startled and upset by the giant's appearance. The cops signed him over to the security man at Mercy Lutheran, then gratefully walked out the double glass doors, back into the beautiful night.

The emergency room staff had a little trouble with the big man. "What seems to be the trouble?" asked a nurse from behind the glass.

"No trouble," said the tall man.

The nurse had just noticed that the giant's head had been stitched—rather nicely—all the way around, from larynx to the nape of the neck and back, in a perfect, neat circle. "When did that happen?" she asked. The sutures were still in the incision. It had happened very recently.

"I don't know," said the man.

The nurse had a funny, quivery feeling in her lower abdomen. Valium seemed called for; for the nurse, that is. "And you say you're not now in any pain?"

"No," said the giant.

"Well," said the nurse, adopting a false, frightened, professional attitude, "if there doesn't seem to be any immediate emergency, I hope you'll understand that we have certain procedures here. You'll have some forms to fill out, and then you'll have to wait with the others in those chairs over there. A doctor will see you in a short while."

The big man stood in a line at the other end of the emergency room's counter. A second nurse slid sheets of paper under the glass partition to the people in the line. The man got one of the forms and a pen, then went to a chair. He stared at the paper for some time. Emergency cases came into the hospital at irregular intervals: auto accidents, drug overdoses, a stabbing, an ancient woman with a failing heart. The huge man sat in his chair for half an hour. An hour passed, an hour and a half. At last the nurse happened by and saw the giant staring at the paper.

"What's wrong?" asked the nurse.

"I have to give this back to you," said the man.

"Well?"

The man gave the paper to the nurse. Not a single question had been answered. "Why haven't you filled in the blanks here?" asked the nurse. "We can't even start to help you unless we have this information. And we have to have your medical history, you know, and your insurance data and all of that. We want to help, but you have to fill out this form. How long have you been sitting out here? Almost two hours, right? You could have gone home by now."

"Home?" asked the giant.

"Oh, Lord," murmured the nurse. "What's your name?"

"Name?"

The nurse chewed her lower lip thoughtfully. "Just a second," she said, and she took the paper and disappeared into a maze of curtained observation areas. She came back in a few moments with a doctor and an intern, neither of whom were in a very happy mood. "See?" said the nurse.

The doctor made a cursory examination of the sutures on the big man's neck. "Boy, is this going to leave a scar," he said. "No pain?"

"No," said the giant.

"No nausea, no vomiting?"

"No."

"Headache, dryness of the mouth, blurred vision?"

"I have a kind of ringing in my ears," said the big man.

"He doesn't know who he is or where he lives," said the nurse.

"Ah," said the doctor. "Is this usually the case with you, or is this a special situation?"

"I don't remember," said the giant.

"Right," said the doctor. "We'll fill out your form later." He turned to the nurse. "Start a John Doe file on him. I'll want to give him a quick examination. Get him in a gown. And then I want him up on Seven East." That was the psychiatric ward. "Put him in the isolation room. All the admitting forms will have to go hang until morning. Let the day shift nurses worry about them."

"Thank you, doctor," said the nurse. She, like the police, seemed overwhelmingly happy to have the responsibility for the big man removed from her shoulders.

"Don't thank me, nurse," said the doctor with a distasteful expression. "After I examine him, I want him shot full of Thorazine. Before he strangles somebody."

"He doesn't seem dangerous," objected the intern diffidently.

"Look at these sutures," said the doctor. "Learn something. In order to do a job like this, whatever it was, someone obviously sedated the hell out of this guy. When that wears off, look out."

"I see what you mean," said the intern, turning pale. Half an hour later the giant was secured in a bare room with a locked door. It was decided by the staff on Seven East to tie him down to the bed. He was, as ordered, also shot full of Thorazine. It was the hospital's policy, especially late at night, to shoot full first and ask questions afterward. Understaffed in the early morning hours, the emergency room and seventh floor crews agreed that the best thing was to hold the big mother where he could do no harm, until the full day staff arrived for work. They'd have a nice surprise to start the day.

The day nurses were not happy, either, at the sight of the gigantic, unknown man in the isolation room. No one entered the room, although hospital procedures called for nurses to check on the big man regularly. There was a small window reinforced with wire set in the locked door, and every hour a nurse would look in. As far as the nurses were concerned, they couldn't care less about his temperature or blood pressure. They waited for the physicians to make their rounds.

About two o'clock in the afternoon, a staff psychiatrist entered the isolation room. The big man was lying on the bed, his arms and legs strapped down so that he could barely move. "Hello," said the doctor, "my name is Dr. Kinsel. You have a pretty shallow file." He held up the file the hospital had begun on the giant. There was no information at all beyond the police report and the write-up from the emergency room. "How are you feeling today?"

"Fine," said the grotesque man on the bed.

"Do you remember anything about yesterday?"

"Just being put in the car by the police and being brought here," said the giant.

"Nothing before that?" The doctor's voice was low and friendly in tone.

"No."

"Still can't remember your name?"

"No, I'm sorry," said the man.

"No personal belongings on you when you were checked in," said the doctor thoughtfully. "Do you think we could remove these restraints?"

"Yes," said the giant, "I'd appreciate that a lot."

"Do you mind if I examine you a little?" asked the doctor.

"Nope," said the man.

The psychiatrist tested the big man's reflexes, gazed into his eyes, ran a sharp object up the man's arms, legs, back, chest, and on the soles of his feet, had the giant attempt some dexterity and balance tests, and went through other miscellaneous procedures. There was nothing noteworthy except that the psychiatrist was personally repelled when he saw, after raising the big man's gown, that the head wasn't the only part that seemed to have been artificially attached. Both arms seemed to have been stitched on at the shoulders, and both legs at the hips. There were similarly sutured incisions at the ankles, where the feet appeared to have been added—they didn't precisely match; one was at least three sizes larger than the other. The hands looked like they always belonged on the arms, however. The doctor shuddered.

"Let me call a nurse." The doctor pushed the call button. A nurse at the station down the hall answered on the intercom; the doctor asked her to bring two prepared medications. "I'm going to give you a capsule and an injection," said the doctor. "They will probably make you a little drowsy. Do you understand?"

"Fine," said the giant. "You're the doctor."

The nurse arrived and gave the man the capsule and the injection. The doctor watched thoughtfully, looking with intense curiosity at the red sutured wound around the man's neck. "Did they put his clothing in the closet when he came in here last night?"

"No, doctor," said the nurse. "It's checked in down the hall."

"Get it," said the doctor. The nurse went out and came back in a short while with the clothes. The doctor went through all the pockets, but found nothing. There was a label inside the sport coat, however. It said:

> *This garment was designed*
> *and tailored exclusively for*
> Victor Frankenstein

"Well," said the doctor, "now we know who you are. Nurse, get that on his record. Help me loosen the restraints. That injection has hit him by now." The doctor and nurse removed the strong bonds that held the giant to the bed.

"Thank you," said the man.

"You're welcome, Mr. Frankenstein," said the doctor. The giant's expression remained blank. "Do you recognize the name at all?"

"No," said the huge man. "Should I?" He stifled a yawn.

"It might not be his jacket, after all, doctor," said the nurse.

"Still," said the doctor. He didn't know what he meant by that. "You probably feel like taking a nap now. I'll look in on you again later."

"Thank you, doctor," said the giant.

No, in truth the sport coat did not belong to the big mother, and his name was not Frankenstein. Which is just as well, because the nurse spelled that name wrong on the giant's chart.

He slept most of that afternoon and evening, and ate some clear broth and a little lemon Jell-O. The nurses dosed him regularly with a strong sedative, and gradually they lost their fear and repulsion. They took his temperature, but not one of them yet had the nerve to feel his pulse or take his blood pressure. The next day the staff doctors gave the big man a battery of tests, psychological and physical, and they were puzzled by the results. The monstrous, ill-shaped man in the bed seemed to be almost perfectly normal in most respects. They could find nothing amiss with his psyche other than a complete absence of memory. And even that wasn't a typical form of amnesia. He hadn't merely blotted out part of his identity. He was truly innocent, as uninformed about much of life as he was about the details of his own identity.

On the third day, before lunch, the door to the isolation room opened and a young woman came in. She was wearing the usual white coat and white slacks, but without a nurse's cap or a stethoscope to indicate that she was some kind of medical practitioner. She was not. She was from the hospital's accounting office. She had blonde hair piled high on her head and sprayed until it stayed there against the will of gravity. She wore a fuzzy pink sweater under her white lab coat, and she chewed gum while she talked to the giant. "Mr. Frankenberg?" she said.

The man in the bed looked up. The young woman's visit had been timed by the psychiatric ward's staff to coincide with the patient's most docile period, according to the schedule of his medications.

"Mr. Frankenberg? My name is Miss Meadow? Of the Accounting Office?" She spoke many of her sentences as though they were questions. Her intent was to catch any mistakes or confusions in her conversation as quickly as possible. The effect, however, was that Miss Meadow herself seemed mistaken and confused in at least eight out of her every ten statements.

"Please come in," said the giant.

"Thank you. We have some questions to ask you about the payment of your account? Are you covered by hospitalization? Blue Cross?"

"I don't know," said the big man. "I don't think so."

Miss Meadow frowned and wrote that information on a form she had trapped on a clipboard. "You do realize then that upon being released from Mercy Lutheran, you or another responsible adult will have to sign a promissory note stating that your account will be paid in full within ninety days. You will not be able to be released without signing this note. Do you understand?"

"Yes," said the man. He didn't understand at all, but nurses and doctors seemed so pleased when he tried to appear helpful.

"May I have your home address and telephone number, please?"

He made no reply.

Miss Meadow hit her forehead with the palm of her hand and laughed. "Boy, am I dumb!" she said. "That's your whole problem, isn't it?"

"In a nutshell," said the giant.

"Then the address and phone number of a relative? A friend, maybe?"

Again, there was no answer.

"Could I have your Social Security number, please? No, you wouldn't know that, either." Miss Meadow read through the form quickly, searching for a question or two that might elicit some positive response. She found none. "Mr. Frankenberg? I think what I'm going to do is turn your file over to the Social Services Department? They'll get in touch with a case worker who'll be able to help you out. This is over my head, you know what I mean? I think we're going to have to work this out together, okay?"

"That will be just fine," said the drowsy monster.

"I guess I'll be going? You'll be hearing from Social Services this afternoon or tomorrow morning. They'll know just what to do. They handle things like this all the time. Don't worry about it, okay?"

The big man was not worried. The doctors and the nurses on Seven East did not want him to be worried, and the capsules and the injections were successful in preventing any anxiety whatever. The capsules and injections made the giant forget all about Miss Meadow even before she left his room. Of course, that was due in part to Miss Meadow herself. She often had that effect on people without any psychological disturbance at all, and who were not sedated by anything other than her own conversation.

An hour after Miss Meadow left the isolation room, the medical staff decided that the big man presented no immediate problem and ought to be released soon. The results of the tests had been analyzed again and again, yet they still indicated only that he was average, possibly above average in intelligence, gentle, friendly, and almost clear of neurotic tendencies. There was no medically pressing reason for him to be hospitalized any longer, and in preparation for his discharge he was moved out of the isolation room and onto a ward; the capsules and injections kept coming at regular intervals, however. Everyone on the ward got the capsules and injections. The only disconcerting thing about the giant—in addition to his appearance, of course—was his total lack of memory and his apparent unfamiliarity with the more sophisticated ways of the world.

On the morning of the day he was to be released from Mercy Lutheran, a representative from the Social Services Department came to see him. Her name was Mrs. Violet Perry. She was tall and too thin, not yet middle-aged but clearly hurrying in that direction. She wore her short brown hair parted carelessly on the side. Her glasses were too large and made her face look like a droll ceramic mug that one kept pencils in. She was the most beautiful woman the giant had ever seen; of course, he had only ever seen eight, all in the hospital.

"Mr. Frankenberg?" she said. She seated herself in a chair beside his bed. She had witnessed, had talked to many people in disturbing physical conditions in her job. She had had to talk money matters with the families of people who were on the verge of death. She had had to make decisions affecting the entire future lives of people whose health, happiness, and purpose for existence had all been destroyed. She had had to make such a decision about the big mother. She waited until her pulse slowed and her dry mouth returned to normal before speaking again. "Mr. Frankenberg," she said, "Dr. Kinsel has decided that there is no reason to keep you here any longer. But the entire staff agreed that it would be a bad idea to just let you walk out onto the street. You are obviously still in need of some kind of care, but we here at Mercy Lutheran are just not set up to provide that. Do you understand me so far?"

The giant nodded. The motion drew Mrs. Perry's attention to his sutured neck. She made a little gasp, then closed her eyes until she was able to continue. "Now, these things are decided by people who know much more about your welfare and your problems than you do. Everyone's trying to help but, to tell the truth, Mr. Frankenberg, you're one of these cases that seems to fall in between categories. We're all genuinely concerned, but we're limited in our options."

"Please don't apologize," said the giant.

Mrs. Perry drew another deep breath. The man was so, well, so *deformed,* but he was evidently very understanding. In fact, he was doing more to make *her* feel comfortable than she was doing for him, and that was her job. Mrs. Perry decided that the monster wasn't really deformed, by a strict definition. He just showed the results of quite a bit of sophisticated surgery. His face, almost always expressionless, was virtually dead, but that was something one might grow used to. The incisions around the neck and joints wouldn't be as noticeable once the sutures were removed. The scars would fade and in a little while perhaps he might be able to walk along a sunny sidewalk somewhere without generating terror. He might learn to make jokes about his height, about his huge chest and immense feet, about the powerful arms and the head that had been stuck on like that of a broken dolly. Mr. Frankenberg seemed to be a good and sweet man, and it was a shame that he had had to go through so much pain. Thank God he couldn't remember it, thought Mrs. Perry.

"May I ask your name?" said the big man.

Mrs. Perry was stunned. She hadn't realized that she was just sitting beside his bed quietly, thinking. She gathered herself together. "I'm sorry," she said. "My name is Mrs. Perry. Now, uh, let me check your file." Three more pages had been added to the chart, although they were like the previous pages, mostly blank, except for Dr. Kinsel's recommendations. "Dr. Kinsel has suggested that you be committed to the Hanson State Hospital for the Mentally Disabled. That's over on Huron Street, you know. They have programs for people in your position. You're not really mentally disabled in the usual sense. That is, you're surely not mentally retarded or suffering from some other disability that would render you unable to care for yourself in the outside world. Still, you very definitely have what must be termed a mental disorder. Now, Mr. Frankenberg, in order to have you committed to this facility, we must have the signature of a relative or guardian. We have looked up the name of Victor Frankenberg in the telephone directory, and there is none listed. There are no records of any such person; neither the city nor the state could help us locate you, and both city and state have tremendous cross-referenced computer resources. You're a difficult riddle for us, Mr. Frankenberg."

"I don't mean to be," said the big mother. "Do you know,

Mrs. Perry, that you are the loveliest person I have ever met?"

Mrs. Perry's eyes narrowed. She felt a flush of anger, but when she saw the ingenuous expression on the man's face, when she heard the words again in her mind, when she recalled his tone, she realized that he was being soberly honest with her. The anger disappeared immediately. The feeling that replaced it made Mrs. Perry want to weep. "Yes, yes," she said distractedly, "but the signature, Mr. Frankenberg. Without a relative or a guardian, you will have to sign this release form yourself."

"Mrs. Perry," said the giant, "I am on a psychiatric ward. This form will permit me to be turned over to a state program for the mentally disabled. What possible worth could my signature have?"

"I don't know, I don't know," said Mrs. Violet Perry mournfully. She did know, however, that it would save Mercy Lutheran the trouble of obtaining a court order. She hadn't felt so miserable in a very long time.

"I will sign," said the monster. He took the form from her and the pen. "What is my name?" he asked.

"Frankenberg," said Mrs. Perry. "Victor Frankenberg. Do you know how to write?"

"Yes," said the man. He signed the form and gave it back to the woman. "Please don't leave me now," he said. When she heard that, Mrs. Perry could not stop the tears from running down her cheeks. She stood. The hideous man on the bed looked up at her. "I'm very sorry, Mrs. Perry," he said.

The woman's feelings were in total confusion. The monster—no, he wasn't a monster, he was a disfigured man, she decided with finality. The man was intelligent. His comment about the validity of his signature demonstrated the quickness of his mind. He was concerned for her feelings, something that was for Violet Perry a rare occurrence in the world. Yet he was being shuffled between institutions like a consignment of clean linen, represented by a thin file of largely insufficient data.

The giant's clothing did not go with him when he left the hospital. He traveled to the state facility in hospital-issue green pajamas, cardboard slippers, and a thin robe. Mrs. Perry rode in the van with him, although technically that was not at all her responsibility. "I'd like to make sure that you get settled all right," she said, still unable to untangle the knot of her own emotions.

"That is so good of you," said the big man.

"Not at all," said Mrs. Perry. She patted one of his hands, conscious of how gnarled his knuckles were. His physical appearance no longer disturbed her quite so much as before. She wondered where his family was, if he had friends nearby, if he were perhaps married. When they arrived at the state hospital, Mrs. Perry rode through the side gate in the van; it was the first time she had approached the building in the same way that the mental patients did. It was like entering a military compound or a jail. Mrs. Perry had thought in her youth that all institutions were basically indistinguishable in many respects: hospitals, prisons, army bases, schools, abbeys, asylums. Those thoughts belonged to her dead days of doubt and wonder, and the resurrection of the idea thrilled her for a moment. Then the dun color of the building and the flat black of the iron grillwork over the doors and windows dismayed her. There were beads of raindrops on everything, and a cold mist in the yard as the attendants led the big mother into the hospital. Mrs. Perry followed behind, herself lost, useless. Immediately inside, it was made clear that she was not welcome. She signed two more papers that would be put into the giant's file, then turned to him. "Goodbye," she said. She felt a great emptiness inside her where something, she didn't know what, had just been hurt.

"Goodbye, Mrs. Perry," said the big man. "Thank everyone back at Mercy Lutheran for me."

"I will," she said. She didn't know what else to say. One of the two attendants helped the giant into a wheelchair. The second man shook his head in amazement. Mrs. Perry looked after him for a moment as he was wheeled away. Then she turned and went back outside to the van. She felt unreasonably upset on the drive back to Mercy Lutheran. When she got back to work, she announced that she wasn't feeling well and that she was going home. She left the hospital, drove to her apartment, took a largish dose of Equanil, and sleepily watched afternoon game shows on television.

The monster, meanwhile, had been given a semi-private room at the Hanson State Hospital for the Mentally Disabled. The accommodations were only temporary, of course. A doctor arrived almost immediately to check the giant's chart and order the first injection of Thorazine of the afternoon. Soon a nurse came to give the shot. "Ugly bastard," she murmured. She couldn't control an involuntary exclamation when she saw how the parts of his body had evidently been fitted together.

Nothing more happened that day, although at dinner that night the big man experienced a new emotion: annoyance. He was given food that he couldn't identify, and the attendants were equally unable to tell him what kind of meat he was eating. It tasted like newsprint marinated in a night's rain. He was very hungry, having missed a meal in transit. An injection and a capsule, however, made all the annoyance go away, just like that.

The giant shared a room with a man named Wallace Mendes, who was classed as a chronic psychotic. Mendes paid no attention to his own appearance or personal hygiene. He could be made to shave and bathe, but only after he was medicated and with a great deal of trouble. Generally the overworked staff didn't take the trouble, so Wallace Mendes remained unshaven and unclean. His hair was matted down and his eyes were red and wet. He wasn't dangerous; not in the hospital, not with the kind of sedatives ordered by the staff doctors. Mendes' medication was much stronger than what the big man was getting. Mendes was beyond rehabilitation. He was being locked away, kept apart from normal people, imprisoned in a sense. The giant thought nothing about Mendes. He didn't see any reason why Mendes shouldn't be receiving exactly the treatment the hospital was giving him. The only thing that began to puzzle the ugly bastard was why he and Mendes were put together in the same hospital. What did they have in common?

The big man learned more two days later. The Chief of Staff, Dr. Weber, came to see him. "Hello, Mr. Frankenbaum," said the doctor, who was escorted by two other doctors and a nurse. It was like a convoy, with the smaller doctors present to keep the sometimes troublesome patients from harrying the battleship Chief of Staff.

"Hello," said the giant.

"My name is Dr. Weber. I'm in charge of this hospital, and I thought we should get to know each other. I think we should give serious consideration to you, to your problem, and to what we're going to do to help you. Do you mind if I sit down?"

The man waved a hand politely to the chair beside his bed. Dr. Weber sat, and the two attendant doctors and the nurse moved forward as well, in formation.

"Do you mind if I smoke?" asked Dr. Weber, taking out a pipe and tobacco pouch.

"I'd rather you didn't," said the giant.

Dr. Weber shrugged and replaced both pipe and pouch. There was a gurgling groan from the other side of the room, beyond the curtain separating the beds. No one paid any attention. It was a familiar sound. "Mr. Frankenbaum," said Dr. Weber in a kind of low, conspiratorial whisper, "surely you realize that you are not in the same kind of state as poor Mr. Mendes, or as most of our other patients."

"I agree," said the ugly bastard. "It's only my memory."

"Well," said the Chief of Staff, tapping the giant's medical records with his fingers, "it does go slightly beyond that, but essentially that's true. Now, though, that *must* be reconciled with our position. We did not ask to have you sent here. We are happy to have you, and you will receive the best of care while you're with us. But we have limited resources, Mr. Frankenbaum. This is a state hospital, and the state legislature has cut our operating budget for this fiscal year in an absurd and unrealistic way. The previous Chief of Staff protested a little too strongly, and so now I find myself as the new head of this hospital. A new broom, in a manner of speaking, with a heavy responsibility both to our patients and the state's taxpayers. Everything that happens in this hospital is my responsibility. So, therefore, I want to be certain that everything that goes on is in the best interests of the greatest number of people. Do you follow me?"

"Of course," said the huge, disfigured man. "You have a job to do."

Dr. Weber smiled, as though the man in the bed were an exceptionally handicapped child who had just responded to the sound of his own name. "Good, good," he said, nodding. The other two doctors and the nurse nodded, too, and smiled pleasantly. "Then you will understand why I have come to the decision that you would be better off in a work-release program of out-patient care, which would also have the effect of freeing this bed for someone more in need. Someone in as much permanent difficulty as Mr. Mendes, for example."

"I see your point, of course," said the man, "but I'll need

help. I don't have anywhere to go. I wouldn't know what to
do."

"Ah," said the nurse, "don't fret about that. We have per-
sonnel specially trained just to place patients in non-threatening
situations. You'll adjust to daily, normal life in no time."

"I appreciate everything you people are doing for me," said
the giant. "I'm sorry to take up your time when you have more
important things to worry about."

"Oh, Mr. Frankenbaum," said the nurse, "each member of
our family here is equally important to us."

"Well," said the Chief of Staff, standing and taking out his
pipe, "it was very nice meeting you, Mr. Frankenbaum. Have
a good day. We'll have a case worker tracking down just the
right place for you, and we'll also make sure you're taken care
of even after you leave our hospital. The doctors have created
a personal drug profile for you, and with proper medication,
proper guidance, and some honest effort on your part, Mr.
Frankenbaum, you'll be able to begin your life all over again.
There isn't a reason in the world why you can't be just like
everyone else in just a short time. You'll be indistinguishable
from all the people on your street."

"I don't know who I am," said the ugly bastard sadly. "I
don't know any other people. I don't know how to do anything.
I don't belong anywhere. I have a body put together with nylon
wire."

There was silence for a moment. Dr. Weber filled his pipe
but didn't light it. "Don't worry," said the Chief of Staff after
a few awkward seconds, "we'll add a mood elevator to your
medication. It will all look better to you by dinnertime." Dr.
Weber looked at the man, decided not to shake hands with
him, turned, and left the room. The other two doctors and the
nurse sailed along behind him.

Outside the room Dr. Weber took out a pen and wrote a
note in the chart of Victor Frankenbaum: "Hospital cannot
keep. No family. Return to social worker for placement."

The social worker, a young, serious man named Moreland,
came to see the huge man in the evening, while the big mother
was in the television room watching a nature program. Moreland stood several feet behind the giant, staring at the livid scar
that circled the man's neck. Moreland hurried out of the television room and back toward the nurses' station. He stood in
the hall for a few minutes, pretending that he was studying his

forms and notes. He waited until the irrational fear subsided. Finally, under control, he walked back to interview Mr. Frankenbaum.

"Sir?" he said, trying to get the big man's attention.

"Yes?"

Moreland was heartened. The monster seemed peaceful enough now. "I've come to discuss your transfer to the work-release program."

"Would you like to talk here?" asked the giant. "Or would you be more comfortable in my room?"

"This is fine. We're very proud of our program, you know. We're getting a lot of people back into normal life, instead of taking up bed space in a hospital when they don't really need to. Our program has had a very high degree of success since we started it under Dr. Weber's supervision. Only about twenty-five percent of our people end up returning to the hospital."

"That's certainly something to be proud of," said the ugly man.

"What we'll do, you see, is give you a job in the neighborhood in one of our rehabilitation centers. You will also be offered a low-rent apartment nearby. Your rent for the first two weeks will be deducted from your first paycheck, and thereafter a regular deduction will be made for rent and maintenance, leaving you with a respectable amount that will allow you to live moderately well. In time, perhaps six months, you will be discharged from the work-release program, and we'll help you find a higher-paying job in the competitive market. You will be entitled to keep your apartment beyond that time, subject to approval by the program's evaluation staff, and as long as you are steadily employed. We're trying to ease you back slowly into the real world."

"Everyone is so kind to me," said the big man. "I can't tell you how important and wonderful that is."

"No need," said Moreland. "It's all part of our in-patient/out-patient continuing package of care designed by Dr. Weber. When you leave here, you won't be getting the injections any longer. But I'm sure the doctors have drawn up some kind of optimum medical program."

"Yes. They've already mentioned something about that."

"Well, then, Mr. Frankenbaum, is there anything else? Any questions?"

"No, I can't think of anything."

"Will you be ready in the morning? We'll drop by your new apartment first, and then we'll drive you over to introduce you to your new employer. There's no reason why we should delay the program."

"I don't have any money," said the monster. "Until I get paid, how will I get around? How will I eat?"

"Family?" asked Moreland. "No. I see here that you're alone. Friends?"

"My memory. I know nothing about where I came from. I have no memory."

Moreland smiled, embarrassed. "That's right. I forgot. You don't know anyone?"

"I know a Mrs. Perry from Mercy Lutheran."

"Would she take charge of you?"

"No," said the giant.

Moreland chewed his lip in thought. "Don't worry," he said, "we'll work something out here. A loan, deducted with your rent from your first or second paycheck. Don't worry."

"I won't," said the man.

"Good," said Moreland. "It was nice meeting you. I or someone else from my department will see you in the morning."

"I'm very grateful," said the big mother.

Moreland left. On the way back down the tiled hall he couldn't suppress a gasp and a shudder.

In the morning the huge man was awakened by a nurse with his final injection. "Last one, Mr. Frankenbaum!" she said. It was impossible how cheerful that nurse could be at seven o'clock in the morning. "Just after the shift change, after you eat breakfast," she said, "someone will come in with the release papers and your prescriptions. You brought no clothing with you, is that right?"

"Do I get to keep the robe and pajamas?" asked the man.

"I don't think so," said the nurse. "But I believe Mr. Moreland said yesterday that you will receive an advance to pay for some clothing and personal articles."

"What kind of job will I have? I'm not able to do anything, and I'm afraid of what people will think when they see me."

"Why, whatever do you mean, Mr. Frankenbaum?" she said. The nurse knew *exactly* what he meant.

"Oh, they'll want to know why my head and arms were

sewn on, and why I can't remember anything about it. I hope it's not too difficult a job."

"Don't worry. They'll just give you some dumb little thing that you won't even have to think about. Remember, you're mentally disabled, or you wouldn't be in this hospital."

"I'm not mentally disabled, or I wouldn't be getting out," he said.

The nurse had a reply to that, but she kept silent. Instead, she punctured his hip with the syringe, a kind of goodbye stab. The scars where his head, arms, and feet had been sewn on were already losing their bright, shocking color, she noticed.

Moreland evidently couldn't bring himself to take charge of the giant himself. About ten o'clock a timid young woman named Molly Calhoun came into the room with a small zippered case. "Mr. Frankenbaum?" she said. She uttered an audible cry when she saw his face and scarred throat. She put a hand to her mouth and took two deep breaths. "I've brought your clothes. Please, change clothes, and then we'll sign you out of the hospital. I'll be right outside. There is a razor and shaving cream, soap, a toothbrush and toothpaste, a comb and brush in there, too. Take your time, Mr. Frankenbaum."

The man got up and went to the bathroom. He took a shower and examined his fabricated body. He disliked looking at it. It made him feel precisely the same way as it made everyone else feel. He shaved and dressed and combed his coarse black hair. Then he opened the door, and Molly Calhoun came back in. She seemed a bit calmer. Now that he was dressed, he seemed virtually normal. He was seven feet tall, of course, and gruesomely ugly, but Moreland or whoever had picked out the clothing had wisely chosen a huge turtleneck sweater to cover the incision at the base of his neck. "Ready?" she said.

"I want to say goodbye to Mr. Mendes."

"Okay."

The huge man walked around the curtained separation, the first time he had faced Mr. Mendes. He had listened to the man's noises and cries for hours on end. "Goodbye, sir," said the giant. "I truly hope you improve." There was a mild, druggy scream from Mr. Mendes, and then the big man came back and took a clipboard from Molly Calhoun. "I sign these?" he asked.

"Yes," she said. "Three places, where the Xs are."

He signed the papers and she took back the clipboard. She led him from the room without grasping his arm, as she would normally feel obliged to do. There was a wheelchair for him to ride in outside the room. He sat in it and she pushed him along. None of the nurses said anything to him as he passed their station. They stared at him as he rode by.

They left the wheelchair inside the hospital's lobby and walked out the front doors. Outside, the day was cool and clear. The air smelled good to him after days of hospital disinfectant. They went around to the parking lot, where Molly Calhoun helped him into her small blue Dodge. He had to sit diagonally on the seat in order to be comfortable. They did not speak as she started the engine and drove away from the state hospital. She headed up a busy avenue for about twenty blocks, into an older, decaying, racially mixed neighborhood. She stopped outside a tenement. "Your new home," she said.

"My first home," he said.

Together they went up the stoop. The inner lobby of the apartment building had no security door. It smelled of urine. Molly Calhoun checked the tag on the set of keys and showed the ugly bastard how to open his mailbox. "That's good," she said, when he succeeded in turning the small key with his huge, clumsy hand.

"Who will be sending me mail?" he asked.

"Oh," said Molly Calhoun, "lots of people. It's almost Christmas. You'll have tons of catalogs and lots of junk mail to look through."

"It will make me happy to see mail in there for me," said the big man. The case worker only looked at him with a pensive expression.

"Let's go upstairs," she said.

"You know," said the giant, "those stairs outside were the first ones I've ever climbed. I think I did rather well."

"Yes, of course," said Molly Calhoun. She was stunned. His first stairs? She wondered what kind of assignment she had on her hands this time. Dealing with illiterates was difficult enough, or people who spoke no recognizable language. But even they knew how to climb stairs and open mailboxes. It was as if she had been given charge of a small child who was just beginning to form his own personality.

The apartment was dreadful. It was small, dark, old, in poor condition, smelled terrible, and decorated in a depressing manner that only emphasized the poverty of its occupant. "It was nicer in the hospital," said the big man.

"Well, the state pays for that," said Molly Calhoun. She didn't know what else to say. She disliked the apartment intensely. She was ashamed of having to make the man live in it. She was leery of touching anything. Even the brown-stained wallpaper seemed laden with disease.

"The state's paying for this, too, isn't it?"

"Only indirectly," said Molly Calhoun. "The state pays for a lot of things only indirectly, so those things pretty much have to look after themselves."

"I will be comfortable here," said the big mother.

"You will?" said Molly Calhoun. "I mean, that's good, Mr. Frankenbaum. With your first money, why, you can buy some pictures for the walls and some flowers and books and make the place seem very nice."

"I will. I'm happy just to have a home. I'm beginning to become a whole person."

The case worker looked around the apartment once more. It consisted of one large room that would be living room, bedroom, and dining area all in one, with a small bathroom with ancient, broken tiled walls and floor, and a tiny kitchen. Situated beneath the stove and oven, the refrigerator wasn't even waist-high. The freezer inside was so small that Mr. Frankenbaum would have the option of keeping something frozen in it or having ice cubes, but not both at the same time. The cockroach situation was out of control. The mustiness of the main room might be alleviated if the three front windows were opened, but Molly Calhoun wasn't strong enough to do that job. The furniture that the state provided was old, shabby, mismatched, and uncomfortable. There were no light bulbs in the lamps or ceiling lights. The floor—even in the living area— was covered with badly scarred linoleum of a strange purple floral design. Painted wallpaper hung in strips and patches in the corners of all the rooms.

"Well," said Molly Calhoun, clapping her hands, "time to go. Time to put you to work."

"I'm looking forward to that, also," said the giant. The young woman wondered if his enthusiasm was an attempt to mock her, if it was genuine, if it was drug-induced, or if the big mother was just plain stupid. She let him practice some more with the keys, locking the door as they left. He started to give them back to her, but she shook her head. The giant smiled suddenly and put the keys in his pocket.

The job was washing bottles and equipment in a neighborhood clinic operated by the same hospital from which the big man had just been discharged. He was happy about that, because it gave a kind of continuity to his new life.

"Mr. Frankenbaum," said Molly Calhoun, "I'd like you to meet your new boss, Mr. Sokol. He will take over now. Remember, if you need anything, you can get in touch with our office on Huron Street. But try to handle as much as you can by yourself. We'll be glad to help in case of emergency, but it's best that you try to get along on your own now. The sooner you become completely independent, the happier you will be."

"Miss Calhoun," said the ugly man, "I will never forget that you were the person who took me out of the hospital and established me in the outside world. I owe you everything, Miss Calhoun. I owe you everything that I will ever be or have."

Molly Calhoun was extremely embarrassed by his speech. "Thank you," she said, "but I didn't do anything special. I was glad to help."

"Through as much pain and suffering as I have endured," said the man, holding up one huge hand and placing it softly on his throat, "it has been the blessing of kind people that has made it all bearable."

"Thank you, Mr. Frankenbaum," whispered Molly Calhoun. "I have to go now."

"Goodbye, Miss Calhoun," said the big man.

The case worker left, and Mr. Sokol tapped the monster's arm. "Come with me to my office," he said, "and we'll take care of the paperwork."

"Yes, sir," said the man. He followed Sokol quietly, shortening his footsteps to stay just behind his new employer.

"Much work experience?" asked Sokol over his shoulder. He didn't seem to be affected at all by the big mother's appearance. Of course, the scars were covered and he was dressed to look like any other grotesquely powerful giant. Perhaps Sokol had had previous encounters with other men well over seven feet tall, nearly four hundred pounds, with shoulders three feet across. Perhaps Sokol was the kind of man who didn't like to display his thoughts and feelings. Perhaps he truly had none.

"No," said the ugly bastard. "No experience at all. Of any kind."

Sokol shook his head. His employees were almost exclusively former patients referred from Hanson State Hospital. He sometimes sighed when he thought about the kind of workers he had to put up with. Loonies and semi-loonies, according to Sokol. According to Sokol, there was no such thing as a "former" loony.

They went into the office. Sokol sat behind his desk, opened a drawer, and took out some sheets of paper. He stuck a remnant of unlit cigar in his mouth.

The giant couldn't sit back in the molded plastic chair provided for him. He was too big, so he had to perch on its edge.

"Let's see," said Sokol, taking the cigar out of his mouth and putting it back on his blotter, "I got your name." He looked up. "First name is Victor, right?"

"Yes, sir."

Sokol wrote *Victor Friedbaum* in the space at the top of the form. "Address?"

The big mother took out the ring of keys he had gotten from Molly Calhoun. The address was on a cardboard tag. "154 W. Garfield Street, Apartment 309."

"Phone number?"

"Pardon me?"

"Do you have a telephone?"

"No," said the man, "I'm sure that I don't."

"Age?"

There was a pause. "I don't know," said the ugly man.

Sokol looked up again. He opened his mouth to say something, but didn't. He skipped that question, then went back and put in an estimate of *30*. "Sex we can agree on," he said, writing in *M*. "Social Security number?"

"I don't have one of those, either."

Sokol was growing irritated. "If you don't have a Social Security card, fella, you can't pay taxes. And if you don't pay taxes, you're not going to get a job. Not here, not nowhere. So you damn well better *get* yourself a Social Security number. Tomorrow. Early. I'll let you work today anyhow, but I've never heard of anything so crazy. How have you gotten this far without it?"

The giant looked unhappy. "Just lucky, I guess," he said.

Sokol scowled. "Yeah, right," he said. He went on down

the form, filling in the job description and pay scale information. "Parents' names? Mother's maiden name?"

The big man said nothing. Sokol said nothing.

There were more lines on the forms to fill out, but Sokol learned nothing more from the ugly bastard. All he knew was that the huge man's name was Victor Friedbaum and he looked to be about thirty years old. He wouldn't even want to swear to that information. "Okay," he said in a weary voice, "I'll put you to work cleaning up with the two Spanish kids. But I'm warning you, you won't get paid until we send in the W-2 form, and we're not doing that until we get you a Social Security number. Got that?"

"Yes, sir. Right. I understand. Tomorrow morning."

"Fine. Now just go out, turn right, go down to the end of the hall. There's a big room there. You'll see two guys sitting around looking at magazines. That's Hermano and Juan. You tell them I told you to tell them to show you how to help them clean up. You got that? You'll be cleaning clinic glassware and stuff. Do you think you can manage that?"

"Will they give me instructions?"

Sokol snorted. "They'll tell you what to do, all right. And remember. Tomorrow. After you take care of your card, you report to me and we'll finish up these forms." Sokol scooped up the papers and threw them back in the drawer. "And I'm supposed to advance you seventy dollars." Sokol took out a large checkbook with triple rows of perforated checks on each page. He wrote out a check to Victor Friedbaum for seventy dollars and handed it to the giant.

"What's this?" asked the big man.

"A check."

"What do I do with it?"

Sokol chose to answer the question with tact. "You cash it. At a bank. Where do you have an account?"

"I don't."

"You ought to. But it figures. You don't have a Social Security number. You don't have a bank account. What are you, an immigrant?"

The misshapen creature stared for a moment. "I don't know," he said at last.

At that answer, Sokol threw up his hands. He had no idea what kind of person he was dealing with. He decided that the best thing was not to deal with him at all, to put him to work and forget about him. "I'll get it cashed at the clinic's accounting desk. You can pick up your money here sometime this afternoon. Just sign the back of it for me."

The giant did so. "Thank you," he said, smiling warmly. "You are as good as Mrs. Perry and Miss Calhoun."

"No, I'm not," said Sokol sourly. "You'll see."

"I'll get to work now," said the big man. He stood and turned to go.

"I'll check on you later," said Sokol. "And watch out for Hermano. Sometimes he gets a little, well, crazy. Don't ever ask him about his wife, got that?"

"Yes, sir," said the ugly man. He left the room.

"That is one dumb guy," muttered Sokol. He guessed that the giant could handle himself, against *both* Hermano and Juan, if he needed to. But Sokol also got the idea that the man was somehow completely passive and gentle. Sokol shrugged.

The job was just as the nurse had predicted: the big man never had any difficulty understanding what was expected of him, although his dexterity was limited and he dropped things often, particularly if they were still hot and damp. The two co-workers decided to let the giant work with the steel pitchers and other unbreakable supplies, while they took care of the lab's glassware, which was more expensive and more important.

The day passed. At five o'clock the big mother stopped by Sokol's office and received his seventy dollars. Then he left the clinic and walked home. He didn't have anyone escorting him as he made his way back to his apartment. It was the first time in his life that he had been all by himself. He had to stop in confusion until someone pointed the way to Garfield Street; he had gone by it and had to walk back toward the clinic a few blocks. He climbed up to his apartment and sat down on the couch. He sat in the dark for two hours doing nothing, just listening to noises from the street. At last, when he got hungry, he went out again and found a supermarket. He bought some food and some light bulbs—at several points angry customers and employees had to direct him and teach him the proper way to shop in a store. He accepted all their help and abuse with the same good grace and a quiet smile. He paid for his groceries, went home, and prepared a small supper with the kitchen utensils the state agency had provided him.

After the meal, the big man sat quietly in his living room

until he began to feel tired. Then he fell asleep on the couch, his long legs hanging over the end; he didn't realize that the piece of furniture folded out into a bed. When he awoke in the morning, he had no idea what time it was. He realized that there were many things—just too many—that he would have to learn very quickly. People seemed ready to supply him with the information, but not voluntarily. He had to do something shockingly wrong before someone would correct him. He knew that there was a clock in the kitchen, hung on a nail on the wall. The face of the clock was clouded with brown drips and splashes of ancient cooking grease. The numerals were barely legible. The clock wasn't plugged in; sometime that day the ugly bastard would have to set it.

He got up and washed, put on his one set of clothes, and set out in search of the Social Security number. He stopped several people on the sidewalk before he found where he was to go. He also learned that most people do not like to be stopped on the sidewalk, especially on their way to work. Especially by someone who looked as frightening as he. One woman, however, decided that they could find his answer by looking in the telephone book. She looked up *United States Government*. The Social Security Administration offices were in the Federal building downtown at the corner of State Street and Santa Rosa Boulevard. The woman also told him how to get there by bus. The big man thanked her and she smiled. He felt for her the same warmth that he had felt for Mrs. Perry, Miss Calhoun, and all the other people who had helped him.

The woman at the Social Security Administration information desk tried to be helpful, too, at first, but she had just never dealt with anyone whose background was as odd and incomplete as the monster's. "Here," she had said, handing him a sheet of paper, "it's just a simple form. Fill it out. You'll need a certified copy of your birth certificate and some form of positive identification."

The monster realized that he was going to have some difficulty. "There's no other way?" he asked.

"What do you mean?" asked the woman. There were many other people with their questions waiting behind the dumb guy.

"I have no birth certificate. I have no identification," he said.

The woman stared at him. "Well," she said with tired cynicism, "maybe we can get your mommy to sign for you."

"I have no mommy," said the giant.

"Aw," said the woman. "Now look, honey, how do you expect the government to know if what you say on that form is the truth? You got to have some identification. Driver's license. Passport. Government employee ID card. Something. You look nice enough to me, dear"—the woman grimaced—"but the computer will want to be sure you're telling the truth."

"Why would I lie?" he asked.

"Go sit down and fill out the form," she said. "When you're done, you'll have to talk with Mr. Farber."

"Thank you," said the man. "May I use this pen?"

"No," said the woman, "that's mine. Borrow someone else's."

The dumb guy did as he was instructed and filled out the form as completely as he could. Like all the previous forms, that wasn't very satisfactory.

"This isn't much information, is it, sir?" asked Mr. Farber, the Social Security representative, some time later.

"I'm really sorry," said the big man. "I know this is a little out of the ordinary, but I'm in kind of an awkward situation."

"I'm afraid I don't understand," said Mr. Farber. He was about ten years older than the giant, almost bald, conservatively dressed. His job consisted mostly of listening to people, day after day, telling him why their stories were out of the ordinary. After fifteen years of listening, Mr. Farber had learned that very few of these stories were in any way unusual, and most could be quickly reconciled with a brief notation, a checkmark in one box or another on the paper, a "yes" or a "no," or by forwarding the whole matter to his supervisor. Mr. Farber was a form of sorting device. He served the same purpose as the unit on a coin-operated machine that rejects the worthless slugs.

"Well, briefly," said the ugly bastard, "as best as I can recall, I didn't exist before I was found by the police earlier this month. I have no past at all. I have been treated at both Mercy Lutheran Hospital and Hanson State Hospital, and I am now in a work-release program. I have been given a job at the Reitsch Community Clinic, but in order for them to process my paychecks I need a Social Security number. So I have come to obtain one, but I cannot supply any of the identification you require."

Mr. Farber smiled. He looked very kindly. He folded his hands and coughed softly. "You have come to get a Social Security number?" he said.

"Yes," said the big man.

"And you have no identification at all?"

"Yes, that's my problem."

"The solution is simple," said Mr. Farber, smiling again. "You can't have one."

The monster was slightly taken aback. "Why not?" he asked.

Mr. Farber shook his head mildly. "Mr., ah, Friedbaum, don't you see that we *must* have that identification? Look at it from our point of view. From the time you had your first part-time job as a teen-ager, you almost surely had another Social Security number. And now you're asking us to give you one more. Well, what if tomorrow you went to another office in another town and acquired a third, fourth, a fifth? My goodness, Mr. Friedbaum, the only purpose I can think of for wanting multiple Social Security numbers is for some kind of unemployment or welfare fraud, or something equally as corrupt."

"But I don't have another number," said the giant.

"Show me some positive identification, and we'll run it through the computers and check," said Mr. Farber. "It's just that simple."

And it would have been that simple, but the big mother had to leave the office without being given a Social Security number. He went back to the clinic and to his boss, Mr. Sokol, in an unhappy and frustrated mood. Sokol wasn't pleased to learn of the monster's failure either. "No card?" he asked. "They wouldn't give you a number? I've never heard of that before. They give *everybody* a number, as far as I know. Even Hermano and Juan have numbers. If they didn't give you a number, they must have pretty good reasons."

The dumb guy tried to explain to Sokol why Mr. Farber wouldn't let him have a Social Security number. Sokol cut off the explanation by raising one hand. The giant fell silent. "Look," said Sokol, "if they won't let you have a Social Security number, then you can't work here. You might as well go home until you *can* get a number. If the problem is identification, well, get some identification. Then get the number, then come back here. Don't take it personally. You'll always be welcome to come to work here, but only when you've got what the government says you have to have. You follow me?"

"Yes, sir," said the man. He was learning more about dealing with people every day. The more he learned, the less he liked it. If he had had a choice, he would have wished that the police had never picked him up that night. He would rather have been left alone to wander mindlessly through the dead fields of the world, like a woodland creature.

"Why don't you take that girl's advice and go back to the hospital for help? You're going to need it, because when I report that you're not working here they're going to take your apartment away from you, and they're going to want their seventy dollars back."

The big mother gasped. "When are you going to report that?" he asked.

"Right now," said Sokol.

"I think I need help," said the giant.

"It's nothing personal, don't take me wrong," said Sokol. "It's just the way the deal works. Sometimes some innocent sucker gets shafted. If I can help in any other way, just let me know. I tell you, you better just find some way of getting the number and identification. That's all."

"Thank you, Mr. Sokol," said the innocent sucker. He knew that Sokol wasn't being vindictive or arbitrary. The giant had no bad feelings toward him. "I'll go see Miss Calhoun."

"You do that," said Sokol, picking up his telephone receiver and dialing a number.

Later that day, as the big man described his problems, Molly Calhoun listened sympathetically. She had been trained to do that. She nodded as she listened and made a few fragmentary notes. "The basic hang-up here, as I understand it," she said, "is that the government isn't able to give you the papers to prove who you are, because you can't prove who you are, because you don't have the government papers. Am I correct in my summary?"

"Yes," said the big man. "Miss Calhoun, can you help me?"

The young woman sighed. "I can't tell you how sympathetic I am. It's one of those unfortunate administrative pickles you get into occasionally in any bureaucracy. They're very funny, sometimes, unless you're personally involved. But as to *help*, well, I'm afraid we can't give you any. This is a governmental problem, and the hospital just doesn't have any jurisdiction or influence there. If it were a medical problem we'd have you back under observation in a minute. We did give you an apart-

ment and a job. After that, what you did with them was up to
you."

"But how will I live now?" asked the ugly bastard in a
pitiable tone.

There was a long silence. "You might consider selling your
prescription drugs on the street," said Molly Calhoun. "But
don't tell anyone I suggested that."

The giant smiled indulgently. "Miss Calhoun," he said,
"would you buy drugs from someone who looked like me?"

She frowned and shook her head. "But I don't use drugs,
anyway," she said.

"Thank you, Miss Calhoun," said the dumb guy.

"I'm sorry I couldn't be of more help."

The big man stood and left her office. He went home, where
he sat thinking on his couch for a few hours. Then he went to
the grocery store to buy food for his supper. This time he
attracted some curious stares, but caused no unpleasant scenes.

The next day the innocent sucker sat alone in his apartment,
from morning until early evening, doing nothing. The day after,
he thought that he might seek help from Mrs. Violet Perry,
from Mercy Lutheran Hospital. There was no reason why Mrs.
Perry would want to help him, but she was the only person the
big man knew to turn to. He waited until after lunchtime, then
took a bus to Mercy Lutheran.

"My goodness!" was all that Mrs. Perry could say when he
entered her office.

"Hello, Mrs. Perry. I'm in some trouble, and I was wondering if you could spare a few minutes to give me some
advice."

Mrs. Perry took a moment to calm herself. She had felt an
odd excitement when the giant appeared, and she needed a few
seconds to get her emotions under control. This was the second
time the man had caused this reaction in her. She did not
understand it. "Please, come in and sit down. I'll be happy to
listen," she said.

The ugly bastard sat in a chair by her desk and went through
the same story he had told Molly Calhoun. Mrs. Perry didn't
interrupt or ask any questions until he was finished. "She didn't
try to help you?" she asked.

"There was nothing for her to do," said the big man. "She
made that quite clear. Her hands were tied. It was just not the
hospital's responsibility."

"*You* are the hospital's responsibility," said Mrs. Perry, feeling indignation at Miss Calhoun's refusal even to try to help.

"Then there is a way out?" asked the man.

"I don't know," said Mrs. Perry. "I have more experience at this, I think, than Miss Calhoun. Let me take a look at what resources we have." She picked up a thick book from a shelf behind her desk. She paged through it for a moment. "Here," she said at last. "Here we have a list of city agencies that are designed to aid disadvantaged, handicapped, or minority-group members who feel they are being discriminated against, for one reason or another. Now some of these are no good to us. But let me make a note of a few agencies you can visit. I'm sure someone there can cut through this red tape. It's criminal, what they're putting you through. Go see these people this afternoon, and tomorrow let me know what results you got."

"Mrs. Perry," said the big mother, "you have more humanity than all the other people I've met combined."

Mrs. Perry didn't reply. She blushed and looked down at her desk. She felt the strange excitement again; she couldn't identify it, but she had an idea that it wasn't entirely wholesome.

The first agency the giant visited was the city's Center for Children with Learning Disabilities. He was made to wait in a small anteroom while the receptionist went into an inner office. Not long after, a tall, stoutly built woman came out, dressed in a long plaid skirt and jacket over a pale blue shirt. She was Dr. Martha Duvigny, the director of the C. C. L. D. "Mr. Friedman?" she asked.

The big man stood up. The woman's voice was cold and mistrustful. She intimidated the giant, and he didn't say anything.

"Won't you please come into my office?" said Dr. Duvigny.

"Thank you," said the innocent sucker.

After she seated herself behind her huge desk, Dr. Duvigny indicated a comfortable leather armchair. The man sat down and waited. "How," said the woman at last, "do you think that we may help you?"

The dumb guy thought for a moment. "I have a problem related to the conditions you are helping your children to overcome. There doesn't seem to be an agency devised precisely for helping adults like me. I came to you with my urgent need, hoping that you might have a suggestion."

Dr. Duvigny nodded gravely. "I hope that we may be of service," she said, though her tone was doubtful. "What actually seems to be the trouble?"

The ugly bastard recited his story for her, just as he had done for Mrs. Perry, for Miss Calhoun, for Mr. Sokol, for Mr. Farber. When he finished, Dr. Duvigny was quiet for a moment. "I see," she said. "Your problem is genuine and very serious, Mr. Friedman."

"I know," said the big man.

"You've come to the wrong place. You are neither a child nor afflicted with a learning disability, am I correct?"

"Yes, but—"

"And you cannot even prove that you are a resident of this city or state, and a taxpayer thereof. My advice to you is that you seek aid from a non-government-sponsored program, such as the Center for Psychotherapy and Human Development, on South Marginal Road."

"They'll be able to help me?" asked the giant.

Dr. Duvigny clasped her hands and made a steeple of her index fingers. "I can't promise, of course, but I'll call over there and let them know you're coming. I'll fill them in and tell them to give you every possible assistance. I'm sorry, Mr. Friedman, that's the best I can offer. It's a shame you aren't about twenty years younger. At your age, you just don't fit into our area of involvement."

"I understand perfectly," said the man. "It is my mistake for coming here in the first place. I'm sorry to have bothered you."

"Not at all, not at all," said the woman. She said nothing more, she only stared. The giant realized that he was expected to leave the office without any further discussion. He did so. The receptionist told him that he couldn't get to the Center for Psychotherapy and Human Development by public transportation, so she called a cab for him. He didn't like the idea of paying for a ride with part of his rapidly diminishing stake of cash, but there was nothing else to be done.

It was a waste of time there, too. Once the interviewing doctor learned that he was already in the out-patient work-release program of Hanson State Hospital, he refused to have anything more to do with the big man's case. "They're handling your problem," he said, "and they know what they're doing.

Anything we'd do would work against their decisions. I'm afraid that we can't help you here. Perhaps if you tried an agency outside of the medical and psychotherapeutic line. Why not investigate your legal rights, Mr. Friedman? That is the nut of the problem, after all, isn't it? I mean, find out what you're legally entitled to. If you're being denied justice, then you can proceed to petition. But there isn't a medical answer to your situation."

"I see," said the big mother. He hated the traveling from one agency to another, looking for a simple answer to what he believed to be a simple problem. He couldn't comprehend why no one was able or willing to take the small yet significant steps essential to the giant's eventual happiness. He left the Center for Psychotherapy and Human Development without a clue as to his own future development. Evidently, at that center, their psychotherapy and their human development came as a boxed set that they didn't like to break up.

The doctor's receptionist made a list of several agencies that might be of assistance to the monster. He studied her list and compared it to the one Mrs. Perry had given him. He decided to visit the four agencies that appeared on both lists. He visited the City Attorney's Office, Civil Division, in City Hall, and was told that he was entirely in the wrong department, that the City Attorney couldn't help him in any way whatsoever, that he had the wrong idea about how to go about getting what was due him. "What did you expect the Attorney to do?" asked the woman at the desk. "Sue the Federal Government for your Social Security number?"

"Yes," said the innocent sucker, "something along those lines."

"Try the Legal Aid Foundation. They're on Newman Drive." The woman at the desk watched as the big man walked away from her. She was appalled at how hideous he was. In her job she met and spoke with thousands of people every month. Yet in all the years she had held that job, she had never seen anyone so completely horrible. She thought that it was no wonder the man couldn't get anyone to help him. She thought that he would get far better results by dealing with people by telephone, so that they wouldn't have to see him in person.

The Legal Aid Foundation was sympathetic, as sympathetic if not more so than Molly Calhoun. But, like Miss Calhoun, there was nothing that they could offer in the way of help. "What did you expect the Foundation to do?" asked one of the eager young legal whiz kids. "Sue the Federal Government for your Social Security number?"

"Yes," said the giant, "something along those lines."

The legal whiz kid laughed. "I'm sorry," he said. "If you were being discriminated against, we could try to help. But that's not the case. The government doesn't discriminate in the issuing of Social Security numbers. They *like* to give them away, one to a person. That way each person becomes an identified taxpayer. You can't earn a dime at a regular job in this country without it being reported to the government. The government can then keep track of who is paying income taxes and who isn't. They *want* you to have a number. But if you can't prove your identity, they're perfectly right to refuse you. In fact, you don't have enough identification and information for us even to take your case on. You couldn't fill out *our* application form, either."

"I see," said the ugly bastard. "Thank you."

"Sorry," said the legal whiz.

In desperation the big mother tried the Mayor's Office of Manpower and Economic Development. He was sent to the Counseling, Placement, and Evaluation Group. The woman at the desk there looked up from her snack of yoghurt and saw him looming above her head. She caught a glimpse of his straw-like black hair, his shadowed, sunken eyes, his black lips and dead face, and she shrieked. Then she seemed flustered. She patted her hair and straightened her blouse. "Oh," she said, "can I help you?"

"I'd like to be evaluated, counseled, and placed, please."

"Did the city welfare people send you over?"

"I come of my own free will," said the disfigured man. "I come seeking aid."

"You don't have the forms from the welfare people?"

"No, ma'am."

The woman at the desk gave him some forms to fill out. The giant glanced at them quickly and saw that they would remain mostly blank, like all the other forms he had been given. "This is more or less beside the point," he said. "I don't have most of the information these forms ask for. That's why I need help."

"Then give them back to me and go away," said the woman. Her brusque manner was a device to make up for her startled reaction a few moments before. "Look, what do you want from us? We don't evaluate *people* here. We evaluate what they put down on the forms. If you don't put anything down, there's nothing for the counsellors to evaluate."

"You are, of course, correct," said the big mother. "I have come to realize how vital these papers are. But I hoped that your agency could help me acquire that information. It wouldn't take much time. It's not that difficult a problem."

"Well, you're going about it the wrong way. You're a grown man, and you can't answer these questions? What's wrong with you?"

The dumb guy shook his head slightly. "Nothing," he said. "I'm a man without a number. I am an exile in a world full of people with numbers. Without a number, a man is home nowhere and no one is his friend. I long only for the day when I may have my number."

"Try Welfare," said the woman at the desk. "They're down on State Street."

The man went down to State Street, to the Welfare Department, Division of Emergency Assistance. The receptionist took out their standard forms and began asking questions. She asked, "What is your name?" and "Age?" and "Address?" and got two out of three answers. When the ugly man said that he didn't know his age, she looked up at him with a disgusted expression. She wrote some more on the form, filling in descriptive information. "Social Security number?" she asked. He said that he didn't have one. The woman looked up, this time even more disgusted. "Here," she said, handing the paper to him, "take this and fill it out, or get out of here. Come back when you feel like cooperating."

The giant was surprised by her sudden vehemence. "I'm sorry, miss," he said, "but I am trying to cooperate. That's my problem, you see. I can't answer most of these questions."

"Then we can't help you," said the woman. "We get enough welfare cheaters as it is. Most of them are a lot more clever than you. Go on, get out. There are other people waiting."

The big mother felt anger rising in him, and he fought to keep himself polite. "Thank you," he muttered, and he hurried out of the office. Downstairs and outside on the sidewalk, he probed his feelings. He had never experienced anger before. The closest he had come had been annoyance and irritation. Anger was a strong and intoxicating emotion, but it frightened him. He was glad when it subsided quickly.

The next day, he reported to Mrs. Perry. The thin woman took off her glasses and rubbed her eyes. She seemed filled with fatigue. She had a suspicion that no one, in any agency or program, would help the giant. It was difficult enough to get through channels with plain straightforward cases. Here, however, in the matter of the ugly bastard, everyone had a simple and direct course of action: deny and dismiss.

"Here are some more agencies you can try," she said after checking her source books again. "These may do you much more good. They're on the state level. The city government may be too narrow-minded to be much help to you. On the state level, though, they may not have such a negative attitude."

"I will give it my best, Mrs. Perry," said the big man. "That truly gives me hope."

"Good," she said. "Let me know how you make out."

The giant visited two agencies after he saw Mrs. Perry. In the state Department of Health and Human Resources, he spoke with a woman at the receptionist's desk and was directed to the Resources Development Unit. He received much the same treatment as he had gotten from the city agencies, except his transformed name "Friedman" somehow became "Goodman." To all the state agencies, he was now Mr. Victor Goodman. After the Resources Development Unit, the big mother stopped by the state Department of Labor to speak with the Unemployment Insurance Appeals officer. That man was so bewildered that he couldn't understand what the giant wanted, needed, or expected from the state. Finally the Appeals officer just said bluntly that he couldn't help, and invited the monster to leave. The monster did so without another word. The ugly bastard hated to create trouble for anyone.

He went home at lunchtime, and was pleased and delighted to see that there was an envelope waiting for him in his mailbox. He opened the mailbox and tore open the envelope. Inside was a letter from the Hanson State Hospital for the Mentally Disabled. It was signed by Dr. Weber. It said that he was aware that the innocent sucker had stopped working at his appointed job at the clinic, that the monster refused to clear up the technical difficulties standing in the way of his gainful employment, and that if the situation didn't change in forty-eight hours the locks on the door of his apartment would be changed and the dumb guy would be forced to vacate the premises. Also, the hospital and the state wanted its seventy dollars back.

The big man was stunned. He would soon be homeless and penniless, unless one of the state agencies came to his rescue. He hurried out again to visit some more offices, bureaus, units, divisions, departments, sections, authorities, boards, services, programs, and centers.

At the state Financial Assistance and Social Services Office, the giant was welcomed by a cheerful man named Mr. Salvatore. Mr. Salvatore had worked in this particular office only three months, so he had as yet little idea of how meager his power and influence were. He was cheerful because he still believed that he could help anyone who came to him in need. He had not yet been dragged down by the accumulating knowledge of his failures. "Mr. Goodman?" he said, indicating a plain wooden chair beside his desk. The giant sat down.

"I have a problem, and I wanted to talk to you about the possibility of getting some financial assistance and one or two of your social services."

Mr. Salvatore smiled. "If you qualify, sir, you will have your pick of all our services, and we have quite a few. I'm very proud of them all."

"Understandably so," said the ugly bastard. He related to Mr. Salvatore his story, including now the additional news of his impending eviction.

Mr. Salvatore listened carefully, nodding at each important point. The smile on his face evaporated slowly, bit by bit, like the water in an abandoned fish bowl. Eventually, well before the big man had reached the end of his story, the smile was gone entirely. "It sounds to me like you're being given the runaround," he said, when the dumb guy finished. "I wish there were something I could do for you immediately, Mr. Goodman. But, frankly, without the referrals from the offices you've already visited, I can't pry loose a dime for you or provide even the most elementary of services. If they turned you away down below, I don't have the power to dole out money or aid. I can't just throw our resources around, Mr. Goodman. That's why the screening agencies exist. By the time someone reaches my office—through proper channels—we're certain that he or she is qualified and deserving of whatever help we can render."

"So it's pointless for me to try looking for help at some of the other departments in this building."

"Now, Mr. Goodman, don't give up hope. I think it's just a matter of going about it in the right way. I think that you're expending a lot of energy visiting offices that couldn't help you in the first place. I would advise you to forget the bottom-level agencies. You already know that you're at the mercy of some weary pencil-pusher who doesn't care about your situation. And at the middle-level, like here, for instance, you are helpless without the okay from the bottom-level, which you are not going to get. So I think the only real alternative is to go straight to the top."

"What is at the top?" asked the innocent sucker.

"Washington, Mr. Goodman," said Mr. Salvatore, smiling again. "They have so many people to take care of, so many problems, that yours won't seem so unusual to them. It's too strange for city employees to deal with, and it's too odd even for state employees. But the federal government is so overworked and frazzled that they will probably just give you what you need in a matter of minutes. You will be just one standard form in an unending river of standard forms."

"That is all that I have aspired to be," said the big mother.

"I will set up an appointment for you right now," said Mr. Salvatore. "This is one social service you are getting free of charge."

"I appreciate it," said the big man.

Mr. Salvatore dialed a number and waited for a few seconds. "Hello? I'd like to speak to Mrs. Dorsey, please." While he waited for the switchboard operator to transfer the call, he looked at the giant. "Mrs. Dorsey is the Regional Director of the Office for Civil Rights," he said. Then he spoke into the telephone. "Mrs. Dorsey? Hello, this is Joseph Salvatore at the state Financial Assistance and Social Services Office. Fine, thank you. I have someone here with a very serious problem, and I can't help him out. His name is Victor Goodman. Yes, it's extremely simple but no one appears to have the authority or inclination to give him a hand. I was wondering if you had a free moment to see him? I think you are the right person to put an end to his trouble. Tomorrow? What time? Wonderful.

Thank you, Mrs. Dorsey. Goodbye." He hung up the telephone. He looked at the man and smiled. "She'll see you tomorrow at one o'clock, Mr. Goodman. If she can't help you, she'll know exactly where to send you. Mrs. Dorsey is a kind woman."

"Thank you, Mr. Salvatore, for your social service," said the ugly bastard.

"Think nothing of it, Mr. Goodman. And I hope everything turns out fine for you tomorrow. Don't worry about it." He put out his hand, and the monster shook hands for the first time in his life.

It was Thursday afternoon. The innocent sucker had an appointment for one o'clock the next afternoon. He decided that if Mrs. Dorsey couldn't solve his problem, then he would have to try a few more offices on the federal level, because no one could help him over the weekend, and by Monday he would be forced out of his apartment. He simply had to get the matter settled by five o'clock Friday afternoon.

Friday morning was cloudy and cold. It was early December, and the weather matched the big man's mood: dark, gusty, somber. In a drugstore near his apartment he used a telephone book to find other offices to visit before and after his appointment with Mrs. Dorsey. He had watched Mr. Salvatore use a telephone book, and he had learned how to find what he needed. He copied down several addresses and telephone numbers, including the numbers of Mrs. Perry's office, Molly Calhoun's office, and Mr. Sokol's office, in the happy event that everything came to a successful resolution. Mr. Sokol could then advise Hanson State Hospital and Dr. Weber that there was no need to evict the ugly bastard from his apartment.

The first place the big man went was the HEW Office of Human Development. Even the title of the program inspired hope and confidence in his heart. He was human, after a fashion, and he desperately wanted to be developed. A woman at a desk told him that he couldn't see an official without an appointment, as they were not an agency that dealt directly with people in need. Instead, they funded programs that in turn developed humans on the community level. The giant insisted on speaking with someone, and his appearance so unnerved the woman that she agreed to ask one of the officials for an interview. The big man was glad that he didn't have to fill out an application form.

A moment later the woman returned to her desk. "Miss Constantine will see you now," she said. She indicated one of several doors behind her.

The big mother nodded and went into the inner office. "Miss Constantine?" he said.

She was a young woman with the air of someone who had just a bit too much work to do. She nodded impatiently. "Please sit down," she said.

He sat. He began his story, but she interrupted. "What we're interested in," she said, "and what we can help you with, is funding for certain areas of the population with special needs. Programs we operate are chiefly geared toward certain targeted groups of individuals. If we find that you fit one of these groups, we'll be able to tell you how to get in touch with the right program in this city. Otherwise we won't be able to help at all. We can't, for example, just write you out a check on the basis of your need."

"I understand," said the dumb guy. "What are these groups under your care?"

"First, children and youth. You don't fit there. Then, the aged. Again no. American Indian and Alaskan natives? No? I didn't think so. We have an Office of Rural Development."

"That wouldn't be any good to me," said the man.

"Okay. How about the Office for Handicapped Individuals?"

"I think that's good," said the giant. "I am certainly handicapped."

Miss Constantine studied him for a few seconds. She agreed that there definitely was something wrong with him. "What precisely is your handicap?"

"I have no past, and I have no Social Security number."

Miss Constantine didn't quite know what to think. "About your Social Security," she said, "you're in the wrong department altogether. We can't do a thing about that. And what do you mean that you don't have a past? Amnesia?"

"In a way, yes, ma'am."

Miss Constantine thought for a moment. "It's not an administrative problem you have. It's a medical problem. Now, Hanson State Hospital has a marvelous program organized on an out-patient basis. It's a work-release—"

"I am in that program already, Miss Constantine."

"Then why are you here? Why are you taking up my time?"

"Because I can't get a Social Security number, and without

the number I can't keep my job, and without the job I can't keep my apartment."

Miss Constantine glared. "Look," she said angrily, "I have a ton of work to do. Don't come to me with your Social Security problem. Go to *them*. We don't have a damn thing to do with them."

"I already have," said the innocent sucker timidly. "They can't help me."

"And neither can we," said Miss Constantine. She stood. "Good day," she said. The big man left without saying anything more. He felt humiliated.

In the same building was the HUD Office of Fair Housing and Equal Opportunity. He was told that he might have gotten some help if he could prove that he was a woman being discriminated against, or a black being discriminated against, or a Jew being discriminated against, or a senior citizen being discriminated against, or a veteran or ex-convict being discriminated against. The disfigured man admitted that he was none of these things. He thought how unfortunate that one of his component parts hadn't come from a black donor. Then at least part of him could get aid from the federal government.

It was nearly one o'clock and time for his appointment with Mrs. Dorsey. Her office was on the same floor as Miss Constantine's. When he told the secretary that he had an appointment, she seemed shocked. She checked the daily list and, yes, there was an appointment for a Mr. Victor Goodyear. The secretary picked up her telephone and buzzed the inner office. "Mr. Goodyear is here to see you, Mrs. Dorsey." There was a brief pause. The secretary looked up at the giant. "She says to go right in."

"Thank you," said the big man.

Mrs. Dorsey was round. She was so plump that she was like a large soft ball with limbs. She had a dour expression from pushing and tugging at the governmental machine for many years, but she was genuinely interested in helping. Her confidence was not as strong as Mr. Salvatore's, but that was the result of a full career of experience. "Mr. Salvatore told me that I might be able to help you," she said.

"I hope so. I think my civil rights are being abridged."

Mrs. Dorsey frowned. "That, of course, is a serious charge," she said. "It's one that ought not to be made lightly, because you never know where you might end up. In the Supreme

Court, making a precedent in a decision for or against you that will affect millions of other people. Just how are your rights being denied, Mr. Goodyear?"

The innocent sucker went through his whole story, although by now he himself was finding it tiresome. It bored him, and if it weren't for the fact that he had only eight dollars left, he wouldn't have continued his quest for assistance. His recitation this time stressed the immediacy of his need.

When she had listened to the facts, Mrs. Dorsey thought for a long while. The dumb guy moved uncomfortably in his chair. He waited for her to speak.

"You're really caught in it, aren't you?" she said. "Look, there is a chance one of our official agencies could help you, but I tend to doubt it. I think you've been behind the eight ball since the beginning, and the reason no one's offered you any concrete aid is because *they* all knew that, too. You're caught in a unique trap, and not many people would be willing to crawl in there with you, Mr. Goodyear."

"I never intended to get anyone else personally involved in my dilemma," said the big mother.

"That's very thoughtful," said Mrs. Dorsey, smiling. "The basis, the very rock-bottom essentials of your case make it hard to proceed on your behalf. Let me explain. Take the case of your apartment. This isn't a matter of discrimination. You are not actually renting that apartment from a landlord. If that were the case, you couldn't be asked to vacate the premises so quickly. You have no actual lease, have you? No? In effect, that apartment is like a private room still in the Hanson State Hospital. The money that would in theory have been deducted from your paychecks is not actually paid to anyone as rent. If you read the papers you signed, I'm sure you would find a nice legal distinction that covers the hospital and makes sure that they can't be defined as 'landlords.' They want to be protected, and they want to avoid all the legal entanglements that a land-lord-tenant relationship can create. Also, your job at the clinic is part and parcel of your therapy. Instead of having you cut out paper dolls and weave baskets in Hanson State Hospital, they have you washing dishes at the clinic. You are not really an employee. It's like asking a prisoner in jail what his oc-cupation is and he says he's a license-plate manufacturer. In those papers you signed, you'll find your employment hedged around with legal quibbles just as beautifully as your housing.

But they still need your Social Security number, because a small quantity of money changes hands, from them to you."

"Everything would be wonderful if I could just get my number," said the giant.

"Do you know what you sound like?" asked Mrs. Dorsey. "You sound like an additional character in the *Wizard of Oz*. If you can get in to see him, maybe he'll give you a number, Mr. Goodyear."

The ugly bastard didn't know what she was talking about.

"As I see it," she said, "the best thing for you to do is proceed through the courts. It's obvious to me that you're being given the royalest of screwings, and I think it would be obvious to a judge as well. You can bring suit against the state, against the Hanson State Hospital for the Mentally Disabled, against Dr. Weber, against his work-release program, and against your supervisor there, too. Doing that will require huge amounts of time and money, neither of which you have. I think, though, that your case is worth pursuing. How far, I can't say right now. This office would be willing to back you up, I think. A lot of research and investigating would have to be done first. By that time, your problems may have taken care of themselves. But if our office decides that you are, indeed, having your civil rights denied, we will carry the ball for you. Let me have your address and phone number. I'll start the paperwork moving, and I'll get in touch with you on, let's see, next Tuesday."

"By Tuesday I will be evicted," said the innocent sucker.

Mrs. Dorsey nodded. "Yes, that's right," she said. "Come see me next Tuesday, then. Is ten o'clock all right? Be sure to tell my secretary outside. Well, it was nice meeting you." They shook hands. "I'll see you Tuesday, and with any kind of luck you'll have all your troubles licked by then, Mr. Goodyear."

"I hope so," said the big man.

"Have a nice day," said Mrs. Dorsey. Mr. Salvatore was right; she was a kind woman. As she watched the giant leave her office, her only thought was "poor schmuck."

Still, out in the bleak weather, the man tried to understand what had just happened. Had he made progress or not? He hadn't been turned away, as in most of the other offices. But he hadn't come out with the tiniest tangible bit of help. He was still in jeopardy of losing his apartment, and he still had only a few dollars to buy food with. Yet Mrs. Dorsey seemed so positive. If she persuaded her superiors to help the ugly bastard, they would be a formidable force to have on his side. He might receive a gigantic settlement from the state. He might be able to live in luxury. He would be able to buy a second turtleneck sweater.

The giant tried three more offices that afternoon but, much as Mrs. Dorsey predicted, none of them was able to offer any help. The big man left the area of the Federal buildings in a much darker mood than he had been in that morning. It was Friday evening; sometime in the next few days he faced the prospect of being turned out into the street. He had only a few dollars left. No one would be able to do anything for him until Monday. It looked like a difficult weekend ahead. He made his way home by bus, wrapped deep in thought, feeling the frustration growing in him until he felt the need to release his anger.

There was an abandoned, burnt-out building at the end of his block. The doorway was covered by a sheet of corrugated metal, but children in the neighborhood had pried it open enough so that they could get in the ruined tenement. It was used as a playground, a meeting place, and a refuge for all kinds of illicit activities. The ugly bastard squeezed into the building and threw chunks of broken brick at the walls. He threw until his arm grew tired, and then he threw with his other arm. After a long time he calmed down. Then he left the empty building and went to the supermarket. He bought enough food for his supper and for breakfast. After he paid for the food, he went home and ate. Then he sat in the darkness on his couch and waited for fatigue to overcome him. He fell asleep early.

He was awakened early Saturday morning by someone knocking on his door. He sat up and rubbed his face. He went to the door and opened it. In the hall were three men, one in a business suit, one in work clothes, and one in a uniform with a peaked cap. The man in the business suit said, "Mr. Frankenbaum? I'm from the Hanson State Hospital for the Mentally Disabled. I represent Dr. Calvin Weber, and I have here an order for you to vacate these premises, after which we will have to change the locks on the door to prevent you from reoccupying this apartment." The man indicated the second man in work clothes. "We're sorry to have to do this, but there are a limited number of these apartments available, and there are many other people waiting to get into Dr. Weber's program."

"No," said the big mother.

"Pardon me?" said the man in the business suit.

"I won't leave," said the giant.

"You have to," said the business suit. "That's why *he's* here." He indicated the man in the uniform. It was the uniform of the hospital's security staff, not a municipal policeman.

"How will he make me leave if I don't want to?" asked the innocent sucker.

"He has a pistol," said the business suit.

"I have a gun," said the uniform.

The big man had seen guns used on television programs. He knew that they killed people. The concept of violent death horrified the monster. "I see," he said. He thought for a moment. No one said anything. "I guess I have to leave quietly, or be shot dead on the spot."

The business suit didn't point out that there were other possibilities open. Mr. Frankenbaum seemed a simple-minded sort, and if he wanted to believe that he had only two choices, the business suit wasn't going to complicate matters.

"I will leave," said the poor schmuck. "I expected this to happen, but not so soon."

"We're very efficient," said the business suit.

"I don't know if that's the appropriate word for it," said the giant. He moved out into the hallway, and the man in work clothes immediately began sorting out the tools in his kit, preparing to begin work on the locks.

"You have to leave the building entirely," said the business suit.

"Okay," said the dumb guy. He went downstairs and out on the sidewalk. The air was colder than the day before. He realized that he had left behind a good quantity of food in the apartment, and that he had less than two dollars in his pocket. He went to the store and bought a loaf of bread and some pears and ate them for breakfast. Then he began to think about what he was going to do.

He didn't have many options. He walked around his neighborhood and watched children playing on the sidewalks. They were all bundled up in jackets and hats and mittens. The innocent sucker was cold in his turtleneck sweater. He pushed his huge hands into the pockets of his trousers, but his fingers were red and painful. His ears stung when the wind blew. He walked toward the Reitsch Community Clinic, if only because he didn't know where else he could go to stay warm. Sokol wasn't there on Saturdays, and neither were Hermano and Juan. No one else at the clinic knew who he was, and they wouldn't let him stay. He thought about going back to the Hanson State Hospital, but if they had been tough enough to chase him out of his home, then he couldn't expect much hospitality from them on their own grounds. He wished that he could talk with Mrs. Perry or even Molly Calhoun.

The day passed slowly. The giant counted out enough money to pay for bus fare downtown on Monday—he had decided to make one last, desperate plea for help. He only had one dollar and thirty cents left over. He bought some fruit and milk with the money and carried the bag back to the burnt-out building near his apartment. He crept into the building and went to a back room. This area had once been divided into several smaller separate rooms, but the walls had long since been knocked down. In the corners of the room were large cartons and boxes lying on their sides, filled with newspapers and rags. Derelicts and fugitives often slept in the building, and these boxes were like private rooms in a dotmitory. Some even had pictures taped to them, making the cartons personalized in the midst of a frozen desert of rubble, trash, and broken glass.

The big man chose a Maytag washing machine carton in the darkest corner of the large room. He slid his mismatched feet into the crate and wrapped his legs with the filthy assortment of rags and newspaper sheets that covered the bottom of the box. He lay on his back and looked up at the charred ceiling. The light from the winter sun made gray patches all around the room, through the holes and windows and collapsed portions of the walls. There was no noise; the big mother couldn't even hear the shouting of the children. Slowly the gray light turned darker. He ate the fruit and drank the milk. He was still hungry. He had no more money to buy food. He was cold, and he tucked himself as tightly as he could into the Maytag carton. He covered himself with the papers and rags, but they did little to keep out the bitter chill. Finally it was night. Through one chink in the nearest wall the ugly bastard could see a few stars. They hardly seemed to twinkle in the icy air. He slept.

Sunday morning was distinguishable from the darkness only

by a mild lightening of the shadows. Surely the sun was creating nothing in the way of warmth. The giant was nearly numb with cold. He didn't stir from his nest in the crate, because there was nothing for him to do. Sunday meant that all the government agencies were closed. He had no money to spend, so there was no reason to leave the ruined building.

His hunger was immense. He hadn't had a good, full meal in days, and his body was torturing him with need. There was nothing he could do, though. He began to get thirsty and he knew that somewhere in the city he could find water to drink without spending any money. Yet the trouble involved in going out and looking for a free glass of water seemed to him at the time too great. He felt paralyzed, immobile beneath his coverlets of newsprint. He thought feverishly that he had to save his strength for the massive effort on Monday, the effort to wrest official recognition from some agency—he didn't care which, or if the agency were city, county, state, or federal. Someone, somewhere, *would* help him tomorrow. In the meantime everything else was secondary. On Sunday the innocent sucker went nowhere. He spent the day watching the weak sunlight stretching across the ceiling, until the light was thin and faint and finally gone entirely. He slept again, hungry, sick, and filled with futile anger.

He awoke on Monday possessed by a determination to get solid results by that evening, or else be so adamant in his demonstrations that he would end up back in the isolation room in Mercy Lutheran. After a moment of thought he realized that wasn't such a bad solution; in the isolation room he would at least be well-fed.

He was filthy, as filthy as the floor of the abandoned tenement. He was unshaven and he hadn't washed for more than two days. His face was streaked with dirt and his hair was disheveled and knotted with bits of wood and brick dust. His clothing, his one set of clothing, was torn, dirty, and rank-smelling. He presented the image of the most offensive sort of vagrant. This image was superimposed over his original image, which was not all that attractive to begin with. As he walked down the sidewalk toward the bus stop, people came to a halt as they caught sight of him. They moved slowly away, into the street or into doorways, out of his path. The big man did not notice the effect he was having. His mind was on one thing: he *had* to find help today.

He was dismayed to learn that he had slept later than he wanted. It was noon before he arrived at the first agency. This was the Office of Economic Development, a program sponsored by the Community Services Administration. He had almost exhausted the Cabinet-level agencies, and he was now working through lower level departments of the executive branch of the Federal government. They were not pleased to see him at the Office of Economic Development. The secretary who was confronted by the monster was driven nearly hysterical; later that evening, after she had calmed down and gone home, she told her husband that she wasn't going back to her job unless they hired a bouncer. When she had collapsed into hysterics at the office, a clerk came running to see what was the matter. The clerk, a young man who couldn't allow the secretary to see that he, too, was verging on panic, asked the poor schmuck what he had done.

"Nothing," said the giant. "I'm only looking for some financial aid. I have a problem with the government."

"Then go bother the government!" shouted the clerk. "Get out of here!"

"Yes, sir," said the big man. "I'll come back when you feel better."

The scene was much the same at the Equal Employment Opportunity Commission. He had a quick interview with a receptionist, who determined that his problem was not based on his race, color, sex, religion, or national origin. Having decided that, the receptionist referred the dumb guy to several other agencies, all of which he had already visited. "What do I do now?" he asked.

"Go away," said the receptionist. He did. He did not mind these two failures, because he was saving himself for his last chance, his last visit of the day. He decided to drop in to see the Community Action Agency and see about their action. He was prepared to go very far to guarantee their cooperation. He was driven by hunger. He was prepared to be as ruthless and cold as the Hanson State Hospital had been, and as unresponsive to reason as every agency he had seen.

"Hello," he said, "I'd like to see someone concerning some community action."

A middle-aged man stood behind the counter. The man stared at the ugly bastard. Behind the middle-aged man were posters exhorting everyone, government worker and citizen alike, on to community action. There were slogans stapled everywhere, urging safety and cooperation and education and brotherhood. The middle-aged man had a low-power job, and obviously this was the first time he had had to use initiative in handling it. He fumbled the ball. "Unh" was all that he could say. He just stared at the dead white, dirt-smeared face of the giant.

"Hello?" cried the innocent sucker loudly. "Anybody else here? Come on out!"

"What's going on out—" A woman carrying a file folder appeared from a rear office. She saw the gigantic man on the other side of the counter and dropped her folder.

"Would you help me, please?" asked the big mother.

"How? What do you want?" she asked.

"I have a problem with the government, and I can't get anyone to help me. They keep sending me from one office to another, and the situation is very desperate. I was evicted from my apartment Saturday, and I haven't eaten very much since then. Would you please call Mrs. Dorsey at the Office for Civil Rights? She'll be able to vouch for me. Maybe you can get me some temporary help while she gets her office ready to take my case to court."

The man's rational speech restored both the middle-aged man and the woman with the dropped folder. "Certainly," said the woman. "Just have a seat by the wall."

"Thank you," said the giant.

The woman went into her office. She hadn't even asked the big man's name, but she didn't need to; she merely described him, and Mrs. Dorsey remembered Victor Goodyear well enough. After a few minutes the woman came back. "Mr. Firestone?" she said.

"Yes?" said the poor schmuck.

"Would you come to the counter?"

"My pleasure." The deformed creature walked up to the counter. He had a slight limp from sleeping two nights in a box.

"We really can't do anything for you here," said the woman. She stopped talking when she saw the expression on the monster's face. She became suddenly afraid. "Look, Mr. Firestone," she said, gasping, "what do you think we can do? What do you want? Mrs. Dorsey said that you should have patience—"

The great, huge man raised one mighty arm and brought his fist down on the counter, splintering it into kindling. The middle-aged man fell to the floor either dead of a stroke, merely unconscious, or faking. The woman dropped her file folder again and shrunk back against the bulletin board. "I am hungry," said the big mother.

The woman nodded. She understood.

"I have no food. I have no home. I have no money."

The woman nodded again. The monster was making himself very clear.

"You will come with me."

The woman nodded. She didn't know why. The ugly bastard wrapped his immense hand around her wrist and dragged her behind him. He pulled her out onto the sidewalk. She was too weak from fright to scream. "Mr. Firestone?" she whispered.

"Yes?"

"Where are you taking me?"

There were a few seconds of silence. The poor man hadn't thought that far ahead. "I don't know," he said. He let go of her arm. She rubbed it and watched him warily.

"Can I go?" she asked.

"Yes," he said. "I'm hungry."

"It's almost five o'clock," she said. "Let me get my coat and purse. I'll buy you something to eat." In fact, the woman wanted nothing more than the opportunity to run back inside and hide in the ladies' room.

"I want my *number!*" shouted the monster. He started down the sidewalk. There was a small grocery at the end of the block. He ran toward it in a loud, lumbering gait. He scooped up an armful of apples and pears and ran with them. The grocer stared for a moment, shocked, then yelled, "Hey, come back!" Then he realized that he truthfully didn't want the big mother to come back. He could keep the apples and pears. But for some reason he ran after the monster. The woman of the file folder ran, too. The brute was something amazing in their lives. He was something frightening yet elemental, something electrifying, something that made the day special. The monster made *them* special, just for having passed by them in his hunger and fury.

Around the corner was a Greek restaurant. It had an open counter to serve people on the sidewalk. Above the counter was a sign that said: GYROS FALAFFELS SOUVLAKI BAK-

LAVA. A woman in a long cloth coat was paying a counterman. She had ordered a falaffel for her young daughter, and a gyro for herself. Her teen-aged daughter was wearing blue jeans and a Navy pea coat. She had not started to eat her falaffel yet when the giant ran by. He grabbed the falaffel out of the girl's hands and consumed it in three gigantic swallows, on the dead run. "Hey!" screamed the girl angrily. She hadn't quite caught a glimpse of the big man's face.

"What's wrong, dear?" asked the girl's mother, turning casually. When she saw the monstrous figure of the ugly bastard running down the sidewalk, she gasped. "What did he do?"

"That guy grabbed my falaffel!" cried the girl. At this point, the grocer and the woman from the Community Action Agency arrived.

"What did he do?" shouted the grocer, slightly out of breath.

"That man grabbed my daughter's falaffel!" shrieked the mother.

"That pervert," snarled the grocer. He started chasing again.

"Mr. Firestone!" cried the woman of the folder.

The dumb guy knew that he was being chased. He looked over his shoulder. Behind him on the sidewalk came the grocer, the woman from the Community Action Agency, the mother, the daughter, the Greek counterman, and several other people who had heard the mother's anguished cry. The big man knew that he was in trouble. As he ran he tried to think of what to do. He ran into an office building and past a row of elevators. He ran out a door onto another street. He thought that he might have eluded his pursuers. He ran into another building and up to a telephone booth. He dug in his pocket for the paper with the telephone numbers on it. He read the instructions on the telephone and put a coin—his last money, which he had been saving to use on the bus—into the slot and tried Mrs. Perry's number. There was no answer. He tried again, dialing Molly Calhoun's number. He was luckier there: Miss Calhoun was working past five o'clock. "Hello?" she said.

"Miss Calhoun?" said the innocent sucker, out of breath. "Maybe you don't remember me. I'm that big man from the hospital—"

"Mr. Frankenbaum? Is that you?"

The monster's heart felt lighter. "Yes, dear Miss Calhoun, it's Mr. Frankenbaum." He explained his present predicament and Miss Calhoun, though by nature a rather shy person, was immediately aware of how much danger he was in. She knew that an aroused mob might well destroy such a naive, unsophisticated, virtually helpless monster as he.

"Where are you now?" she asked. He told her. "Stay there," she said. "I'll come get you and take you back to the hospital."

"Thank you and thank God," said the dumb guy. He hung up and waited for her.

A moment later the pursuers ran by his telephone booth. He waited until they passed, then he ran in the other direction. "There he goes!" someone shouted. He ran and ran, not caring in which direction; he just tried to lengthen the lead he had over them. He was stronger, and he knew that they couldn't chase him forever. Finally, though, he began to tire. He realized sadly that he couldn't run away, that he would have to stop sometime and try to explain his plight. Whether or not the angry crowd would listen was another matter. He hoped that Molly Calhoun would be able to find him and help him. He ran. He turned a corner and found himself on a residential block, one much like the block uptown where his former apartment had been. There were three abandoned buildings on the block, and the monster climbed over the rubble and dashed into one of the buildings. He thought that he could hide from his pursuers in a Maytag carton in the dark. He could hear the angry voices from the sidewalk.

"He's in there!"

"I saw him! He ran in there!"

"We got him now!"

"What did he do?"

"He assaulted a girl, back there, right on the sidewalk!"

There were twenty-five or thirty people in the mob now. Bits of information and rumors passed among them. The story of the big man's crimes grew. A member of a youth gang in the neighborhood came by to investigate. He heard the story. "He's in there?" asked the young gang member.

"Yeah, we got him trapped," said the grocer.

"He raped a girl? Right on the street? In broad daylight?"

"He's an animal! We got to get him!"

The gang member announced that no one, *no one,* raped girls in their neighborhood and got away with it. Not on *their* turf. This was a chance for the 5th Street Emperors to demonstrate their civic consciousness. They gathered and had a quick meeting. They decided to torch the building and flush the monster out, and then beat him to a pulp with baseball bats. They began to implement their scheme just as Molly Calhoun arrived. When she saw what was happening, her face went white. She shook with fear. She almost turned and ran away, but she knew that poor Mr. Frankenbaum was trapped, unable to understand what was happening. "Mr. Frankenbaum!" she screamed.

"Mr. Firestone!" screamed the woman of the folders.

"His name is Firebaum?" asked a man in the crowd.

The gang members poured gasoline around the inner entrance and hallway of the building. One youth lit a match, and soon the abandoned tenement was a burning holocaust of orange fire. The crowd made low, odd, moaning sounds and moved back, across the street. Three members of the gang waited for the dumb guy to run from the building.

"What's going on here?" asked a policeman, running from a patrolcar that had appeared around the corner.

A woman turned and pointed to an upper story. A man's form could be seen in the empty frame of a window, lit by leaping flames behind him. "He did it, officer!" screamed the woman. "He raped a little girl and then ran in there. His name is Firebaum."

"He raped a girl and firebombed himself?" asked the policeman.

"Right, officer," said another man.

"Then he's getting what he deserves. Everybody stand back. I got to call the fire department."

High above the sidewalk the figure of the innocent sucker gestured and waved. No sound could be heard from him; the noise of the fire and the screaming of the crowd overpowered his voice. The billows of smoke and the curtains of flame grew. The silhouette of the man vanished as he jumped back into the room. A great thundering sound accompanied the collapse of the roof, and a mighty geyser of sparks and fire flared into the sky.

"There!" cried a woman. "That got him!"

"Oh, Mr. Frankenbaum," wept Molly Calhoun.

The building was entirely consumed by fire. The heat was too intense, and the crowd moved down the block a short distance. Sirens could be heard in the crisp December air.

Not far away, as she walked from her bus stop homeward, Violet Perry saw a glow lightening the sky above the apartment buildings ahead of her. She saw the yellow aura flickering, and she saw the dark smudge of smoke rising above the corona of firelight. Her eyes opened wide. She quickened her pace. She felt her heart beat faster. Ever since she had been a little girl, the magic of great blazing fires gave her a peculiar thrill. She hurried toward it.

THE CARE AND FEEDING
OF EARTHLING GEORGE

by Lois Wickstrom

The author calls "The Care and Feeding of Earthling George" her first big sale and identifies herself as a project of Ed Bryant and Tom Disch. Here, Wickstrom steps outside society to paint a clear picture of our misconceptions and misconduct in the eternal battle between female and male—and between generations.

The typical cassowary is approximately six feet tall, and weighs about 120 lbs. While cassowaries are not obviously dimorphic, it is possible to determine their sex by turning them upside down and looking in the right place. One of the first things you learn when you turn a cassowary upside down, is that it doesn't like it. Cassowaries have been known to kick a human being over an eight-foot wall. For this reason, very few people sex cassowaries.

Until recently, no cassowary offspring were born in zoos because zookeepers did not like to see them fight.

Zookeepers feared that instead of mating, the birds would kill each other, and then the zookeepers would have no examples of this species to house. Normally, a four-foot wall is sufficient to contain cassowaries. However, during mating, the female repeatedly kicks the male over the wall. The zookeepers keep putting the males back inside the compound. When the male reciprocates and the zookeeper finds the female kicked over the wall, it is general knowledge that there will be babies soon.

—a Denver zookeeper

Forl carried the earthling, and Banna carried the empty scrapbook that the adoption agency had given them. They both wore the smug grins of those who have just done a good deed for selfish reasons.

At the agency, the happy couple had sat in a large mock-nest of shredded polyfoam and cooed as they gave $10,000 to the agency bureaucrat. The bureaucrat perched on a rung at the edge of his desk and deposited the bills into a cash register. When he shoved the drawer shut with his claw, the register rang a full-sounding ding and an albino wearing a nurse's hat brought in their earthling, wrapped in a down quilt. The albino placed the earthling on top of the happy couple's feet, and left the room. The bureaucrat then gave Forl the scrapbook.

"In the front of this book you'll find instructions for the care and feeding of earthlings. I'm sure it will be of use to you for years to come. And in the back of this book you'll find blank pages. These are for you to write on and paste pictures of your earthling as it grows. When the earthling is old enough, these memories will help it appreciate its heritage. And if you ever get tired of the earthling and sell it to another happy couple, be sure you give them the book. It is part of our agreement with the earthlings."

"Oh, thank you," the couple cooed.

"Enjoy your earthling," responded the bureaucrat.

As soon as they were out of the office, Forl and Banna unwrapped the earthling. They had never seen a naked earthling before. The earthling had bumps on its skin, just as if it were going to grow feathers.

"We'll give it a much better life than it could have had on its own world," said Forl, hugging the little pink earthling with his wings.

"Yes, we can give it nice clothes, good food, and a wonderful education," said Banna as she put a claw on the infant's cute button nose.

"It's a very lucky earthling to have found fine liberal folks like us to take it in," said Forl as he tickled the baby's tummy with his beak.

"Yes, but you know what they say about earthlings. They're not as bright as we are. That's one reason they have so many babies." Banna removed her claw from the cute button nose.

"But they have a natural mechanical sense." Forl began tickling harder.

"Yes, we are lucky to have one. They say it's just as easy to learn to love an earthling as it is to love your own." Banna started to stroke the baby's head, catching its hair in her claws.

"We should give it an earthling name, so it can feel ties to its own heritage."

"Yes, something strong, like George."

"And we'll have to get it an earthling costume so it can see what its ancestors wore."

Banna and Forl pasted Earth pictures and baby pictures in the scrapbook. George wet its pants and ate pieces off decorative sculpture. Friends and relatives traveled kilometers to see the new baby and congratulate the happy couple. They also ate much of the couple's food. And they had earthling stories to tell.

There was the explorer whose brother got raped by an earthling. There was the broadcaster who still couldn't believe his boss had promoted an earthling over him. "But," said another, "you should see them with a socket wrench. They'll fix your buggy in a jiffy. And they get things real clean when they set a mind to it. But their personal habits . . ."

"Don't you think at least some of that is cultural?" asked Banna.

"Maybe some of it," said their guests, "but be sure you loan it to me after it starts repairing things."

And George grew, and went to school, where it mainly broke things. Forl and Banna dutifully recorded all George's adventures in the scrapbook. They included a picture of George shivering in the rain, followed by a picture of George all warm and dry. They had coated it with black, sticky roofing compound, and then rolled it in plumage swept from the floor at the barber shop. Now George was feathered just like them. They hoped one day to be able to point out to the earthling that it had been clumsy as a child. To show George that it had improved.

George did not do well in school. It insisted on doing math with all its fingers instead of in base six, like it was taught. It was not good at flying. It refused to read and said the stories were boring because they weren't about earthlings. And worst of all, it showed no inclination to tinker with machines. The teacher said George had no leadership capacities, and was socially maladjusted. The other children would not play with it.

Forl and Banna felt like failures. Adoption had failed to free their own procreative powers, and their child was not responding to the advantages of a good upbringing. The relatives were generous: "Perhaps the deficiencies are genetic. You did the best you could. Earthlings are simply inferior." Still Banna and Forl dutifully placed George's papers and art projects, and report cards into the scrapbook. George, too, was adding pictures and words to the book. It drew a picture of the meal they ate on their first rocketship ride together. George had eaten the plates, too. Why anybody would eat that indigestible starch was more than Banna and Forl could figure out. True, they pecked at earthling plates and ingested the shards. But they stored those shards in their gizzards. The book said earthlings don't have gizzards. The book warned the happy couple not to put their claws into the earthling's mouth after it grows its own stones. "Earthlings grow small stones in their mouths when they are small and big stones when they are big. But unlike most stones these can cause the earthling pain if they are broken or if you try to remove them."

"That earthling may grow up to be a juvenile delinquent," said Banna.

"Maybe we should send it to a trade school," said Forl.

"Yes, that might bring out its natural talents."

"Unless of course it might do better in the military."

"Yes, I have heard that earthlings are good at that, too. Still, we should give George one more chance."

"George isn't even good at standing on its perch at school," Forl looked at Banna's tearful eyes, "maybe I should ask the teacher to let it stand where it likes in whatever posture it chooses."

George's grades began to improve. It was particularly good at gathering fallen grain, and it showed interest in disassembling anatomical models. Perhaps, its parents hoped, George would become a doctor, one of the higher-paid tinkering trades. Still, when they had adopted George, they had had hopes that it would rise above its class, and take a good job like ballet dancer.

George was getting tall and its breasts were growing, as if it were preparing to migrate. It was eating second and third helpings of food it used to despise. Its parents were worried, since George had flunked map reading and star gazing. If George migrated, where would it go, and how would it get back?

But George showed no signs of preparing to leave. It packed no bags, as the book said earthlings were known to do. And instead of getting sleep like any normal person before a trip, George began to spend its evenings at school functions. When it returned, it hugged them.

Forl dutifully noted all this down in the scrapbook. Banna became more upset.

"I've seen George dancing with Nesh. Do you suppose it's contemplating interspecies sex?"

"We haven't taught it about sex. We don't even know which sex it is, so how could it figure that out?"

Banna pulled the book away from Forl with her claws, and flipped pages with her beak. "Oh, how embarrassing," she chirped. "It says here that George's growing breasts are a sure sign of George being a female. And the name "George" is in the list for males."

"That gives me an idea," said Forl, "we could breed George and sell the babies."

"Yes, the book says that earthlings breed best in a dark place at 23°C."

"We can arrange that. What else does it say."

"Earthlings like to have a party with cake and fancy old-fashioned earthling costumes before their first sexual experience. They also like to repeat this party with different costumes for each new partner."

"That could get expensive. And what do we do if George wets the costume? The rental agency won't like that."

"Oh, don't worry. We'll get the money back when we sell

the babies. Do you think the Herds would let their earthling mate with ours? They got it nearly eight years ago, so it must be old enough."

"Not the Herds. Their earthling, Lynn, is so badly behaved. And how do we know if it is male?"

"I saw their earthling just last month in the orchard. I thought it was very well behaved. It ate the fruit on the ground and left the nice ones on the branches for the rest of us."

"Maybe it has learned manners since I last saw it. And it does look a little different from George between the legs. We could invite them and try it."

"Do you suppose the Herds will demand a stud fee?"

"Quit worrying about money. We'll get it back when we sell the babies. How many do you suppose earthlings lay at once?"

George wore a long white earthling costume. Lynn wore a short one. Forl wore a black earthling cape and said some magic words from the book. Then George and Lynn fed each other pieces of cake.

"They didn't break any glass," said Lynn's mother. "The book says Lynn should break some glass."

Quickly, Lynn ran to the kitchen cabinets and began removing dishes and throwing them onto the floor. George joined in and threw glass at its parents as well as the floor.

"Is that enough glass yet?" asked Forl.

"I think so. Maybe just one more dish," said Lynn's father. "We must do this right, you know."

George threw another dish and a shard of glass bounced back, piercing her thigh.

"Don't worry," said Lynn's mother, "the book says that females bleed before their first sexual experience can occur."

"Should we cut her some more?" offered Banna.

"She's bleeding pretty much right now," said Forl. "I'm sure it will be enough."

Banna led the two earthlings to the specially prepared dark room. Then she closed the door and joined the other parents sitting in the main room. They waited. And waited. "Do you think we should go in and help them?"

"Let's wait a little longer."

The door opened and Lynn walked out. "George's belly button smells bad, and she doesn't move any more. I don't want to be in the room with George. I don't like it."

"Maybe you should kick George, dear," offered Lynn's mother.

"Or shove it around," said Forl.

"George tried to kiss me," shouted Lynn, and he ran out of the home.

"Give us the money back," said Banna.

"And don't try to mate Lynn again 'til you've taught it better manners," said Forl.

"Well, you should have washed George's belly button," said the Herds as they ruffled their feathers. They strutted out of the house.

George was lying in the polyfoam nest with a puddle of blood around its leg. George was not conscious. Forl and Banna removed the dress before the blood could clot and ruin it.

"I'll kick George, myself," said Forl.

"Now, now, we mustn't impose our culture on it," said Banna.

"Well, at least, I'll clean out its belly button."

George recovered and returned to school.

"Ha! Ha! I hear your parents tried to mate you," teased George's classmates.

"And you tried to kiss Lynn. Ha! Ha!"

After class, another earthling, named Mart, walked George home.

At George's door, Mart said, "Gee, I'm sorry it didn't work with Lynn. I'll show you how it's done."

"You can arrange that with my parents. They have to pay your parents and then we have to have a party and we have to break glass . . ."

Mart grabbed George's watch. George slapped Mart's face. Mart smashed the watch on the sidewalk. "There, I broke some glass. Now will you do it?"

"I have to bleed first."

Mart punched George in the nose causing blood to run down her face and breasts.

Forl and Banna looked on through their window.

"Now they'll do it," said Forl.

"We'll have earthlings to sell," said Banna.

"And it didn't cost us anything," said Forl.

As Mart threw George to the ground and George screamed, Banna said, "We'll have to tell the agency that their book is wrong."

They climbed up to their perch to get a better view.

A CHILD OF EARTH AND HELL

by Jessica Amanda Salmonson

Those of you familiar with this author's work may be expecting a tale about swordswomen, or at least something with an Eastern flavor to it. But Ms. Salmonson has a greater versatility in her writing abilities, and this story will prove it. It is the haunting, compelling, frightening story of a most unusual half-breed: "A Child of Earth and Hell."

I had spent many years in search of my parents, whom I remembered without clear detail: my mother weeping and hugging me and telling me what to say to whomever found me, my impatient father pressing her to hurry and his face now and then grimacing as from pain. It was a simple yet nightmarish recollection, and I suspected even then that they were gone upon a life and death mission to which they would not imperil my life with theirs. Her tears made me cry also; and the crowded concrete sidewalk was a frightening thing in itself, to a child accustomed to soil and woodlands verdant.

63

My father, who had stood almost dispassionately in the background whilst my mother bid her sad good-byes, suddenly staggered against the wall and began to groan. That was when my mother with agonizing effort forced me through the huge door of the railroad station and I saw neither of them again, save in my uneasiest dreams of where they might have gone.

After minor efforts on the part of the authorities to find my parents and learn my identity, I was declared a ward to the state of Washington and placed in a foster home outside the suburbs of Seattle, the city where I'd been abandoned. It seems that the state had no orphanages, which were deemed dehumanizing, and in many cases it was necessary to place children in less than amiable situations merely to provide them any home at all. I was treated abhorrently by my foster family, except on those days, often months apart, when the welfare caseworker dropped by to see my circumstances.

Once, as I recall, I did try to inform the caseworker, during her visit, that I had not been kindly treated. But she could see I was not unhealthy or beaten or dirty, and she surmised, I presume, that I was lying, perhaps out of jealousy of the two older boys, who were my foster parents' own by birth and but one cause of my various distresses. Surely the caseworker recognized my conditions were less than adequate, but she never seemed to grasp the true extremity of the non-physical violence I endured. And it was, after all, especially difficult to find homes for deformed children.

My foster mother, after the caseworker left, locked me in an emptied closet as punishment for trying to be a "tattle-tale," as she called it. I was fed, twice daily, mixed scraps from the family's table, which I suppose was ample feed; and my box-sized room was cleaned daily, so I was at least as well kept as any caged house pet. My false brothers would torment me outside the door by describing the taste and flavor of candies and ice creams they were eating, or by pounding on the door and yelling until I was cowered so far into the corner that I could only withdraw into myself for further escape.

I was not released until a month later, on the occasion of the welfare worker's return visit. I was the epitome of good manners and obedience, complaining naught, for I knew she would not believe anything so outrageous as my being locked away all that time since her last visit, and I did not wish to be so punished for another month as well.

My gratefully accepted reward for being good and silent was my usual run of the basement. I did not mind being kept there at all, for I was seldom bothered except when food was delivered or thrown down the wooden staircase; and I had a private toilet there, several makeshift toys scrounged from the debris and stored items, and even a mange-scarred rat for company, with which I shared my adequate if motley food supply. My one true friend, the rat would generally eat with me, but he was too high-strung ever to let me touch him; he was, after all, wild, and he never came closer than arm's length. His was the first moral lesson I ever learned: a friend, but at a distance.

I should not belabor the cruelties of my childhood, for they lend either an air of disbelief or bitterness to my tale, however true the case may be. And I confess a vile detestment for that family, which emotion is bound to corrupt my memory of early life. But the fact that I spent much of those six years in the dank cellar of a foster home is important to my tale, for certain barely tangible occurrences, I now believe, were early clues to my heritage.

It must be said here, to state it mildly, that I was no handsome child. No attractive child would have been subjected to my treatment. My appearance, I feel, is a large reason for my being placed in a home with people whose only concern was receiving the added monthly income provided by the state for the care of its wards.

No hair graced my pate, and I was regularly taunted by my enemy foster siblings for that baldness. My fingernails were blunt, black, hard things that had to be cut almost weekly lest they grow into useful weapons against my hateful and hated brothers. Beyond these two abnormalities, I was reasonably ordinary and was never accused of being more than merely overgrown and homely.

During these six years of cellar life, I came to appreciate the darkness, even to prefer it. I went so far as to make a willful attempt to seal off the metal grid which allowed fingers of sunlight to stray into my domain each morning. But more, my senses were driven to acuteness. Not only were my eyes grown keen and accustomed to the night, but my sense of touch and hearing were so finely attuned that I could detect underground sounds and movement with uncanny accuracy. I had, by ear and fingertips, learned where the rat's every tunnel weaved, and I envied his smallness, his ability to explore those dark passages.

One of his tunnels I judged to be made of metal, probably a fragment of buried pipe; and one chamber was large enough to cause a perceptible echo of the old rat's padding feet. I thought also that I had detected passages which the rat never used, and I was curious as to why he limited his territory. If it were me, I reasoned, I would methodically conquer every reach of my domain of miniscule caverns and crevices.

One night, as I lay with only the thin coverless cot-mattress between me and the floor, I blocked from my mind the sound of the late television shows upstairs, and listened to the rat scramble underground, questingly. I wondered what had him so busy. Then I heard something extraordinary, a faint noise that might ill-fittingly be termed "slithering." Whatever it was, it seemed to have entered the chamber which was the rat's chief lair, only a few inches beneath the cement floor. My heart beat hard, for I feared some rodent-eating snake had found its way to my one friend's main nest. But in the next moment I knew it was no serpent, for I heard a beguiling purring sound which began to accompany the abrasive slithering on the tunnel floor, and this was confounding when one considered that no ophidian could make more than a hiss.

I sensed and heard my mammalian friend approach his favored lair and stop, sniffing the rank sub-cellar air for signs or odors of the unwanted guest which had risen from deeper, more sinister passages. The rat squeaked uneasily, uncertainly, as though unsure of the alien presence. I envisioned its sensitive whiskers dancing quizzically, its nervous tail, hairless as my pate, twitching. I wondered why the mangy little beast didn't flee; could it sense less than I the presence of the other? I knew the rat to be a wily, crafty sort—but perhaps senility was upon him at last. Or maybe the thing that purred had no odor the rat could perceive, and echoes made him uncertain which way to escape. *Run*, my mind was thinking, but the rat stood fast, either of senility, enchantment, foolhardiness, or the territorial instinct to stand against an invader.

The thing, the purring slitherer, at last struck. I heard their underground tussle and knew the elongated slitherer was trying to loop itself around its biting prey. The rat squealed loudly, furiously, so I knew that he was in peril. In my own panic for his well-being, I began pounding on the cement floor and screaming at the slitherer to go away, leave my rat alone, when suddenly the key rattled in the basement door.

My foster father, a shadowy hulk against the blinding light from the kitchen, beer can in hand, descended the steps in his untied shoes and approached where I lay. He kicked me in the face and two of my teeth were broken out. Without our exchanging a word, and without my whimpering, he left the cellar and relocked the door. That was my first really physical attack, but somehow it was less detestable to me than was the day-to-day revilement and spite I suffered without physical contact of any kind.

As I spat blood and bits of my teeth, I listened for the rat. The slitherer had gone, scared off by my shouting or by the larger footsteps. And the rat had not been killed. It crawled out through the crack in the concrete floor, its manged fur matted with dark blood, its yellow incisors dripping with ichorous slime. It stood there on the ledge of that small crevice, badly shaken by its ordeal, and that night we shared our mutual pain.

Several days later I was called up from the peace of the cellar and cleaned and clothed afresh for the benefit of th woman from the department of social services. Of course the caseworker was curious about my shattered front teeth. She was told by my foster mother that I had fallen down the base ment steps. The caseworker demanded that she see the basement, as it was part of her job to see that the homes of state wards were not unduly dangerous. My foster mother hedged, refused, but with her husband gone, she hadn't enough backbone of her own to resist the caseworker's insistence that she be given access.

I followed innocently, precociously, as the caseworker carefully took the darkened stairway one step at a time, appalled by the stench and disrepair of the place. On the floor, she spied my toys: pieces of blue and green glass from shattered Bromoseltzer and antique canning jars, rusty cans and tools, an old brass water-hose spray-nozzle.

My foster mother was fidgeting with her own fingers and explaining nervously that the basement was almost always locked and no such accident would ever happen again. But the caseworker was not a complete fool and could see the area had been played in with regularity. My rat had been getting a drink from the stained porcelain toilet when we intruded; the case-worker choked back a cry when she saw it dart toward the crack in the floor. Dumbfounded, she stood at the base of the steps. She saw my blue-striped, filthy cot-mattress in the corner, stained with blood not yet turned brown, where my mouth had bled off and on for two nights running.

"Oh, that," my foster mother tried to explain before the question could be posed. "That's just an old thing my husband threw down here."

Still being true to my act of innocence, I passed the case-worker at the foot of the steps and walked with an almost casual stride to my mattress, where I laid myself down as to take a nap, facing the wall so that my insuppressible smile would not be witnessed.

Shortly after, I was taken from that place, and when most of the facts were learned, I understood that my foster parents were to be prosecuted for various offenses. The caseworker discovered that I had not, in my six-year stay, been enrolled in any school, and that my ex-foster parents were guilty of welfare fraud as well as breaking out my teeth and keeping me like an animal. Yet, they never came to trial. I was by then an estimated eleven years of age, large for the age yet in many physiological ways underdeveloped. Whatever my true age, I was old enough to have developed a keen and compelling need for revenge. I doubted that the sentences they might receive would equal my torturous six years, and I knew with a certainty my two pseudo-brothers would escape any kind of punishment, for they were young and would not be held responsible for their part in my cruel treatment.

I did nothing overtly. Even mentally, I did not willfully cause the thing to happen. It was merely a dream I'd had—a dreamland wish-fulfilment, which afterward proved to be the physical reality. Perhaps I inadvertently made the thing happen by some sinister ability unrecognized even by myself, or perhaps I was only an astral witness and not the cause. Or possibly it was coincidence. Yet so strange was the circumstance, I cannot but think it was somehow linked to me. It was too bizarre a happening to be dismissed.

The dream was this, and I had it the second week following my removal from that foster home: I was viewing the familiar cellar and it seemed my spectral self was located near the ceiling, judging by the angle of my panoramic vision. I was calling, spiritually, to the purring slitherer, which I had longed to see since that night less than a month earlier when I heard it beneath the floor. "Slitherer," I called. "Slitherer. Come." I think I heard my voice command aloud, an echo in the darkness, but I knew no one else could hear me. None but one.

The rat, dear untouchable companion, scurried frantically out from the crack and ran madly toward the toilet. He jumped atop the back of it and stood there twitching his tail and squeaking wildly.

The slitherer was coming to my call! I was overjoyed by this newfound power. When I saw it ooze its abominable snake-like, slug-like flesh up from the small crevice, I was tempted to further test my power over it. "Up the stairs," my whispering voice echoed, chanted. "Up the stairs. Up the stairs."

It glided smoothly, leaving a trail of slime to mark its path. The length of it, when entirely distended from below, was several meters, perhaps as many as six. It reared its flattened head with the slow purpose of a snail, and under it I saw the circular razored maw of a lamprey. It seemed to be testing the air by whatever senses it possessed in the four eyes dancing on stalks. A single hole on the side of its long body, immediately behind the head and which I imagined to be a gill or other breathing apparatus, fluttered rapidly, producing the purring sound. It started obediently for the steps, veritably *flowing* upward, matching the contour of the staircase.

My dream continued on and I was experiencing a high degree of delight over the success of my orders. Its slimy flesh squeezed under the door, stretched itself across the length of the kitchen's linoleum floor, and at my mental insistence sped its way around a corner and down a narrow hall, then through an open doorway to where the two boys slept in twin beds. It slithered up one bed post, its air-hole purring with excitement. Unfelt, it attached its razored suction disc to the sleeping youth's neck. With a barely perceptible sucking sound, the boy jerked once, and was instantly leeched to whiteness.

The sticky maw drew away from the punctured jugular and the insatiable, blood-dripping, hideous little head with waving eyestalks looked toward the other bed.

"Hurry," my echoing voice commanded. "There are two more in the other bedroom."

I awoke then, witnessing no other nightmarish feasts, not suspecting until years later that my command had been obeyed even after I woke from my dream. The authorities evidently kept the strange slaying unpublicized, and of course I was never told of the occurrence by my new keepers.

At first I was presumed retarded, but I was not responsible for my lack of education. Their initial judgement was born of other factors as well, aside from my low level of general knowledge. An abnormal growth rate made me seem awkward, though I later became exceptionally coordinated when the speed of my growth subsided and my physiology caught up to my size. I had always had a speech impediment, worsened by the loss of two front teeth, which grew back at an unusually slow pace. My teeth and skull and even the length of my arms particularly intrigued the doctors who initially examined me. My increasing ugliness must have added measurably to the overall appearance of a mentally deficient child. I bore some resemblance, in fact, to a leering spastic with little command over facial muscles, though I venture to say I was actually facially coordinated in my own way.

Because of my presumed mental handicap, I was moved from the Seattle Orthopedic Hospital to a virtual children's sanitarium in the town of Buckley, a goodly distance away. My new home in Buckley was the nearest thing the state had akin to an orphanage. The defective, sickly sorts were kept there—children no one could be expected to adopt, children who needed specialized training or constant care. My playmates were the spawn of inbred minorities, unwanted children of decadent or poor families—some blind, deaf, or mute, or combinations thereof, with birth defects, or scars acquired after birth, and a great many mentally retarded cases. We all had in common the single fact that no one wanted us, though I think no one was as fully cognizant as I of our shared trait.

I did not enjoy their company, and I think I might have gone truly mad and thereby adapted to my situation, but for one saving grace. I was given the opportunity of an education, as it was of primary concern to the establishment that as many residents as had the capacity would be raised into self-sufficient members of society, to one degree or another.

I relished the education, and it was quickly evident to all that I was not, after all, in any way mentally handicapped, though I think they still considered me somewhat deranged, a condition they may have attributed to my traumatic childhood history.

Told a thing once, I remembered it, and I had reached sixth grade level within a few months. I was recognized as exceptional, but a special tutor was beyond the resources of the ill-funded home and my teachers remained the same people who were trained to aid the underdeveloped mind, not the overly intelligent. I was my own best instructor anyway, once the fundamentals were at my command. I read voraciously, everything and anything I could lay my hands on, until I was adjudged as being at the college level of education and still accelerating. The teachers and hospital staff were easily overawed, however, and something inside me always reminded me of my basic inferiority.

My studious efforts were not well organized, thus I went through phases. I had books of more advanced and variegated subjects delivered regularly from neighboring libraries to the sanitarium on loan. For a while, I was deeply interested in prehistoric mammals especially of the ice age. The likes of the woolly mammoth and the sabertooth awakened what might well have been racial memories, sparking in me an academic intensity that was not quenched until I exhausted all available information, much of it exceedingly technical. Eventually I moved on to another obsessive interest, then another. American Indian lore held great fascination to me for a long duration. And though it would be ludicrous to suggest this attraction was also born of some genetic link to the past (for I was obviously kin to no Indian) there was always something barely beyond my grasp that was definitely familiar about those cultures. There were other phases as well that rendered me superficially expert in archeology, world history, philosophy, mythology, and all manner of subjects that had intrigued me fleetingly.

Always there was a feeling of emptiness after I'd completed a study, for though I did not know what it was I was hoping to discover, it seemed certain that I had not found that for which I quested.

And these studies kindled my sleeping imagination—or perhaps awakened an array of memories locked by heredity into my DNA. I would see as vividly as life the glacial ice and the great hairy beasts that roamed there, and in one such dream I saw a grey-robed old man sitting dwarfed astride the neck of a mammoth with long, widely curved tusks. That man was sombre of face and in my dream I could not be sure if the man were an aged and wizened version of myself or of my father. In another dream, I watched savages in a forest gather around a great, tall totem pole, and all the faces of the totem looked like my father. The savages knelt all around it in wonder, and they chanted a weird song in a tongue that was not their own.

That song I remembered even after I awoke. I chanted the words in the manner I had dreamed them, for I liked it better than the nursery rhymes the younger children were obsessed with, though the words were meaningless to me. One doctor took an interest in my dreams for a while, and I think he recorded the sounds of the chant I learned in my sleep. But his time was sparse, and his interest in me was aborted. So my dreams, like my studies, were largely private things, and I largely a private person.

I lived in the sanitarium only two years, until I was thirteen or fourteen. I had grown to astonishing proportions for my age, and the doctors suspected a thyroid problem. I was too large to be kept with normal-sized children any longer, and too intelligent to be left there to waste away. But I was too young to legally be on my own or to start any job rehabilitation program. These sorts of things were talked over in my presence, and I was told one day that I would probably be placed once again into a foster home and allowed to enroll in a regular high school. That circumstance did not appeal to me, however, so I ran away. It was simpler than I had imagined it would be, leaving.

It was not totally without preparation or purpose that I left, for I had two small clues to help me discover my true parents' identities, and I intended to find them. Being tall and intelligent, and too ugly for anyone to guess my true age, I had little trouble adapting to the outside world. Labor jobs, though paying poorly, were not hard to find. Additionally, I stole. My needs were few, but my search made travel necessary, and I learned the crafted art of thievery to make up the difference in bus or train fare—though I honestly did prefer to work for my subsistence whenever possible.

One clue to my identity was acquired from sanitarium files, during my quest for reading material and out of conniving curiosity. The file contained not only medical and educational records, but also a resumé of my earlier life as seen by old caseworkers. Portions that interested me were the areas covering my earliest known history—vague or completely forgotten by my own memory. I was presumed between four and six years of age when found wandering in Seattle's King Street Station. At the time, I carried a wrinkled lunch bag prepared by my mother so that I would not go hungry during the time it took some official to realize I was lost and abandoned. On the old and oft-reused brown paper sack was written a fragment of an address, possibly scrawled by one of my parents. It had been the police department's only clue, but it led them nowhere since it was a rural street address without the name of a town or county, and it might not even be a Washington state residence. Nowhere else in that file was there a tangible clue, though I found out in that one reading how many misconceptions persons had about me.

The second clue was dredged out of my own blocked memory, or from my dreams. Often I had awakened, frightened by some terrible horror, with the stifled cry of "Momma Lydia!" almost bursting from my lips. Possibly I cried out to a Momma Lydia rather than simply Mother because my father called her that, I could not be sure. But at least the name Lydia was one clue I had of which no one else had been aware.

Then, too, I had the potential of remembering more, of seeing something that would trigger recollections of tothood experiences or places. Not three months on my own, one such memory tugged faintly at my mind. My first job was as a berry-picker, and it brought back something of that childhood train-ride to abandonment: we had passed farms of a huge-leafed vegetable, which I suspect was rhubarb, though on that point my memory cannot say for certain. And people were bent among the agricultural waist-high forest, chopping the leaves at their bases. That was all: only a rhubarb field, and it wasn't of much help. But if more memories of the countryside returned, perhaps I'd be able to place myself on the map somewhere near where my parents came from, with me, on that train.

Early detective work consisted of learning from where every train had come, that day I was abandoned. The train schedules were available from the newspaper morgue. It was a futile gesture, I knew, for it was ground covered by authorities when the trail was fresh. And the number of stops at towns and cities was incredible, the additional number of potential transfers incalculable. But I was determined to visit every single burg. Traveling, at least, I had a chance of spying something that would bring back memories.

Several years passed while I lived the life of a road tramp—a singular life, lonely but for the occasional hobo who would befriend me temporarily. From one tramp, as ragged and unkempt as any, I learned that the life of a hobo had once been noble in its way. In his youth, such wayfarers as we, he told me, could find their way into a sub-culture and network of carefully hidden hobo villages, colorful tagrag communities with boisterous elected officials, proud rail-riders, and friends returned from, say, Chicago or New Orleans or San Francisco, all with grand stories to tell. But alas, I was told, that life had died, though there were yet half a dozen or so hobo villages strung up and down the West Coast. Melville, for instance, around the northern Cascade region of Washington, could still boast a fairly large community, completely unknown to the remaining inhabitants of Melville itself.

Bells rang when I first heard my fellow tramp mention Melville in connection with a hobo village. I remembered, so very faintly, the tramps my father used to hire a day at a time to chop wood or plow or tend the vegetable gardens. Why Melville should trigger that recollection, I could not be certain. But that one previous clue, that rural address minus town, was imbedded in my mind.

For one reason and then another, I did not make Melville for several months. The cold season was upon the land when I slipped out of a box car as the train approached that commercial forestry town. Snow splotched the ground sparingly, the really heavy snows not expected for another month; but the biting cold rain was already generously available. Collar up and hands thrust deep in my pockets, I walked away from the tracks, along a muddy narrow road through the trees.

It proved a fruitful journey. Set back among the Douglas firs far along that little-used road, I found that rural address, and it filled my heart and lungs with nostalgia and yearning. Though it smelled no differently than any number of abandoned barns and houses I'd used as shelter over those years, it had a quality all its own when joined with a familiar vision. Hadn't I played near that very porch, now sagging and ready to fall with the rain pouring off and through it? Wasn't that rotted rope on that lone elm's branch the remnant of a rubber-tire swing my father had once made?

It was a painful vision and my eyes blurred. I began to weep, though the tears were not distinguishable from the freezing rain that numbed my high-boned cheeks. There came an urge to turn and flee, not as from unknown terror, but as from an unbearable emotion, a commodity so long pent up in me and threatening to burst forth all in a single flood.

There, in the now crumbling house and barn, walked the ghost of a man who never lived—myself. My ghost: me, as I could have been if some mystery hadn't driven my family to abandon me in a far city and then go on to some other life or place.

I was shaking all around at the shoulders, and my weeping became whimpering as I tried unsuccessfully to control myself between the elm and the firs. Crying for no specific reason to determine: for the atrocity that had been made of my life, for the loving childhood which was the best part but least recalled of my youngest years, for my parents who must have deserted me only by their own sacrifice.

With a few deep breaths, I managed to contain myself, and even managed a methodic countenance as I searched through the rotting timbers. Vulturous persons had been there before me, salvaging anything of value. Thus I found little but rubble and familiarity. Nothing noteworthy awaited at the top of the dangerously creaking stairs, and all I found in the main floor room was a broken bed-frame and a few dry logs some hunter had left unused by the still-sturdy fireplace.

Miserably wet and cold from the subsided rains which still dripped from the eaves and leaves outside, I shook out my long coat, built a fire, and sat on a bed-frame plank across two logs, watching the flames that glowed orange on my face and hairless pate, and I thought.

There were flashes of memories tugging at the back of my mind—impressions almost tangible, here in this place where, quite likely, I was born. But the memories were not useful, merely teasing visions of my father sawing boards laid over a wood-horse or pitching hay or milking the single cow, and my long-skirted mother bent over a steaming pot on a wood-burning stove which now lay rusted and broken in the weed-grown back yard.

Then, suddenly, I jerked forward, staring into the flames, mesmerized by the memory I envisioned there:

I crouched in a nightshirt at the top of the stairs, unseen between the rails of the banister, as my father answered the rap at the front door and my mother stood immediately inside the kitchen. My father bore a shotgun, but the man outside stepped in with a wicked, twisted smile, unafraid.

"Leave us alone," my father demanded.

"You know I can't do that," a deep voice said calmly. Like my father, like me, this man was bald, as I saw when he removed his brimmed hat. "It was not easy to find you. But you can't hide your mind from ours, especially as the Time draws near, as the Change alters your metabolism."

My father cocked one side of the two-barrel shotgun.

The other did not plea, but said, "There will be others after me. And if there were not, would you die here?"

"I would *live* here!" my father shouted angrily, raising the gun to fire and cocking the companion barrel. But his finger tensed and he lowered the weapon. "I have never before begged," he said, in a tone I had never heard from this seemingly callous but truly caring man. "I beg you."

"To what avail?" The mysterious stranger shrugged.

"I have, perhaps, another month. Give me that long. Then I will return."

"Or you will die," concluded the other flatly.

My mother gasped from her listening place and hurried from the kitchen to my father's side. She exclaimed, "Why are you threatening us?"

"Shh," my father said. "He did not mean it as a threat." Then to the tall man—tall as my father and enough like him to be his brother—he said, "Come for me in a month if I have not come of my own accord, and there will be no resistance. Let me live a true life while I can."

The eyes of the other were without evident emotion. But behind that mask of uncaring, compassion must have rested, or pity, or even envy—all these feelings and others, carefully hidden and unexercised. After a cold, glaring minute, he turned abruptly and left without a word, the door slowly swinging shut behind him.

My parents clutched one another in terror, her terror that of not comprehending, his of comprehending too well. His almost claw-like hands ran gently, lovingly, down her back, and he spoke so quietly I almost couldn't overhear, "At least he knows nothing of our son, Momma Lydia. It may be that your blood has made him different from me. In what time I have, I must find safety for him, away from their clutches."

And then, before his beloved Momma Lydia's wondering, frightened eyes could search his with questions, he turned to the crackling fireplace and wrestled loose an unmortared stone. There, in the hollow, he retrieved a parchment tied with string, and he faced his wife again, to tell her with dour expression, "Lydia, were I a poet, I would recite you a verse of love. But instead, I must read to you a grave horror and truth, that you might know me as I really am."

Though sore afraid, strength and dignity was in her, and she promised, "Even then—I will love you."

There my memory, my vision, ended. How much, I wondered, originated in my own locked thoughts, and how much was relayed mystically in the flames now dying before me, like tattling ghosts of a haunted ruin. The fire, or my own mind, had given up its secret, and my fingers fumbled expectantly at the unmortared stone, pulled it loose, let it thump to the floor.

Inside the hollow lay two pieces of paper—my heritage.

The first paper, laid flat and face down, was a yellowed and faded photograph of my father, mother, and myself. My mother was plain, but not unattractive, my father like a brute beside her, smiling fawningly at the baby in her arms. On the back were written all our names, and at last I knew my identity, or part of it. It read, quite simply, "Bennet, Bennet, Jr., and Lydia Strlpretner."

So, I am Bennet Strlpretner Junior. Strlpretner—German? Swiss? Or something more arcane? It was anyone's guess. I tucked the family photo in my ragged shirt. The other paper, rolled and tied, was of rare parchment, so dry and brittle it gave a crinkling complaint as I unbound it. It was in a strange script; serpentine letters crawled across the scroll, familiar somehow, but beyond my reckoning.

I stood staring at that paper held taut between my hands, wondering if I really wanted to know what it meant, what it said. Here were things my father meant to protect me from: horrors he deemed more dread than anything the mortal world could mete out to an abandoned child. Before the last embers of the fire I stood, unmoving, uncertain, and I fancied shadows darker than the shadows reading over my shoulder and whispering among themselves. I let the paper roll shut, and in a desperate pang of fear I held ready to fling the parchment onto the coals. But I did not. I had come too far and suffered too much to throw it away now. I smashed the sides of the scroll flat, folded it lengthwise, and tucked it in my pocket.

I could not sleep there, for my own ghost would haunt me. The hobo village was not far, for it was from there tramps would come for handouts or a few hours work when I was a toddler. There I went, and was welcomed half-heartedly, and begrudgingly spared some hot beans from a campfire. My coat was heavy and usually served as mattress and blanket, but tonight I would sleep with a real blanket, tattered thing though it was, proffered with the same slow reluctance. I was a stranger, and a beggar of beggars, and these were hard times for their kind. Perhaps in other years, they were warmer people who lived like these. Or perhaps they were warmer now, to their own kind; much as my mien resembled theirs, I was yet an outsider.

Before turning in, I sat with a few others around their fire, exchanging pleasantries so that they might more easily accept me, for a few days if necessary, while I collected my thoughts and laid the most tentative of plans. When I removed my hat, the oldest among them gasped in apparent surprise, though he was nearly as bald and not much handsomer than I. His eyes then looked down at my hands, the nails of which I had not cut in some time and were long, black, sharp. For a moment I feared he recognized me as a monster—for such I feared myself to be. But he asked again what I'd said my name was. I had cast off former titles; now I called myself Bennet Strlpretner. His eyes seemed to glisten then, for he had known my father, and worked for him upon occasion. "A generous man," he said. I was thereby linked to their company, and accepted so fully that their propriety and good nature was embarrassing.

I stayed a week, and learned much of my father's personality from the codger. But more, I learned of a strange circumstance following what the man admirably termed, "the sudden disappearance of the Strlpretners." It seems a huge dark traveler came into their village of lean-tos shortly after my family's home was vacated. "Could have been kin to you and your daddy," said the tramp, and he asked questions about "Bennedictus Strlpretner." When the group of bums kept mum (as it was their rule never to aid detectives in finding someone who wished not to be found), the great tall man became violent.

"We all ganged up on 'im, though," the old man said, laughing. "He swung those hands like ball-and-chains, nearly killed ol' Pipeline Henry, but he couldn't out-match us all with our rusty knives and broken whiskey bottles. He turned and beat a track out of here, and I cut him up the arse with a busted wine jug as he went. He didn't bleed, though, so I figure I didn't get deep. Strange feller, that one, no offense now, I mean because I said he was a bit like you."

"Hairless like me, you mean?"

"Can't say; wore a hat. But those hands. Huge! And nails like claws, like yours, like your daddy's. What causes that anyway?" He passed a puzzled look over my fingers and I closed my fists self-consciously to hide the nails. "I don't know," I said.

Shortly after, I was gone—at once sad to leave that supportive atmosphere and pleased to be free of their constant closeness.

I had to have that parchment translated, but a tramp cannot simply walk up to a language professor or an eminent archeologist and ask a favor. It was months before the time was right. I finagled my way into a gardener's job on a community college campus in Seattle. Did a right good job, too, and made certain I came to be on "howdy" terms with all the language teachers. With the meager wages, I rented a cramped room in the skid row district and slept in a bed for a pleasant change— a small bed, but with fewer lumps than the ground. Bought myself some new Salvation Army clothes. Then, one day after classes were done and I noticed one of my "howdying" professor friends had remained behind for whatever reasons, I walked into his empty classroom with my arcane scroll in hand.

He was immediately intrigued. I told him I did not know its origin, or what it said, but that it belonged to my father and I'd greatly appreciate it if I could find out what it said. He ventured that it might be Arabic, Turkish or some derivative, but he didn't know enough about it. If I'd let him keep it awhile, he said, he might be able to get one of his colleagues to look it over. I thanked him kindly, then spent the next few weeks quietly gardening about campus, betraying no impatience.

But I was impatient—for strange visions, waking dreams, were beginning to visit me; and I felt certain that the parchment would contain not only clues to my heritage, but lend purpose to the psychic phenomena I began to endure. At the same time as my occult experiences were beginning to unfold, my old affinity for darkness returned anew. Or perhaps that affinity had never left but, if anything, had only been suppressed.

Each afternoon, my gardening duties fulfilled on the campus grounds, I would escape to my cramped, windowless room, away from the dread sun, and sleep out the day. Come nightfall, I would roam the skid row streets, from the dark waterfront wharves to the decrepit and historic relics of First Avenue, preserved in their decay. From midnight to three a.m. the drunks and sexually disturbed and prostitutes were my unspeaking company; I would pass among them as a shadow, almost unnoticed. Once, a native American Indian, in the grip of sotted delirium, fled from the sight of me, bellowing in his tribal tongue. By four in the morning, the whores and homosexuals would be gone, the winos and alcoholics hidden into stairwells and abandoned buildings, and I would walk alone between the bleak exteriors of pioneer architecture a hundred years old.

But this architecture was young compared to what lay below the city streets. In another era, the whole of Seattle was gutted by fire. Instead of leveling the sturdy, burned out structures, iron girders were laid down and a new city built atop the old. Every year, new portions of that elder city are unearthed or rediscovered, for miles and miles of tunnels worm from one underground building to the next. Some of them are mapped, others are suspected to exist but have not yet been reached. Underground tours are conducted daily through the safest, tamest areas. In Pioneer Square itself, the underground buildings have been sandblasted clean, so that gift and novelty shops run amok, turning these confined areas into tourist ghettoes. Few among the plebeian horde ever stop to realize that these obtainable areas are only the smallest fraction of the entire rat-infested complex beneath the shops and hotels of their mundane world.

I was attracted to that low and gloomy realm. A hound for the macabre, I sniffed out secret or forgotten entries and passages. My clawed hands had minimal trouble pulling up a manhole cover, and I walked beneath the nighted streets, an occasional police car or other vehicle the only sounds above, rumbling over my roof. I came to a section where the walls were interrupted by low archways, seldom visited but not unknown. I entered each building I found, scrutinizing worthless artifacts. The roofs were so low I had to stoop, as none of that early generation was so tall as me. I needed no light, though the eyes of another would be blind in such darkness. Soon, I had discovered places doubtlessly unseen by human eyes since the days they were paved over and forgotten.

Each night I would widen the outskirts of my territory, until dawns arrived and I'd perforce return to my rooming house, bathe at the end of the hall, and go to work, hoping each day for word on the translation of the script. Hearing nothing yet, I would grovel in the gardens beneath the horrid light of day, then bus to my room once more to sleep out the sun, and complete this cycle when returning to my explorations.

I had discovered a place on one of the lower side streets where the boards far behind a tall wooden staircase could be pulled loose and I could enter underground Seattle, then replace the board behind me. I disappeared into that corner, to the consternation of a night patrolman cruising the streets, who shone his spotlight my way an instant too late to see who'd been there.

I made my way along paths known to no other—I, and a few giant wharf-rats. But even they were not common in the specific area I had grown fondest of, and that was odd in itself. The stone-walled, rat-shunned building had once been a drugstore. Among the antiques I found in the strewn mess were many out-dated pharmacy utensils, and in one area a pile of pill bottles fused together by the heat of that historic blaze. A blackened porcelain syrup fountain lay crashed on the floor. There was nothing overtly special about the place, but it attracted me, and I knew by psychic intuition that this would come to mean something.

Near a wall was a perfectly round hole that may have been where a sewage or water pipe once led. One night, I heard noises from that hole, which at first I took to be mere rats. But rats do not speak.

Out of the jumble of many voices, I picked the word "Benedictus" many times. It grew louder, but no easier to understand with so many blending undertones. And then I had my vision, not unlike the vision I'd seen in the flames of a fireplace many months before. Like a genie from a lamp, a ghostly vapor rose from that opening, and it took on the transparent, tenuous shape of a woman in ordinary dress, her arms held out to me as her form wavered into solidity. Her forward-held arms did not invite me, however. The way she held herself, I knew that she was warning me away.

"Go back!" I read her lips saying, though I could not pick her voice out of the other ghostly sounds. "Go back" was the message her mouth was forming.

"Momma Lydia," I called quietly, and walked forward, hoping to touch her, longing for the embrace of her loving arms. I begged to know: "How can I come to you?"

She shook her head, and warned me back vehemently. And then she vanished, like a popped bubble, rejecting me and abandoning me once again. And with her went the haunting sounds. I was left dumbfounded, empty, but not afraid. I was determined to carry on. Her very warning was proof of my nearness!

All morning as I tended the flowers, though the bright colors had come to offend me, though I affected a show of loving my endeavor, I reflected on the spectre of the night before.

When first I began venturing into the eerie catacomb-like hollows of old Seattle, it was merely the longing for darkness, I had thought, which drew me on. Only the instinct of a burrowing, nocturnal beast—for surely I was that, or made myself that, or had been made into that. But now I suspected premonitory, psychic ability, untrained, unrealized, native to my being, which had brought me to the depths below the city *on my quest*.

I remembered, or it struck me, suddenly, like a flash of lightning, a thing that had never before dawned on me, though it seemed so obvious in that instance of enlightenment. My true parents had abandoned me in the Seattle train depot, but *they themselves had never entered*. The train station was on the southern verge of underground Seattle. Indeed, the tracks leaving Seattle were themselves underground railways, buried beneath city traffic.

I had searched in Washington, Idaho, Oregon and Canada, when all the while they had been here. They had never left the city. And my instincts, my sixth sense, or some subconscious logician, had at last led me to their self-imposed burial place.

In my glee of realization, my strong hands broke the handle from the trowel I'd been using to lay rows of marigolds. I stood anxious from the chore, and would have fled downtown to re-enter the maze of buried buildings and dark passages, never to return until I'd found where my parents had gone, or died in the trying. But I did not rush back then, for Professor Bunting was in my path, and the sight of him brought my fitful thinking back from plans of a sub-city existence, subsisting on rats captured by swift bare hands, drinking what seeped down from the gutters above.

What expression was on my visage, I could not know, but it must have frightened poor Bunting, for he stepped away from my hulking height as though I might be dangerous. But after composing my manic thoughts, I smiled amiably, and he reddened as though embarrassed by his moment of foolish terror. He said he had good news.

"The translation?" I asked.

"I imagine so," he told me with a nod. Young men and women hurried down the campus sidewalks to their next classes. "Professor Fennerson of the University of Washington has suggested I have you come by his office. Here—I have the directions written down. I expect he wants to know more of your parchment's origin. He's a noted archeologist, and when he says he's got something slightly phenomenal, you can bet the word 'slightly' is his modesty creeping in."

After minor pleasantries, we parted company, and I left knowing with a passion that I'd not return to that miserable daylight job. I had what I needed now. Or, rather, it awaited at the end of the bus connections to the opposite boundaries of Seattle.

Late that afternoon, I walked into Professor Fennerson's office. Skulls lined a shelf behind his desk, ranging from some tiny primitive primate's to a modern man's. Indian artifacts were hung in random attractiveness all about the room, with an unmatched pair of African masks glowering from among its Northwest cousins. After greeting me with a warm handshake and cordial manner, Fennerson, who was grey with years flesh-wise and hair-wise, tottered to a cabinet from which he removed my parchment inheritance. He set it on his desk, using two ancient-looking pieces of carved stone to hold it flat, then opened his notebook beside it.

"Have a seat! Have a seat!" He waved in a direction and I pulled up a chair to one side of the desk he sat behind.

"I'd never seen a script like it," he was saying. "It's not

that I was too busy to get to your request sooner, my friend. In fact, I set other matters aside to work on this every night. It simply took this long!" He was most apologetic as to the length of time I'd waited, as though his time had been worth nothing. But now all I cared about was the meat of the matter, and I craned my neck in an effort to read his notebook while he talked not of the work involved, but of the extremely interesting nature that made the work worthwhile.

"I worked with Leonard Styles on an expedition, oh, back before the war, in an area still considered Palestine. Styles, rest him, would have known more of this, I think, and would have delighted in it as well. He was always dabbling in arcane matters, forever trying to make some ancient spell or magic work. Poor fellow! He was a genius of archeology, but ignored by his peers for his eccentricities." Fennerson smiled then, mischief in that look. "And he *was* eccentric, I suppose. Never did get any of those spells to work—used to blame it on inadequate phonetics. Said he thought he had the right words, but the pronunciations were wrong."

Fennerson chuckled, and I was growing secretly impatient with his almost senile fondness for relating the past. Then his humor waned a moment and he added, "But no one ever knew exactly what became of Styles. Vanished utterly from his home in England after retirement. I often wonder if he finally got his pronunciations right." The humor that marked Fennerson's brow returned again and he completed his recollection: "I'd like to fancy he did, at last, herald some doom upon himself; he'd have liked that, I think—knowing in his last moment, after a long life, that he was right."

"Please, Professor. I don't mean to be reticent, but I'm dying of suspense. What precisely does the parchment relate?"

"Oh, yes!" he said, as though suddenly realizing the present. He fingered a pair of round spectacles from the pocket of his vest and wrapped one wire stem around each ear. Then he focused on the parchment, his lips pursed, and looked to be reading the Sunday paper spread out before him. Then, bursting into recital, he seemed to be reading directly from the text:

"We came before the French came down from Quebec, before the Spaniards from California. We were first to witness the Straits of Juan de Fuca. First missionaries to the shores of Puget Sound. Before Cook, before Lewis and Clark, before all others of Europe, we came.

"Constantinople was still a power then, from whence we fled. We sailed from that adopted homeland, ostracized, our numbers much reduced by attempted genocide, avowed to settle nowhere near the likes of civilization, nor where it soon might come.

"No martyrs had we been—only sources of heroism for Turks and sometimes Moors, who would prove their bravery by the slaying of a wizard. We sailed. By the sorcery of lost Mu, we crossed the wide Pacific, across seas that covered our once-proud nations. Our numbers dwindled further on the journey. But the strong survived, by tooth and claw and necromancy.

"There were cannibals on Puget Sound then. But it was ritual cannibalism, and the natives would not foul their honored heritage by adding the flesh of outsiders to their own. So we were unmolested. The tribes were peaceable, and always preoccupied with bizarre customs of greed and prestige: who owned the most baskets, who caught the most fish, who held the biggest feasts, who built the tallest totems. These were important among them; and they were, for their needs, a rich people. And we were, for the first time since our land was destroyed by angered gods, free of persecution."

The professor stopped here, took up a tissue to dry watery eyes. He smiled at me and said, "Imaginative, yes? A queer history, or a well-spun yarn? There's more."

He returned to the long page of tiny, snake-like marks.

"One day a young brave spied us fishing without nets. He carried this tale to his people. The story spread, and when it came back to us, we were already legend. Monstrous salmon, said the tale, threw themselves on the shores at our feet, in multitudes unequalled. By their custom, our prestige was unrivaled.

"We feared we might soon become objects of superstitious terror. Instead, the innocent people revered us. The natives made pests of themselves. They built their longhouses on the outskirts of our small community. They came to us begging and praying. We craved solitude, and could not stand their incessant curiosity, interest, reverence. But we could not smite them when they were as children or affectionate dogs.

"Three chiefs we took into our confidence, or made them think as much. We taught them small magicks: how to control a bear or sasquatch and make it do their bidding. How to conjure a ghost, though we were guarded enough that they could not also learn to summon demons. And how to leap uninjured from high places. Several medicine men we taught to heal wounds or cure certain common diseases by reciting incantations more powerful than their own. And we taught them to raise small rocks without touching them, which useless sport pleased them more than any. We were this generous, and more, but only for our own good.

"We knew the medicine men would want the workings of their new abilities kept their own secrets. And the chiefs would want no others to learn the same magicks that would equal them in prestige and power. So it was the medicine men and chiefs came to insure our solitude, keeping their people from coming to our region and learning the same things they had learned.

"A cult sprung up around us. The sons of chiefs and medicine men, and the daughters of priestesses whose line had been more powerful in earlier generations, came to us each autumn with payment of gifts, to be our students. A mystic aura was given us, cultivated by the leaders of the tribes, so that we were no longer bothered save by the few young and honored students.

"Years passed. A century. Our numbers were still not great, but our survival seemed secure. And then one night we were attacked by an army of black bears, and we knew the magicks we had taught, though minor in themselves, had been turned into a weapon of some might by the combined efforts of all the chiefs. We were reduced to the border of extinction, and we were angered. For the first time, we proved our mightiness.

"We set upon one tribe a gigantic spectral raven whose wings produced hurricanes against their villages. This was a dread horror for them, for Raven was their greatest benefactor, creator and uncreator of the world, and they thought certainly they had incurred the wrath of their most honored god. On another village, whose chief and medicine man had betrayed us, we sent a likeness of their honored Thunderbird, who burned and ravaged their community beyond repair. Into another tribe ambled a grizzly bear that dwarfed the black bears beset us, and it killed every brave before it was completely subdued and died of its many wounds taken. Their nights were harried by the presence of soaring white owls, their symbol of eternal darkness and death. We caused crops to wither and fishing nets to come untied at every knot and our temper was so beyond our own control that we did not stop these evil sendings for three days.

"And then we mourned our own sins as much as our dead. We had gained nothing. Vengeance is so hollow. And so we saw that our past history of oppression was not all undeserved, and we deemed our kind unfit to walk with other races of humankind. Thus we cast repentant and repulsive spells upon ourselves that would last unto the hundredth generation. We condemned ourselves to a self-made hell in the depths of the earth, there to live in our so-precious solitude for all our lives, and our children's children's lives, accursed to the sun, accursed to all who might summon us from our living death."

The professor finished the script with a wry smile, and when he looked up to the chair I'd been sitting in, I was not in it. He glanced over his shoulder in time to know his fate. He slumped forward without a grunt, the top of his skull caved in by the carved rock I'd taken from a shelf behind him. I then left with his notebook and my parchment, and threw both into an incinerator before leaving the university. I made my way to downtown Seattle on foot, shunning the close proximity even of transit passengers. The shops were closed by the time I attained the downtown area, but it was not so late that the movie crowd had yet deserted the streets. I felt lost in a sea of oppressive flesh while I made my way to the secret place behind the steps. All the crosswalk lights had seemed to work against me.

With the strength of my inhuman hands, I madly ripped away a large portion of the bricked and boarded section leading underground. I did not regret leaving my entryway more easily discovered, for none would follow so far as I intended to go. A ferret in the night, I found my way through areas none but I knew. There was a chamber, I knew by sense of hearing and touch, existing where I had been unable to find passage, deeper in the earth. I came to the stench of a long-buried, fire-gutted brick structure, and I cried out in despair: "Show me the way!"

My voice echoed with a commanding power and I felt a slight tremor, an earthquake that few would notice though the Richter scale at the University would tell of its passing. A section of the floor gave way beneath me, and I fell, screaming, and fell, screaming, and fell, screaming.

And from the depths of the earth resounded my cry . . . the name of my mother.

AMANA MAÑANA

by Freff

Without literally describing something, Freff is able to
create clear and striking visual images—such as the
last moments of this story. Couple this with humor and
the result is a rememberable story. Add an unusual
scenario and you have a memorable story, one which
leaves the reader wondering how he or she would react
in the given situation. And conversing with one's refrigerator is certainly unusual...

APPENDIX A: SELECTED EXCERPTS FROM THE DIA-
RIES OF THE FIRST, compiled and edited by Felix A.
Amerson, M.D. (Frozen Windfall Press, Mecca Institute,
Bensonhurst Colony #6911, ⊗ 1991):

October 18th, 1981 (second day)
    I've got to tape this, got to get it down. I've got to get it
down *now*, before I flip out again. I sure the hell can't tell
anybody about this. Who'd believe me? Adriana? Hah! She'd

just say I was doing drugs again and dump me. Well I *was* doing drugs, of course I was doing drugs, but it was only acid and that's not so bad and besides oh christ on a goddamn crutch what am I gonna—I can't even tell Amerson. He'd probably strap me to his couch and call Bellevue. Do they still cart off lunatics?

But I'm not crazy. I'm not I'm not I'M NOT . . .

Christ I can't breathe. Anxiety attack.

Paco, Leo, the other guys at work—can I tell them? Nah. They'd come up here, grooving on the gag, but when they saw what was on my refrigerator they'd—

I don't want to think about it.

No way. They can't call you paranoid if you keep it a secret from all of them. Mum's the word. Handle this myself. But when I think about going back in the kitchen I feel like I'm gonna throw . . .

I I I I IIII

Too much can't cope Oh *God*

Lots calmer now.

It's six p.m. I threw up a few times, drank some scotch, took some Valium, managed to get some sleep. I don't feel much better. In fact, I feel terrible. But maybe I can face this thing, or pretend to.

All right, I'll pretend I'm being logical.

Who is involved? Me. And the refrigerator, of course.

What's happening? Damned if I know.

Why is it happening? [*incoherent laughter*]

Skip *where*. *When*, at least, I can sort of answer.

It started about three a.m. Saturday morning. I'm not exactly sure; I was on my way down from a trip, so my time sense was all blurry. I started feeling hungry, so I went into the kitchen to feast. That's when I noticed the little sign on the refrigerator. It was green and about the size of an index card. There were purple letters on it.

PLEASE DO NOT OPEN. I AM NOT YET ACCUS-TOMED TO YOUR PLANET'S TEMPERATURE RANGES.

That's what the card said.

I must have laughed for five minutes. Everything's a little funny on acid, but this was right up there, a prime practical joke, like something out of an early Firesign Theatre riff. Right away I blamed Paco. I mean, he sold me the stuff, and he knew I planned to use it, and he knew where I kept my party key, so I figured he must have snuck in while I was tripping under the headphones. Paco is that kind of guy. I spent a few minutes trying to think up ways to get even, but I kept being distracted by wall textures and stuff. For a while I even forgot I was hungry.

The refrigerator door wouldn't open.

If I pulled real hard on the handle it would give, ever so slightly, but that's all. It wouldn't open.

And then I noticed that the little green sign was pale blue, and the purple letters had turned glaring neon red, and they spelled out I ASKED YOU NOT TO DO THAT. I jammed my nose up against it. Whatever it was, it wasn't paper, and there wasn't any edge. It seemed like . . . like it was *in* the door, not on it.

That's what dropkicked me from euphoria to bananaland. I got out of there so fast I nearly broke my toe on the goddamn doorframe and didn't even notice it. I think I was screaming, too. It's a little vague now.

Three hours later, when I was sure I was down all the way, I worked up enough courage to go back in.

The sign was green again.

WE CAN WORK THIS OUT, it said.

I . . .

I don't want to think about it.

October 21st, 1981 (fifth day)

It's a good thing the Costanzas are off on vacation, because I *was* screaming the other night. Hell to pay if I'd woken up my landlords and their kids . . . bad enough that old bitch Trenini across the street called the cops. Said she'd heard a "hippie mass-murder." The pigs have been up and down the street ever since, on foot, in patrol cars—twice already I've had to play dumb.

Having a real persecution complex instead of a neurotic one is no fun.

The refrigerator's okay, though. I mean: relatively. It's still possessed or whatever but I'm not terrified now. Amazing what you can get used to. Nervous I am, very nervous, but not terrified. Dr. Amerson calls it Coping. He also says I'm no good at it (why else would I be seeing him?) but I'm down to two Valiums a day and that's good enough for me.

It's like trying to drive late at night when you're flatass tired, and the only way to hold it together is to concentrate so ferociously that nothing else exists but the road, you know? I go to my job. I paint my share of shutters. I joke with everybody, get high on the fumes, come home and listen to records or watch TV or sleep. I sleep as much as I can. But most of all I try and look normal. Sometimes when the sane line narrows up I imagine I hear people whispering about my refrigerator. I know it's paranoid, but knowing doesn't help. It happened coming home today, and even though it's cold I sweated through two shirts and part of my jacket.

I hate this. Why me? Why not some other schmuck? I can't bring people up here. Adriana thinks I'm having the place painted. I live in absolute fear of hearing that door open, *all by itself*.

For breakfast the last few days I've had toast and peanut butter. At least I still have strategic control of my pantry.

For now.

October 22nd, 1981 (sixth day)

This morning I went into the kitchen and stared at the refrigerator for a long time. (Know Your Enemy.)

The kitchen is small. There are drawers that stick and cupboards that open at inconvenient angles and molding you have to keep shoving back into place and lots of coffee stains. No roaches, thank God. And there's the refrigerator. Standard white enamel job. One door and a chrome handle. Piece of wood shoved under one leg to keep it level despite the cruddy linoleum. Magnetic strip on the front with lots of recipes and bills under it. Three hooks and two potholders. The dent I made hauling it up the stairs . . . all normal.

Except for that little sign, mute proof that I'm not crazy.

Or that reality is.

Big difference.

It hasn't printed anything since I took off screaming. Caution, maybe. I'm leaving it alone, and it's leaving me alone. But quiet or not the goddamn thing is still there, like a piece from the coat of many colors: blue, green, gold, white. Once it was pinstriped. No matter how long I stare, I never actually see it change. But if I look away or blink—bam! It's very frustrating.

Also, the refrigeràtor motor is running all the time now.

It must be really cold in there.
I could unplug it . . . but that's too risky. I—
I think I'll wait.

October 24th, 1981 (eighth day)
I either made a breakthrough or I'm about to die.

I can't believe I just said that. I'm sitting here waiting for dinner and I feel like an idiot. Also nervous and curious as hell and scared shitless, all at the same time, but I'll be damned if I'm leaving this room before that timer goes off.

Last night Dr. Amerson and I talked about habits. He knew something else was bothering me, but I wouldn't talk about it and he never pushes when he can glide, so we shot the whole hour with me bullshitting about habits. I'm real good at them. I told Amerson that I thought everything in the world was really habit; he loves that kind of blanket statement. And then I told him that survival of the fittest actually meant being able to get into necessary new habits *fast*. That makes me very fit, 'cause look at me—in a little over a week I've gone from terror to collaboration.

This "journal" (hah)—there's a new habit, a good example of what I was talking about. Every night, just like religion. Now I lay me down to tape. Maybe it will give me perspective when this is over. And if not that, if I'm poisoned tonight or go completely bughouse, then Amerson can at least get a few laughs and a monograph out of it.

That's what the breakthrough—breaking point?—bit is all about.

Adriana and I went out for lunch today at La Gioconda, the one under the elevated on 86th. Maybe she got suspicious because we've been eating out so much, or maybe I was just too twitchy. Anyway, she asked me two different times what color I was painting the apartment.

The first time I said white and the next time I said blue. *Idiot!*

She started screaming, right there in the restaurant. Said I wouldn't take her to my place because I was keeping some other woman there, and I said, *"No, I'm not,"* and she said, *"So take me there right now and prove it,"* and I said, *"I can't,"* and that's when she threw her scallopini in my face. I tried to grab her. Figured I could calm her down, get her outside, something, *anything*.

She kicked me in the crotch.

God, that hurt.

Where was I? Oh yeah, breakthrough.

The one led to the other, see. When I finally got home I was so angry that fear got crowded right out of my brainpan. I'd bought a crowbar on the way back. One way or another, I said to myself, it ends now, even if I have to beat the goddamn refrigerator into scrap metal.

I rounded on it and took aim. One mighty swack to show it I meant business, and then I'd give it my demands.

New words flashed onto the card. They were dark grey on light grey.

DO YOU LIKE YAMS?

That was it. The fabric of reality was eaten through by moths.

"I hate the fucking things!" I screamed.

YAMS DO NOT FUCK, it said.

All of a sudden I couldn't hit it. I was nulled out. I mean: flat, empty, drained. Imagine, two years wasted on an analyst when I could have been doing primal screams.

Besides, it had a point.

"You have a point," I told it.

THANK YOU, it printed, in tiny sparkles of silver. LET'S TALK.

"I don't trust you."

YOU'VE GOT THE CROWBAR.

That was two hours ago, and now I'm about to eat its peace offering.

I wrote down everything it printed out, all the different colors and such, everything, but for now I just want to get the conversational feel.

"Who are you?"

ME.

"What are you?"

ME.

"Straight answers or I bash the door off."

OKAY, OKAY. I'M A REFUGEE.

"From what?"

THAT'S CLASSIFIED. BUT DON'T WORRY, IT ISN'T GOING TO MAKE THINGS HOT AROUND HERE.

"Dammit, you take over my refrigerator, you scare me silly,

and that's all you have to say?"

I CAN'T SAY ANY MORE THAN THAT. ON THAT SUBJECT. ASK SOMETHING ELSE.

"For now I'll let you get away with that. Why me?"

PURE ACCIDENT. IT WAS AN EMERGENCY KIND OF SITUATION.

"Then this isn't a permanent thing? You don't intend to stay in my refrigerator forever?"

I SHOULD HOPE NOT. THE ACCOMMODATIONS ARE LESS THAN STRIKING, EVEN WITH TEMPORARY IMPROVEMENTS.

"What do you mean, improvements?... No, strike that. What do you mean, temporary? *How* temporary?"

SIXTY-SEVEN DAYS. YOUR DAYS, THAT IS. FROM NOW.

"And what happens then?"

CLASSIFIED.

It went like that for a long time. I kept pushing to know why it was there, and it kept refusing to tell me.

"You're an alien, aren't you?"

NOPE, YOU ARE.

"I live here!"

ALL IN YOUR POINT OF VIEW.

I kind of dug the thought that it was an alien. I mean, I'd seen *Close Encounters* and looked for funny lights in the sky and all that stuff. Aliens! Sure! Made perfect sense. Well— some sense, anyway. I admit I'd expected something flashier than an index card on a refrigerator. Actually, my biggest emotion was relief at finally having some answers. I didn't even care if they were lies. Anything beat the big Not Knowing.

I'D LIKE TO PAY RENT.

"Huh?"

PERFORM SOME SERVICE. MANAGE A RECOMPENSE. PAY MY DUES.

"I still don't quite follow."

I AM STUCK HERE FOR AT LEAST SIXTY-SEVEN MORE DAYS. I WILL BE AN INCONVENIENCE TO YOU. DO YOU LIKE YAMS?

"I told you before, I hate them. Why are you so on about yams? How come you know anything about earth vegetables, and our language, or anything like that?"

CLASSIFIED. I MENTION YAMS BECAUSE THEY

ARE NUTRITIOUS AND HAVE A PLEASING COLOR.
SINCE I AM OCCUPYING YOUR FOOD PRESERVATION
CENTER, HOWZABOUT I COOK FOR YOU?

"Howzabout?"

CLASSIFIED.

"'Howzabout' is classified? It's just slang."

MY APOLOGIES. I THOUGHT YOU SAID 'HOWZA-
BOUT.'

"I did!"

CLASSIFIED.

I lifted the crowbar.

JUST KIDDING. WHAT ABOUT MY OFFER?

That took a lot of thought. It was weirdly easy to imagine
a dumb horror movie plot, in which aliens possessed refrigerators, made wisecracks, and then poisoned people.

Maybe I *was* hallucinating the whole thing.

I'M WAITING.

"What do you know about cooking for humans? You're not
from here!"

JULIA CHILD. GRAHAM KERR.

"What?"

THEY DO TELEVISION SHOWS. WE PICK THEM UP.

Then it printed a shopping list. Yams had been scratched
out.

The bell just rang.

Me and the alien reached a deal. If I like this trial run, then
it suggests the food, I buy the food, it cooks the food, and I
eat the food, the only precondition being that I stay away during
meal preparation. The whole thing reminds me of Pandora's
box but I'm too damned hungry to care. I can't face any more
peanut butter and toast and warm Coke.

It kept buzzing CLASSIFIED at me when I asked it why
it wanted privacy. Maybe it's really ugly, or shy, or maybe
. . . maybe it's scared of *me?* Wouldn't that be a trip. But I
don't care about that, either. I just want the next nine weeks
to go by fast and with no more trouble, after which I'll probably
throw all these cassettes into the Narrows and never watch
Twilight Zone reruns again.

Smells pretty good in the kitchen. Guess I'd better check
it out. I wish me luck.

• • •

Christ, it's a four-course meal!

Shrimp cocktail for an appetizer, mushroom and veggie soup with Monterey Jack cheese and spices, this gorgeous steak with broccoli and cream sauce, and mandarin oranges in gelatin for dessert. Whoa!

The gelatin is blue. That's a little disturbing.

But everything else . . .

Still, I'd better go slow. One bite of the shrimp, first. Now I understand why medieval kings had tasters.

God, that's good.

Five minutes gone and I feel fine. My stomach is growling, but that's hunger, not pain. Funny. I never noticed it before, but hunger has an edge on it that's a lot like being high.

I should take another bite and wait. I should.

But then the food will get cold, you know.

I'll wait.

That steak looks so *good*.

I'll wai—

The hell I will. I'm too hungry. We who are possibly about to die give in.

Oh wow. Wow ow wow ow WOW.

Food, glorious food/Cold sausage and custard/When we're in the mood/French-fricasseed Bustard . . .

Oh wow.

This stuff is wonderful! I have never eaten stuff so wonderful in my whole entire life by God! Screw you and your casseroles, Adriana! Screw greasy sandwiches at dirty delis! Screw health food! God save my gracious refrigerator!

And I want me to know we *mean* that. The edge has turned into a razor. Razor's cut my tongue. Tongue's loose, loosed moorings loose on waves of flavor that are sweeping under my tongue and through my stomach and in the room like big blue gelatin oceans of warm diamonds, you know, just like diamonds, and when I finish-finish-finish this I think-think I'll eat the puh-*lates* 'cause everything in the world looks and tastes and smells and feels and sounds wonderful what a rush THE COLORS look at that bloody index card go . . .

Moremoremoremoremore!
I'm nine hundred feet tall—*Did you know that?*
And I'm gonna *take over the world!*
Can I have another helping? Prettyplease?

October 25th, 1981 (ninth day)

It's eleven-thirty p.m., and I'm down now.

I think.

At least, I've been listening to the tape of me raving and it no longer makes the tiniest bit of sense, so I guess I must be straight again. And I feel great—how about that!

In fact, I'm kind of sorry it's over. That was without a doubt the finest culinary and/or drug experience I have ever had. Julia Child never whomped up anything like that.

No side effects, either. No sore muscles like acid, or dizziness like grass, or nausea like psilocybin. I'm going to the bathroom an awful lot, but that's understandable. Judging from the plates on the table and in the sink I not only ate dinner, but also a buffet breakfast and a brunch and a lunch and some snacks and another four-courser, all of which have now blended into one glorious stereophonic 70mm technicolor blur.

It begins to look like the next nine weeks won't be so bad after all.

November 16th, 1981 [*date approximate: reconstructed from other sources*]

This is the first entry I've been able to record in over a week. It's all turning to shit. I can't go on like this.

I've lost my job. I've lost my girl. I'm losing weight. My clothes don't fit any more (but what does that matter—I'm so feverish all the time I can't stand to wear much anyway.) I'm nervous and twitchy and more paranoid than ever before and my Valium prescription has run out and I don't dare go to Amerson for more because he'd restrain me now, I just know he would, and I can't keep food down unless it's stuff my refrigerator fixes, everything else I just throw up, and, and . . .

Does this sound like I'm complaining?

Damn straight!

The last two weeks I don't have any grasp on *at all*. It's all fuzzy, just random scenes, no continuity. Did I take a swing at Paco before or after Adriana said she didn't want to be seen out with a drug addict? Did I tell Adriana that lie about giving her the clap before or after she swung the vacuum cleaner pipe at me? I can't find my car! Where the hell did I leave it? Was it stolen? Did I *give* it away?

I don't remember.

I'm scared to go outside. There are people out there. They'll stare at me. I mean, how often do you see a guy plowing through two feet of snow in a T-shirt and cutoffs—and sweating?

I've got all the windows open and the air-conditioning on and there's unmelted snow on the foot of my bed and I'm *still hot*.

I remember now why I lost my job. It's because I wasn't working. I was taking my refrigerator-fixed lunches into the john and blissing out.

Actually I was in the john all the time anyway. I just can't seem to stop.

That's another reason I can't go out. How far would I get before I couldn't help myself?

What's happening to me?

It's the alien's fault. It can't be anything else. But if I smash the fridge or pull the plug out or bug out now there'll be no more food fixes. I'd starve. I can't give those up. Before I'd do that I'd—

Oh goddamn damn *damn* not again!

[*The remainder of this cassette contains nothing but the regular sound of plumbing.*]

November 22nd, 1981 (37th day)

Right now the question is: Do I kill myself or go on with this crazy nightmare? I've never been a believer in noble suffering—just the miserable selfish greedy kind. I admit it. So why should I throw away everything that ever defined my life, when I could just go run in front of a snowplow? It's come down to that. The way of the fridge-alien and whatever it's turning me into; starving myself to death; or ending it quick and clean.

They're invading. I'm sure of it.

But I'm getting ahead of myself.

After the last entry I tried to run away by running straight into it. I ate everything the fridgething served up. I fogged out all over again; you know—the little death, 'cause I couldn't face the thought that I might have to go for the big one. Christ, was that ever a mistake. I finally woke up yesterday morning, sick and filthy, curled over the arms of my wicker rocker. Let me catalog the changes brutally. If I'm blunt they don't seem so scary. (Distancing techniques courtesy the good doctor A.) I'm shorter. I'm a lot shorter, down from 5'11" to 5'7". *I am not imagining this.* I weigh less, of course. That must be why my proportions don't seem a lot different. But other things . . . my palms and fingers are lumpy and calloused, like I've been doing hard labor. They're all red. And hair? Hair! Hair everywhere, except the calloused places, like my hands and—did I mention the soles of my feet or the area just around my eyes? No. Well. Excuse me, imaginary person I'm taping this for. Lately I've been confused. My moods swing a lot. Your moods would swing pretty wildly, too, if you'd shitted and pissed away thirty pounds of yourself.

I haven't eaten since I woke up yesterday. Haven't slept, either. The pain is pretty bad, like little critters with claws in my gut. Toilet paper is running low. I either go out, like the fridgething suggested, or I start in on old copies of the *Post*.

I've had two talks with it since I woke up. The first one didn't accomplish much, but this morning's was productive. I'll read my notes to you. (To the future me? I wish I could be sure.)

DON'T BOTHER ASKING ME FOR THE TRUTH. IT'S STILL CLASSIFIED.

"I'm not going to ask. I'm just going to tear you apart."

HO HUM.

I didn't like the sound of that, and said so.

I'VE TAKEN ADVANTAGE OF MY TIME HERE TO BUILD SOME FORTIFICATIONS. IF YOU ATTEMPT ANY KIND OF SABOTAGE OR VIOLENCE YOU WILL RE-CEIVE AN ELECTRIC SHOCK CAPABLE OF KNOCKING YOU OUT.

I dropped the crowbar, but my fists kept bunching and unbunching.

REALLY, NOW. IT'S JUST SELF-DEFENSE.

"Self-defense! *Self-defense?!* Just who the fuck is attacking who around here, anyway? How do I defend myself from your lying, and your goddamn addictive food, and and—"

IT'S FOR YOUR OWN GOOD. TRUST ME. YOU'LL BE

FAMOUS AND HAVE A WONDERFUL TIME.

"I'll be a freak!"

NOTHING OF THE SORT.

I grabbed up the crowbar again and swung it.

When I woke up I didn't feel like ever doing that again. There was fresh food on the table. It smelled delicious—as usual—but I wasn't buying.

"I'm not going to eat that. I'm not going to let you poison me any more."

SIGH. NOW YOU'VE CAST ME AS A BORGIA. I'VE ONLY YOUR BEST INTERESTS IN MIND. PLEASE LISTEN VERY CAREFULLY. THERE ARE NO MIND-ALTERING SUBSTANCES IN THAT MEAL. THAT STAGE OF THE PROCESS IS OVER—I COULD KEEP INCLUDING THEM, IF YOU INSISTED, BUT THE RESULTING EMOTIONAL SPASMS WOULD BE COUNTERPRODUCTIVE. BELIEVE ME, I'D LIKE TO TELL YOU WHAT'S GOING ON. I'M AN ETHICAL SORT. BUT I CAN'T YET, AND THAT'S ALL THERE IS TO IT. WHAT I MUST INSIST ON IS THAT YOU KEEP EATING. IT'S VERY IMPORTANT.

"Oh yeah? How important, you lousy sneaking—"

QUITE.

"You must think I'm a jerk. Well, I'm not that gullible. Not any more."

PLEASE UNDERSTAND. IF THERE WERE SOME OTHER WAY THIS COULD HAVE BEEN DONE, IT WOULD HAVE BEEN. YOU ARE IN THE MIDDLE OF A VERY DELICATE PROCESS. IF YOU DON'T KEEP EATING . . . WELL, YOU'LL DIE.

After a moment it added: I REALLY WOULDN'T LIKE THAT.

And in the end hunger wins another round. Hunger always wins, with me. I'll bet it was counting on that. I wish I could con myself into believing that staying alive is as courageous as killing myself would be.

Bloody hell. This pelt I'm sprouting has started to itch.

November 30th, 1981 (45th day)

I've been listening to some of my older tapes, and I'm pretty disgusted with myself. No sense of stability. Always jerking from one state of mind to another. But now I feel like I have a direction.

I remember this movie... what was that title, again? Ah yeah. *The Incredible Shrinking Man*. Ol' Incredible and me, we have a lot in common. Bigger worlds, narrower focuses.

Funny, I can't remember precisely when I finally started to like this. Maybe the alien's been putting tranks in my food. But I don't think so. I've done downers before and they never made me feel like this. I feel... good. Together. Everything is finally stabilizing. My attitude, my sense of temperature (for the record, anything above thirty degrees is pretty unbearable), the times of day I have to go, everything except my height. Every morning I measure that against the fridge. Inevitably it has gotten lower.

I think I understand Adriana better, now that I'm small. Easy to be nervous when nearly everyone's bigger than you. I learned that at the bank today.

What an adventure!

What a drag.

First thing I had to do was prepare. I began with a cold tapwater bath (a bit on the muggy side, but pleasing.) Then I shaved everything that I'd have to expose, my forehead, cheeks and nose, neck, some of the upper chest, back of my hands, leaving just a full beard. This fur is getting *thick*. I crapped out a pair of scissors doing the first hack, and it took two razor blades to finish the job—which is already sprouting out again. Crazy. Anyway, then I started modifying my clothing. Ripped the guts out of my winter coat, stuffed some giant garbage bags in. Filled the bags with ice supplied by my helpful fridgethingie. The coat hung well below my knees and looked lumpy—but then, it had looked lumpy in the first place. I'd just have to be careful not to bump into anybody.

Under the coat all I wore were some jeans I'd cut down, and sandals. I'd decided I could get away with those.

The world was accommodating. There was this lovely sleet storm going on, so I didn't have to wear the coat until I got near the bank. (Not my regular one—a branch. I couldn't take a chance on being recognized and having to explain myself. "Oh, it's nothing. I've just been a little sick, lately." Right.) The storm kept on helping after I got inside. What few people were there were wet, miserable, and thoroughly self-occupied.

Tall, too.

I hadn't been out since the shrinking became overt. It made me nervous being loomed over by little old ladies.

But it made me more nervous, getting grilled by the branch manager. The teller couldn't make such a large withdrawal without approval, so she sent me to him. And he called my old bank, and got approval there, and satisfied himself that my signature matched up with my ID, and generally had to admit that he was going to let me withdraw all my money, but . . . damned if he was going to let me do it easily. He kept asking questions and squinting his little piggy-eyes at me. As if closing out my own account was a sin.

Or maybe he was just prejudiced against midgets.

It got intense. I was *very* uncomfortable, even with my icecoat. The place was an oven. Once in a while someone would come through the doors and a blast of cold air would accompany them; it was all that kept me going.

Sweet relief, then, when I finally got back outside, a roll of bills in my pocket.

After that, a few errands. Standing orders at the grocery. Certain things from the hardware store. More razors, just in case. Two cases of toilet paper. And a note for my landlords, with advance payment of the next two months' rent. As long as they've got their money they won't bother me.

December 17th, 1981 (62nd day)

I had guests tonight. Scared them away, too. A regular David and two Goliaths scene.

The sound of them on the stairs woke me up. Those big people are so *clumsy* . . . they shouldn't bother trying to be covert. It's like thunder trying to sneak through the sky: impossible, ludicrous. I was out of sight under the table and ready for them before they even made it to the apartment door.

But they did surprise me. It was Adriana . . . and Paco. Paco who knew where I kept my party key.

They were holding hands.

So silly, the way their eyes were all wide and their shoulders hunched. Paco fumbled the light switch on and they stepped all the way in.

"Mike? You there, Mike? Where you been hidin' the las' few weeks, man?"

No way in hell I was going to answer. But how to get them out?

"Jesus, it's cold in here!"

They solved my problem for me by going into the living room first, instead of towards the bedroom. Once their backs were turned I charged across the floor and leapt for the light switch. Made it first try. Paco hadn't yet gotten the living room lights on. Everything went black.

Adriana screamed quite satisfyingly.

Then I ran past her leg and poked at it. That scream was even better. She grabbed Paco. I kicked his ankle. He grabbed at it in pain and the two of them got tangled up, going over like cows at a packing plant. Hah!

They did get away, finally. But not without bruises.

Just after they left I deadbolted the door (an intricate maneuver, that; had to use a chair and some books) because I was afraid they might come back with reinforcements. But there's no chance. They aren't very imaginative people. Given a little time they'll rationalize it all as bulb burnouts and bumping into furniture, and the fear beneath the rationalization will keep them from coming back and making sure.

Big people are so *stupid*.

December 25th, 1981 (70th day)
A Christmas soliloquy:

It's beautiful tonight. I'm sitting on my west-facing windowsill. It's in a blind corner; I can see, but I can't be seen. The sun set an hour ago, and now the afterglow is gradually being replaced by the crazybright glitter of thousands of strings of Christmas lights, staining the snow on the eaves and roofs and windowsills with little pools of color. Just over the buildings, looking close but really far away, is the Verrazano Narrows bridge. From here it's just another string of lights. Christmas . . . people spent today opening presents and eating glorious feasts. Me, I had a feast and no presents, but that's okay. That's fine by me. I've got something better.

I've got peace.

That sounds silly to me, even as I say it, but it's the truth. I've never been happier. All the troubles I had before came from not fitting in; now that I don't have to bother, all the pressure is off. There's lots of room in the world for me, all the room I could possibly ask for.

I'm not entirely sure what I'll do when my savings run out, but there's plenty of time yet to think about that.

And in five days, on December 30th, I'll know The Secret. The fridgething has given me notice.

I wonder what it is. When I thought I was being poisoned it made sense to assume that some kind of invasion was going on. But that was a half-assed idea. Then I thought: a test? Am I being used as a guinea pig by other intelligences? Or maybe I'm the class project of some artist in alien biologies...

The thing is, it doesn't matter *why* it happened. I'm just glad it did.

And I may not be such a freak, either. Looking out over these thousands and thousands of roofs makes me wonder if there might not be more like me out there. Could others have been running the gauntlet with little cards on their refrigerators? Are they sitting on their windowsills now, thinking the same sorts of thoughts as I am?

No matter. There are carolers in the street and the air is clean and icy cold and a breeze is ruffling my fur. I think I'll take the tape recorder back in and then climb onto the roof and roll around naked, making snow angels.

Merry Christmas to all, and to all, a Good Night...

December 30th, 1981 (75th day)

Well, it's gone now. But it left a note.

HI, MIKE. SORRY TO RUSH OFF LIKE THIS, BUT TIME IS CRITICAL IN THESE EARLY STAGES. THANKS FOR BEING SO GREAT ABOUT EVERYTHING. I HOPE THIS NOTE WILL HELP YOU UNDERSTAND WHAT WAS GOING ON...AND, WELL, I HOPE YOU'LL WANT TO KEEP "DOING BUSINESS" WITH US.

SEE, IT WAS ALL AN ACCIDENT. WE DIDN'T MEAN TO MESS UP YOUR SUN. NOT REALLY. IT WAS JUST AN INSIGNIFICANT LITTLE EXPERIMENT THAT KIND OF...BACKFIRED. ONCE THAT HAPPENED THERE WAS NOTHING WE COULD DO TO REVERSE IT. OF COURSE WE RAN COMPUTER SIMULATIONS IMMEDIATELY. THEY SHOWED THAT THE ONLY CHANGE OUR FAUX PAS WOULD CAUSE (THE ONLY ONE WORTH MENTIONING, ANYWAY) WAS A RADICAL SHIFT DOWNWARD IN YOUR PLANET'S AVERAGE TEMPERATURE. BYE BYE HUMANITY.

WE COULDN'T LET THAT HAPPEN, COULD WE? THERE ARE FINES FOR THAT SORT OF THING.

I'M SURE YOU'LL APPRECIATE BOTH THE DIFFI-
CULTY OF THE TASK AND THE ELEGANCE OF OUR
SOLUTION. WE DECIDED THAT INSTEAD OF SUPPLY-
ING YOUR PLANET WITH BULKY, COMPLICATED
PROCEDURES FOR OFFSETTING THE CHANGE (WHICH
WOULD MEAN TALKING TO YOUR GOVERNMENTS,
AND WE WEREN'T SURE THEY'D BE UNDERSTAND-
ING) WE'D JUST ADAPT *YOU* TO *IT*. IT WOULD BE
SEVEN OR EIGHT YEARS BEFORE THE WORST HIT,
ANYWAY. THAT WAS ENOUGH TIME.

TAKE ONE SOMETHING. MULTIPLY IT BY TWO.
MULTIPLY AGAIN BY TWO. MULTIPLY *THAT* BY TWO,
AND SO ON, AND SO ON, AND SO ON . . . PRETTY SOON
YOU HAVE A VERY LARGE NUMBER.

YOU, MIKE, ARE OUR NUMBER ONE. SIXTY-SEVEN
DAYS OF TREATMENT HAVE TURNED YOU FROM
HOMO SAPIENS SAPIENS INTO *HOMO SAPIENS FRI-
GIUM*. (I'M OFF NOW STARTING ON NUMBER TWO.)

I KNOW THIS IS A BIT UNEXPECTED. YOU—AND
YOUR PEOPLE—HAVE EVERY RIGHT TO BE ANGRY.
BUT WE'LL TRY AND MAKE IT UP TO YOU, REALLY
WE WILL.

IN THE MEANTIME, I'D LIKE TO MAKE YOU A
PROPOSITION: WOULD YOU LIKE A JOB? THE HOURS
ARE FAIRLY REASONABLE, IT'S CHALLENGING, AND
IT INCLUDES ROOM AND BOARD. (IF INTERESTED,
JUST PRESS THE BLUE BUTTON ON THE INSIDE OF
YOUR REFRIGERATOR DOOR.)

January 2nd, 1982 (1st day)

Well, I'm all set and eager to start. The card is in place.
The door is wired shut from the inside (that's just temporary;
I'll come up with something better.) All my stuff is moved in
and the first drug treatment is ready to go.

Now all I have to do is wait for the Costanzas to get home.

Partially I chose to start with them because of convenience.
They're just downstairs from my old place, after all. But mostly
it was the math. I worked it out. If I got one person this time
around, and we each got one the next time, and so forth, in
a little under six years there would be 4,294,807,296 of us.
That's one hell of a graduating class.

But there are *seven* people in the Costanza family . . .

By that one action alone, according to the numbers, I can knock three months off the Plan! (Of course, there are problems. Mrs. Costanza is Very Very Catholic. I hope she doesn't try to have me exorcised.)

I wonder how long it will be before this whole thing goes public? Before people start lining up to be converted? We could make a big sales pitch to folks on environmental grounds: little people use up less of our resources, that sort of thing. It'll foster teamwork, too. Any slackers in the foxholes are going to get buried when the glaciers start rolling.

I just thought of a riff from an old fairy tale. "Seven at one blow," indeed. Ha ha.

Awful warm, even in here. Oh well. I think I'll go lie down in the freezer until they get home.

[*Editor's note: The tapes from which this (highly) abridged appendix have been drawn were given to me by Mr. Michael Demarest, formerly one of my psychiatric patients, at the end of my own Conversion. Mr. Demarest's current whereabouts are unknown, but certain reliable rumors place him in Manhattan. We at the Institute hope to verify this next July, when the mild summer season allows reshoveling of the Brooklyn Bridge trade routes.*]

A NOTE OF EXPLANATION

People keep asking us, "Who is this Freff person?" Freff himself hasn't fully figured it out, and we present the following as a brief glimpse into why.

YOU ASKED FOR IT, I WARNED YOU, NOW PAY THE CONSEQUENCES OF YOUR RASH MISDEED (BIOGRAPHICAL MATERIAL ON FREFF)

Since appearing in THE BERKLEY SHOWCASE #2 my life has been a mad swirl of parties, honors, and acclaims. Any recent week will serve to illustrate. For example:

MONDAY, OCTOBER 12th: Notified by Nobel Committee that my thinly disguised autobiographical work, "Wembly at the Zoo, Vol. 6" has won. Can I be in Stockholm for the ceremony by Thursday? Sorry, no clean socks. I decline. The Swedish Embassy in Kansas City, site of my upbringing, is closed in a gesture of retaliation that I choose to ignore. Go to movie. Recognized. Good sweater and new jeans ruined by screaming mobs of older women. Home again, mail contains latest royalty figures; I'm in my fourth new tax bracket in as many months. Investment counselors advise purchase of small island near Mauritania. I make a bid on Coney Island, instead. I like real estate I can see from my window. Drop load of socks at the cleaners.

TUESDAY, OCTOBER 13th: Have hair cut and hennaed. Have cat's hair cut and hennaed. Have Mercedes upholstered in yak hair, and cut and hennaed. George Lucas calls—Where are script revisions for VADERS OF THE LOST ARK? In mail, I promise, lying. After lunch I dash them off on some table napkins and give them to my messenger service for posting. Party tonight at Bo Derek's. No clean socks. I send my regrets. Successful people must have no mercy. Instead I eat dinner at home with my wife, Amelia Sefton, and a few intimate friends. Something, it is decided, must be done about the balance of payments. If Japan exports much more to us, my stock investments will send me to the cleaners.

WEDNESDAY, OCTOBER 14th: George calls again. He loved it. Socks come back from the cleaners. To celebrate George's call, I send them back again for a second rinse.

THURSDAY, OCTOBER 15th: Birthday. I reflect on my twenty-seven years. The Oscars, Emmys, Nobels, Grammies, Purple Hearts, third-grade good citizenship awards . . . somehow, today they all seem empty. Mail contains song publishing royalties. Change my mind. Bo calls. Linda calls. Jackie calls. Marie calls. Sylvia calls. Woody calls. I agree to go out with him to the Proust Film Festival at the Lone Star Cafe. Fly to Boston to take my socks to a special cleaner I've heard of in that city. Drop them off and fly back. Sweden sends letter of complaint to White House concerning my no-show.

FRIDAY, OCTOBER 16th: A good day. In the morning I find a theoretical proof for the Lominsky Interface Paradox, refute

Kant on the immutability of consciousness, and go buy bagels. Ronald Reagan calls, asking me to please invent time travel so that I can go back to attend Thursday's ceremony in Stockholm just as soon as my socks are clean, thus averting war with Sweden. After lunch I do that, but as I'm about to step into the device another me shows up from the future and says it wasn't worth it; the veal at the ceremonial dinner was strictly from hunger. But I'm in need of a break before the afternoon conference with the Defense Department, so I hop in and spend a few years herding prehistoric animals into the La Brea tar pits. (You think they would have been stupid enough to get into that muck themselves? No way.) Come back with a nice tan; everybody at the Pentagon says so. Sweden makes first move at economic war, banning sales of hand massage units and blondes to this country. Alan Alda calls to tell me he thinks I'm sincere.

SATURDAY, OCTOBER 17th: Go to opening of my play, EVERYBODY SINGS LOTS OF SONGS AND WINDS UP RICH OR HAPPY OR BOTH; my homage to Ibsen. Richard Nixon is there. He's heard of the time machine, asks me if he can borrow it and go "to the best of his recollections." I stall. Hard to get out of Times Square due to long lines around military recruitment offices. America is responding to the Swedish threat with renewed patriotism. I do my share, shipping all my socks (dirty and clean) to the USO. At least I know our boys won't be losing any toes to the Swedish snows. Decide that's a good, snappy slogan. Sell it to Young & Rubicam. Gary Trudeau calls—do I have any good ideas for DOONESBURY? I pass on Nixon conversation. Andy Warhol calls. Dan Rather calls. Miss Piggy calls.

SUNDAY, OCTOBER 18th: Buy new socks, and rest. Sweden surrenders.

And I owe it all—the honors, the improved tempo of my urban existence, the glory of celebrity—to my appearance in THE BERKLEY SHOWCASE. What new heights might I scale after appearing there once more? I dare not guess.

THE SAILOR WHO FELL
FROM GRACE WITH THE VOID

by Karl Hansen

Here, in Hansen's bone-jarring, mind-jangling style, is an extraordinary retelling of the story of the eternal triangle. It is a story of passion, deceit, regret, atonement, and punishment. It is a timeless story, one destined to be lived and told over and over again *ad infinitum*. This is as good a one as you will ever read, set in a perfectly visualized future and positively seething with life.

Jupiter looms in the sky overhead. But I know this orientation is mere illusion—I am fooled because Ganymede's gravity by definition pulls *downward;* the other direction, then, arbitrarily is *up*. I know that in reality the Jovian mass is below always. Ganymede perpetually falls around Jupiter. I irrationally fear the wires of centrifugal force will break and I'll plunge into the Jovian atmosphere. Sweat beads along my spine. Firestorms rage on the gas giant's surface, reaching for me. Their

111

albedo dims the surrounding stars. My heart pounds in my chest. But I cannot look away.

Then tiny new stars flare quickly along the halo of the planet, as gravships flash from shadow into sunlight, and solar fire shines from taut gravsails. The racers stream down from the planet like sparks from a carbide wheel, shoot past overhead, and disappear behind the horizon as they make one orbit around Ganymede. Then they appear again settling down to their anchorages, like dust motes dancing in air.

I watch all this through the blister dome of my club, which is perched on the rim of the great crater of Chalise. The other domes of the city are clustered like berries on the crater floor below.

I was once a sailor myself, a long time ago, when the void was disrupted by noisome nuclear rockets. I once had my own fuship. I once tempted the energies. Sometimes I wonder what it's like to be a sailor now. Do their hairs still tingle with ionization? Are their eyes still seared and frosted by fire and ice? Are they as afraid of the blue empty—so scared it's better to know what's out there than to only wonder. I think not. Not these new sailors who are not men.

I go back to polishing glasses.

The ships are in port. Soon the evening crowd will arrive. Business will be brisk. It always is during the races. Especially if your club is considered chic this season. *Critical Mass* is very chic this year.

Nostalgia as a state of mind is *de rigueur* this season. Suddenly, all the new sailors yearn for the bygone days of fusion rockets, when spaceships spewed plasma-hot particles from their thruster nozzles, when sailing the space-lanes was tempting death. Sailing is safe and sane now. Gravships sail on currents of gravity, whispering in from the void as graceful and serene as the flight of the extinct birds of Earth. Crashes are rare. Ships are seldom lost. Radiation leaks are not possible. Danger is unknown.

And sailors are not men entirely.

So *Critical Mass* panders this wave of nostalgia for the nuclear age. The club's dome is constructed around the standing hull of an ancient fuship freighter. The old radar pod protrudes from the vertex of the dome. Cargo pods are now dancing surfaces ringed with lucite tables and chairs. Crew quarters are now lavatories and powder rooms. The control cabin has been converted to a private dining room. In the center of it all is the old fusion thruster, still humming with nuclear life: rings of helium-cooled, super-conductor magnetic coils still generate a bottle of magnetic field; hydrogen still fuses into helium and heat; plasma still squirts from the nozzles of the thruster, but only a dribble, as now the power has been dampened to the minimum level before complete shutdown would occur. The energies are asleep. Clever deflector shields turn the jets of plasma upward, where they stream harmlessly into space, like a fountain of light. Very impressive after dark. Sailors are lured to it like moths to a candle.

Sometimes they even know the proprietor of *Critical Mass* was once a sailor himself, that he once raced in the Jovian Cup. Of course, it was a pitiful race compared to one with gravships. Fuships were so much slower and clumsier. Even twelve-meter racers. Nothing at all to be proud of. Pride is a luxury I forsook long ago.

Soon I see the first of the sailors approaching. They come in small groups, leaping from dome to dome across the crater floor, gliding fifty meters in the weak gravity of Ganymede. With the vanity of hybrids, they disdain the more conventional means of ingress to *Critical Mass*—the airlocks and connecting tunnels of Chalise. They can easily survive up to an hour in vacuum without oxygen or protective suits. Hybrids incline to be obvious of their advantages over non-hybrids. And why not? They can do things true men can only dream. Their jumps remind me of the grasshoppers I used to watch as a child on Earth. I also think of ants. Some childish fable dimming in memory.

A liftube drops from the dome of my club a thousand meters to the floor of the crater, opening into a commons dome of Chalise. Behind this transparent cylinder, is a cliff of glacial ice. The sailors forsake the lift's convenience. Instead they scale the cliff by clambering up the outside of the tube, clinging like tree frogs to its smooth surface. Before long, they enter my club through the blurred orifice of the outside doorfield. Ions spark around them briefly, like corposant, as the static they collected when passing through the charged field of the door is dissipated into the air. Even St. Elmo shares his fire with these new sailors, as well as his patronage.

My hostess greets them with a kiss and sticks a radiation badge over their hearts. My guests love this cunning touch of verisimilitude. As the evening progresses, the badges slowly change color. A simple chemical reaction, not excess radiation. Rads would be harmful to my staff. But the guests don't know the difference. They're charmed by this simple trick.

Sailors are splendid creatures, and they know it. They are long and lithe, with smooth musculature rippling beneath skin as black as wet obsidian. Their eyes are the blue of flawed turquoise, when not hidden behind silver nictitating membranes. Sonic jewelry glitters from fingers and toes, dangles from ears, and hangs around slender necks. They wear only capes of fine spidersilk clasped around their shoulders, having need for neither clothing nor modesty. Their heads are bald. Vitalium wires form convoluted ridges beneath scalps gleaming with transducer gel. Sailors are creatures of both flesh and metal. They are cybernetic hybrids. They are not men. Hardware in their skulls allow them to become an integral part of a gravship. But their software is not entirely human either. Xenogenes from several other species were used to modify their tissues. They are adapted to the void. They have no reason to fear the blue empty. Anti-radiation pigment granules in their skin absorb energies from ultraviolet to cosmic rays. Sweat glands secrete a monomer that insulates them from both temperature and vacuum. Brown adipose tissue stores oxygen. Ocular membranes protect their eyes. Ears and nostrils have sphincters to close them. Fingers and toes are equipped with suction pads that can grip polished surfaces.

Sometimes I wonder if their genes are confused by hybridization, if their soma is not disturbed by being a chimerae— a blending of frog, bat, whale, bird, and human tissues. I know their thoughts are different than mine. Their brains are not human brains. And the changes are more than a little cyber-surgery to implant wires, electrodes, and transducers—though those have been implanted. Motor and sensory cortex and cerebellum have been expanded. Their brains must drive more servos and receive more data from sensors than any human mind could handle. When a cybrid sailor places his navhelmet on his head, he becomes a part of his gravship, as well as a gestalt consciousness. His mind fuses with the minds of two other sailors and in turn with the mechanical physiology of their gravship.

I wonder if there are not dim urgings of racial memory from the animals whose xenogenes were used to modify their brains—secret yearnings to fly in the breezes of Earth beneath a moon of night. If so, Brit would not tell me. And I asked her more than once.

The sailors sit together on cushions on the floor or at tables. They laugh at the clever things they say to each other. Or maybe they laugh at me, or the contrived antiquity of my club's decor. Maybe they are amused by synthetic danger. Pseudo-fear is funny. No matter. They keep coming back for more. Their chargrings transfer credits to my account. I have been laughed at before. I once looked up the meaning of geek. There are worse fates.

The evening has deepened; only Jupiter-light shines outside. Inside, music emanates from sonic crystals hanging from the dome. Tendrils of song swirl among dancers like dew-coated cobwebs. Their bodies become tangled in the filaments of music. Naked skins gleam with monomer sweat. Bodies embrace, release, embrace again. Waiters ply among the tables with silver trays, offering mnemone, peptides, and rare liquors. Intoxicating fumes fill the air. Laughter from a thousand throats blends into a cacophony of noise, beneath which drones the endless hum of fusion.

I stand at my place behind the bar, watching numerals flash from a display register as transactions are tallied, smiling as the cumulative gross steadily increases. Business *is* brisk tonight.

My eyes glance about the club. It has become crowded. Music swirls. Dancers dance. Euphoria shines from a thousand eyes. The mood is right. I press a call-button beneath the bar, then lean back with my arms folded across my chest, smiling smugly. I *am* rather clever.

An old sailor appears in the liftube. He stumbles out and shuffles across the dance floor, heading toward the bar. He too is a relic from the nuclear age—radiation scars pucker his skin; his eyes glitter with cataracts; scraggly patches of hair hang like clumps of dried grass from his pate; a black cancer grows like a fungus from one cheek. The energies have left their mark on him.

I pay him a trifling wage to come to my club each night. When the time is right, I summon him to make his appearance. He is very popular with my guests—almost as much as the throbbing fusion thruster at the center of *Critical Mass*. The old sailor is worth the pittance I pay him. Authenticity need not be expensive. His ravaged countenance is my *pièce de résistance*. And why not? The new sailors are immune from radiation damage, even though there are no longer any un-shielded rays. Their bodies have protective adaptations. They can afford to laugh at an old man mutilated by too many rads. They can easily snicker at the effects of the wanton rays of a bygone age. Such deformity is not seen much any more. There's money to be made pandering morbid curiosity.

The old sailor totters over to the bar. I pour him a glass of Earth wine. This one luxury I allow him. I let him remember in the wine the Earth he'll never see again: warm sunshine, cool rain, gentle breezes, rich, moist soil. I can afford that much. I pay my debts. I have a reason to give him wine. My own reason. From my past.

He gulps the wine greedily. Red liquid dribbles from lips too scared to seal properly and drips from his chin to stain his shirt. His glass tips over when he sets it down. Then he wanders along the bar, tugging on the capes of real sailors. "Have you been to Earth?" he asks anyone who doesn't shove him away. His speech is garbled by scarred vocal cords. A woman laughs delightedly. "Have you been there?" he asks her.

The woman smiles. "Yes," she says. "I've just come from Earth." Sonic earrings flame.

"Is it as beautiful as it once was? Is the sky still blue, the clouds white? Do lightning and thunder still crash from roiling skies? Does the dew still sparkle? Are the forests still too green to believe?" Bright intensity shines in his eyes behind glittering cataracts, as he remembers a youth squandered to the raw energies of fuships. "Is it still the Earth I remember?"

"I suppose," she says. "But it seemed rather plain to me, all green and brown and blue. I'd rather look at more vivid colors. On Mercury, there are yellow lakes of molten sodium in which to splash. On Mars, one can ski on carbon dioxide snow that sparkles whiter than any snow of water. On Titan, liquid methane drips from the facets of crystal trees. Old Earth has nothing but dirt, and water, and smelly plants. I couldn't leave there soon enough." A single strand of sonic pearls hangs between her breasts, blazing like a string of neutrons. Her teeth shine when she smiles.

"But what about the animals? Are they still there? Do hawks still wheel in thermal updrafts, do eagles still pluck fish from lakes? Do whales still spout in the sea?"

"I don't think so. Not very many, anyway. They were all used up years ago. Their genes were harvested by bioengineering combines. The DNA was needed to make people into hybrids, who could populate the other planets and moons. A small sacrifice," she adds, and smiles again.

"No animals?" the old sailor mutters. "Then I'm glad I can't go back to Earth." But his eyes are downcast. He meanders among my guests, begging sniffs of mnemone. Soon synthetic memory glows from his eyes. He becomes lost to pleasant reverie.

The young sailors love him. They coax him out on the dance floor. He stumbles amid bright filaments of music, becoming tangled in swirling wires. He totters on legs deformed by radiation-contractured skin. Musical strands wrap themselves around his arms and legs and seem to tug on them. He dances clumsily. Taut lips try to smile. He trips and sprawls on the floor, becoming covered with musical silk.

Young sailors go back to amusing themselves.

Jupiter has now climbed to zenith and hangs directly overhead, casting ocher light into the crater of Chalise. There are no shadows in the city. The radar pod atop my dome points into the eye of an angry vortex swirling across the planet's surface.

I avert my eyes, looking downward. Another pair of eyes stare into mine. I know the look I see within depths of shattered tourmaline. I see it often.

The woman sailor laughs. Teeth shine. Her friends have abandoned her for other amusements. Sonic pearls sing their song in light.

I laugh with her. I know the game she plays. "What's your name?" I ask.

"Greta," she says, smiling. She looks to the edge of the dance floor, where the dancers have hauled the limp form of the old sailor. He is still covered in a blanket of optical music. "Don't *you* want to ask me questions about Earth?"

"Not I, said the fly."

"But you also sailed in the old days." It is not a question. She touches the smooth, unflawed skin of my face, then lets her fingers run down my neck and slips them inside my tunic. Suction pads pull gently. "Where are your scars?"

"My scars don't show."

"Ah, a tormented soul. You must write poetry?"

"On occasion." I signal Pierre, my assistant, that he should take over the bar. He knows the routine. He knows where I'll be if I'm needed. Then I walk around the bar and take Greta's hand in mine.

"Where are we going?" she asks, laughing. But she knows. She has heard. She knows who I am.

"Sunbathing."

She touches her tongue to the edge of fine, white teeth. "But it's night." She smiles. She knows.

"Somewhere it's always night," I answer by rote, then lead her away from the bar.

My bed chamber is carved into the solid rock beneath the dome of *Critical Mass*, centered on the axis of the hemisphere. A circular staircase winds down past thruster nozzles to a door marked PRIVATE. A deflector shield forms the ceiling. It is carefully tuned to avert all energies except a little of the visible spectrum and the near ultraviolet.

Greta and I lie together on pulsating wombskin. Her skin shines with monomer sweat, mine gleams with PABA oil. A few minutes ago, we made love. Now we lie together basking in the glow of used love and the brighter glare of controlled novae. For if one looks directly up at the ceiling, one can peer into the interior of a fusion chamber. I wear contact filters in my eyes. Greta's nictitating membranes have closed. Even though the deflector shield turns away all but a fraction of the thruster's energies, unprotected eyes would quickly go blind in the glare of the remaining light.

My body is covered with tiny red circles made by the suction pads on Greta's fingers. One earlobe bleeds where she nipped it with her teeth.

"Do you sleep here?" she asks. "With all this brightness?"

I nod my head. "If I close my eyes, I see an image that has resided in my mind for a long time. It's easier to sleep in blinding light."

"An image?"

"A swirling vortex in crimson."

She looks at me. "Why a Jovian firestorm?"

I pretend not to hear.

Warmth beats into our skins. My hand touches a control knob.

"Why does he want to know about Earth?" she asks.

"Who?" I take my hand away from the knob.

"The silly old sailor upstairs."

I pause. The glass walls of the bed chamber shimmer with light. I answer: "Because he can never go back home again. He's exiled here on Ganymede."

"Why is that?"

"His body suffered certain strains once, and was exposed to too much radiation. He took a risk he should not have taken. He tempted the energies once too often. No matter. Though he survived, his body would not tolerate even the stress of one G. Blood vessels would rupture. His heart would leak. Earth's gravity would kill him. So would the acceleration of a departing gravship. He cannot leave this lovely moon."

"Then what they say is true?"

"What do they say?" But I know. I've been waiting for this question.

"The stories about you and him. And a Lady. They speak of a Lady too." She looks at me closely. "Are the stories true?"

"I suppose."

"Then *you* tell me the story." She giggles. "I want to hear you tell it."

"I need to know something first. A question for you?" I have asked them all the same question.

"OK."

"What is the substance of your dreams. I dream of fire. What images bother your dream-time?"

She touches her finger to my chest, tugging on a nipple. "I'm not sure I can describe my dreams to you—we're not the same. I'm not even sure the thinking part of my mind can describe them. I have different ancestors than you—my brain is part bird, part bat, part whale. My racial memories are a blending of four. Only the thinking part is pure human. My dreams are those of air and water and concern feelings you cannot understand." She laughed. Eyes and teeth both shine. "Is that an answer?"

"A confirmation." My fingers seek the control knob again.

"Now it's your turn to tell me a story—about the Lady and the sailor who fell from the void."

I stare upward, gazing into thermonuclear fury. My hand rests comfortably on a control knob. Fire pushes away other images of fire. I whisper, telling a story by rote I have told before and will tell again, until I'm exorcised of its demons. But there is another way. My fingers sweat. If only I had the courage to twist the knob. But I don't. So I keep whispering instead.

Those times were tempestuous, those days at the end of the nuclear age, before gravity was harnessed and sailing became safe. The energies they used then were wild, barely controlled, like nuclear genies straining to escape their magnetic bottles. Accidents were common; radiation leaks were expected. Life was dangerous. Death was always near. No one wanted to live forever. Few did. Space-men lived with wild abandon: riches were easily accumulated, more easily squandered. Risk was taken without second thought. And what was greater to risk than one's life?

Settlements clung tenuously to the surface of the outer moons. Every depravity was pandered: sex, drugs, gambling, pain, and death all had their houses.

And the people were still true humans—fragile and easily broken.

Then came the first of the hybrids—creatures who had been adapted for space with graftings of xenogenes.

One of them was a Lady.

Her name was Brit von Yee.

She was a sphinx—part human, part cat. Her kind had been bioformed to build New O'Neil. They were sleekly furred and had eyes that could see in the dark. They had an uncanny sense of balance and could move with lithe grace as they scrambled easily among the girders of the space colony, assembling its far-flung pods. When the construction was finished, they wandered about the system, rich from accumulated bonus pay. One of them was Lady Brit von Yee.

On Ganymede, she found a sailor...

Chalise was a port city. The space-port lay in the center of a great crater twenty kilometers across, and consisted of a ten-kilometer disk of fused rock upon which nuclear rockets landed, with hangars, depots, warehouses, and terminals ringing the landing area. Beyond the boundaries of the space-port proper was the Combat Zone—a ring of bars, peptide parlours, mnemone dens, and mind casinos. Legitimate hotels and businesses lay at the edge of the ice cliffs that lined the walls of the crater.

Brit von Yee prowled the nighttime of Chalise. She had only recently arrived on Ganymede, coming sunward from Titan. She had tired of the diversions there, and had heard they were better in Chalise. She'd heard of blue-space racing. She was going to give it a try. But first, she needed a sailor.

She entered a cabaret. Heads turned; eyes stared. Sailors were not yet used to seeing hybrids. Sailors were still true humans. But she was worth staring at. She wore only a spidersilk cape. Silver fabric was contrasted against the orange and black of calico fur. Her eyes were amber; their irides were contracted into vertical slits even in the dim light of the cabaret. Her ears were pointed and tufted with red hair. She had long arms and legs with supple muscles. Her belly was flat. Her breasts were faint bulgings beneath the fur on her chest. A ruby choker circled her neck.

She walked in long, graceful strides across the room, past tables of gaping sailors. Her eyes looked beyond them. Her nose wrinkled.

Then she stopped suddenly.

Her eyes stared.

She stood before a table where two sailors were seated. Candlelight flickered across their faces, but to her eyes the dimness was as bright as carbon arcs. The sailors couldn't see, but the fur rose at the base of her spine, where her tail should have been. Her eyes glanced back and forth between their faces. Her throat quivered.

Both sailors stared back at her. They looked enough alike to be brothers, but they were not. Both were young, with short-cropped hair the color of wheat. Their skin was tanned deep bronze. One had eyes the green of jade, the other steel grey. Muscles bulged under skin-tight shirts of golden polymer. One draped his arm over the other's shoulder. One rested his hand on the other's arm.

For a long time, the only movement was that of their eyes: nystagmus in green, grey, amber.

Then one of the sailors coughed. The spell was broken. Green-eyes spoke: "You seem to know us. But that's impossible. For I would remember meeting you."

"Perhaps in dreams," she said, then paused.

"Dreams?"

"Maybe we've met in the dream-time?" She laughed a rough sound out of her throat. "Maybe our thoughts have mingled in the blue empty."

"I would have remembered that also. But we are being rude. We enjoy a Lady's company, as well as our own. Won't you join us, Lady?..." His voice trailed off with the implied question; his eyes glanced to an extra cushion.

"von Yee. Lady von Yee. But call me Brit." She seated herself at their table.

Green-eyes spoke again: "And I'm Jacob Stevenson. I go by Jake. My friend is named Ston Kurtner."

"Does he talk?" Her bare foot stroked someone's leg under the table.

Grey-eyes smiled.

"Sometimes," Jake answered. "When something needs to be said. Otherwise I talk enough for both of us."

A waiter passed, carrying a tray of mnemone sticks. Brit grabbed a handful and stood them in a ruby vase. She picked one randomly and snapped it open, inhaling the fumes deep into her lungs. She then passed one to each of the sailors. They repeated her ritual. Soon the edges of vision blurred, as synthetic memory began its intrusion into sensorium.

"What do you find so intriguing about us?" Jake asked. "Why pick us, out of a room full of sailors?"

"Instinct," Brit answered, placing a slender finger against her lips.

"And what do your instincts tell you?"

"I want to make it with both of you." She smiled, licking her lips with a pink tongue.

Jake laughed. Ston stared straight ahead, peering through appositioned fingers. There was brightness in his eyes.

"Rather direct, aren't we?" Jake asked.

"Someone has to be."

Brit's hotel room was the penthouse of the Ganymede House—a persplex pyramid capping a kilometer-high crystal spire that rose out of Chalise crater beside cliffs of ice. On one side could be seen the cracked and cratered surface of Ganymede. On the other, far below, the city of Chalise lay shrouded in hydrocarbon mists. Jupiter hung overhead.

Brit held the sailors' hands and led them from one side of the room to the other, showing them the view.

Then they lounged on cushions on the floor, sipping Earth wine from emerald goblets.

"How long have you been sailors?" Brit asked. Something showed in her eyes.

"Long enough," Jake answered. "Ston and I crewed together for a few years, as free-lance sailors, working every run in the system. Then we got lucky. United Radioactives needed to move a load of unstable isotopes from Cronus to their power plants in orbit around Earth. If the isotopes decayed before they reached destination, they'd be worthless. U.R. was willing to pay a big bonus to anyone who'd risk a high-G trajectory. I talked Ston into taking a chance with me."

"What were the risks?" Her eyes flicked back and forth.

"The isotope could have blown at any time. But besides that, you always worry about a high-G run. The continuous acceleration does bad things to your body. Sooner or later, a blood vessel will blow. Or your heart will rupture. There's also a greater likelihood the magnetic bottle of your thruster will spring a leak. All it takes is a weakening of the field. Then you're fried alive with rads. The longer you pull the G's, the more likely something will go wrong."

"But nothing happened."

"No. We lived to collect the bonus."

"So how did you spend it?" She laughed. Brit knew how to spend bonuses.

Ston spoke softly: "The only way I let Jake talk me into going with him, was to make him give me control of the bonus. I bought a freighter with it. In both our names. Free and clear. We sail our own ship now. Some risks are worth taking. Others aren't. Sailors learn that early. Nuclear energies are too wild. We haven't tamed them—just learned to control them a little. They're alive, waiting to break free. They'll kill you if you give them the chance. So you don't give them the chance very often. Only when you have to. And only for good reason."

"He does talk," Brit said. "And gives speeches too." She got up and walked around the edge of the room, taking long, graceful strides. Her eyes caught and held Jupiter-light, shining red. She stopped in front of a table and opened an ivory box sitting on it. She picked up a small vial and rolled it between her fingers. Iridescent liquid swirled within the vial, brighter than her eyes. She laughed. "Who wants to take another chance?"

"Peptide?" Jake asked, licking his lips.

"Of course. High-grade endorphine. Nothing but the best for sailors. Warm you up inside. Care to take a hit?"

Jake nodded.

Brit looked at Ston. He shook his head.

She went over to Jake. He lay back on his cushion. She knelt over him, straddling his torso with her legs. She took the cap from the vial and dipped her tongue into it. A drop of opalescent liquid clung to the tip of her tongue. She lowered her protruding tongue toward Jake's face. He opened his eyes wide. The drop on her tongue enlarged as saliva mingled with neuropeptide. Then it fell, dripping into Jake's eye. He blinked, then closed his eyes. Facial muscles twitched. He moaned with narcolepsy.

Brit ran her fingers along the seams of Jake's suit, opening static closures. She stroked his bare skin.

She felt hands on her shoulders, releasing the clasps of her cape. Ston lifted spidersilk fabric away from her shoulders and dropped it to the floor beside them. He took the vial from her hand. "Your turn?" he asked. "Medicine for you?" He smiled.

"No, none for me. I have no need for synthetic passion. I've enough of the real kind."

Ston closed the vial and let it roll across the floor. "What is it you want from us?" he asked abruptly.

"Nothing. Just a good time. A few laughs."

"What else?"

"No more. Are you jealous of me? Afraid I'll take him away from you. Are you worried he'll be overwhelmed by my passion? Don't worry. I want both of you. If you'll take a chance again."

Ston smoothed the fur on her back, letting his hand linger over her buttock.

Beneath them, Jake stirred, opening his eyes. His pupils were black pin-points. He reached up, pulling both Brit and Ston close.

"I wonder," Ston muttered.

Brit giggled. Delight shone from retinal reflections.

Stars shone steadily overhead. Stark shadows were cast about the room. Starlight gleamed from three naked bodies intertwined on a bed of wombskin. Brit lay between Ston and Jake. Each of them stroked her fur from neck to thigh. Static crackled and sparked blue under their hands. A vibration formed in her throat.

"What is that noise you make?" Jake asked.

Brit smiled, showing her teeth. "Something I do when I'm pleased."

"We please you then?"

"Very much."

"You'll stay with us then?" Jake asked, not seeing the look that came into Ston's eyes.

"For a while." She placed a hand on each of them, caressing limp members. Softness stirred to firmness beneath her fingers. "Where do you sail?" she asked.

"Lots of cargo moves about the outer system. We find work whenever we want. We know all the runs."

"Have you ever raced?"

"A little. When I was younger."

"Or sailed a twelve-meter racer?"

Jake's eyebrows arched. "Once. Just once. Again when I was young and foolish. An old sailor invited me to go sailing in his. He wanted a little favor in return for the joy ride. But it was worth it. Dogs, it was worth it."

Brit smiled. Her fingers continued to do their work. "I need a pilot for my twelve-meter racer," she said casually. She paused, enjoying the effect of her words. "Would either of you like to be my pilot?" She glanced back and forth between their faces. "I want to race in the Jovian Cup. I've already entered my ship."

"You have such a craft?" Ston asked, in the same voice an addict used when asking about medicine.

"Of course. I just recently purchased it. From Lord Vichsn's shipyards, I believe. They tell me it's one of the fastest ever built. But I need someone to fly it. Interested?" She looked at him.

"No," he said with finality. "I have my own ship. I sail for myself, not for hire. And I have more important things to do than race fuships. The energies are hard enough to manage under controlled circumstances. Racing is a needless risk."

"But a twelve-meter racer," Jake said. "They can pull thirty G's. I could break the Jovian Cup record—I'm that good a sailor. I know I could. And the prize money is up to a million this year."

"A million . . ." Brit said, smiling.

Ston snorted. "A lot of money that will do no one any good if they're trapped in orbit around Jupiter or roasted alive by the energies. Rash foolishness. Such bravado serves no useful purpose. Sheer folly."

"Which is exactly the reason to try it," Jake said. "Quit being such a fuddy-duddy. Don't you want to appear in holos all over the system? Couldn't you use a million credits?"

"No. I'm content with my life the way it is."

"Well I'm not. I could use the bucks. How 'bout m'Lady? Are you ready to race?"

"Of course," Brit answered. "Why do you think I sought you two. They told me you were the best sailors on Ganymede. When can we start?"

"Tomorrow," Jake said. "The race is only a week away. Scant time is left for practice. Not that I'll need much."

"Not tonight?" Brit laughed, eyes gleaming wide. She leaned over to kiss Jake's chest.

Jake laughed with her.

Ston got up from the bed and began dressing.

"What's the matter with you?" Jake asked. Brit's lips nuzzled the hollow of his belly.

Ston didn't look at Jake and Brit. "Nothing," he said. "There's nothing wrong." He paused. When he spoke again, there was something the matter with his voice. "How much do you want for your half of *Kestrel?*"

"I didn't know I was selling my half," Jake answered.

"You won't want to sail a bucket-of-bolts freighter, not after racing a twelve-meter fuship. I'll make monthly payments."

"Let's think about it."

"I have thought about it. You won't be coming back. You can't tempt the energies and win. They're too wild. Sign *Kestrel* over to me. I don't want trouble with your estate."

"Don't be hasty. We'll talk tomorrow."

"Maybe." Ston finished dressing and walked to the door. He looked back briefly, then left.

Jake lay back on the wombskin.

"I didn't mean to come between you like this," Brit said.

"Yes you did. But it doesn't matter. I was getting a little tired of Ston. He's a bit serious. And superciliously arrogant. And smug. Besides, he'll wait for me. He'll watch the fort while I'm out playing with the Indians. Good old Ston." Brit's tongue was rough against his skin. Jake smiled to himself.

• • •

Race day.

Port of Chalise was a glowing disk in the middle of its crater—the fused rock of the rocket pad was hot with stray radiation. Commerce didn't stop because of races. Confusion was everywhere: fuships came into port balanced on bright streams of plasma, or left port engulfed in nuclear flame. Groundcrew scurried about, attaching moorings, opening hatches, filling fuel tanks with water. Stevedores loaded and unloaded freight. Sailors sauntered about, wearing skin-tight spacesuits with phase-effect oxygen bubbles around their heads. Tourists gawked at the iridescent domes of Chalise. Ice-cliffs shone in sunlight. Pleasure craft circled overhead in orbit, awaiting the start of the race.

Brit's twelve-meter racer stood in line with nine others. *Wyvern* had sleek lines—two long, tapered pods with a shorter one in between. The middle pod was transparent crystal—its front half was the control room, the back half was a single cabin with two berths. The two lateral pods each contained a fusion thruster. Nozzles directed the flow of plasma for guidance purposes. There was not a faster, more maneuverable craft made. But there were nine her equal. At least on paper. Of course, sailing skill had something to do with the outcome of a race.

Brit leaned over to fuse her oxygen bubble with Jake's. "Are we ready?" she asked. "Can we win?"

"Of course." He laughed. "Come on. I can't wait. Let's get going."

He broke a sensor beam. A transparent cylinder dropped from the aft surface of the central pod to the fused silica of the launch pad. Brit and Jake stepped through a field-effect orifice in the side of the cylinder. It telescoped into the pod. They rose with the tube, soon disappearing within the pod.

Inside, oxygen bubbles melted into air. The cabin was luxuriously appointed, with teak paneling and iridium trim. The bunks had ocelot coverings. But Jake scarcely noticed. He hurriedly ducked into the control cabin.

Overhead, the ship's nose was a crystal spire. Two acceleration couches lay side-by-side, with a control console between them. Jake quickly strapped himself into his couch. Brit followed his example, although more slowly. They pulled helmets over their heads and snapped down mirrored visors. On the inside surface of the visors could be seen display monitors, registering data collected by the ship's sensors. The display panels were one-dimensional and semi-transparent, so one could see through the visor when sailing under visual control.

Jake's fingers played over the control console. Green images flicked from navhelmet visors.

"Ready?" he asked.

"Any time you are."

Jake rested the heel of his hand on the power bar, curling his fingers around. He held his thumb over the strain gauge, careful not to touch it.

The starter began counting down.

A flare arced high into space.

Jake let his thumb drop. Thirty G's of acceleration smothered them. *Wyvern* shot away from Ganymede, spewing twin jets of plasma. Nine other fuships rose simultaneously, balanced on their own nuclear jets.

Jake eased off the thrusters. They could breathe again. He tilted the power bar. Nozzles, bent in turn, changing their thrust vector. *Wyvern* arced toward Jupiter.

"How is she sailing?" Brit asked. "Have you had enough practice?"

"All I need. I could sail this sweet machine in my sleep." He looked at her with eyes hidden behind mirror. "Let's take the plunge." He laughed.

Jake nudged the thrusters back to max with his thumb. An uncomfortable thirty gravities settled over them. Oppressive. Impossible to breathe in. But a membrane oxygenator perfused blood through their skin. Breathing was only a psychological necessity.

Jupiter inexorably neared.

"What's your strategy?" Brit asked with a hiss as she forced the words through lips stretched tight against her teeth. When her lungs were empty she wouldn't be able to fill them for more speech.

"No plan." Jake clipped his speech short also. "Make as close a trajectory as we think we can escape from. Try to escape then. All balls and bravado. No plan." He stopped speaking. It was too much effort. His belly began to ache from viscera pulling on their mesenteries. His balls started throbbing.

• • •

Jupiter filled their field of view. A crimson storm covered ten percent of the visible Jovian disk. Jet-streams were caught up in the vortex of the storm and bent into its substance.

Ten shining sabers arced through black space toward the planet.

Jake cut the engines. Giant hands stopped smothering them.

Brit gasped, sucking her lungs full of air. "What now?" she asked.

"We fall around the planet, matching residual velocity to gravitational field-strength. The closer you get to the center of the Jovian mass, the greater the gravitational force, so the faster you must be going to escape on the other side. Like a comet's orbit around the sun. Too close, we'll be caught by Jupiter's gravity. Too far, we'll lose the race. We want to make a trajectory as close to that balance point as we can. But stay just above it. Watch your visor displays. The navcomputer is plotting vectors."

Brit focused her eyes on her displays. A red disk showed, around which a blue dot was inscribing a blue line. Dotted lines showed possible trajectories for various velocities. The computer knew the maximum thrust *Wyvern*'s thrusters could generate.

Jake's thumb pressed on the power stud. Acceleration waxed like approaching thunder clouds. Behind, disassociated matter streamed into space. The roar of novae throbbed in the metal of the ship. The scream of stripped nuclei resonated in ultrasonic harmonies. A blue dot dipped closer and closer to a red margin.

Jupiter now appeared to be below them. Firestorms raged silently across the surface of the planet. Stars disappeared overhead, replaced with bright sunshine. The particle trails of other racers were visible on both sides. But they gradually fell behind. On her visor displays, Brit saw their blue dot ahead of the others.

Wyvern dropped from one plotted curve to another. Her thrusters drove her ever faster. Soon there was only one tighter trajectory possible. Its blue dotted line almost touched the red fringe of atmosphere.

"Back off a little," she gasped. "We're ahead now. No need to take chances."

But Jake must not have heard. *Wyvern*'s blue dot dropped to the final orbital curve. The other dots fell farther behind.

"We're going for the record now, Lady," Jake whispered into his throat mike. "No one has ever cut this close." He *had* heard.

A red glare appeared on the horizon of the planet. For a moment, Brit wondered if it could be a sunrise, then she realized the sun was still overhead. The red glare curved nearer. She saw it was a Jovian storm. An angry vortex swirled with unrestrained fury in thick hydrocarbon atmosphere. A giant cast wind like handfuls of sand.

Slowly they approached.

The storm raged as it had for centuries, collecting jet-streams in its whirlpool like tangled silver thread. *Wyvern* was going to pass directly over it. The other ships eased into higher orbits, further widening the gap between themselves and *Wyvern*.

Brit wondered why the others had backed off. Jake knew. He was a sailor. He knew the ways of Jovian storms. He took a chance.

The storm was large enough to enclose a moon. In its center, solar temperatures were approached. Light flared, bright as a fusion flash.

Jake growled and pulled back on the navhandle. *Wyvern* nosed upward. Too late.

A finger of swirling gas reached up. Turbulence buffeted them. A blast hit from below. Suddenly, they were tumbling. G-forces fluctuated, kneading flesh and raising bruises. Tortured metal screaked.

Twelve-meter racers were deep-space craft—blue void sailers. They could neither enter nor leave atmosphere. Aerodynamic stresses were too much for them to handle.

In a moment, it was quiet in the cabin. The energies were silent. Both thrusters rocketed away, sheared from their struts. Acceleration ceased. What was left of *Wyvern* tumbled in a wobbly orbit around Jupiter. Jake and Brit stayed strapped in acceleration harness. Their faces were alternately flooded with sunlight and red storm-light, in a periodicity of about thirty seconds.

"What happens now?" Brit asked. Her eyes shone crimson.

"Nothing." Jaked laughed. "Until our orbit decays."

"Why nothing?"

"It costs too much to rescue stranded sailors. It's too dangerous. Shipwrecks are a risk sailors take. You don't expect to be rescued. You wouldn't rescue someone foolish enough to crack up his ship. *C'est la vie!*"

"How long?"

"Look at your visor displays."

Brit saw green numerals flashing down. Less than six hours were left before burn-out. She took off her navhelmet and unstrapped her harness.

"What are you doing?" Jake asked.

Brit stood up, balancing herself on the edge of her couch. No human could have kept their balance in the tumbling craft. She stepped over the control console and landed lightly on Jake's couch. Kneeling over him, she lifted off his helmet. Her eyes peered into his briefly. Then she kissed his mouth, slipping a rough tongue past his teeth. Her fingers unfastened his restraining straps.

They drifted into the air. She held Jake and kicked them away from his acceleration couch. With prods of her feet, she kept them from bumping into the walls. A vibration formed in her throat. Jake closed his eyes, letting his thoughts wander as his body moved toward love with Brit.

Jake opened his eyes.

Brit watched his face. Her irides shimmered as her eyes beat back and forth. Beyond her face was the transparent wall of the aft cabin. Stars and sun and roiling Jovian clouds formed a kaleidoscope of images. He wondered how long before their orbit decayed. Soon, he thought. The time must be near. Sunlight flashed from a silver wire curving over the planet's horizon. Then bright stars appeared again. He must be hallucinating, he decided. No one was coming. They were alone.

Brit's eyes continued to stare at him. Then he realized they weren't focused; she was looking through him, seeing images residing in her mind. He imagined he could see flickerings behind the vertical slits of her pupils. But just glimpses. Nothing substantial. Ghosts of memory.

He leaned up to kiss her nose.

Her eyes focused.

"Where were your thoughts?" he asked.

"In a fugue. Lost to pleasant reverie."

He raised his eyebrows in inquiry.

"I stalk the nighttime," she explained. "I sneak through forests of night."

"And what do you hunt there?"

"Men. Tender men, of course. I mean, true humans. My roar paralyzes them with fright. Men, women, children. They stand as still as statues when I charge. Only their eyes move. Pupils widen as they wait to feel my claws and teeth. Nothing tastes as sweet as human blood. No flesh is finer than man-flesh."

"I see," he said.

"Do you?"

"I think so."

Beyond her face, the planetary horizon rotated into view. A gleaming saber thrust toward them. With a *single* edge. He was not imagining it this time. The image was real. Help was coming.

Brit glanced over her shoulder, then turned back to face him. "I saw the ion trail a couple of hours ago," she said. "He's had a little difficulty matching orbits."

"You know who he is?"

"Of course. Who else would risk his ship and his life to save you? No one would to save me, certainly. He's not coming for me. You shouldn't treat him so shabbily. He deserves better than you."

Jake laughed. "I guess he does," he said.

Kestrel had matched orbits with *Wyvern* and lay about fifty meters away. *Wyvern* still tumbled, but fortunately her motion was restricted to one axis. Ston had skillfully parked his ship on *Wyvern*'s axis of rotation, so from his perspective, *Wyvern* spun like a wheel.

Kestrel was a deep-space freighter—not very pretty, but functional. A central thruster was surrounded by stubby struts protruding symmetrically around its longitudinal axis. Cargo pods were normally attached to these struts. But not now. *Kestrel* was not on a cargo run. All unnecessary mass had been removed. Only the control pod and two fuel tanks were attached to the thruster. Anything else was excess mass. *Kestrel* would need every newton of thrust she could muster to lift even her stripped mass out of the Jovian gravity field.

Jake and Brit had donned space coveralls and crawled out on *Wyvern*'s hull. They carefully worked their way over the hull until they stood in the center of her rotational axis. *Kestrel* lay directly beside them.

A line shot out from *Kestrel*. Jake caught its end and snapped it to his belt. He held Brit with one arm. The line tightened. They were pulled across fifty meters of space to *Kestrel*'s entry hatch.

Ston waited inside the cabin. For a moment, Jake and he stood and stared at each other. Then Ston grinned. "Damn you," he said. "I don't know why I bother to be your mother duck."

"I'm good on the wombskin?"

"That must be it."

They both laughed, then embraced.

Brit watched silently. But the fur rose along her back.

Twenty G's pressed against them. Hydrogen melted into helium. The fury of annihilated matter was held within a magnetic bottle. Almost. Stripped matter roared from thruster nozzles and streamed into a glowing cylinder behind *Kestrel*.

Three lay on two acceleration couches. Ston by himself, Brit curled around Jake. A control console separated the couches.

Jupiter still lay below. Firestorms played violent music within dense atmosphere. *Kestrel* strained against a giant's hands. Plasma spewed forth in an orgasm of fusion. But gravity would not release its grip.

"We don't have enough thrust," Jake whispered into his throat mike. "Thruster temp is already nearing red-line."

"Overload it," Ston said. "We've no other choice."

"The bottle will blow."

"A chance we've got to take."

Jake pressed the power stud down a final centimeter. Five more gravities kicked against his body. Vibrations coarsened. Metallic matrix screamed with resonating stress. The temperature indicator blinked red. Jake ignored the warning light and pressed his thumb a little tighter. His thumbnail whitened. More G's nudged against him.

Kestrel shook herself free of clinging gravity. Jovian fire receded.

Somewhere, unheeded, a radiation gong clanged.

Greta traces muscle lines on my chest and abdomen with her finger. Brightness warms our skins.

"The old sailor?" she asks.

"Of course."

"Why was there only one of you?"

"The thruster's magnetic bottle developed a pin-hole leak. Hardly big enough for a whole atom to squeeze through. Only a narrow beam of radiation escaped. Narrow enough so that only one of us was speared by it. A random event, a chance occurrence. A quirk of the energies. *C'est la vie!*"

She moves her pelvis in rhythmic thrusts against my hip. Her mouth encircles my breast; teeth nip at the nipple. "The Lady?" Her eyes smile.

"She bought another yacht. But I saw her prowling the clubs for a time. Before she found another sailor."

"Not you?"

"Not me." I look at her. "You don't see radiation sickness much anymore. Their bowels run foul water. They vomit constantly—green bile until something tears inside and blood starts coming up. Hair falls out. Sores develop and weep yellow serum. They don't heal for a long time, and then scar."

"Sounds terribly unpleasant."

Her mouth wanders: licking, nuzzling, kissing. Slick skins slide over one another. She kneels above me, settling her pelvis into my groin. We couple. Movements synchronize. She spreads her legs wide to more deeply receive my thrusts. Her shadow falls across my face.

I see the fire again.

My heart races. Sweat beads from my skin. My bowels twist into knots. I glance frantically about the room.

The door is open!

An old sailor stands in the doorway.

Greta's undulations do not break their rhythm.

I know the brightness of the room can penetrate even his cataracts. He can see us. He will remember the passions of youth. Passions now lost to radiation-induced progeria. But his face remains lax. Scar tissue puckers the skin into a mummy's mask. Drool drips from the corner of his mouth.

I realize he can no longer see. Scarred retinae have been burned further. He is blind again. Mercifully.

He leaves. I hear him stumbling up circular stairs.

Later, Greta moans as her orgasm ripples through smooth muscles. Platysma fasciculates her skin.

She opens her eyes. There is a distant look within them. A look I have seen before. I know she flies on night winds, swims warm ocean currents. She has dreams I cannot share, racial memories I cannot imagine. But I can guess. I see a winged shape dropping from the sky with sharp talons outspread. A figure stands on the ground below. Eyes wait to receive the thrusts of claws. Or a grey torpedo streaks up from the murky depths. Toothed jaws open. A pale figure swims on the surface, unaware, until bones crunch and blood stains water red. Her eyes clear.

I briefly wonder if some day there will be no more true humans. Will we pass the way of the other animals of Earth? Will all creatures be hybrids? All bastards of recombinant DNA?

"I wish I could take you sailing," Greta says. "But our gravships develop a hundred G's. Such acceleration would kill you, of course. You were not engineered to be a sailor. Real sailors could make love in a hundred G's. But I could be easy on you. Why not? Come sailing with me tonight? After all, you were once a sailor. I'll be gentle to your poor flesh."

My hand touches a control knob. Every night it so lingers, when Jupiter fills the sky. I'm tempted to twist it. But I resist the urge. With one twist of the knob, deflector shields will flip away and, simultaneously, liquid hydrogen will squirt into the thruster chamber. Protons will fuse. Plasma will then spew from nozzles. A thermonuclear roar will be heard once more. Raw energies will be unchained. *Kestrel* will tear away her moorings and sail the blue empty one final time.

My hand doesn't move; it's not yet time to use the old energies. I wait for another with whom to share the fire. She'll come back some day. Our thoughts have mingled in the dreamtime. She's getting older; teeth and claws are becoming dull with age. Soon she'll be so slow she'll need to hunt wounded prey. She will have heard of *Critical Mass*. Hunger will overcome caution. She'll come back, lured by the scent of a staked goat.

When she does, I'll let the old sailor join us, for a final

ménage à trois, so our atoms can mingle together before becoming dissipated into the void.

Until then, the energies must sleep. You only want to tempt them once.

NEW OLYMPUS

by Ronald Anthony Cross

This startlingly beautiful and exotic story has to do with
one of the most wondrous and frightening things in the
world: growing up. Such simple words for such a complex, weighty, never-ending process. It carries with it
the realization of responsibilities, the maddening loss
of one kind of security and the sometimes-reluctant
gain of another, and so much isolation. "New Olympus"
is undoubtedly about a good deal more than the loss
of one's childhood. Cross's stories, his visions of life,
are as complex as the finest poetry and similarly leave
the reader with singular, recognizable, yet hard-to-de-
fine feelings. This one left us feeling awash in admi-
ration.

I. THE RIVER

The waterbabies were noisily at play in the middle of the
river. It was a bright sunny summer day on the Storm King's
asteroid, as usual. He had seldom exhibited those rainy-day

blues of late: he was all sunshine and flowers.

These were fun days for the babies old enough to be let out of the nursery to play all day in the cool swift running river. The only fear was that the Storm King would magnify the sun up too bright and roast all the kids. Except for the fear of Maneagle.

They were supposed to be watching the sky for the Maneagle. Which was why they spotted Silverflash standing in the middle of the waterfall, right at the top, just before it goes over the edge and falls and falls, and changes into white frothy foam, like they all blew off the tops of their icy mugs when Mama brought them root bear and said, "You have all been good babies and now you may all have a good drink of root bear to cool you off," and they laughed and laughed because they all felt so good and Mama was so good, and root bear was good, and 'bear' was funny, only Mama said it wasn't really 'bear,' silly, but 'beer,' which men drank and drank and then got silly after they drank it too much. And they fell down. So all the waterbabies always got silly and fell down after they drank their root bear.

Silverflash was waving to them now, sinking a little into the water: he liked to let himself get heavier than the waterbabies did because he ran so fast he liked to let his feet sink in and get more of a purchase.

They knew it was him because the sun glinted off his round silver hat. They shouted and waved back because everybody loved the Silverflash messenger boy, he could run faster than anybody in the whole world and he was just a little boy like them—well, maybe bigger than that, like a seven-year-old or eight-year-old, but he was the oldest little boy ever. He was over two hundred years old.

So all the waterbabies shouted, "Silverflash, Silverflash," over and over, and waved over and over, and Silverflash waved back from the top of the waterfall, only something was wrong because he was waving too fast and then he shot over the edge and popped down into the bubbles like a cork. That made everybody laugh, only he came up out of the bubbles and skimmed across the top of the river right at them, shouting something they couldn't hear, and then one of the babies was shouting "Eagle, eagle," and they were all screaming and running for cover.

One of the babies was scrambling in terror toward the shelter of the trees along the bank, when the shadow fell on him.

Then he heard the scream of death and the whistling sound of something plunging to him from a great height.

At the same time Silverflash was coming at him across the surface of the river—so fast. He didn't know what to do. He just froze up crying, "Mama, Mama," until Silverflash smashed into him and sent him rolling off like a ball and something hit Silverflash and plunged underwater with him.

And it hurt so much where Silverflash banged him, but he just kept scrambling, and all of the babies got away into the trees, and just kept going, screaming and all.

They didn't see Silverflash and Maneagle bob back to the surface again. But they heard them. Maneagle was screaming mad. The only thing that had saved Silverflash was that Maneagle had been aiming at the waterbaby and had not gotten a good grip on the messenger boy. On top of that, he had hit the water wrong and both of them were stunned by various impacts followed by submersion: water had forced them apart.

Now the vicious but soggy Maneagle was flapping and scrambling around on the surface of the river in one last futile attempt to get his claws on Silverflash. But he had missed his only chance. Wings weren't that good once you were down, and nobody could catch Silverflash now. Maneagle, for all his screaming and thrashing about, rather resembled a grouse playing wounded to lure you away from her chicks.

Finally he gave up the chase and tried to lift up off the river, but he was all tangled up in water and he couldn't even start to take off. In fact, had his wings been any less powerful he might have been in danger of drowning. But he sort of thrashed his way across to the bank, fluttering and flopping along.

When he got there he was surprised to see that the Silverflash messenger boy had followed him. He had expected that kid to flee in terror.

"I'll kill you, I'll kill you. Go back to your own asteroid and don't ever bother the waterbabies again. I swear I'll find a way and kill you. I swear it!"

Maneagle was amazed. "A messenger boy threatens the Gods," he said, waving dry his wings. "I wonder how the Storm King will reward his servant for such effrontery?"

But he was bluffing and they both knew it. The Storm King was fast becoming annoyed that Maneagle had been preying on his waterbabies. It's true, they were only servants. But it was a nuisance to incubate them and then there was the upkeep on the clone mothers, and then they just get old enough to go out and play, and Maneagle uses them for target practice. No, he wouldn't be the one to approach Storm King with that story.

Ignoring the furious messenger boy confronting him from the shallows of the river, nevertheless still standing on top of the water with the magnified sunlight sheening off his absurd little round silver helmet, Maneagle lofted into the air and flew away. Soon he was a dot in the blue lake of the sky.

Silverflash watched him until he disappeared. Then his hostile act fell apart and he began to cry. He was two hundred and thirty years old, but he was just a little boy and he was angry and frightened and sore all over and tired, and yes, even hungry.

He lightened up his body weight a little and ran slow (for him) and light, downstream.

II. THE BABIES' HOUSE

Soon he ran around a bend in the river and there was the babies' house, which was more like a temple than a house, Doric columns and all that. It looked great among all the shrubbery with the river running by. Silverflash had been born and raised there by the clone mothers. It was the only home he had ever had. He still felt a sentimental rush at the sight of it.

By the time he got inside he was weeping uncontrollably. "Oh no, I'm regressing" (he had learned that word from the clone mothers, who were psychiatrists and doctors, of course), he said to himself. But he couldn't help it.

The first room was the grape purple room. The babies' living room. The playroom. The floors and walls were made of some soft spongy material—deep purple, of course. One of the clone mothers rushed over to him and at once hugged him to her with sweet passionate calm.

"Don't be blue, Silverflash, the babies told us all about it. You should be proud of yourself. Yes, you should. Ohh, Silverflash, come on, let me get you some root beer. We'll all have some root beer."

The babies all looked up from their games on the immense spongy floor. Root bear?

"I can't stay," Silverflash sobbed, "I've got to talk to the Storm King about this Maneagle business right away. I've got to get him to take action against that Maneagle. He—he almost killed me today. He's got no right to prey on the babies either. Only I don't know how to—" He broke off, overwhelmed by another fit of crying.

"There, there, Silverflash. It's hard to be two hundred years old and just a little boy at the same time. But you're doing fine. Just remember we love you because it's our nature to do so. You don't have to ever do anything to earn it."

"That's what mothers are for." One of the other clone mothers, who had been nursing an infant, had put it down to sleep on the spongy floor in the corner and come over to join them. And a third had come out of another room. He couldn't tell them apart.

They were identical in appearance, with their long rich brown hair and sweet calm expressions. They were small and curvy with melodious voices.

"Come into the infants' chambers with us, Silverflash. We want to show you something of an enigma, before you go."

"What's an enigma?" Silverflash asked them. His sobbing was subsiding. Being here always put him in a good mood.

One of the mothers (the same one?) picked up the sleeping infant and the four of them passed through a doorway into an inner room.

The blue room, the bathroom, several babies were splashing around in a giant icy pool of water: a sunken bathtub or a shallow swimming pool. Another mother was in the pool with them.

"Sunburns," one of the mothers said as they passed on through. "You could ask the Storm King again about turning down the sunlight a notch. Just mention it, Silverflash."

They passed on through into the infants' room. Pink sponge.

"It doesn't do any good to ask him, because he doesn't care about anything but himself, the same as Maneagle. All they care about is what they want!"

Another mother was sitting on the spongy floor with her back against the spongy wall.

"Men," she said. "Or Gods, as they like to see it. How few of them ever grow up. When they are babies they play with their toys. When they get older they play with the universe. Outward and outward, dominating and penetrating. The only thing that changes is the amount of damage they are able to inflict."

The four mothers exchanged rich ironic yin glances. All four of them smiled and shook their heads.

In one corner of the room the babies were learning to function under anti-grav conditions. Later they would have implants like Silverflash and the three-year-olds. But for now the gravity in that corner of the room was turned way down so they could practice.

They were playing a game. Many brightly colored clown heads popped out of the ceiling on long springy necks. Then all the infants kicked and waved their arms excitedly. The gravity was so low that this action propelled them up into the air, where they batted and kicked the clown heads, squealing delightedly. Then they slowly floated back down to the spongy floor, and the clown heads withdrew momentarily back into the ceiling. Then the whole cycle started up again. The infants did not seem to anticipate it or get tired of it.

But a bigger baby sat in the corner. Not watching them, not participating, not doing anything. Something was obviously wrong here. He had a rolled-up piece of paper clenched in one hand and now he excitedly began to tap himself on the head with it in a strange agitated manner. He emitted a low humming noise like a machine.

"Is he the enigma?"

The mothers smiled. "Yes, he is, Silverflash. How quick and clever you are. How terribly perceptive. He is the enigma. His name is Wilbur. He is older than he looks. We've been hiding him here. He appears to be suffering from severe mental illness, and well, we just don't know why. That's why he's an enigma.

"Our experience with him and our intuition tell us that he's suffering from constant fear arising from a life-threatening situation. But there is no such threat to be found anywhere in his present environment."

"We believe," one of the other mothers continued, "that he is somehow seeing into the future. Finding himself threatened there."

"It's a vicious circle, do you see?" the first mother continued. "He sees he is going to be destroyed by the Storm King for being autistic and therefore defective. But his fear of being destroyed is keeping his mind disorganized and incapable of relationship.

"We have, of course, been keeping it a secret as best we can. But we trust you, Silverflash. Our women's intuition—"

"Psychiatrist's intuition," one of the other clones interjected.

"Quite right, both intuitions—tell us to trust you with everything. Give you all the information we can and well, we know you'll do your best to help us out if you can find a way. You are our only representative to the Storm King."

"Our little warrior." Two of the lovely little mothers hugged him from either side.

The weird little boy fascinated Silverflash. He darted over and sat down in front of him.

"Hi," he tried. But the little boy didn't acknowledge his presence at all, unless...Yes, it was subtle, but the agitation in his movements had increased.

Everything about the little boy reminded Silverflash of himself. His darting eyes, the weird humming sound that occasionally emerged from his depths, the quick jerky movements, the nervous tapping with the piece of paper: all of these things suggested speed.

"He looks like me, he's like me—it's more than looks—somehow he's like me."

The clone mothers exchanged glances and came out exactly even. One of them nodded.

"He's your little brother, Silverflash. We weren't going to tell you, but you're just too quick to keep anything from. The Storm King wants to engineer another messenger boy for some reason. So that's why we have to tell you. We just can't keep it a secret much longer. A few of the special operations need to be performed on Wilbur fairly soon. The Storm King will check on him. And he'll destroy him, of course."

Silverflash was swept with turbulent feelings he didn't understand. This was often the case with him.

"He'll never grow up. He'll never get to grow up. Even if they let him live. They'll operate on him and make him like me and he'll be a little boy forever." He was shouting with rage.

"Is that so terrible, to be a little boy forever?" one of the mothers asked in her sweet voice.

Silverflash darted over to her and hugged her.

"It's the worst thing in the world to never grow up into a

man. To never blossom. To never grow a mane or a deep voice. To never come into your power. But to feel inside you the hint of all these things and know they will never be fulfilled. Oh God, it's the very worst thing in the world."

III. THE STORM KING'S CASTLE

Silverflash stood peeking over the edge of a spongy white cloud down at the Storm King's castle. Its magnificent spires jutted up from the highest mountain on the largest asteroid in the belt.

All these pseudo-Gods planted their castles up in the air so they towered up over you, but Silverflash always got up above them and looked down. He was smiling now. There were some things about being Silverflash that just had to make you smile. Everything changed so quickly, his thoughts and moods tended to shift dramatically in relationship somehow to the dramatic shifts he experienced in scenery. A short while ago he had been running the river; now, a little lighter and he was in air. His spirits soared when he was in air.

He kicked the fake cloud mischievously; it bounced off like a balloon. Storm King had bunches of them floating about merely for purposes of decoration. He dialed away the real ones unless he felt like rain. Then he dialed up a bunch all at once and rode around in his phony little cloud car shooting electric flashes at the unlucky trees and local inhabitants from his mighty thunder stick. Lucky for all his victims, he couldn't hit the ocean with a stone if he was swimming in it. You were only safe if he was aiming at you, Silverflash thought with malicious pleasure.

Then he darted down and hassled a crow, which swam slowly (or so it seemed to Silverflash) but steadily through the warm, rather thick atmosphere. Crows hated to be disturbed, so Silverflash always made it a point to disturb them. They always had some important business to attend to and flew with gruelling regular strokes to some specific, carefully chosen location. They never tarried, slowed down, speeded up, or altered their course for anything.

So Silverflash altered their courses for them. The bird seemed so cumbersome and ungainly beside him, as did every other living being. Except perhaps for Maneagle. Silverflash frowned at that thought.

He upped his body weight to very heavy and shot into a whistling dive like a stone, after the manner of Maneagle, in fact; except that he had less control in the air because whereas Maneagle had great strong driving wings, Silverflash had none, unless you count the phony little white fluffs on his helmet. They were, like these pretty little fake clouds, mere decorations.

No, when he traveled the airways, he traveled them faster than any living being, but he did not depend on the use of wings. He traveled the currents of air, shifting his molecular density with exquisite practiced precision, shifting his weight up and down as only he could. Blowing along like a leaf, sinking like a stone to a different current, shifting the weight to feather, upping the density in his left leg or right arm, steering around a curve and into the face of a blast of wild screaming wind and suddenly the big shift and all weight off and being just a part of the wind only arms out like a surfer, swept away in the curve of some huge invisible breaker charging across the ocean of sky.

The atmosphere was dense and small on the Storm King's asteroid. The currents were small and subtle. But of course, they related to your weight. There were always currents racing across every sky, if you could relate to them with your weight.

With his gift for understanding and navigating air currents, polished for over two hundred years, Silverflash was a part of the ecology of air, but against Maneagle that left him with this disadvantage: his skills depended on the prevailing conditions about him; Maneagle's did not. The Maneagle flew in whatever manner he wanted to regardless of air currents or weather— well—almost. More than any bird Silverflash had ever seen, Maneagle powered his way straight to where he wanted to go. Rather like this stupid crow, only with more of a vicious grim purpose. Which was maybe the reason that Silverflash was taking time out to razzle-dazzle the poor bird. As if he needed a reason! He was what he was.

His divebombing carried him just past the crow's left wing and down, and suddenly he caught a current that puffed him back up until he floated alongside the complaining bitter black bird, lying on his back with hands behind head and left knee crossed over right leg, comically at rest.

Then he lightened up and tumbled around the furious crow in a circle. The crow screamed at him, he screamed at the crow. But he was, thank the God of crows, tiring quickly of the sport. Every crow on the Storm King's asteroid knew and hated the Silverflash messenger boy.

He abruptly forgot the crow and drop spiraled, drop spiraled, around and down to the castle. He shot through the electrical field that protected the castle successfully from everyone but him. His molecular density altered along with molecular flux as he became momentarily one with the electrical field.

He was still buzzing like a hive of bees when he came back to himself as he flowed through an open window and dropped into the great hall.

A few moments later, as he was changing his clothes in his little room in the servants' quarters, he was still gathering back loose thoughts and feelings that had zipped away somewhere. Merging with electricity was total ecstatic dispersal of being—kwatz. Only momentum carried him on through, and then there seemed to be some sort of automatic rebirth that took place, gathering back his body and mind, ego and heart.

Most of what he did with his molecules was done on fully automatic: he was the only one who could do these things (with the possible exception of his autistic clone brother, Wilbur). His body and brain were genetically engineered to house the perfect servant. Operated on and chemically altered into a beautiful eternal child.

Ironically enough, while the so-called immortals could only extend their glorious existences, it seemed to be theoretically possible to keep someone alive indefinitely by forcing him to remain as a child. Silverflash had made it. His childhood had been extended into infinity, and probably his lifespan along with it.

A few fleeting moments and Silverflash had flashed through a brief shower and donned his official royal silvers. Silver helmet and silver running slippers with matching white wings and a silver silk track suit, which sported royal golden lightning bolts zigzagging across the front and back of the tank top. This, of course, to point out to everyone that he was in the service of the Storm King.

He allowed himself a brief look around his tiny room, chosen, no doubt, to remind him of his stature, both physical and political, in the Storm King's arena. Yet the small living quarters pleased Silverflash because they also always reminded him of other things that were unintended. They reminded him that he was a part of the Storm King's castle only in token. That his true home was the sky and the river, the House of Infants, and even the dark spaces between asteroids: he was at home in movement and not at rest, and thus he could never be truly owned or controlled by anyone.

Then he was out and running down the plush purple carpeted funnel of the main royal hall. Gaudily dressed guards, like lavish ornaments—which they were—were strategically placed along the hall, bearing ornate useless weapons but looking good.

Silverflash didn't throw them a glance. These clods were truly owned, lock, stock and barrel.

"The Silverflash messenger boy doth present himself before his lord, the master asteroid ecology builder, the lord of the dark cloud and the bright smile, the God of art, the immortal Storm King Henry II," the effusive, rather daintily built but splendidly attired little royal announcer announced.

Another poor fellow genetically engineered and coaxed into the Storm King's precise work of art: the asteroid he called New Olympus. For the fact of the matter was that art was the Storm King's main raison d'être. He controlled not only every stone, every cloud, every genetic make-up and every costume on the asteroid, but he also had a good grip on the relationship between himself and the other immortals on the neighboring asteroids. Though some of them, like the Maneagle, were hard to keep under control, there was no question in any immortal mind but that Storm King Henry II was the dominant factor among the asteroid belters. And the main reason was simple and clear: he was the best asteroid engineer. He was the best asteroid engineer because he was the richest engineer. He had gathered together the best crew of maintenance engineers, over a lifetime of ninety-some years, at enormous expense. He had inherited some of the best mechanics and engineers from his father, who also was rich, but was just plain engineer Henry without any aspirations toward royalty or immortality or any numbers after his name. He had been, however, a shrewd tough businessman and a top engineer who had made a fortune as an asteroid mine consultant in the bad old days.

Like most engineers, Storm King Henry II confused engineering with art and thus aspired to immortality all ways at once. This had dragged his mind, in Silverflash's opinion, somewhere off the deep end, where he floundered somewhat awkwardly: artists were at home in those waters.

"Did you see the sunset last night, noble traveler of winds and waters and of fire if need be? Sunsets are my best work, and last night . . . But an artist must not speak of his work; alas, we are at the mercy of the critics. And everyone's a critic these days."

"The sunset was great. The sun went down, or at least we were given that illusion; the moon came out. The winds blew. And I lived through the whole affair. What more could I ask?" The Silverflash messenger boy hoped to dispense with the frills that way. It was the same genetic stroke that made him so quick and sure of foot in the most precarious areas of travel which also had made him so quick and caustic with words. He always wanted to cut through everything like a sharp knife, taste the heart, toss it away and get the hell on to something new.

But the Storm King was not pleased. "Take care, Silverflash, I gave you the special gifts of quick tongue and quick feet and so I am lenient with you. After all, you are one of my finest pieces of this great work, the New Olympus. Yet you are only a piece. You can be replaced should your impudence offend me. And the work will go on."

"The Maneagle is thinking along those same lines, my liege. He nearly removed me from your work of art this morning, with very little thought given to the matter of my replacement."

"Surely he was poaching babies and you got in his way. I don't begrudge him a few babies. He is a free spirit, as are most denizens of the air. And besides, he's kind of flapped himself a little bit over the edge with his weird predatory lifestyle, flying around all day long screaming and divebombing everything in sight and living in that weird dark aerie on that ugly austere asteroid of his. I think he's not quite right in the head."

Who is? Silverflash thought but didn't say.

"Still, he wouldn't be so bold as to attack you. Why that would be . . ."

"But he was so bold, my lord," Silverflash lied glibly. "He attacked specifically and only me: there were no babies on the river, they aren't allowed outdoors of late because you've got the sunlight up too bright and it's burning them to a crisp. At least you could filter out more of the ultraviolet rays!

"Anyhow, I was alone on the river when, without warning, the Maneagle divebombed me. Luckily, we were separated by the water or he would have killed me and hid my body, no doubt. You would never have known about it. I tell you, I don't know why he would do it. That is for you to figure out. I am but your messenger boy." He bowed an elegant yet somehow mocking bow.

The Storm King rose up from his throne and held his palm out in a gesture signifying silence.

"Silence," the royal announcer announced, "the Storm King Henry II demands silence that he may . . ."

"I said, 'Silence,'" the Storm King roared. Some days it seemed to him that he was just a second-rate engineer and that everyone around him was party to some giant conspiracy to put him on.

But he was a beautiful figure of a man. His musculature was archetypal perfection. Computers balanced his hormones and electricity had spasmed his muscles until they had blossomed into exactly the ancient Greek ideal. He was the exact replica of an ancient Greek statue of Zeus. A minor but impressive example of his own engineering skills.

As was Silverflash. But when Silverflash witnessed the Storm King pacing back and forth before him, lost in dark thought, displaying the mantle of ideal physical male maturity as carelessly as would a fully grown male lion in the peak of power, the eternal messenger boy was caught in a riptide of disorienting emotions. Like any little boy, he longed for manhood with all his heart and soul, and he knew it would never come to him. Again he couldn't control a sudden flood of tears. He fought it back quickly but not in time.

"What, you shed tears? I'll never understand you." The Storm King's voice was rich and full (he had gotten that gene combo from an Italian tenor).

"What now, the heat is burning the babies? Try to remember, my most valued servant, the babies are made for Olympus and not Olympus for the babies. Do you understand? Babies are easy to replace. A perfect sunny day with a sunset like last night is a perfection which can never be duplicated again. But you don't understand that. Of course not. No one understands the artist. No one understands the art. And yet I will go on with it, forever."

Silverflash could not resist asking, "Why?"

"That's the wrong question, my little messenger boy. There is no reason or reward of any sort involved. It is just simply what I will do, no matter what or why.

"The babies? They are not worth the worry. As to the Man-eagle, however, you are, for once, correct. Something must be done about him, and done soon. He can only have attacked you as a minor part of a major effort to take over New Olympus. It will perhaps put you at ease to know that this surprise attack has not really caught the Storm King by surprise at all.

"For some time now I have been suspecting it from one source or another. Alas, my work of art, New Olympus, has been blessed with the fatal flaw of all perfection. She is too beautiful to exist without creating envy in the hearts of lesser immortals. I knew it was only a matter of time before a group of them, living on their grotesque floating garish chunks of rock, would attempt to steal all this—" He waved his arm lavishly out to encompass the whole asteroid, his precious work of art.

Silverflash was stunned. What mortal could have dreamed? Power corrupts, indeed, he thought, it just plain drives you clear crazy.

The Storm King continued ranting. "I have noticed of late (how could I not?), at the grand parties, how a certain group of immortals has split off from the rest of us. Whispering things, planning things. Oh, it's all been very subtle, but it's there all the same, for the subtle mind to grasp.

"It was then I realized that my suspicion, even if it were no more than just a suspicion, should be acted upon if I wanted to remain, as I always have, one step ahead of my pseudo-peers, the so-called immortals.

"It does not surprise me that their intention was to first eliminate you. No indeed, my faithful messenger, it only helps me to reawaken my understanding of how invaluable to me you are. For you are my most valuable source of communi-cation. My ambassador. My spy."

He drew this last word out significantly and paced back and forth a bit more. His manic expression became for the first time shadowed ever so slightly by doubt.

"Well, I haven't told you quite all of it. They are stronger than I gave them credit for. Their spies are everywhere. Some-how they've got wind of my most secret plans.

"I told you I was on to them. I was forced to take measures. Picture this, another messenger boy identical to you. He can penetrate anywhere. He can ride the winds, run across the waters—yes, survive the empty spaces between asteroids and go through the electrical protective fields. No one can keep him from penetrating wherever he wants. And in fact if they see him they will think he is you, delivering a message from me. And so he shall. The ultimate message. The message that lasts forever.

"He's like you in every way, with one fatal difference. He's a living bomb. His heart is the timer. The bomb is implanted and set to go off in so many beats. He penetrates to the control room, explodes, the gravity goes off, the atmosphere disappears. He not only blows up the palace but he destroys that whole world. Maneagle no more, aerie no more, Eagle World, if that mordant dungeon can be called a world, no more.

"I was experimenting along those lines. I've cloned you, but we haven't got the bomb right yet. It's a tricky step that we're still working on, and I'll admit we're a ways from it.

"Well, don't you see? They found out about my plan. They attempted to eliminate you. Then they plan to eliminate your clone as well as any others I produce."

He paused dramatically and shook his fist off at outer space. "Well, I've got your message. But it won't do you any good at all. I've got back-up plans to cover any emergency."

Silverflash had been standing still without fidgeting for the longest time in his entire two-hundred-and-plus-year career. He was so stunned he had no idea what to say or do. The Storm King was totally mad, with enormous deranged paranoid delusions. He wished the clone mothers were there to diagnose the situation for him.

And my little clone brother, poor little autistic Wilbur. That is who he plans to use for his first human bomb.

And this is what Wilbur sees. The clone mothers were right, he sees into the future, which means that as of now this is not just some grim possibility. This is what will happen for sure. Unless I can do something to change things. I'm so helpless. A little boy with a little boy's attention span and strength. Can I go up against the immortals?

But the Silverflash was a very smart little boy with two hundred years of experience to draw upon. He knew the answer. There was no choice.

"My back-up plan, once again, my most trusted servant, depends on you. A move no one will ever suspect until it is too late. I shall be here in plain view of all, keeping open friendly lines of communication.

"No, better than that—" he clapped his strong hands to-gether theatrically—"How ironic, I'll give a party. A grand ball. They'll all be here celebrating with me in the most lux-urious palace ever conceived by the mind of immortal. A grand costume ball. All stops out. And while we are all dancing, romancing and celebrating our general invulnerable lifestyles, do you know where you will be, my Silverflash?"

Silverflash was shaking visibly now. "I was afraid to ask," he said.

"Always the wit," Storm King said, "or at least, halfway so. You shall be traveling the dark spaces in between, to the asteroid of the oracle. You shall penetrate to the oracle, subdue the priests with my own weapon, the devastating lightning gun. You shall then consult the oracle for the key the future holds to my true domination of the asteroid belt. I will assert myself at last. No longer as a mere semi-immortal confined to New Olympus, but as royal God-King of the entire asteroid belt, and everyone in it. From there . . . ?"

But Silverflash wasn't ready to go anywhere yet from there.

"That's totally impossible. Nobody can penetrate the aster-oid of the oracle. Not even I. They have an enormous electrical field that covers the whole asteroid. I change consciousness in electrical fields. Only my momentum carries me on through them. But there is no way to drift through this one, it's every-where. And even if I could, I couldn't subdue the priests with your lightning gun. It's a toy to them. Their technology is a million years beyond yours. I mean, begging your pardon, sir."

"How dare you? You really have gotten out of hand, haven't you? Well, I'll forget about it this time. It's obvious you're under a great deal of pressure.

"Just the same, I'm disappointed in you. I expected more. It's true that I've given you your most difficult task, but it is also your hour of shining glory. There are risks, of course, as in any bold plan. But the rewards justify the risk in this case: one small messenger boy's life against dominion of the entire asteroid belt.

"Don't you see, I have no choice and neither do you. Good luck, my brave messenger, may you succeed; and if not, may you go out as you have lived: a silver flash of glory, the messenger of the lord of the dark cloud. I salute you."

He actually saluted.

"And if you should fail—well, I have other plans. And plans within those plans."

And plans within plans, Silverflash said to himself in an effort to keep from screaming.

"Good, it's settled then. I'll leave the details to you. Do your best is all I ask. My blessing goes with you. Now come with me to the control room. I'm thinking of dialing up the heat a bit more. I'll rain it up a bit tonight just in case, but I think the shrubbery will handle it well enough. As for us— well, the Storm King's palace does come complete with air conditioning, ha ha ha."

Dazed into submission, Silverflash followed his boss, the mad immortal.

At the door to the control room, King Henry II turned back to him with a sudden worried expression. He was clearly showing the effects of stress. But he was so manic and filled with wild plans and energetic power that he only showed this side of himself in the incredibly brief moments of quiet.

"Besides," he said, "if the priests of the oracle have such great technology why would they wish to live the way they do? Quiet, and bleak surroundings. Nothing but empty knowledge. Dark plain garb and drab plain meals. No, they would live like me. I'm certain of that. They would surround themselves with glory and..."

His voice ran down and stopped like a mechanical toy. And in that brief moment of silence, and in a flash, as was his way, Silverflash saw completely into the core of the Storm King's soul. He was completely and utterly alone. Terrifyingly alone. Alienated by his insane pride from every other living being in the universe. He could not touch or be touched other than by himself. He had achieved what he was aiming for, he was utterly self-enclosed. And if he succeeded in his plan to expand until he absorbed the entire universe it wouldn't matter to him in the long run because he would find nobody home but himself.

IV. SPACES IN-BETWEEN

Silverflash had a few days to himself before the Storm King's ball. As he thought that these would probably be his last days of life, he felt committed to make the most of them. And he somewhat surprised himself to find that he spent them no differently than he would have anyhow. Ordinary days were the best: running the winds and rivers, hassling the irate crows, quarreling with the babies and the band of masked raccoons that haunted the river banks at night. Mostly just traveling light and fast to visit all his special ordinary places.

Silverflash's life was visiting places. New Olympus was the Storm King's creation, but it was Silverflash who most intimately knew her and every creature in her, who combed her with an eager scrutiny to unravel her living secrets, who loved her. He was at once a part of New Olympus and her witness.

And soon, he felt he would be leaving New Olympus for the last time. To be swallowed up by the dark in-between, forever. Yes, it was the fleeting beauty of the ordinary day that he cherished, with all its conflict and petty quarrels, with all its foolish misunderstandings, with all its plainness.

"The asteroid of the oracle arrived from no one knows where and settled into the belt a few hundred years ago," a clone mother was telling Silverflash. "Not much is known about it. Only three times have outsiders been allowed to land and consult the oracle. Anyone may request a consultation by beaming in from their ship's com. And doubtlessly thousands have done so. But all but three have been refused the right to land. The entire surface is covered by an enormous hot electrical field."

"What are the priests like?" Silverflash asked the mother psychiatrist historian.

"Who can say? They wear robes with hoods. Talk mystical nonsense. Much like other priests, I suppose. You'll never survive the electrical field, little flash. Listen to your mother and run away. Forget about us. You're clever and quick, you can get to another asteroid and . . ."

"And they send me back or face a war with New Olympus. No, I've made up my mind. This is my fate, clearly. I am destined to travel in between worlds and find death or answers at the asteroid of the oracle. Mad as he is, the Storm King is right, we have to seek solutions through greater powers than our own."

As Silverflash was talking he was pacing back and forth in front of the clone mother on the banks of the river. He was never still. A large sly trout popped its head out of the water to catch a glimpse of the world above. He found it lovely but austere. Quite harsh. He appreciated the fluid darting movements of Silverflash on the bank, then dropped back into the cool wet waters of relief.

"What did you say were the questions accepted by the oracle? I was distracted by the light on the water, the singing of the river, the call of a crow and that sly old trout that just jumped up over in the shadow of that willow tree," Silverflash said.

The clone mother smiled her sweet smile, "You're always distracted, Silverflash, by every pretty noise or color. Try to listen carefully at least when your life depends on it.

"The three questions that were accepted by the oracle were:
1) 'How can I grow giant grapes the size of oranges?'
2) 'Why is God so angry with us?'
3) 'How can I murder my wife and get away with it?'

"The electrical field was dialed off. They landed and were escorted by the priests into the center of the asteroid. Well, technically I guess it's not an asteroid. They say the entire thing might be a giant machine. A computer spacecraft. No one knows, of course."

"What were the answers?" Silverflash asked the historian mother.

"We don't know. The answers weren't in the form of words or simple formulas. The men were hooked up to the oracle and they experienced some sort of transcendental vision. They were changed by the answer. The question they had asked was changed.

"As you well know, we don't have grapes the size of oranges. But a giant variety of orange was developed. Without seeds. Delicious.

"The man who asked why God is so angry with us said he was ashamed of all of us, but he broke with his church forever and never went inside once again. He professed himself to be an atheist from that moment on; but nonetheless he said he understood why God was so angry, and seemed to feel that all churches and churchgoers of every religion that ever existed were responsible for God's wrath.

"The last fellow returned home to his wife and finished out his unhappy life with her. 'She's already dead,' he answered to a news commentator's questioning about the experience of the oracle.

"Perhaps you can persuade the Storm King to give up his

plan of attack and simply ask permission to consult. Who knows what criteria they use? You may be the fourth to be accepted."

But Silverflash did not know if he wanted to be the fourth to be accepted. Although he didn't want the Maneagle to continue poaching babies and generally preying on the denizens of the forests and rivers of New Olympus, he didn't want the insane Storm King to dominate the asteroid belt either. He really didn't know what he wanted at all.

He spent his last free hours studying his sad little clone brother, Wilbur.

The boy didn't seem to see Silverflash at all. But he was seeing something. He darted about on his tiptoes making a high-pitched squealing noise and inventing frantic magical gestures with his hands. Then all at once he went over and lay down flat on the spongy pink floor. There he lay as if dead, until finally Silverflash left once again for the castle.

Just as the guests were arriving at the palace for the grand costume ball, they shot the Silverflash into space in a simple slender capsule with the automatic directional finder geared to the asteroid of the oracle.

As the capsule popped out of the small, contained atmosphere of New Olympus, Silverflash felt the darkness of in-between seep into his body and mind. He would need no oxygen or heating system; he could live there. Become part of the silence. Or rather, his body could resurrect itself after that death of deaths.

His thoughts sprayed out, his breathing stopped and suddenly, nothing. Absolute—nothing. An eternity of . . . Kwatz . . .

V.   THE ORACLE

At the bottom of that well is a little black dot that is a well. At the bottom of that well is a little black dot that is a well. Sinking and sinking and . . . Kwatz . . .

Sprinkle of little bright dots, electric dots. And at the bottom of that bright well is a blazing dot of light that is a well. And at the bottom of that well is a blazing dot of light that is a well. Rising and rising . . . Kwatz . . .

Awake awake awake. Bubble bubble bubble. In a bright water world live gleaming fish swimming in Silverflash's flashing mind. Everything is light. Everything is light. Everything is . . .

The three trout are talking to someone. Who? There isn't anyone. In the dark. In the light within the dark. Is there?

"Ask your question, space traveler."

"What question?"

The wise old fish slithers around, opens and closes its mouth. "Ask your question, space traveler."

"What should I ask?"

There is an explosion of bubbles. A giant king of fish is jumping up breaking the surface. More light pours in. The fish swims around and around. Light is blazing and blazing off his silver form. Crackling with electricity.

"Your question has been accepted, space traveler. You may land your . . . whatever it is. Or should I say we will land your . . . whatever it is, and you may consult . . ." Around and around. A whirlpool of light, of dark, down and down into a funnel of dark, of kwatz.

"The oracle."

Silverflash opened his eyes. He was in an enormous room full of machinery. He couldn't see the end of it, and he couldn't make sense out of it.

"I said your question has been accepted, space traveler, you may consult the oracle."

Silverflash sat up, abruptly, as he did everything. His head swam.

"I survived?"

"Another fine question." The being in the dark robes spoke from the depths of a hood. You couldn't see into it. It was as dark as . . . oh no, you don't. I'm not going there anymore, Silverflash thought.

"But you could hardly improve upon your first one. *'What should I ask?'* You are the first being who has ever thought to ask us that question in all of these hundreds of years. The blind fools seem to just keep driving themselves on when they don't even know where they're going.

"We must have listened to a million questions, all the wrong ones. We accepted one here and one there to keep you coming. But we had almost given up hope. Until you. A child.

"Tell me, how did they expect you to get back? Your capsule would have been destroyed in the electrical field. If you had survived, then what?"

Silverflash hopped off the table and darted over to the open shell of the capsule. A pile of his belongings lay beside it. He snatched up the Storm King's rifle and ran over to the hooded priest and handed it to him. "I was supposed to subdue you all with this and take over the oracle. And then after I'd consulted the oracle for the Storm King I was to signal to New Olympus to send a ship to pick me up. Or force one of you to send me back, or..."

The hooded priest was making a loud frightening noise that caused Silverflash to jump back. It was, he realized, laughter.

Still laughing in a peculiar hissing style, he took the gun from Silverflash and quite suddenly shot a huge bolt of electricity into his hood.

There was a blaze of light so bright that it momentarily blinded Silverflash. The robes burst into flames. The creature within the flames, still laughing, was revealed.

It was not like any man Silverflash had ever seen. And yet, it was faintly humanoid. It was obviously a machine.

"You—the priests are robots?"

"As is usual among transient life forms we have studied the universe over, you revert to the habit of asking questions without thinking about them first.

"No, I am not a robot. I am not anything. There is no 'I' here. All this," he waved around him, "is a response machine. These parts you think of as beings are not separate from it. It is neither a spaceship nor an asteroid, although it travels through space. Nothing in it is separate. No function is separate. All there is is one enormous response machine. These mechanical forms of priests are parts of that machine molded to fit the minds of the creatures whom it answers. Those parts will be disassembled when the machine no longer needs to express itself in that manner. There is nothing here but oracle. Nevertheless—follow this part—" (More weird laughter.)

VI. SILVERFLASH'S MIND

Silverflash, the quick far traveler, had entered another new world. It was the world of his own mind amplified by the giant space-traveling machine called the oracle.

He was lying strapped onto a bed-table with a special helmet on his head. His eyes were closed; he could not open them.

But he was in communion with the fantastic machine. Pictures, odors, sounds flooded him in response to his slightest whim, and these were somehow stronger and more real than he had ever experienced before.

And yet the oracle would not initiate, it would only respond.

Silverflash knew beyond all doubt how important it was to ask the right question. It was everything.

What should I ask? he thought. Pictures of the babies, his brother, the Storm King, flashed through his mind.

I'm too confused to know, he answered himself.

Who is it that asks what should I ask?

Was that him or the machine? Confusing images rose up, not quite coming clear.

The machine could only respond, but what about himself? Silverflash? Could he only respond? Could anyone or anything exist outside of relationship?

Who was it, asking what to ask? Images came clearer.

Relationship with other beings: with the clone mothers, with babies, with Storm King, with . . .

Relationship with things: with food, with possessions, with . . .

And most of all with places: rivers, lakes, the wind, the babies' house, palaces, space, electrical fields.

The flood of images was overwhelming. Images of . . .

Suddenly he had it. He had been racing around the edges all this time.

It was images. The relationship of images. The being he thought of as himself was totally composed of a chain of images fished out of a memory pool. There was nothing really there at all.

How could mind ever sort it all out to ask the right question? It was the same mind creating the confusion that was trying to ask . . .

Suddenly doors opened everywhere. And doors within those doors, and doors within those . . .

Mind let go.

Nothing.

But in that nothing, images disintegrated and dispersed into void, in that nothing, relationship lived on without the image. True relationship.

It was love. Relationship without the image was love. He knew what to ask.

"What is the best possible world we can create for Wilbur?" he asked the oracle.

VII.   THE FUTURE

A man sat at an enormous desk, fishing through an immense pile of documents. He was a slender man who moved with delicate precision. Yet strength was there. But he was weary. He looked up. Smiled.

"My little big brother. How long have you been there? Why didn't you say something to me? Oh, how welcome you are to me, little far traveler. How precious to me are these moments of rest from my endless negotiations and coordinating and . . ."

He shook his head, smiling. His softspun silky brown hair re-formed itself into new rivulets and pools. His sweet sad expression was amplified by eyes so mischievous, so bright and shining they seemed out of place on a human, as though they really belonged to an elf, or perhaps a raccoon.

This is the man I would have become, Silverflash thought. How beautiful, how far beyond the animal elegance of the Storm King. This is Wilbur, my big little brother.

"The raccoons along the east riverbank are unhappy with their situation," Silverflash heard himself reply. "The babies are always pulling pranks on them. They ask you to put some restraints on the babies' territory. The clone mothers want a bigger house and more sunshine, only . . ."

His own voice droned on and on without him following it. He was there before Wilbur making a report of some kind, and at the same time he was observing the scene from some outside point.

Again the man shook his head and spoke. He had a sweet voice, not nearly so imposing as the Storm King's, and yet just as strong—no, stronger—the mixture of cerebral distance and emotional involvement was balanced and blended into a different kind of strength. A strength where brashness and flashiness were tossed away with other useless ornaments. It was the strength of a concerned man who knew he was doing his best.

"Everyone wants more all the time. That's why it's so difficult to be a good..."

"King?" the confused Silverflash suggested. He felt himself being drawn back to some other time and place, but he struggled to remain.

"Why, no, little brother, what a strange thing to say. I'm not a king at all. I was going to say, that's why it's so difficult to be a good servant. Isn't that what we both are, each in his own way? Servants? You bring me the messages, the demands, and I feed them through the computer, and then you carry back the compromises, the suggestions, and then it all starts up again. It never ends. To be a good servant you have to give up everything. And what's left when you give up everything?" He smiled his haunted smile.

Silverflash felt himself being inexorably drawn away from the scene, as though a powerful rubber band attached to his back had suddenly reacted to the pull upon it.

"No!" he tried to shout, but it was lost in the astral wind.

And then he was back on the table, eyes still shut, still asking questions.

"How do I...?"

But who would know how, except himself. If the scene he had witnessed was possible, the answer must lie within himself. Or within relationships. Within his relationship to the oracle? Could he, like his brother, give up everything?

VIII. THE COSTUME BALL

The new Silverflash fizzed through the electrical field and into the open window of the palace two nights later, only to find the lavish costume ball still in full flower.

The prince and princess of fairyland asteroid were dressed up, as always, in outlandish medieval-style outfits, all sparkle and glitter, cold and distant as stars. They were floating around the hall on a large spongy indoor cloud, playing weird sex games with two of the maids. All four of them fully clothed.

Silverflash ignored them and continued on his way to the grand ballroom, ignoring the floating clouds that wanted to carry him along. He never rode where he could walk, run, fly or crawl.

It was dark in the ballroom. Red pulsing lights were lit here and there. The room was so vast it rolled out before him like a dark plain lit by campfires. The ceiling was an invisible endless void.

Savages were milling around the campfires. Savages in fancy costumes. Savages with weirdly altered minds and bodies. Savages with an incredible technology at their fingertips. But savages none the less.

Silverflash said to himself, Let there be light. And there was light.

Startled cries, from drugged minds, confused hearts. They held up their hands, arrested in their eating, drinking, fornicating, they shrank from the light.

One small familiar figure shook its fist at him from very far away.

"How did you do that? How dare you?" it roared.

The new Silverflash said nothing. Like the oracle, he was waiting for the right question.

"Why did you do that?" Storm King demanded, advancing on Silverflash in a menacing manner.

"The dark ages are over," Silverflash said.

The words along with the dazzling flood of light had a momentary sobering effect even on the Storm King. He pulled up to a halt before the new Silverflash with all the anger drained out of his gestures and expression. Curiosity seemed to have taken the upper hand.

"The oracle?" He didn't know quite what to ask. To everyone's astonishment, the huge viewscreen automatically lowered itself into place at the far end of the ballroom and turned itself on.

It was obvious to everyone what it was showing them. It was the asteroid of the oracle. It just sat there for a moment, doing nothing other than what asteroids do, and then quite suddenly it rushed away at unbelievable speed, diminished and disappeared. Nothing was there at all anymore. The viewer just showed space.

"It's gone," Storm King muttered somewhat redundantly.

"It did what it came to do," Silverflash said, "it answered my questions; or rather, we answered our questions."

The Storm King's limitless confidence suddenly poured back into him. He grinned his manic grin.

"And what was the answer?" he asked.

"As always, the answer to the question was the questioner.

I was the answer. Only the question changed me. The answer changed me. Silverflash is no more. What stands before you is the new servant of New Olympus. Having merged with the oracle and having merged with all this," he waved his hand about him and then he smiled, "I am no longer your servant; this form is the servant of your work of art. You see, in a way you were correct. Your work of art has gone beyond the artist. It has taken on a life of its own. It no longer needs to limit itself to the distorted ego of the artist, it is truly alive and I am its servant. I am its eyes and its ears and its mouth. I am its subjective viewpoint and I am its focus of power."

For once in his immortal life, the Storm King appeared stunned. His handsome jaw was slack, mouth open. His thoughts were searching every which way at once and not finding.

"You mean the computer?" he whispered in awe.

"Indeed, that is part of it. I am still part eternal little boy, but I am also part machine. To put it more exactly, I am also a remote control for computers." He removed his funny little silver hat to display a silver plate in his now totally bald head. He let everyone have a guess at what had been put there, he really didn't know himself.

He tossed the lightning gun into the air; it floated there.

"Ugly tool," he said. Suddenly it shot across the ballroom and everyone's attention followed it until it raced out one of the windows.

Once again the screen lit up, and this time followed the lightning rifle's wild flight across the skies faster and faster until it ignited from friction and went out in a blaze of glory.

"Maneagle?" Silverflash demanded.

"He wouldn't come," one of the guests stammered. "He's at his aerie."

Instantly Eagle World appeared on the giant screen. It was a view of the aerie atop the highest cliff. For a moment it perched there quite bleak and predatory. Then it shot off into the air where it raced across the sky. The camera followed it until it exploded.

"You know how merciless a child can be," the new Silverflash said to everyone in the ballroom. "You would do well to remember. The penalty for poaching babies is death: by freezing."

The temperature in the room suddenly dropped, people cried

out and huddled together, shivering.

"By cooking."

The temperature in the room suddenly climbed, a woman swooned, everyone breathed in great rasping heaving breaths, faces turned red.

"Or by . . ."

And the Storm King flew into the air and started to whip across the room, suddenly slowed and was set back on his feet again. Clearly and utterly dethroned and defeated, his manic energy did not desert him. He did not beg. In fact he grinned his crazy grin.

"So the servant becomes the King. Now what, your majesty?"

His mind was already wheeling and dealing with the new situation. And probably, the new Silverflash realized with a start, coming up with all too many answers instead of too few. His only problem was that he never put to it the right questions.

"Now, ordinary days," the new Silverflash said, "and ordinary nights. The servant is still the servant, and the little boy is still the little boy. Little boys can't rule the world, and regulate the earth, the wind, the fire and water. Little boys can't govern the affairs of men, and I will never grow up.

"One is coming, however, for whom ruling means the chance to serve. Who will balance his maturity and strength with his heart. And when that one grows into his obligation the dark ages will have truly ended. Till then, continue playing the game the way you always have."

He turned and started back the way he had come. But then he turned again before going out the door. They watched him in stunned silence.

"I'd advise you to lower the heat a notch or two, Storm King. Just try and remember—as of now, New Olympus was made for the babies and not the babies for New Olympus."

The Storm King nodded, still grinning, still full of ideas; the new Silverflash felt the familiar rush of mixed emotions flash across his child's body.

IX. WILBUR'S MIND

Wilbur looked up. He actually looked up when Silverflash entered the room. One of the clone mothers was feeding him cereal when he actually looked up at Silverflash. She was so startled she forgot to feed him and just sat there holding the spoon, cereal all over her and Wilbur.

They were in the yellow room. Little yellow tables were all over the spongy yellow floor. Some of the babies sat there being fed by other clone mothers and some of the older babies sat crosslegged feeding themselves.

Funny vacuum machines that looked like nervous little anteaters scurried about sucking up spilt cereal here and there with furious gurgling noises.

Wilbur was looking at Silverflash. Wilbur had never really looked at anyone before.

Silverflash darted over and sat down crosslegged directly in front of his clone brother. They just sat there studying each other.

Then Wilbur took some cereal from his mouth and patted it onto Silverflash's arm, and with solemn dignity leaned over and slowly ate it up. Carefully he licked it clean. Then he took another handful of cereal from his bowl and patted it onto Silverflash's arm and began to eat it.

Silverflash laughed. It was so funny. The babies were always funny. He loved to be here.

"What does that mean?" he asked the clone mother.

"It means he needs you to help him get well, Silverflash. It means you are his sustenance. It means he's changing."

And later that night, just before bedtime, one of the clone mothers said, "Oh, you cut off all your hair, Silverflash. It will grow back in a while."

"No, it won't ever grow back again," he said; and suddenly unable to stop himself he blurted out: "I conquered the Storm King, and I killed Maneagle, and I made them turn down the temperature. I can make them do anything you want."

Some of the older babies were yelling, "Yea, hooray for Silverflash," but a clone mother just shook her head and laughed her musical laugh.

"Oh, Silverflash, you silly child, don't tell the babies stories like that. You know that little boys can't conquer the immortals. Anyway, it's a nice thought and we know you mean well. I'll tell you what, this calls for a celebration. Root beer is on the house, babies."

A cheer went up and soon they were all clinking together frosty mugs in their lovely little blue living room. Everyone was laughing and squealing or just shouting in excitement, "Root bear, root bear." Everyone, that is, except new Silver-flash.

"Silverflash, don't cry, Silverflash. Why are you crying?"

Suddenly time stopped. Silverflash's spirit soared outside the house, and he was one with the wind, the river, the night sky, the little family of gypsy raccoons thieving and chattering along the riverbanks, the fish gliding in their cool secret depths. Then he was just there again, in the cozy little blue room, just a little boy, with a little boy's heart and soul.

"I don't know," he said, "and I guess I never will."

EPILOGUE

The writer puts down his pencil in the pencil pool and staggers to the window. He lets in some light. It's twilight in this world, he thinks. He still hasn't pulled himself out of the other one, the one he's just created. I'm the only one who can do these things, he thinks. It's a fantastic world, better than this one. He looks out the window: cars, kids, etc.

Sometimes I wonder if I am not creating them both. I can do anything, he thinks. His eyes glow with that manic glow. His thoughts rush fearlessly outward, all directions at once. He is quite gloriously mad. His psyche spreads out to cover this universe as well, and everything in it. He becomes it, it becomes him. He is God. But he is alone. He puts down the curtain. He isn't afraid of the dark, or the light.

The pencils beckon to him, the notebook. I've been sitting here writing alone in the dark. How could I see what I was doing? I can do anything.

He begins to laugh, a loud, raucous, obviously disturbed cackle. He settles down on the floor still hissing and choking. He hasn't eaten all day or moved from this spot. Still cackling, the crazy bastard picks up a pencil and starts in again writing in the dark stuffy room—alone.

ENCROACHMENT

by Kevin O'Donnell, Jr.

This is a portion of O'Donnell's novel, CAVERNS, which didn't make it into the actual book. But you don't have to have read CAVERNS, or know McGill, Jose and Pat Feighan to understand and enjoy this. "Encroachment" is the story of a fiercely proud father with an unusual son. Only through a near-disaster can the father accept that he is *not* all his son needs.

Patrick Sean Feighan was a big man, and Cleveland cramped him. They built the cars small and the ceilings low: to conserve, they said. They squashed the houses together and shrank the lots: to make green belts, they said. *And most of the time I don't mind,* he thought. Most of the time he scrunched his shoulders indoors and stepped carefully outdoors, pretending the world had room for an ex-tackle of two-meter-ten. When the fans remembered and the women whistled, it worked out just fine.

It was when they forgot that the bleakness set in.

Like everybody alive he was really two people, the surface and the core, and wistful melancholy infused his inner self. He had been the best, but that was past. The years had dimmed his fame. Once, everybody knew him; now, he could give his name and half the time draw no response. In another ten years, who'd recognize him at all?

The city reached into his house to squeeze him. The sports-news printout, aswarm with youngsters jostling to erase him from the books, crackled between his hands. It used to banner *his* picture, flaunt *his* achievements. *How long's it been since they even mentioned me?* Leaving the locker room that last time had been like stepping off a bus a thousand klicks from nowhere—and having the bus go on without him.

From the den came a child's delighted hoot. He glanced down the hall, through the half-open door. His young son McGill was sweeping checkers off a board saying, "I beat you again, Jose."

"You sure did, kid," said the grey old man.

"Wanna play another game?"

"I don't know, kid—I'm getting awful tired of losing. Why don't you get your father to play?"

"'Cause I'd rather play *you*. He doesn't like checkers. And I don't feel like playing football right now."

"All right. But only one more game."

"Then I better beat you *real* bad this time." With a little boy's exuberance, he bounced into the air, grabbed the old man's shoulders, and hugged him hard.

Panic expanded in Feighan's throat. Gasping a ragged breath, he pushed out of his chair and pounded upstairs. His gut spun hollow and empty. The world closed in like a too-tight suit of clothes. It was a bad way to feel just before a fortieth birthday.

I've got to get out of here! Though he knew his impatience for a fault, he couldn't control it, not when the urgency was on him. He had a temper and a bull-headedness and an impetuosity that had gotten him into scrapes before. After each, he could analyze and even regret the forces that had driven him—but during the compelling, his considerable intelligence rode as cargo, not crew.

With quick, brittle movements he packed a knapsack, kissed his wife, and traced the route to the forest he'd bought in his last year as a pro—the hundred acres Nicole wouldn't live on because, she said, there were too many bugs and not enough neighbors. He checked that he had food and fishhooks, then called his son.

"I'm going camping," he said, when the boy and his seventy-year-old shadow appeared. "You want to come?" He tried to keep the need out of his voice, but Schwedeker's brow-twitch told him he'd failed. "Good weather for it."

"Sure!" said McGill. "We love camping, don't we, Jose?"

Feighan began. "Ah—" but stopped himself. He didn't want the old man along, but had to let him come. Custom and unwritten law said so.

The boy was a latent Teleport; Schwedeker, a retired one home from the stars. The thin grey man had discovered the child's Talent two years earlier. In the vernacular, he'd "rung McGill's changes." That gave him rights—he slept upstairs, sat to dinner with the family—and a responsibility. On his bowed shoulders weighed the burden of seeing that the Talent survived to maturity, when it could fend for itself.

The ability to "Fling," to shift a mass from one place to another through a psi-cut "doorway," came rarely, and left easily. It needed an environment which accepted it, which believed in it though it had yet to show itself. Schwedeker provided that environment, and that brought the two together. It gave them a culture of their own, a language of tongue and dream that no outsider could fully share.

While the two grabbed their gear, Nicole looked sharply at her husband. "No trouble, Pat," she warned.

He shook his head. "None."

"You leave him alone—he's doing good for McGill."

"I know, I know." Footsteps thudded on the stairs. "Here they come—see you in a couple of days." Pack over his shoulder, he headed for the garage and unlocked the hovercar.

The two climbed in thoughtlessly, piling into the back seat though there was room up front, laughing about things they didn't explain. Grey Schwedeker was saying, ". . . didn't know which was which, since they were both out cold, so by the time their Ambassador got there, they'd sent the gringibeast to the hospital, and dropped its handler off at the vet's."

Feighan looked into the rearview mirror. His son's brown eyes sparkled at the change-ringer. McGill said, "I bet you never did that, huh, Jose?"

"Well, right at the end, I got a little sloppy. Happens to the best of us, kid," he said expansively. "It's nature's way of saying it's time to retire. But not before then, uh-uh."

"I didn't think so," stated McGill with a seven-year-old's loyalty. He leaned across the old man to point out the window. "Let's play license plate!"

All the way down, Patrick Sean Feighan felt like a hired hand.

That fine September evening in 2090, the two men watched a campfire consume itself. The wind that shook the flames bore the smoke up to the forest's rustling leaves; sparks rode it, too, but winked out in mid-air. Nightbirds called, some harsh, some plaintive. The underbrush crackled a hundred meters away.

Feighan cocked his ear to the sound of snapping twigs, then nodded. "It's a deer." He leaned forward, picked a leg-sized log off the pile with his fingers, and added it to the fire. It felt good when the football muscles moved surely and smoothly. They hadn't lost their cunning, not yet. That pleased him, and he smiled to himself.

"You like it out here," said Schwedeker. When he stirred, his ratty old coat opened at the neck and let the brilliance of an energy tunic spatter on a silver birch trunk. He crimped it shut. The rainbow vanished.

Still happy that he'd handled the huge log so effortlessly, Feighan turned his head. For the moment, resentment lay as far from him as the city. "You could say that," he mused, as the mood to declaim crept over him, "were you given to understatement. Like it? Man, I love it! It's the scale that enchants me, all towering and sprawling . . ."

"Room to breathe, huh? I know what you mean. Ever since I retired I've felt cramped."

"Ahh, but there's more out here!" He waved his arm grandly. "The age of these moss-backed trees! My God, they're older than this country—imagine all they've seen? To think I own them . . ." He chuckled at the presumptuousness of the idea. "And the richness of this sweet-smelling ground. Hunker down to look at it, really look at even one square meter, and you'll see more complexity than your mind can hold . . . Ah, Jose, it's space that a forest offers, and permanence, and variety so dazzling that after a hundred trips here I still don't know the half of it."

"Very poetic," said Schwedeker dryly.

He felt rebuked. The new log caught; a dozen more flames rose wobbly and bright. He blamed them for the warmth in his cheeks. "The loquacity ends in the morning," he sighed, "but I babble the first night out of the cage. It's the release from self-consciousness, you see. I can swing my arms when I walk out here, and it hits me like strong champagne. It's temporary, though."

"I don't envy you your bulk." Schwedeker nodded to the boy in his bag. "At least you didn't make McGill go the upsize route."

"One ape in the family's enough," said Feighan sharply. Then he shook his head. When he spoke again, his voice had softened. "I never wanted to be a bonecrusher; my da' did, God rest his soul. It was pride he was after—All-N.Amer, All-Globe . . ." He snorted, and scratched at the corner of his eye. Then he cleared his throat. "What I wanted, you see, was a son. And even if he hadn't been"—his hand rolled over on itself in the dark—"Talented, I could never have put him to the drugs. God, it hurts to grow that extra bit. For years you sleep bad. All of you aches, from head to toe, and your skin's so tight you feel it'll split if you bend too quick. Naah, even if he'd been normal, I could never have done it."

"I'm glad," said Schwedeker simply.

A note in the old man's voice jarred Feighan. He peered through the shifting shadows. "I've been wanting to talk to you," he began, picking his words carefully because he sensed their power to ignite his temper, "about you and my boy."

"The kid and I have gotten real close," answered Schwedeker.

He heard it again: a touch of smug, a streak of kinship: taunts, almost, like Schwedeker was claiming something Feighan didn't have. A subtle fear spread through him—could the old man be right? "It's my understanding—" stiffness straightened his phrasing "—that you're supposed to be teaching him how to teleport."

With a laugh, Schwedeker stretched, raising his arms to the boughs uplifted above. "Not really. I'm a change-ringer, sure, but—" He yawned into his hand.

"And what is that?" said Feighan, taking the pause as an insult, "if it isn't a Talent trainer?"

"Pat," he protested, apparently sensing the mood swing, "it's everything *but!* God only knows when he'll Fling his first thing, and until he does, I—" He coughed suddenly. "He has to get the Talent before he can be taught how to use it."

"Are you saying there's a chance he hasn't the Talent?"

"Hell, no." Shoulders tense, the old man hunched towards the fire. "He's got it, all right—" he closed his eyes "—I can feel it like I feel these flames here, hot, bright, and pure gold— but it hasn't risen yet." Firelight danced on his tilted face while he groped for the explanatory sentence. "It's not mature enough; it's not ripe. The kid can do a trick or two—catch himself in a stumble, slow a fall—but the full Talent hasn't popped out yet. Hell, I was fifteen before mine did."

Feighan stood. He looked down at the man who had moved into his life to share his son. Schwedeker's collar had drooped open and colors sparkled through it. Feighan's belly churned like an anchor-slipped ship in a storm. He was jealous and afraid, but had to deny it because he wasn't supposed to be. He was supposed to be pleased about his son's future. He waxed angry, instead. "Why?" he demanded, keeping his voice low and hoarse so as not to waken McGill.

The change-ringer lifted his red-webbed eyes. "Why what?"

"Why is it you've come before you're needed?"

"Pat—" He spread his hands palms up, half imploring, half confused.

"Why, dammit?"

"I am needed. Now."

"For what?" he snapped.

The old man took a breath, and let it out slowly. Shadows filled the hollows of his cheeks. "McGill needs a role model, Pat. He's got to have it now, before his Talent matures."

"And I'm not good enough?"

"Pat—"

"Shut up!" Sourness fouled the back of his throat; he clenched his jaws and looked into the darkness. His nerves ran in parallel lines of hot ire and cold fear. His hands made fists of themselves, which he jammed into his pockets lest he be tempted to use them. He had rarely been so angry—and never quite so hurt. What right had Jose to call him a bad father? What did he know? He had never been a father, never raised a son . . . Who gave him the authority to steal Feighan's boy?

Somewhere hooted an owl. The night breeze blew the smoke away. The burning logs spat at each other.

"Pat—"

"No." He swung around. His size and his strength surged, offering themselves as tools of retaliation, but he pushed them down. To use them on a dried-up husk like Schwedeker would cheapen both them and him—and would, he knew with bleak amusement, prove the change-ringer's point. "No. I've heard enough from you, old man, and I'm not of a mind to hear more. McGill and I leave in the morning. Alone." Bending, he seized his sleeping bag, and unfurled it with a flip of his wrists. "Let me know where you want your things sent."

Schwedeker was silent for a long time, but then, just as Feighan started his drift into a troubled sleep, he whispered, "Sorry, Pat. Where he goes, I go."

Birds twittered at the dimness until the sun gave in to their pleas and rolled above the eastern horizon. Feighan sat up in his sleeping bag, yawned so hugely that the tendons of his jaw popped, then blinked his eyes open. Arms around his bent knees, he listened to the change-ringer snore, and watched McGill toss in the restlessness of his dreams. A heavy dew had fallen overnight. It glistened where stray rays of sun knifed through the leaves.

He stretched again, feeling the muscles ripple one against another like notes in exquisite harmony. "Aahh," he breathed.

It was a soft sound, but it startled a squirrel that leaped up the trunk of an ancient elm. Feighan's eyes followed the flash of its brown and grey tail, then came together in a frown. *Damn tree's dead,* he thought. He hadn't noticed it the night before. Leaning back onto his hands, he stared into the elm's canopy. Bare branches all. Not a leaf in sight. *Dutch elm? Old age?*

He got up, shook his son awake and nudged Schwedeker, then pulled the ashen blanket off the slumbering coals and brought them back to consciousness, too.

"Can I help cook?" asked McGill.

"I can use some wood," he said quietly, "and then we'll see about breakfast."

"How much?"

"Oh—" He held up a piece as thick as his wrist. "If you get them about this size, then a big armful should do the trick. No, wait," he said, as his son started to turn away, "let me see the length of your arms."

Puzzled, McGill held them out.

"Ah!" said Feighan. "Just as I thought. You've gotten so

big that a full load would be too much. Half full will do it."
He gave his boy a wink, and a pat on the butt. "Off with you,
now. My stomach's growling already."

"I'll be right back!" He ran for the underbrush.

"Nice," said Schwedeker, from the far side of the fire. It
was his first word of the morning, to Feighan at least. "That
put a glow on him."

Feighan nodded. "'I know mine,'" he quoted, "'and mine
know me.'"

"Then you've got to know you can't fire me!"

"I know nothing of the kind," he said stiffly, as he took the
eggs from their styrofoam container.

Schwedeker sighed. "Pat—"

"Here you go, Dad!" panted McGill, stumbling back into
the clearing with a load of sticks. One slid off the top. He
made a face, and dragged it along with his right foot. "Is that
enough?"

Relieved to drop the conversation with the change-ringer—
yet faintly discontented with himself for feeling relieved—he
goggled in sham wonderment. "Just drop them here, Paul Bun-
yan." He patted the ground next to the fire. "Did you leave
any for next time?"

"I saw a squirrel, and a blue jay. They were shouting at
each other. It was really funny. You want to see them?"

"After breakfast, maybe." He broke the eggs into a pan,
and stirred them with a fork.

"Think you'll have time?" asked Schwedeker.

He raised his eyes to meet the old man's. Smoke from the
dew-damp wood tugged a curtain between them. "For a nature
walk with my son? Oh, I think so."

McGill looked from one man to the other, eyebrows quirked
in worry. "What's the matter?" he asked abruptly.

"Nothing," said Feighan. He reached out to tousle his son's
black hair. As his fingers brushed the bumps of McGill's skull,
he suddenly sensed how it would feel to extend his hand—and
touch nothing. An empty yet massive pain shot through all of
his soul. He had to clear his throat. "Nothing at all, McGill
my boy. Breakfast will be done in fifteen minutes—I'll holler."

"Okay," he said, backing hesitantly away. "I'll, ah . . . I'll
go see the bird's nest."

"You do that," he called after him. Then he blinked, and

wiped his eyes with his fingers. "Damn smoke."

"Shifty wind," agreed Schwedeker solemnly. "Do you speak Gaelic?"

He sat back on his haunches, fry pan in hand, and said, "What?"

"Do you speak Gaelic?"

"Erse?" He shook his head. "Why on earth do you ask?"

"Why don't you speak it?"

Totally confused, he raised his shoulders high and let them fall. "I'm an American. I was born here, raised here— What is it you're driving at?"

Schwedeker picked an ant off his shoe, and set it carefully down on the ground. "Last night I said something about a role model—"

Feighan glared across the flames. "That you did." He reached for the package of ham, to lay out the slices in the pan.

"Hell, I wasn't saying you're no good!" He stood, shoved his spotted hands into the depths of his coat pocket, and took a deep breath. "Pat, will you open your mind and listen to me?"

He came to his own feet, unwilling to concede the old man even the barest of psychological advantages. "If there's something you have to say, yes."

"All right, then. At its simplest: I didn't join your family to replace you. I'm in it to show McGill a way of thinking, a way of viewing the world through . . . from the perspective of his Talent. That's all. You don't speak Gaelic because you weren't raised by people who spoke it. To be the best Flinger possible, McGill has to grow up with someone who speaks teleportation. That's all."

He gritted his teeth. The man made sense, he had to admit it—and in the daytime, when he could see where he stood, he didn't feel the anger he had the night before. Icy fear still lay unmelting in his stomach, though. "Sure, and those are fine words, if you live up to them. But how am I to know if you do?"

Schwedeker searched his face and apparently found sincerity. He said, "Yeah. You've got a good point, there. How can you tell if I'm doing my job, when there's almost nothing to see . . ." He thought a moment, then nodded. "Something I can

show you—" He turned his head. "Hey, McGill, come here!"
To Feighan he explained, "It's really not much more than a
parlor trick, but for a kid his age, it's damn good."

"What?" he asked, but his son joined them before the answer
came.

McGill tugged at the old man's jacket hem. "What do you
want, Jose?" he panted. "I was watching the blue jay again."

The Flinger ruffled the boy's hair. "Your Dad's never seen
you jusmo."

McGill wrinkled his nose. "I don't call it jusmo any more,
Jose. You know that. I'm not a baby. It's ad-jussing mo-men-
tum. See?"

"Let's show your Dad." He picked the boy up with a grunt.
His jaw and neck tendons bulged as he swung McGill as high
as he could reach. "Ready?" he gasped.

"Ready!"

Schwedeker let go. "Jusmo!"

Shocked, Feighan lunged forward—but his son drifted
down like a feather. "What in the name of God—"

"Attaboy, kid," said the old man as McGill touched the
ground lightly. "Real good, real good." Then he looked up to
Feighan. "It's momentum adjustment. A Flinger's got to be
able to do it because the place you teleport to is just about
always moving at a different speed and in a different direction.
What the kid did was fall maybe a meter, then cancel out his
downward velocity. For that long—" He snapped his fingers.
"—he just hung there. Then he fell the rest of the way."

"I can do it from the ground, too," said the boy, face up-
turned to the two adults. "Like a rocket!"

"Not yet," said Schwedeker absently. "You've got to rest,
recharge your batteries, remember?"

"I'm not tired, I can do lots more. If you'd stop arguing,
I could show you."

"We're talking, McGill, not arguing," said Feighan. "Off
with you now, you can show us later."

"Bet you don't watch then, either," he grumbled, as he ran
back to the underbrush.

The Flinger spread his hands to the father. "This is what
I meant, Pat. It's no reflection on you that I can teach the kid
something you can't. All it means is, I've got a skill you don't.
And that's Flinging, nothing else."

"Sure, and that much is true, but—" He halted, unsure of how to express his resentment that this old man seemed so much closer than he to his own son. "I—"

"Hey, watch me!" called a thin, high voice.

Both men raised their heads. Grinning, waving, McGill perched on a branch ten meters up the dead elm. Schwedeker shouted, "Don't! Get dow—"

McGill jumped.

Feighan started to leap—remembered momentum adjustment—and stopped, puzzled by Schwedeker's alarm.

Before he could ask what was wrong, though, he saw for himself: his son stopped in mid-air and floated motionless just long enough for a double-take. Then he plummeted once more, shrieking as he, too, realized he couldn't pull the trick off again.

Feighan charged. Huge quick legs driving him forward, he lunged for the spot where his son would land, praying *Mother of God, help me now!*

"Jusmo!" bellowed Schwedeker hopelessly.

A single image blazed in the ex-pro's head: catching his son on the run, like a special teams' man racing under a punt, absorbing gravity's pull on the shocks of his arms—but he'd been too good a pro not to see he couldn't make it. He'd be two steps late. He sobbed.

McGill's feet thumped. He folded down upon himself, head whipping forward to strike the ground.

Feighan's blood froze. He was moving too fast to stop. Hurdling his huddled son, he dug in his heels and whirled about as soon as he'd caught his balance.

McGill's jaw hung slack. Blood trickled from his hairline.

Feighan dropped to his knees beside the boy. "McGill!" Gently, he touched the bloody spot. A sponge of skin and bone mushed beneath his fingers. "Oh, sweet Jesus!"

Twigs crackled beneath him as Schwedeker pounded up. "Is he—"

Weakly, he rose, "His . . . his skull is crushed."

Even as they watched, the young cheeks sallowed. The boy's respiration barely lifted his back. Schwedeker squinted. "It's not that bad—but he needs a doctor, quick."

Feighan fought down a wail. He wanted to cry, to vomit, to tear out the elm by its roots and beat the thing into toothpicks with his fists . . . An icy cold settled on him, and he knelt again. "McGill, don't die, please, hang in there, we'll get you to a doctor—"

"Find me the most colorful bottle or can you've got," snapped Schwedeker.

Feighan turned, bewildered. "What?" he said, his hands still on his son's shoulder. "What did you say?"

The old man was scribbling on a piece of paper. "A can or a bottle, the brightest, most eye-catching you've got."

"Have you cracked?"

"No, dammit!" He tore the sheet off its pad, and waved it in Feighan's face. "I know the nearest hospital; this note tells them to send an ambulance. I put it in the bottle, Fling it to their Emergency Room, and the color or whatever makes 'em notice it. They'll read it. By the time we get McGill to the road, they'll be there."

He could have cried with relief. In that instant he understood what the change-ringer had meant about growing up with one fluent in the language of teleportation. Urgency had driven rational and memory from his own head. Schwedeker was a Flinger! McGill was saved! Then the comprehension that had slapped him on one cheek back-handed him on the other. He frowned. "But why the note? Fling McGill!"

"I—can't." His hands busied themselves with pocketing the pad. "Get me the bottle."

He fountained to his feet and caught the ratty old lapels in his hands. Light scintillated between his thumbs. "Why can't you?"

Schwedeker shrank inside his coat. "I—I'm retired."

"You're crazy."

"No, I—"

"First that 'Jusmo!' trick didn't work—"

"Of course not," he said quickly. He trembled under Feighan's glower. "You have to rest between, and I knew he'd adjust too soon—that's why I told him not to jump. You heard me, I told the kid, don't."

"Then why the hell can't you get him to the hospital?" He shook the old man, but not too hard.

"Do you think if I could I wouldn't? I've lost it, that's why I'm retired, I don't have the control any more . . ." Tears ran from his age-yellowed eyes. "Pat, if I tried, I'd set him down wrong, I'd give him velocity or take some away—don't you understand? I'm old. I can't control it! Even if I could get him on the floor, he'd slither across it and bang himself up—"

He understood. His fingers petaled open. He nodded. "You'd bounce him off the walls, then?"

Schwedeker, too, nodded.

He sank to the ground and scooped his son into his lap. "Then I'll be his cushion," he declared, gripping those frail bones while he curled himself around them. "Fling away, man!"

Schwedeker froze—seemed to ponder—then slipped into position next to Feighan. "You keep his head and upper body; I'll take his legs."

They readjusted themselves.

The Flinger breathed, "Ready? Set—"

"GO!" hissed Feighan.

The forest disappeared.

They left time behind, so the next instant was eternal, infinitesimal, and everything in between. They shed space, so they became all of creation and the smallest part of it simultaneously. They abandoned reality, so insanity enveloped them.

An Emergency Room appeared.

A meter beneath them.

And headed ten centimeters per second east.

They dropped, and Feighan grunted as his butt slapped the carpet. His heels plowed its pile; its fibers abraded the backs of his calves. He hung on to his son for dear life, and prayed that Schwedeker could, as well.

They stopped with the soles of their shoes a meter from the west wall.

The rest was a blur—orderlies, carts, ointment-bearing nurses who couldn't understand that the rug burns didn't hurt, not at a time like that, and cold fluorescent lights, and hard plastic waiting room chairs, and endless cups of lousy coffee . . .

And, finally, a doctor, white-coated and weary, saying, "He's out of it now. He'll be all right." He took Feighan's arm. "He's asking for you; come calm him down so he'll go to sleep. That's what he needs most, now."

When Schwedeker made to follow, the doctor stopped them.

"I'm sorry, only immediate family are allowed into Intensive Care."

The old man's lined cheeks drooped. Shoulders slumped, he started to turn away.

And Feighan said, "Come on, Jose." To the doctor, he explained, "He *is* family. Let him in."

THE NINTH PATH

by Mike Conner

The author got the idea for this story when he read about a lecture tour the ex-patriate, 14th Dalai Lama was making in towns all over the United States (he has since been invited by the Chinese government to return after 22 years in exile). The thing that fascinated Conner was whether the Reincarnation of Chenresig had adjusted his religious tenets to cope with the unpleasant political realities in his home country. He and his forebears had got along fine with the eight-fold path to perfection. Perhaps now a ninth was necessary. You don't have to know beans from bacon about Buddhism to appreciate this decidedly ironic supposition of where that ninth path—rooted in pragmatism—might lead.

One

The figure of the Buddha had been painstakingly sculpted from a nine-hundred-pound block of yak butter. It seemed to smile in the guttering flames of the butter lamps set before it, nodding as the light shifted. Meanwhile the low, echoing hum of chanting monks gave way to the tinkle of brass chimes as other lights came on, gradually materializing the vivid designs of the silks hanging from the walls and ceiling.

Then a single, harsh-red spotlight snapped on. The chanting ceased, and saffron curtains parted to reveal the person of Tsangyang Gyatso, fourteenth Dalai Lama of Tibet, seated upon a dais of red and gold flowers.

The Thunderbolt, *Gyalwa Rinpoche,* Ocean of Wisdom, Reincarnation of Chenresig himself, allowed himself a satisfied smile as he gazed upon his audience. He touched his fingers to his scant moustache, cleared his throat, then said, in surprisingly unaccented French, "Ladies and Gentlemen of the press, representatives of the international fashion industry, welcome. It is my honor to present the first showing of our new line of silk afternoon and evening wear."

He raised his hands with a rustle of his crisp gown, intent on summoning the first model. But as he clapped, he felt a tightness constricting his neck, felt white-hot wires shooting suddenly through his left arm and leg. The smile had not faded from his lips before he fell back, swallowed by his cushion of flowers.

His personal physician, rushing to the stage, overturned the sculpted Buddha and the votive lamps. The resulting fire was quickly extinguished. No one noticed, as the ambulance attendants arrived, that the face of the Buddha had escaped both flames and chemical foam.

Or that it continued to smile.

Despite the late-season cold in the high passes, the old *Panchen Rinpoche,* Trisong Detsan, slept in the open protected only by his yakwool blankets. The spiritual equal of the long-exiled and now deceased Dalai Lama slept fitfully, anticipating the dream which had assailed him every night for almost two years, since the word of Tsangyang Gyatso's untimely death had reached Lhasa.

It was always the same: the blackhat dancer approached, deadly-sharp *phurbu* cutting the air above his head as Trisong Detsan waited, sluggish and gravid with the evil he had taken willfully into himself. The dancer would come to cut off his head, then disembowel him and cast the entrails into the wind to exorcise the demons subsumed by Trisong Detsan. Yet, as the sword approached, as Trisong Detsan felt the air pushed before the blade, he realized that his preparation had been incomplete. He looked up, trying to scream, to halt the dance, knowing the outcome would be a murder, not a mystic cleansing.

The touch of the sword shook him to his bones just before he woke, sweating, to bare dawn and the dry rattle of wind through the passes beyond the Oracle Lake. Trisong Detsan shivered, sat up, and pulled his cold boots on over his feet. The sensation brought a smile to his lips. He could remember the time when he traveled with his nomad family as a young boy, sleeping outside the tent in the bitterest weather with Bo, the great mastiff, lying atop him. *Always take off your boots,* his mother insisted. To fail to remove them could mean the loss of both legs. It was not yet winter by the shore of the oracle lake called *Lhama Latso,* but Trisong Detsan retained old habits, even after seventy years of monastic life.

He pulled on the government-issued parka and saw that his entourage—three young monks from Drepung and a representative of the Autonomous Region Religious Liaison Committee—were busy with their breakfast. One of the monks scrambled over, offering food with a hopeful expression. But, as he had for the last month, the *Panchen Rinpoche* declined the broiled meat and accepted only a bowl of buttered tea, feeling guilty at the look of disappointment and fear which clouded the boy's features. Trisong Detsan patted his cheek.

"Attend to your devotion and then break camp. Load the rover. We shall know in an hour where the *trüllku* of the *Gyalwa Rinpoche* is living."

The monk ran back, barely able to contain his joy. As he told the others, Trisong Detsan saw the Liaison Committeeman kick the gravel with a disgusted expression on his flat, Han Chinese features.

Trisong Detsan turned away, hoping his pronouncement had been correct.

After a laborious climb along a bank of loose brown stone, the old man reached a little shelf of rock whose surface was worn smooth as that of the lake itself. It had been used many times through the centuries, whenever the oracle lake had to be consulted in the course of the search for the *trüllku*—the reincarnation—of a deceased *Gyalwa Rinpoche.* Trisong Det-

san had himself been here twice before since Tsangyang
Gyatso's heart attack in Paris. Neither time had the crystal-
blue depths yielded the secret of the rebirth, nor had anyone
in the country offered up a candidate. It was whispered among
the people—more loudly among the representatives of the secular government—that the prophecy of the thirteenth Dalai
Lama to the effect that his successor would be the end of the
line of Chenresig, that the religion of the country would be
forgotten, and that no one would henceforth search for rein-
carnations had in fact come to pass. Only Trisong Detsan, it
seemed, believed that this was not so. And yet his search for
a sign—any sign—had produced only discouragement and the
empty howl of wind sweeping across the icy waters of this
lake.

I have not prepared myself properly...

He shuddered and stared into the rippling water. The sun
rose above the peaks behind his back, reflecting off the waves
in tiny triangles that dazzled him. This time, something was
there.

After a time, Trisong Detsan rose. He was pale, and felt
too weak to traverse the gravel bank a second time. But he
knew that if he did not, the thirteenth Dalai Lama's prediction
would indeed be correct. When he finally reached the campsite
he was nauseous with fatigue, accepting without protest the
supporting arms of two of the monks.

Not until he was in the landrover was he able to speak.

"I've seen him. *Changchub Sempa.* The living Buddha."

"Where, master?"

"Not in Tibet, but to the West. Far, far to the West." As
soon as he'd spoken, Trisong Detsan collapsed into a deep,
dreamless sleep.

Lhasa, city of the Dalai Lama in a mountain valley more
than two miles high, had, in the old times, been two things:
above all, the Potala—the High Heavenly Realm—a palace
in red and whitewashed stone straddling the Red Hill seven
hundred feet over the valley floor; and the Jokhan, the golden
temple built by the first Tibetan king converted to Buddhism.
Beneath its foundation is the underground lake, Tsulag Khang,
where visions of the future may be seen. This temple, once
the object of thousands of pilgrimages, had now been swallowed up by the new Lhasa, its beaten-gold spires a glittering

island in a sea of corrugated roofs protecting foundries and factories that turned out bicycles and sewing machines for the new Tibet.

But nothing could conceal the presence of the great Potala palace, and the Chinese had never tried. It remained, in the era of the People's Autonomous Region of Tibet, the one edifice in Lhasa which compelled attention no matter where in the city one happened to be. Its red and white brickwork seemed broad enough to straddle the mountains on either side of the valley; and when the sun caught the giltwork tombs of the eight deceased Incarnations built upon the highest levels of the palace, it seemed as though the roof of the world itself had somehow caught fire.

In the first years of their occupation, the Chinese had tried making a museum of the Potala, carefully preserving the apartments of the Dalai Lama in the event of Tsangyang Gyatso's return. But as his stubborn, and (as the Chinese government insisted until the day of his death) self-willed exile continued, the building had become something of a silent reproach to the Chinese hegemony. Therefore they had scrubbed six hundred years of butter-grease from its walls, strung electric lights through its thousand rooms and seemingly endless and baffling corridors, installed modern plumbing and even an elevator, thus converting the High Heavenly Realm into the seat of the People's Government of the Autonomous Region. There, in a room which had once been a chapel dedicated to a demonic aspect of the protector of Tibet, Chenresig, was the office of the Chairman of the PGTAR, Han Dao Peng.

He was a stocky man with iron colored, crew-cut hair who had continued a chain-smoking habit of thirty years even at Lhasa's altitude. From his window he could see Serpent Lake, fed by springs issuing from the Red Hill, and the road to Norbulinka, the summer palace of the Dalai Lama.

He finished his cigarette and stubbed it out contentedly; the phone connection to Chengtu had been bad, but he had been able to learn that his daughter, Kam, was healthy, and would soon give birth to what he hoped would be his first grandson. Bothersome as his agenda for this morning was, Han Dao Peng wished nothing to diminish the happy pride he felt now.

There was a sharp rap at his door; the Chairman knew his wish might be a difficult one.

"Chairman Han—" came the impatient voice.

"A moment, Comrade Deng, a moment." Han buttoned the top of his tunic, composed himself, then opened the door. In strode a visibly upset Deng Ka Xhong, Second Alternate for the Party Committee of the TAR. The Chairman suppressed a smile and let the door gently close.

"I've reviewed your order of the twenty-third, Comrade Chairman—"

"Please. Sit down."

Deng frowned, but complied with Han's request. "I'm not certain I find your orders appropriate."

Han slowly tamped the end of a cigarette against his desk pad and applied a lighter to it. "Really? You object to accompanying Trisong Detsan to America?" His face was hidden in a swirl of smoke. "I'd have thought you'd appreciate the opportunity to broaden your education, Comrade Deng."

"That is a positive aspect, of course. My objection is based on political considerations.".

"Such as?" Again, he had to force himself not to smile at Deng's distressed expression. Long ago, Han had discovered the usefulness of combining relaxed attitude and forthright questioning in struggles of a political nature.

"I do not believe it is correct to pursue the Panchen Lama's fantasies of reincarnation. The priest-ridden feudalism which existed here before the revolution has been destroyed. Why remind the people of the old ways? It encourages a dangerous revisionism among those not dedicated to our system."

"A valid criticism. But surely you don't believe we have succeeded in excising religious notions from the hearts and minds of the people here?"

"No," Deng admitted. "Superstition clings to them like the fungus that sucks the life from the strongest trees." Or like the rancid smell of butter clings to these rooms, he thought.

"There is a principle of political action, Comrade," Han said. "Deny people a thing, and you amplify desire for that thing out of all proportion to its worth. The people expect a search for the *trüllku* of their deceased Protector. We intend to follow the formalities to the letter."

"But to go to America! I do not see what good can come of such a mission."

"Then you are concerned too much with your own objections, Comrade Deng. Do you fail to understand that, by traveling to America, you and the Panchen Lama will give the people the opportunity to rid themselves of the fungus, as you so aptly describe it? If in fact Trisong Detsan proclaims the infant he's seen as the *Gyalwa Rinpoche,* a double purpose is served: first, the American mother will never agree to allow her son to be taken across the world by a band of chanting monks. And even if she would, the people here would never accept such an infant. They would, instead, finally accept the prophecy of the thirteenth Dalai Lama. Their Chenresig would have left them alone at last. We do not suppress religion. Instead, religion suppresses itself. Could you point to a better example of the working principle of the dialectic?"

"If the situation proceeds as you predict, no."

"Good!" The Chairman smiled warmly. "You southerners are quick to understand when the facts are presented properly. Now let's go. I've scheduled an audience with him for ten!"

Trisong Detsan occupied apartments in the bowels of the Potala, on a level untouched by the recent renovation. Holding an electric torch, Han Dao Peng led the way himself, hesitating only once, at the juncture of three dark, tunnel-like corridors.

"Not a place for the claustrophobic, eh, Comrade Deng?" Han said as he lighted yet another cigarette.

"Surely the only demons in Tibet were those who conceived of this infernal place." Deng eyed a hideous, grease-blackened fresco laid over the wall of a gallery which rose higher than the beam from the Chairman's lamp could reach. Han chuckled.

"Courage, Comrade. The ladder is just ahead."

They turned a corner and reached it, bare wooden poles whose rungs were lashed on with yak leather thongs. It was at least forty feet to the open trapdoor in the ceiling.

Deng blinked in amazement. "How does the old man make such a climb? Surely they have to carry him, or hoist him up with a rope."

"Trisong Detsan's hearty enough. Do *you* require assistance?"

Deng said nothing, but mounted the ladder and scrambled rapidly upward. A few rungs from the top, saffron- and crimson-sleeved arms caught him and pulled him through the door. Deng's surprised grunt echoed through the gallery as Han stubbed his cigarette out on the smooth stone floor and followed his companion. He too was pulled through by the Panchen Lama's attendants into a musty room illuminated by dozens of guttering butter lamps. Almost before he could seat himself on a rug, a monk thrust a bowl of the ubiquitous buttered tea into his hands. The Chairman nodded ruefully; in all his years in the TAR, he had never been able to accustom himself to the taste of the beverage. The bowls would be kept filled, he knew, until he and Deng left.

Trisong Detsan entered and dismissed the monks with a glance. Han was glad to see him looking somewhat better since his return from the high country. He made a respectful bow, which both the Chairman and Comrade Deng returned.

"Trisong Detsan," Han said in serviceable Tibetan, "I bring good news. Your visa has cleared the foreign office. And I have had assurances from the American ambassador that their State Department will do anything it can to assist you in obtaining an interview with the parents of the Incarnation." Han saw Deng shift uncomfortably, but the Panchen Lama appeared not to have heard him. He was on the verge of repeating himself when Trisong Detsan said, in perfect Mandarin:

"The child has only a mother."

"As the case may be. A flight out of Lhasa will be arranged for you whenever it is convenient."

"Deng Ka Xhong accompanies us?"

"As representative of the secular government, yes."

Trisong Detsan said nothing, but appeared on the verge of toppling from his pillow. Finally, he said, "Thank you." Han wished for a cigarette.

Deng finally spoke up. "Does the honorable Panchen Lama know where he will be seeking this boy?"

"My monks have brought me the maps. We shall be traveling to W'yo-ming. Near a city called Paradise, in the County of Carbon. W'yo-ming," he repeated, as if he were unable to believe the improbable-sounding name.

"Contact us when you're ready then," Han said in a strangely pinched voice. Trisong Detsan had brought a cup of steaming tea to his lips, and the Chairman realized with a start that the cup had been fashioned from a human skull.

He was glad to return to his office and get on with the ordinary business of the day.

Two

Sheriff Lee Bateman wiped sweat off his forehead with his sleeve and leaned back in his chair for another look at the pair of black Caddy Fleetwoods that shimmered in the afternoon heat outside the front door of the Paradise jailhouse. He wanted a beer. Hell, he wanted anything but to have to deal with this Washington bird in his dark suit and shiny shoes. But the order had come straight from Cheyenne: fullest cooperation, no ifs ands or buts.

He wondered if Cheyenne knew this Goodwin dude had a half dozen Chinamen in tow, soaking up the air conditioning in the back seats of those Caddies...

"Come on, Sheriff," Goodwin said. Bateman was glad to see him looking a little wilted. "You've read the file. Is there or is there not anybody in your jurisdiction who matches this description?"

"Might be," Bateman admitted. "But I'm not so sure I'd want to tell you if there was. We don't have many Chinese in Carbon county. Why, I doubt if there's more than a couple dozen in the whole state of Wyoming."

"These are *Tibetans*."

"And I damn well know there ain't *any* of those around here. What are they gonna do if they find this little booda they're looking for? Shanghai him?" Bateman chuckled and scratched his neck.

"You have," Goodwin said, teeth practically clenched, "the assurances of the Department of State that nobody's going to be 'Shanghaied.' Now can you help me or not?"

I just bet he'd start crying if I said no, Bateman thought, But he got up and handed Goodwin his folder back. "Well, I ain't gonna tell you I believe this Pancho Lamo fella came up with this description in China or wherever the hell it is he comes from, but yeah, there is somebody matches these particulars. Young widow girl, Lacey Cunningham. Her little boy Kenny just turned two last month."

"*Thank* you," Goodwin said, looking like a granite block had been pulled off his back. "Where may we find Mrs. Cunningham?"

"*Miss* Cunningham. She's living in Roy Bronken's old place on the Five Sixes Ranch—twenty, twenty-five miles from here."

"Mr. Bronken was her husband?"

"Everything but. Would have been if she would have asked him, but he wasn't much for legal niceties and she wasn't either. Tough thing, Roy gettin' killed the way he did. Folks tried to get her to move into town, but she's a proud girl. From what I hear, though, she's doing all right."

"Would you mind calling her, Sheriff, and tell her we're on our way."

"Now just slow down, Mister Goodwin. First place, she ain't got a phone. Second place, she's gonna have to decide if she wants to see your Poncho Lamo friend or not. Why don't you get yourself some rooms in the Continental Hotel, and I'll send one of my deputies up to break the news. She gives the okay, you can send the whole Chinese army up there for all I care. Says no, well..." Bateman shrugged.

"All right, Sheriff, I suppose that's fair. Will you send word to the hotel when you know?"

"Now don't you worry, friend." He shook Goodwin's hand. "Hey, and want some advice?"

"What's that?"

"Get yourself out of that suit."

"Jimi! *Damn* you Jimi, let go of that line, you hear me? Let *go*—" Lacey Cunningham ran for the big mastiff, but it was too late—he'd pulled one end of the clothes rope down and now four dozen wet diapers were lying in the dirt.

"You asshole!" Lacey grabbed the loose skin behind the dog's massive head and pinched as hard as she could. Jimi snorted, twisting free, and loped over beyond the woodshed, where he stood slobbering and grinning at her. "You keep smiling when you're sleeping outside tonight!" she yelled. Well, her horoscope had been right on the button for a change. *Little things stall big projects*. She hoped she had enough Pampers to get Kenny through tonight, because she sure as hell wasn't going to touch that wash again today.

Most days, Lacey would have smiled about how ridiculous the whole thing was: *here I am, stuck with a kid and a retarded dog with a thyroid problem, scrubbing and mopping and hoeing, just the way I was in Turlock*. She'd left home precisely because of shit like that, figuring she'd find a way to get to Ibiza and spend the rest of her life on the beach. She looked damn good in one of those string bikinis, but things hadn't worked out the way she'd planned. She'd made it to France once on a one-hour layover during a long weekend with a commercial pilot she'd met in the Marina Safeway in San

Diego. But that was as far as her *push* had ever gotten her, not counting the way she'd picked up Roy Bronken the night of the barbeque at the Grand National Rodeo in Denver. The kid and the dog and the house were hers after that, all the difference in the world from Turlock, and she could afford the smile. But it was getting too hard since Roy'd been killed, a year ago last June.

Not that it was so bad at the Five Sixes. Roy had left her the cabin, his truck and his tools, and a little money, even though they'd never got around to getting married; Frank Macomb, who owned the ranch, had sweetened the pot enough so that Lacey wouldn't have to worry if she watched her budget. And the air was clear here: afternoons you could sit on the porch and watch the anvil-clouds piling up over the brown, hump-backed Seminoes. For some people, it might really be Paradise, but not for Lacey, not lately. Her *push* was coming back, and she was having a hard time sleeping nights because of it.

I'm gonna have to leave here, she thought, kicking her hiking boots off at the doorway. *Me and Kenny, and hell, even that big idiot dog out there . . .*

Kenny was sprawled on the rug, doodling on the back of an old calendar in time to the Cheap Trick cassette he'd put in the player himself. Right now, it was more than she could stand, so she turned it off. Kenny did not even look up. He continued his slow scribbles, singing to himself: "Um, paddy-hum, um hum . . ."

"Hey, honey, you feel like eating? Got some macaroni."

He looked up at her with serious, ice-blue eyes. Just last week, he'd got his first haircut, something Roy would have been proud to see. Kenny had cute little ears, almost like flower buds. When he rolled over, smiling now, Lacey could see the little strawberry birthmarks, one on top of each of his shoulders. She touched his stomach with her toes, making him giggle.

"Come on now, you silly boy, you want to eat or not?"

"Uh-uh. 'obby."

"What?"

"'obby," he repeated. "'obby hum, paddy-hum."

Lacey frowned and went over to the kitchen window. Sure enough, dust was rising from the Five Sixes road as a black and gold four-track popped over the last rise before the cabin.

More than likely it *would* be Bobby Darwin driving that county truck. Kenny seemed to have a knack for announcing visitors before they arrived.

"You got good ears, Kenny," she said, trotting out to get Jimi, who was woofing loudly in the yard. Sure enough, she spotted Bobby's dark, curly hair as the deputy got out of the truck. Maybe it wasn't so strange, when you thought about it, she decided. After all, Bobby'd been looking in on her more and more often these past few months.

"My hero," she called. "How'd you like to take that wash into Paradise for me?"

Looking embarrassed, the deputy clipped his sunglasses onto his uniform pocket. "I'm on official business, Lace. Lee'd kill me."

Lacey grinned, because Bobby Darwin was always worrying about something like that. "All right, Deputy Robert, what can I do for you?"

"It's sorta complicated. Can we talk inside?"

"Sure. Come on." They went into the kitchen, and Kenny clambered into Bobby's lap as soon as the deputy sat down. "You want a beer?"

"No thanks."

"Ice tea then. Come on, Lee won't yank your badge for that." She put Kenny in his high chair and gave him an ice cube before setting a tall glass in front of Bobby. *What on earth's the matter with him?* The deputy was generally shy, almost courtly around her, but this time he seemed at a total loss for words. Finally, he tapped the envelope he'd carried in with him and leaned forward.

"Lacey, there's a man, Goodwin, from the State Department, who wants to talk to you."

"State department of what!" Lacey snapped. "Didn't Lee promise he'd take care of all that permit shit for me?"

"It's the Washington, D.C., State Department. This Goodwin's brought some, um, foreign visitors with him who want to see you too."

Lacey tried to think if she even *knew* any foreigners, and came up with nothing. She hadn't even been able to get off the plane that time in France.

"Here, Lacey," Bobby said, "why don't you read this. Explains everything better than I can."

Lacey opened the envelope and began reading the same file

Lee Bateman had seen in Paradise. She struggled with some of the pronunciation, but the State Department summary was quite clear and concise. Bobby went over to the baby and played some ice-cube hockey on his high chair tray while Lacey finished. Finally, she stuffed the papers thoughtfully back into the envelope.

"They think *Kenny's* King of Tibet?"

"Something like that. As I understand it, when the old Lama dies, his people believe his soul finds a child about to be born and takes it over. Then it's up to the Regent—that's this Trisong Detsan character—to find out where he is. They've been looking in their own country ever since the last Dalai Lama died, but they haven't had any luck. Old man claims he saw Paradise in a vision."

"Paradise, *Wyoming,* you mean. Big difference."

Bobby smiled tiredly. "Guess that's true. But it's the damnest thing I've ever heard. They're all down at the Continental right now, waiting for the go-ahead to come up. You ask me, they're nuts."

"I don't know . . . sort of flattering when you think about it." She grabbed Kenny's bib, put it over her mouth and spun around gracefully on her heels. "What if they decided Kenny was the one they're looking for? Think they'd make me a princess?"

Bobby frowned. "You can say no. They'd go home if you did, heard Goodwin say that myself."

"Now why on earth would I do a thing like that? I'd love to meet every one of them. You tell them they can come on up tomorrow at one. That'll give me some time to get ready."

"Lacey—"

"Don't give me an argument, Bobby Darwin. Go tell Lee I said fine."

The deputy stood up, opening his mouth as if to protest further. Instead, he gathered up the envelope, and his hat, and walked out without saying another word. Lacey watched him go, slight smile playing her lips.

"Damned if I didn't make him mad," she said to herself. Maybe there was some hope for Bobby Darwin yet.

Trisong Detsan sat on the floor of his room at the Continental Hotel, drinking tea to the snowy white light of the untuned television behind his back. It had been too much to hope that the Hotel kitchen might have a store of yak butter; still, the Parkay margarine had proved a serviceable substitute, and Trisong Detsan felt the pride all travelers who succeed in maintaining habits in unfamiliar places share.

The visit to the boy had been arranged for tomorrow, and this too was a source of satisfaction. Not that he had ever doubted the strength of his vision at the *Lhamo Lhatso;* but there had been a moment of uncertainty when the old man boarded the battered propeller-driven plane that took him out of Tibet for only the second time in his life. Would the power of the *Sakyamuni Buddha* sustain him, even in this strange land of W'yo-ming?

So far, it seemed, it had. But Trisong Detsan's thoughts darkened as they turned to Tsangyang Gyatso. If the young boy was indeed the *trüllku* of the *Gyalwa Rinpoche,* what was the meaning of such an event? Had twenty-five years in the West corrupted the Ocean of Wisdom into perversity? His death had been sudden, unexpected, there had been no time for the traditional preparation, the whispered reminders of the purpose of suffering intended to prepare the dying one for the forty-nine days of *Bardo,* the time of cleansing between death and rebirth. Would Tsangyang Gyatso—in his new form, of course—recoil at the sight of his former teacher? Would his spirit then flee his new body, to take residence in another even farther away, in a place where the old man could not possibly pursue him?

Such doubts do not strengthen your cause, he reminded himself with annoyance, reaching under the bed for the silken bag of effects he had brought from Tsangyang Gyatso's Potala apartments. Trisong Detsan pulled out two seemingly identical turquoise rosaries. One, with a golden clasp, had been the favorite of the Dalai Lama in the time before his exile. The other was a duplicate intended to test the candidate. The real *trüllku* would have no trouble distinguishing the two.

There were other objects as well: a wristwatch, with numerals in Tibetan script, and a silver prayer wheel, turned by means of a battery-powered electric motor concealed in its handle. Tsangyang Gyatso had always been enamored of mechanical things. On his thirteenth birthday, Trisong Detsan recalled, the boy had been presented an automobile, the first ever seen in Tibet, brought over the passes from India piece by piece on the backs of willing monks. Trisong Detsan had not disapproved. Even Siddhartha himself had chosen to remain in the world after his enlightenment, had seen and felt and tasted all the world had to offer.

He was considering this when the door to the room opened with a crash and the lights snapped on. Deng Ka Xhong, red-faced and weaving, stared down at him.

"Abominable American beer," he said, and then he began to laugh.

"You do not set a good example, Comrade Deng," Trisong Detsan said, drily.

"And who are you to tell me that, old man? Sitting there with your trinkets like a common peddler." Deng Ka Xhong crawled across the bed toward the Tibetan. "Peddle your miracles, hoping to make short change. But I understand you now. Oh yes." Deng got up on his knees and laughed harshly. "At first I believed you were serious. Yes! I was mystified that you succeeded in locating this miserable place. Was there something to this old man? I asked myself. I was no different from one of your greasy, timid servants, in awe of the power of the great Incarnation of Opame!"

Deng Ka Xhong lifted his hands high over his head. Trisong Detsan watched him, making no comment, even as the face of the Second Alternate began to change, becoming darker, broader, the nose pushed up, teeth lengthening, their sharp points gleaming. And was that a sword in his hand? Had his Executioner come at last?

"It's all to buy time, isn't it? You won't find the boy you're seeking here, and meanwhile a suitable candidate will be brought over from the revisionist emigré camps in India or Nepal! You intend to begin a counterrevolution, return your accursed country to the old ways..."

Trisong Detsan steeled himself, emptying his mind as the Executioner danced ever closer. He could hear the click of the Demon's claws against the sword-hilt, felt hot spittle from its tongue, smelled its foul, sulphurous breath...

"Han is a romantic fool," Deng went on in a rasping voice. "But he shall soon be asked to retire when we return—*with* the boy. Do you hear me, old man? I will do everything in my power to persuade his mother that a life of unbelievable splendor awaits her in Lhasa! City of the Dogs! She'll come, if only for a week, and it will be enough to destroy what's left of your demonology. When the people see your yellow-haired round-eyed Protector they will turn their backs on him—and on you. The liberation of the Tibetan people shall be completed at last!"

Is it my time at last? Trisong Detsan thought as the blade swept closer to his neck. He wished there had been time to perform the *Chöd* ritual, the dance which would have drawn all the evil of this place—Deng's evil as well—into his own person, to be obliterated by the touch of the Executioner's blade. *Are my entrails to be snatched from the sky by the crows?*

From out of the void came the answer like the wind, like the great crossed thunderbolt, *Dorje Gyatram: not yet, not yet . . .*

"Do you hear me, old man?" Deng Ka Xhong took him by the shoulders, shaking him violently. "Don't pretend you cannot understand me! Don't—"

Trisong Detsan caught his antagonist's wrists; Deng grunted in surprise and tried to pull free, but it was as if steel vises had clamped on the bones. Slowly, the old monk rose, as Deng giggled nervously. Then, with the force of a thunderclap, Trisong Detsan pushed him back onto the bed.

Deng Ka Xhong bounced, rolled over once, and was still until morning.

On the Five Sixes road, the pavement ran out ten miles from Lacey Cunningham's cabin, and even the Fleetwood's shocks had trouble absorbing some of the ruts and chuckholes underneath the gravel. With every lurch of the big limousine, the representative of the People's Government of the Autonomous Region of Tibet groaned painfully. Up in the front seat, Sheriff Lee Bateman and Goodwin, the man from the State Department, exchanged grins. Last night had been the first—and probably the only—time they'd ever help get a Chinese Communist shitfaced.

"Gonna make it, Mr. Chong?" Bateman asked.

Deng replied through clenched teeth, "How much farther?"

"Mile or two. You'll see Lacey's place over the top of this rise here."

As Comrade Deng nodded miserably, Trisong Detsan seemed to become aware of his surroundings for the first time. He leaned forward and peered out his window just as the Fleetwood reached the top of the ridge. Suddenly he could see yet another rise and below it, tucked in a protected fold of the hillside, the green cabin he had seen in the waters of the *Lhamo Lhatso*. There was no mistake. The brown hills, and the rounded mountains in the distance—even the downed clothesline and the white smoke rising lazily from the metal chimney—were all as the Oracle Lake had revealed them. Inside, he was certain, would be the boy, Tsangyang Gyatso's *trüllku*.

Trisong Detsan closed his eyes, suffering a pang of regret. He remembered that fateful morning in the high summer camp of his nomad family. His mother and sisters had just finished churning the hot buttered tea, and the smell of roasting barley, to be ground into the *tsampa* for mixing with the tea, seemed to cover the whole mountainside. Then the strangers had come, dressed as merchants, though they had not spoken like merchants. They had spoken briefly with his parents, and then he, Trisong Detsan, had been called from his chores into the darkness of the family tent. There, the visitors had laid out their baubles, and the boy had been asked to choose.

Without hesitation, Trisong Detsan had picked up a silver incense box, its lid inlaid with a turquoise-and-jade three-clawed dragon. He had also selected certain other objects, prompting the visitors to draw back and confer among themselves.

And then an impulse had seized Trisong Detsan, one which had changed his life irrevocably. Walking over to the tallest of the merchants, he tugged on the man's sleeve and said, in perfect court-dialect: *I know you, Pa Ter Gen-Den. Why do you come here disguised, as a thief might?* At these words, his visitors had fallen to their knees, and by nightfall Trisong Detsan had been traveling with their caravan to Sera Monastery, to begin his initiation into the ways of the Gelukpa sect. He had been taken from his family screaming and kicking. Even now, he did not know why he had said those words to Pa Ter Gen-Den. Trisong Detsan was an Incarnation who remembered nothing of his previous existence.

And now it was his duty to cause another to suffer what he himself had suffered. Only how much more for this youth, and his mother? The *Sakyamuni Buddha* had said the world was an endless round of suffering, but was there never any release, not even for the Incarnation of Chenresig himself?

"Good," the old man heard Bateman say, "Bobby did make it up here after all. He's taking this whole thing pretty hard—thinks Lacey's ready to pack up and leave. Hell, he might be right. It's sorta lonely for a young girl like her, out here all by herself."

Trisong Detsan saw Comrade Deng smile, just as the Fleetwood pulled to a stop next to Bobby Darwin's four-track. Goodwin slid out of his seat, and went back to open the doors for the two visitors. It was not quite so hot as it had been yesterday.

The door to the shack swung open as the Panchen Lama got out of the car, silk bag in hand.

"Dammit, Lacey—" the voice of the deputy followed Lacey Cunningham to the porch. She was dressed in a silk blouse, new jeans, and cordovan boots pulled up to her knees, her silver-blonde hair pulled back and tied with a yellow ribbon.

"Hello," she said, nervously clasping her hands together. Goodwin led the procession to the steps.

"Good day. I'm Hugh Goodwin, State Department."

"Hi." They shook hands.

"I'd like to present Mr. Deng Ka Xhong, of the People's Government of the Autonomous Region of Tibet."

"How you doing?"

"I have been better." Deng said, taking her hand.

"And his Holiness, Trisong Detsan, *Panchen Rinpoche* and Regent and Acting Chairman of the Committee for Religious Affairs, PGTAR."

"You're the man who came all the way from Tibet to see me and Kenny. You're certainly welcome." Lacey bowed, then sheepishly extended her hand as Deng Ka Xhong began translating. Trisong Detsan cut him off.

"I understand. Thank you, Miss Cunning-ham." He reached into his bag and pulled out a yellow and red silk scarf. "You will honor me to accept this. Offering."

"Why thank you, Mr. Detsan," she said, admiring its vivid pattern. "Why don't you come in out of the sun? Kenny just got up from his nap." Goodwin and the Sheriff stepped back to allow Deng and the old man inside first. When Trisong Detsan's eyes became accustomed to the light, he noted the presence of a uniformed young man, obviously angry, glaring at them from the kitchen table. When Sheriff Bateman cleared his throat, the young man got up, though reluctantly.

"I know you folks like tea," Lacey said. "All I had left was some Morning Thunder, if that's all right."

"Please, Miss Cunning-ham. I wish to examine the child."

"All right. I just have to get him dressed."

"Not necessary."

"Okay. This way. Help yourself to some cake—and there's coffee if you want it, Sheriff."

Trisong Detsan followed Lacey into the bedroom, which was cool and dark, smelling faintly of bleach. A poster of Big Bird was nailed to the wall over the child's crib. Kenny bounced happily when he saw his mother, and the old man's heartbeat quickened.

"Kenny, this is Mister Detsan. He wants to have a look at you."

"Hum!" Kenny said. Lacey lifted him out of the crib.

"Do you want me to set him on the bed?"

"Yes, please." Kenny watched as Trisong Detsan opened the curtain a little. His eyes were wide as the monk came toward the bed, but he did not shy away as he usually did with strangers. Gently, the monk grasped his neck and turned Kenny's head from side to side. The ears were indeed the proper shape. And on the downy skin of either shoulder was the mark signifying the vestiges of an extra set of arms. Chenresig's arms.

The *Panchen Rinpoche* said nothing, but brought out the twin rosaries from his bag and dangled them before the boy.

"Oh look, Kenny, a present. One of those'll be enough, Mister Detsan—"

"Shh!"

Kenny looked toward his mother, then without hesitating took the one with the gold clasp from Trisong Detsan's finger.

"Um!" he said, smiling. "Um manny-paddy hum!"

"You know, he's been singing that funny little song all morning."

"Yes," Trisong Detsan said. "It means, 'Hail to the Jewel in the Lotus.' This child is the one."

He heard Lacey's gasp, mingled with the boy's giggling and thought, *What have you done now, Tsangyang Gyatso, what in Heaven and earth have you done?*

Three

The afternoon had turned dark with the threat of rain by the time the *Panchen Rinpoche* completed his examination of the boy. Informed of his determination, Hugh Goodwin looked dutiful, knowing he'd spend Sunday on the horn to Washington.

Sheriff Bateman merely shook his head. His deputy had gone for a walk somewhere. Meanwhile Lacey sat at the kitchen table stirring tea almost numbly and feeding Kenny bits of cake. After a while, Trisong Detsan emerged with his bag from the bedroom, went outside, and sat down in a plastic lawnchair below the porch. Jimi ran over almost immediately, thumping his big tail into the ground as the old man sadly scratched his ears.

"Well, guess that about wraps it up," Bateman said. "You've got a big decision to make, Lacey. Best have some time alone to think about it. Thanks for the cake. Come on, gentlemen, last train for Paradise's leaving immediately."

"A moment, Sheriff," Comrade Deng said. "I'd have a few words with the young lady before we depart."

"That all right with you, Lacey?"

"Sure." Her voice sounded very tired. "I'll talk to you tomorrow, Lee. Nice meeting you, Mister Goodwin." The screen door swung shut with a snap that made her jump. Deng remained where he was, leaning up next to the stove, saying nothing at first. Lacey looked out the window. "Mister Detsan doesn't seem very happy about this," she said.

"Should he be?"

"Well, it's something like a miracle, isn't it, coming all this way and having Kenny speak to him in his own language? Seems miraculous to me. Kenny always *has* been a strange sort of little boy." She pinched her son's cheek. "Haven't you? Huh?"

"But surely," Deng Ka Xhong drawled, "you don't believe in his nonsense."

"Why, I'm not sure. I've never been very religious."

"Let me tell you something, Miss Cunningham. The old fool has surprised himself with that bag of tricks. I have it on good authority that his trip to your country was intended solely to buy time for those who oppose the lawful government of Tibet. He fully intended to reject your boy. For some reason, he's hesitated, but that should be no concern of ours." Deng smiled. "Let me simply say that on behalf of the People's Government of the Autonomous Region of Tibet, I am inviting you—and your son—to visit our country, and to stay for as long as you wish as our guests. Lhasa is a fabulous place—and you will be one of the few Westerners to view its wonders."

"I've done some reading," Lacey said, "and I *would* like

to see it. But what about Kenny? If he's supposed to be your new king..."

"Since the revolution, very few believers in the Buddhist superstitions remain, and those that do are very old. But what harm is done if the boy—and you—take part in a few simple ceremonies? There would be a procession, and perhaps they would dress you both in some rather ridiculous costumes, but that would be the end of it. You would make many people happy in Tibet by consenting to return with us."

Lacey looked at him, unsure if Deng was a man to be trusted. She felt that way about Mister Detsan, but he'd been so silent, like he was going to let anything that was going to happen happen. She gave Kenny a drink of cold tea and said, "All right. We'll go." It was her *push* talking, but she wasn't going to overrule it, not with a chance like this. Triumph flashed in Deng's eyes, but he rose with dignity and shook her hand. His was damp and cold.

"We'll return tomorrow for you with final arrangements. Thank you, Miss Cunningham!"

She nodded and looked past him out the window, but Trisong Detsan had already entered the Fleetwood. His lawnchair rocked silently back and forth in the gathering breeze.

The wind had picked up considerably by the time Lacey went into Kenny's room after dinner and made a survey of things she would have to take along on their trip. She felt the old adrenalin rush traveling used to give her before she'd met Roy, and in a way it made her feel disloyal to his memory. Roy had wanted them to stay on the Five Sixes a long time, and even showed her plans for a bigger house once, to be built along a nice creek in the next valley. He never would have gone for this reincarnation business, but damn it, Roy was dead, and you couldn't make your life around the plans of a dead man...

She heard the screen door banging on its hinges. Tonight there was going to be one hell of a storm. Lacey hurried out to fasten the latch and saw someone—wild-eyed and soaked, standing in her kitchen. Her fear turned to anger when she realized who it was.

"Bobby Darwin, what the hell do you think you're doing!"

"I gotta talk to you, Lace. I—"

"Keep your voice down, you'll wake up Kenny."

He continued in a whisper nearly as loud. "I heard what you're gonna do, Lacey, and I think you're out of your mind."

"Nobody asked what you think. You been walking around out there this whole time?"

"I had some thinking to do." He half-pouted, struggling with his emotions. "Lacey, you just can't leave like this."

"And why not?" She faced him defiantly, waiting for an answer, but he averted his eyes and said, softly, "Roy wouldn't want it that way."

"Roy! Roy can't want anything because he's dead, he's been dead for as long as I can remember, and I've been up in this damn shack trying to take care of his kid and his tools and that damn truck of his and I'm sick of it, Bobby, sick up to here! I'm done planning my life around Roy Bronken!"

"Gonna plan it around some dead Chinaman instead? You'd think you'd have more loyalty to Roy."

"That's the trouble with you, Bobby Darwin, you always were nothing more than Roy Bronken's pet! You'd do anything for that man, even make sure his girl stays in line after he's gone. Hey, I bet Roy's resting real easy, knowing you're around to take care of things for him. Good old Bobby Darwin!"

"I'm not here because of Roy," Bobby said, controlling his temper.

"Oh? What are you here for, Bobby?"

He said nothing.

"Come on, we're all waiting."

"This isn't the time or place to talk about it, Lacey. Goodnight." Then he walked out. Lacey rushed to the door after him, screaming above the rolling sound of thunder. *"Damn* you, Bobby, don't you come back here. Don't you ever come back!"

By the time Bobby Darwin got back to town, the storm had moved in with a vengeance, tossing curtains of rain across Paradise's nearly deserted main street. The young deputy had almost run off the road a few miles back, mostly because of the thoughts that kept turning round and round inside his head. He could not decide what to do: beg the Sheriff to put Lacey and Kenny under protective custody, or kidnap them himself, or even let the air out of the tires of both limousines.

All he knew was that something had to be done, or Lacey Cunningham would be gone before the first of the week. And she'd never be back to Paradise, he was damn sure of that . . .

As he drove past the Continental Hotel, he suddenly slammed on the brakes, realizing that the one person who could do something about it was up on the second floor. Asleep or not, that old bald-headed monk was going to have to listen to a few things. Tracking mud across the lobby carpet, mumbling something about "official business" to the open-mouthed desk clerk, Bobby went up the stairs two at a time, ran down the hall to the room Lee'd said had been assigned to the Panchen Lama. Bobby rapped on the door; when there was no answer, he hit the wood with his fist.

"Deputy Sheriff. Open up." He felt a little ridiculous as he tried the door, found it unlocked, and pushed it open with his shoulder. The TV was on, it's snowy screen like a square sun in the otherwise darkened room. A couple of people were sitting on the floor, softly chanting things Bobby didn't understand. He flipped on the lights.

"Where's Trisong Detsan? I've got to talk to him."

Sharp Tibetan words greeted the intrusion, and a couple of young monks jumped up and grabbed him, ready to throw him out. Bobby was ready to fight all of them—until the old man looked up and clapped his hands together. The monks released the deputy, and silently left for the adjoining room. *Jeez, he's all dried up,* Bobby thought. Trisong Detsan blinked watery eyes in the harsh light from the overhead fixture, and Bobby shut it off.

"Thank you. You have a message from the Sheriff?"

"You know why I'm here."

"Do not credit me with powers I do not possess, Deputy."

"No. You're right, maybe I shouldn't. It's about Lacey and the boy. You can't have them. It's not right."

Thunder rattled the windows behind Trisong Detsan's head. "He is *Gyalwa Rinpoche*. I did not wish it to be so. But he is the Protector and Refuge of my people reborn."

"That's where you got it wrong, sir. He's Roy Bronken's son. Now, I know you never knew Roy, but he was one of the best the town ever had, a hell of a man. I heard about the last words he ever spoke, and he made me promise to look after Lacey and his boy! How am I gonna do that if you take 'em away? How'm I gonna—" Bobby paused, tears blurring his vision. He thought he could see the old man smiling at him, making fun of him.

"What about your Chinese buddy? I heard him talking to Lacey this afternoon. He called you an old fool! Said by bringing Kenny, Lacey'd be helping the Chinese government. Is that what you want? He's using you, Mr. Detsan. You'll bring that blonde-haired boy back to your country and your people'll laugh at you. Don't you know that? Don't you—"

"You blame me," Trisong Detsan said, "for your inability to express certain feelings to Miss Cunning-ham. You let the memory of a dead man interfere with your own life."

"Aren't you doing the same thing?"

Trisong Detsan shuddered, and for a moment, Bobby Darwin was afraid the old man had suffered a stroke. But he got to his feet, finally, his wrinkled features pulled into a mask of infinite sorrow.

"Will you take me there now?"

"Where? Out to Lacey's?"

"Yes."

"Damn right I will!"

"Softly. We do not wish to alarm Comrade Deng."

As Bobby left the room, he saw that Deng Ka Xhong had been passed out on the bed the entire time.

They saw ball lightning split a pine tree open on the approach to Lacey's cabin, and the old man didn't even blink. Trisong Detsan had been concentrating on cleansing his mind as much as possible, though it was difficult with the anxious energy radiated by his eager young companion.

"We must slip in and go directly to the boy," Trisong Detsan instructed as Bobby set the brake. "His mother must not see what I am about to do."

"All right." As the Deputy opened the door, however, Jimi ran over, barking furiously, and kept on, despite Bobby's frantic attempts to quiet him, until Trisong Detsan grasped his huge brown ears.

"Sleep, Bo," he said in Tibetan. The dog yawned once, then disappeared groggily into his house.

It wasn't hard getting into the cabin, since Bobby had a key. He made sure the door to Lacey's room was closed before signalling the monk. Trisong Detsan entered Kenny's room, and looked down at the sleeping boy.

"Stand aside, Deputy, and do not make a sound, no matter what you should see. I shall perform *Rolag*, which is the raising of the dead." Gently, he reached into the crib and pinched the boy's ankles and wrists until Kenny rubbed his eyes and rolled over.

"A word with you, Tsangyang Gyatso," Trisong Detsan said. Kenny smiled back, and it was not the smile of a baby still in diapers. It was a weary smile, older than the world itself, a smile whose weight pressed the old man down to his knees. Trisong Detsan let his mind slip swiftly into trance, until he heard the whisper of the Executioner's sword once more cutting the air above his head. He reached out—and caught the wrist of his old tormentor. The Black Hat tossed his head back to fierce, mocking laughter.

And Trisong Detsan saw that his face was the face of Tsangyang Gyatso.

Old Teacher, have you come for me again? To try and force me out?

No. To ask, with respect, as your spiritual Father, to leave this house and occupy another.

Simply as that? I like this body, old man, and I intend to keep it.

You have no right. You are *Changchub Sempa*, the living Buddha, and you must return to nourish your people.

There is nothing to discuss. Leave me!

Take another's body. Take mine.

Yours? Infirm and lice-ridden as it is? The Sakyamuni Buddha gorged himself on unclean pork when he wished to leave the world. You ask me to do more than that? Tsangyang Gyatso again laughed, but his face had changed to the hideous visage of Chenresig's demonic aspect. He breathed flame, and held his Executioner's sword high overhead.

If you refuse to leave willingly, then I must force you.

Then do so, if you can—

The Demon lunged with the sword, but Trisong Detsan avoided the blow, reaching upward instead to grab the Executioner by the throat. Howling in fury, it attempted to gouge out the old monk's eyes with its claws, but Trisong Detsan held fast. "Leave him! Leave him—"

"Kenny! What in the name of God—"

Bobby Darwin held her back. "Let him finish, Lacey!"

"He's choking my baby to death! Let me g—" Just as she twisted free, the entire cabin shook as if it had been struck by lightning. The child's scream seemed loud enough to break windows, and for a moment, Bobby thought another set of features, red-eyed and hideous, passed over Kenny's face, only to fade as he collapsed to the bottom of the crib.

"It is done," Trisong Detsan said, weakly.

"Still breathing," Bobby said, checking Kenny's pulse, which seemed impossibly slow. His mother picked him up, patting his cheek, trying desperately to waken him. The red marks on his neck were beginning to turn purple; Kenny was like a rag doll in her arms.

"What have you done!"

"It is an empty vessel now. The *Gyalwa Rinpoche* has taken another form. A child just born in Chengtu, in western China. Now you must let me finish my work. Give me the child."

"We've got to get him to the hospital."

"Please."

"Don't you understand, he's all I have left!"

"No, Lacey. You've got me," Bobby said, taking Kenny's limp form away from its mother and giving it to Trisong Detsan. "You've got me. We'll wait outside."

Trembling, Trisong Detsan cradled the body in his arms. As he slipped again into trance, he was comforted by the thought that form indeed had the power to alter spirit . . .

The Executioner waited across the room, face hidden by the Black Hat. *I am ready,* Trisong Detsan thought, opening his arms as he felt the sweep of the sword, and the first touch of its infinitely sharp blade against his neck.

They found Kenny tugging on Trisong Detsan's lifeless arm. "Hum!" he said. "Paddy-hum algone!"

The Chairman of the People's government of the Autonomous Region of Tibet, Han Dao Peng, held the morning's dispatches in one hand as he stood at his window, thoughtfully smoking a cigarette. He could hear the snap of prayer-flags in the freshening breeze as he reflected upon the failure of Deng Ka Xhong's mission to America.

It might not be such a bad thing, he decided. Deng had been a thorn in his side for many years, and his failure to bring back the American child might earn him a stint in a barley-farm cadre, or worse, if Beijing decided to take offense at the death of Trisong Detsan.

At any rate, there was happy news from Chengtu. Kam had

given birth to a son with ears like rosebuds and a birthmark on each shoulder. And Han supposed her transfer to Lhasa might be easily arranged.

SANDY LUST

by Gregory Benford

Gregory Benford is known for his hard-science SF novels and one might not think of him as a man who writes
poetry. But here is a poem, his third, that proves Mr.
Benford to be a writer of many facets: "Sandy Lust,"
the ultimate Ode to One's Beloved—of the future.

I think clouds and moments ring like bells
swelling to be heard, because
of sunlight, eager shaping into swells
of fog. Moist waves—

No, really, remove your claw
from my thigh; I jest, I admit.
I didn't mean to factor in
our sloppy oceans, lush beyond your imaginings.
I carry that same saline fraction in me, a hollow
knocking in my veins

as the knotted pump clenches, noisy, wanting
  work.
An improbable shambling thing, I know, three-
  quarters
ripe liquid, sloshing as I—

(Tough, crusty skin rumples beneath my hand.
Making peace,
I caress a flank not born but budded
in sand caverns, far back in inky shadows,
safe from crisp UV that would
have stirred the genetic soup with
erasing energy. So runs the gospel
according to the Division, or
ExterrEco, as the techs call it—
The subject has no heart.)

Yes, there's time. You rasp against me, a brittle
rustle as circuits close beneath a rippling face.
Your circuits grew as naturally as my dendrites,
my love, but still I think of them
as stringy transistors, junctions
P or N as nature wanted,
germanium-tin forged by competition, not in
  laboratory's heat.
This truth whirls in me, finds no purchase—

Libido, a universal, trips home.
Right; let's be efficient. (Communication is best
that cites shared values,
fundamental constants,
standard wavelengths;
that's how we met.)
Lie back a bit
and use the pillow, there. Hoist me up—ah.
Like a purr in deep dry engines.

Our genes conflict,
argue,
recoil, your chain molecules
twine opposite. You are mottled
with the colors of jungles and jewels

and I—Moisture can be
stern and chill, when frozen, but
in all justice, it comes cloud-soft
and warm, when rising as steam's vapor.
Two bubbles of biospheres,
once muffled from each other
by huge vacuum,
now intersect in your sandy loins.

Quaking quick, you hum
delirious, a consuming rattle.
How like me to give you fluid
in return for your tingling snap,
each using the coinage clinking in the pockets,
and sacs. Silicon has its own gritty flavor, and yet
I sense in you a need, something more.
Of course things dim with use; a light bulb
knows the socket too well.
Something, something—

Well—we can, if you wish,
pretend you're not my bride.

WATERLOO SUNSET

by David Bischoff

Bischoff's London is a magical place somehow removed from time but containing all time within it. Here
a simple man can find all his pleasures, from Shake-
spearian theatre with Will himself present to rock 'n' roll
from the future. Or he can ride a train from the 1800s
with a woman who transcends time and learn that easy
pleasures are not always enough, and that being afraid
is no excuse for being alone.

LONDON June 8, 1973

The National Theatre of Great Britain, unaccountably, was
back at the Old Vic today. The morning *Times* presented me
with this fact which, in itself, was interesting if unspectacular.
I generally peruse the entertainment section over Mrs. Harri-
son's breakfast table, a meal that comes with my bed in her
rooming house in North Kensington, and as I pride myself on
my obsession with the English theatre it was only natural that
this fact should be absorbed. However, what piqued my interest

the most were the facts that the production was *The Tempest*, that Laurence Olivier was presenting his farewell performance as Prospero, and that William Shakespeare himself would be gracing the audience with his presence.

I decided that an early morning trip across the Thames was in order, that a matinee ticket might be procured. I assumed that such an august production was most likely sold out, but the government-subsidized National Theatre saved its standing room and effluvial seats to be sold only on the morning of each performance.

I was gratified to find that the number 12 bus grumbling down Bayswater Road this morning was fairly modern. At times I have had to take horse-drawn omnibuses to central London, and the smell and jogging about is appalling. My appreciation of the history of this great city has somehow grown rather ambivalent with direct participation in some of its history's sensory experiences.

The day was gold and silver with sunshine. There was a cricket game in Hyde Park that I was tempted to leave the bus to watch, if only to try to understand the game. But I kept to my seat, paid my 15P to the frazzled conductor with shiny elbows on his uniform and nicotine-stained fingers. The bus forged its way through Oxford Street, down Regents, past Piccadilly and Trafalgar Square. I left it on the south side of Westminster Bridge, and strolled along the south embankment to Festival Hall. The entertainment notices in the *Times* had not been entirely reliable; the Kinks would indeed be there, the signs said, as usual. I bought a ticket, then hurried through Waterloo Station, then up the Cut past the vegetable market to the Old Vic ticket office. There was a line. I waited.

The area was not the best; a frayed cuff of a neighborhood, stained by pigeons and age. A derelict was pawing through a trash can in the corner park. The ticket office itself was a little hut of a place, ramshackle, adjacent to the Young Vic: a hollowed-out warehouse.

I was just about in the door when I saw a Watcher.

It was walking along the sidewalk, like a TV with legs, its insides aclick and ahum, its huge glass eye taking everything in. Except for my face, which I was sure to hide from it. It ambled on its automaton way, evidently unaware of me, but still I was worried. The things had radio-leashes. At the other end of this one's leash would be a Visitor. I have never liked the Visitors much, and generally keep my distance.

And indeed as soon as the glass and wood door was opened and the ticket office swallowed me safely up, I saw one coming down the Cut, its robe trailing behind it. The large cowl was up, as usual, and inside that cowl was darkness. They must use light-bafflers for masks.

The Visitor shuffled along slowly on the other side of the street. In its gloved hands was a box, to which it did things from time to time. I watched it pass.

From the corner of the window-wall of the building, I could just see it cross the Cut's street. It stopped just short of the park's trash can. Its black robe, loose about whatever was within, rippled in a breeze. It stood there a moment, watching the derelict. The old man took no notice. He pulled something out of the trash which seemed to please him, clutched it to his side and bustled away, out of sight. The Visitor paused a moment, then pursued.

I bought a ten-pence slip seat. At the corner newsstand I bought a 1964 copy of *Melody Maker* and read an article about the Beatles while I sipped tea at the counter of a small over-lit cafe. An hour remained until the locals opened, and three hours till the 1:00 p.m. matinee. At least, my watch said it was 10:00 a.m. I bought it in a Montgomery Ward's back home in the States, half price. Generally, I never gave enough attention to time back home to buy a watch. But I figured I would need one for my trip here.

A couple of air raid wardens were in the booth behind me, casually discussing last night's bombing of the Victoria Docks. The Germans had miscalculated a great deal, and mostly blown up a good deal of Thames water. The men laughed and chuckled.

I paid for my tea, and went to a small park by Blackfriar's Bridge. I picked out my radio from my jacket pocket and listened to a live *Goon Show*. Then I switched to BBC One and it started acting up. In the middle of a Stones tune, it jumped time-refs straight into Roxy Music, then all the way up to bits and pieces of music of the future top ten I'd never heard before. I turned it off, and went to the local pub where I drank Watney's Red Barrel and ordered shepherd's pie. In my second pint, it occurred to me that there was absolutely nothing to prevent the Cut from undergoing a time-ref change in the interim before 1:00. I might arrive and find myself at a performance of Osborne's *Look Back in Anger*. But I decided not to worry.

At 12:30 I ventured out once more. The street had changed. I hurried off for the theatre. I felt slightly high from the beer.

The Old Vic had not changed, and I immediately saw that its time-ref had not altered. I took to the side entrance, negotiated the steep flight of wooden stairs up to the balcony, where I purchased a bottle of Guinness to sip, waiting for the play.

I made my way down the upper circle to the slip seat along the top left side of the stage. If special lighting is needed for any production, the slip seats go to make way for the spotlights. I was early enough to take my pick of spots on the wood bench.

Halfway through my Guinness, another playgoer arrived at the cheap seats. She wore an outfit from the mid-1920s, and was quite attractive. Her hair was short, bobbed and brown. Her nose had a faint upturning lilt to it. Her eyes caught mine, and I indicated that, yes—it would be a pleasure if she shared my choice space. She smiled and settled.

She opened her program and began reading.

I said, "I don't think I can finish all of this beer."

She turned to look at me. "Pardon?"

I held up the beer and the glass. "Shall I get another glass?"

"No thank you." Eyes back to the program.

The rest of the theatre was rapidly filling. Others began to sit with us. I said, after a while, "I guess we're privileged."

"Yes, quite," she said, turning a page of the glossy pamphlet. I estimated she was perhaps two years older than my own twenty-one. "Marvelous cast."

"Yeah."

She turned to look at me. "You're a Yank?"

I nodded, though I did not like the term or the connotations. "I'm an American."

"Money?"

"Not much."

She laughed. "Of course not. You'd be down in row one if you had money."

"I came over here to vagabond Europe on the cheap."

"How long have you been in England?"

"I'm not really sure, now."

"No. I suppose not. Time makes no difference anymore, does it?"

"No."

"But it *is* interesting." She looked at me closer. "Where from in America?"

"Washington D.C."

"Oh. I'm so sorry. Your parents—"

I grimaced. "Yeah. Everybody, I hear. Lots of other cities, too."

"All over the world. Except Europe. Curious, isn't it?"

"Yes. Curious." I shrugged. "Oh well. Puberty was just as bad for me."

Her mouth opened a bit, her eyes widened, and she laughed. "I'm glad you're not disassociated atoms now. But you are sort of stuck here with much of the States a slag heap."

"I'm not planning to go back, if that's what you mean."

"Staying in England?"

"No. I'll bop around the Continent, I guess. Figure stuff out."

"A worthy goal."

Our conversation was cut short by the darkening of the theatre, the ascent of the curtain.

It was quite fine. David Garrick played Sebastian, and Robert Newton was a properly slimy Caliban. Olivier was breathtaking. And the woman who played Miranda was the same woman who was sitting with me.

At the interval, I bought her tea at the balcony lounge. We stood by the window. It had a fine view of Christopher Wren's in-progress St. Paul's Cathedral.

I said, "You're an excellent actress."

"I can see faults from up here."

"Getting an objective view?"

"Yes. I find it helps."

I sipped at a Bass Ale. "I've never seen anyone do this before."

She shrugged. "You live, you learn."

I finished the ale. "I haven't seen Shakespeare."

"He's not coming."

"You know him?"

"Yes. In fact, I left him drunk at a bar."

"Oh."

The lights flicked on and off. The interval was over.

On the way down to our seats, emboldened by the ale, I said, "You're the most stunning woman I've ever met."

She did not respond.

After the play, I asked her for her name.

"Look on the program," she said.

I did. "Elizabeth Hardesty," it read. "Elizabeth, can I buy you dinner?"

"You can walk me out of here, for now."

"Sure."

We descended to the street. It was five o'clock. The sky had grayed with clouds. It was chilly. I buttoned my corduroy jacket.

"Dinner?"

"You are a persistent fellow."

"Yes."

She struck out toward Waterloo. "I've a train to catch, actually."

"Oh."

"Yes. At five-thirty." She did not seem to mind the cold.

We walked through the vegetable market. The outfits people wore looked Edwardian; but then, amongst the working class, clothing styles are not so clearly delineated by eras. I bought Elizabeth an apple at a stall.

"This will do for dinner," she said.

"I had something a bit better in mind."

"What's your name?"

"Gerald. Gerald Hook."

"Gerald, what about tomorrow night?"

"Excuse me?"

"I wouldn't mind seeing you again. Tomorrow night."

"There will be no tomorrow night. There is no tomorrow. Only today."

"You know what I mean. The day after this."

"Okay. Where?"

"Cheshire Cheese. At six. You know where it is?"

"Sure. West End."

We strolled amongst the scattered trash and squashed vegetables, the strewn fruit, silently. From the next to the last booth, a Visitor emerged, confronting us. I was surprised. So surprised I stood quite still. The thing took no notice of me. It looked toward Elizabeth.

It occurred to me that I ought to do something. A bit of directed violence might have been appropriate. But then, I'd never seen the Visitors do anything but scurry about, like tourists with amnesia. Simply because they pricked up my paranoia did not mean this one would harm Elizabeth or myself. She looked at the thing a moment, placidly, then took my arm. "Let's go," she said. And led me around the thing. It swivelled around, watching us leave. But it did not follow.

She let go of my arm. "Come. I've a train to catch."

We went through the huge Waterloo Station doors. She found her platform, and boarded the train, which seemed circa 1881. She put down her window in her compartment so that we could talk a little more. The other occupant, a Victorian civil servant, rustled his *Guardian* in polite disapproval.

"Where are you going?"

"You mustn't ask such things, Mr. Hook." Her voice carried no expression. The station was filling up with fog. Steam hissed from the big engines, adding to the grounded cloud effect. We chatted quietly until the whistle blew. Quickly, she leaned out and kissed my forehead. "Tomorrow night." She lifted up the window and sat in her seat.

The train lurched with squeaks and grunts, and then drifted grindingly down the tracks. We waved goodbye until the fog engulfed her window.

I occupied my evening with dinner at an Indian restaurant, and a stroll though a Georgian night. Later on, I managed to find a modern movie theatre facing Leicester Square. I watched the Hitchcock double-feature on display—*The 39 Steps* and *The Lady Vanishes*—and then caught a hansom cab back to my Kensington boarding house.

The only light available came from candles and gas lamps. I went to bed instead of sitting up, reading.

I had forgotten about my ticket for the Kinks concert, and did not realize it until I emptied my pockets, looking for the theatre program, hoping for information about Elizabeth.

I could not find the program.

I wondered if I would really see her again.

LONDON June 8, 1973

As usual, over the tea and eggs and kippers and sausages set before me for breakfast, I checked the date of the morning *Times*. It had not changed. It had not altered, by my reckoning, for an equivalent of at least one month. June 8 seemed the center of the confusion, the point of regularity upon which the whirling, waving top of troubled time had landed.

After breakfast I spent the morning in Hyde Park upon a bench, reading Graham Greene and John D. MacDonald. The air was quite pleasant and the sun shone agreeably, but the carefully wrought words before me had the tendency to turn into so much stamped ink as my thoughts began to wander over Elizabeth's memory. I went from *The End of the Affair* to *Bright Orange for the Shroud* as a confused bee might buzz between two flowers, spending most of its time suspended somewhere in between them.

I inexpensively lunched on chicken and chips after a walk through the park. It all resembled one of the mornings I spent in London as a simple just-graduated college student walking in a city he had always loved from afar, chastely through pictures, television, movies and books. But the illusion was ruptured with the advent of not one but two Visitors staring up at the Albert Hall, as though sizing it up for transport. Not far from them a Watcher jerked about, missing nothing but myself. I chose a path previously unplanned.

I walked farther, then caught an omnibus. I sat on the upper, open-air level. Through breaks in the buildings I could see the cityscape, shimmering with change.

I stepped off the bus at Whitehall and heard some sort of commotion to the west. There were thousands of cheering people lined up on one side of The Mall. Queen Victoria's coronation procession was coming from Westminster Abbey. On the opposite side of The Mall there was at least as many people, though they wore turn-of-the-century outfits, and black armbands. There was a dark, somber procession moving to the slow beat of mourning music. It was Queen Victoria's funeral procession headed for Westminster Abbey.

The two processions passed, each ignoring the other—or perhaps not *seeing* the other.

I struck off on foot by St. James's Palace, up Piccadilly to Shaftesbury Avenue. I found myself humming a Kinks song, "Waterloo Sunset," as I walked contentedly.

Around me was the steady, random transition of buildings, of people. I could close my eyes in Restoration London, open them in Regency London. I could stare at a building, watch it lose cracks and become new again; or watch it crumble, disappear, to be replaced by another.

The afternoon I idled away at various pubs, listening to conversations. When the pubs closed, I found an open movie theatre from the fifties and watched *Bridge on the River Kwai*.

When I left it was close to six. I crossed the Strand to where my guide book said the Cheshire Cheese was situated.

The tavern was there, where it should be. I entered, scuffling along on the warped wood floor, trying to grow accustomed to the dim lighting.

A hand plucked at my sleeve.

"Good evening." It was Elizabeth, in a barmaid's outfit. Her eyes were bright. She smiled. She was beautiful.

"Hi."

"Come here." She grabbed my arm. I allowed her to lead me to a booth flickering with candle-thrown shadows.

"I'm off in a little while. Meantime, there's someone you should meet. Sit down, and I'll draw you a pint on the house." She indicated the bench under the booth's table. I mutely obeyed.

With a flurry of skirts she sped off, waving away the appreciative remarks of a pair of drunken noblemen at the bar.

No sooner had I seated myself than I heard a frightful series of sounds deeper in the booth, across from me. Something like a hog, aswill in its trough. I stared into the shadows, wondering what could be causing the mushy din.

As my eyes learned their way through the dim light, I saw that a man sat by himself there, eating from a plate mounded high with a thick mutton stew. He was a big man, slovenly, unkempt, whose motions as he stuffed his face with black bread or lifted a tankard of ale to wash it down were awkward, even disgusting. He barely noticed my presence, so absorbed was he in satisfying his seemingly voracious appetite. Indeed, so riveted to his plate was he, so involved in his repast, the veins in his swarthy forehead stood out, and I thought I saw perspiration beading up below his slightly off-center, unpowdered wig.

Not until he had wiped his plate clean with the last of his bread and popped that into his maw, followed by a pull of his drink, did he deign to acknowledge my presence.

"Sir!" he said in a deep voice. He extended a greasy hand for me to shake. "Elizabeth told me you might create interesting company."

He punctuated his greeting with a resounding belch.

"Gerald Hook," I said. He raised his bushy eyebrows in question. "That's my name."

"A name, sir, makes a poor calling card. I should prefer a satisfactorily constructed explanation of yourself. You seem to reek of America."

"I'm afraid I can't help coming from America."

"No. I suppose not." He picked at a nostril with a long ragged fingernail. "Were I cursed to be born there, I should not be able to help coming away from America as well. As to my identity, as you seem not to perceive it, I am Doctor Samuel Johnson."

"Oh."

"Oh? Merely 'Oh'? By that 'oh' might I take it you recognize the name? It is not unknown in literate circles."

"Yes. Back home I read some of your works in an English class."

"Ah! My estimation of America is slightly improved. I have been known to swear love to all mankind, save an American. But then I do not cherish the Scotch, yet I number Bozzy among my dearer companions. There can always be exceptions. And you *are* young."

"Yes."

"Ah, your American eloquence dazzles me!" He chortled. "Sir, I love the acquaintance of young people; because, in the first place, I don't like to think of myself as growing old. In the next place, young acquaintances must last longest, if they do last; and then, sir, young men have more virtue than old men: they have more generous sentiments in every respect. I love the young dogs of this age: they have more wit and humor and knowledge left than we had. But then, the dogs are not so good scholars."

"There are other types of ignorance."

"All too true. A man may know himself, yet not the morrow."

I was so intrigued by his conversation I did not notice Elizabeth's return until she set a mug of ale in front of me. I looked up, she winked, and was gone.

"A good girl," said Dr. Johnson.

"I've only just met her."

"Do you find this city to your liking?"

"Very much so."

"I thought as much. London has as much variety as any-place, and much that is uniquely its own."

"I remember my teacher telling me of your love for London—how seldom you left—ah, *leave* it."

"Sir, I am London. My blood and bones are as much a part of it as any of its buildings. Its air is in my lungs. I would live on no other air so well. London, sir, has all civilization can boast of, all that the human spirit can yearn for short of a meeting with its Maker. It is like a fine wine with a bouquet to delight the heart's desire. Its music is the tune my soul dances to."

"Have you heard 'Waterloo Sunset' by the Kinks?"

A raucous confusion burst from the doorway. Both of us leaned over to determine its cause.

Two men, leaning together to support one another, wobbled down the aisle, splashing beer about. They seemed Elizabethan, perhaps Jacobean, by their garb.

Dr. Johnson sighed. "Lord protect us. Willie and Ben are drunk again."

Elizabeth intercepted them. She pointed them in our direction. They stumbled over and leaned into the booth.

"Sammie!" said the bearded one with an earring. "I have just read what you have written of me. Your pen was dipped in flattery. It is an ink I like."

"Good evening Bill—and Ben. Sit down, please. Gentlemen," said Dr. Johnson. "My companion is Gerald Hook. Gerald, I should like you to meet William Shakespeare and Ben Jonson."

An expression of astonishment must have crossed my face.

"The lad is impressed, I see," said Ben Jonson. "You have seen my plays."

"Yes. I am familiar with both your works. Particularly Mr. Shakespeare's, I must confess."

"Ah," said Ben Jonson, shrugging off history's evaluation. "I like Bill's stuff better myself."

"How gratifying," said Shakespeare. "But a shame. I do them merely for the money, you know. What is it you say, Sam Cham? Only a fool writes for else but money? But look who's here. Elizabeth. We'll have some more drink, if you please, girl."

"Sorry, but I have the remainder of the evening off. Shall we go, Gerald."

I considered. I weighed the possibility of a conversation with three of the world's greatest literary lights against an evening with Elizabeth. Something unusual stirred within me.

I said, "Excuse me, gentlemen. Perhaps some other time?"

We supped at a Chinese restaurant in Soho. We sat by the window, and watched the change through the dangling duck, chicken and pork carcasses. By our table an Italian movie director sat with a bored Englishman: this I gathered from snippets of conversation. The director spoke of a big budget film depicting the imminent downfall of American capitalism in allegorical terms. The Englishman smoked Camels and drank Perrier water.

We ate our food with chopsticks. Elizabeth said, "Have a good day?"

"Yes. Quite a few interesting experiences."

I noticed then that her hair was no longer short and bobbed. It was long—a flow of autumn brown, down to her collar. She had changed to a modest early-seventies midi-dress. She could have been merely an attractive secretary.

"You like plays?" she asked.

"Yes. And television. You know, TV is much better over here. I could sit all evening and watch it."

"Really?"

"Some of your series are very involving."

"Yes."

"I quite enjoy reading as well. And movies, and dance, and opera, and concerts."

She smiled, and set a half-nibbled shrimp back into its rice-bed. From a brown purse, she picked out a ticket packet, set it out in front of her. "Concerts? You want to go to this one?"

I opened the packet. The tickets read: June 8, 1973. THE KINKS.

I could not contain my enthusiasm and surprise. "You like the Kinks too?" She was sipping her tea, and I saw a smile through the wisp of steam.

"Always have," she answered. "I have all their albums they've ever done, will ever do."

"Ray Davies is a genius."

"I think so."

"Rock plus."

"Yes. Plus much more."

"They say he's the most English songwriter of the sixties and seventies—in the style he uses."

"And the words."

"Yes. I get very carried away by his stuff."

"You get very involved in music and other sorts of entertainment?"

"Only if it's good."

"We have a little while before the concert. Tell me about yourself."

It did not take me long. What more was there to say than the dull specifics of my youth. Parents, siblings, friends. School, church, house. The exact facts did not seem important, though I supplied them. I spoke much, though, of my vicarious involvements. My reading, viewing... and my writing.

"Oh. You would like to be a writer?"

"I can't draw, or sing, or play music. I can't dance."

"What sort of things would you like to write?"

"I don't know now. Things have changed. It doesn't seem important—not in the same way—anymore."

"What did you want to write about once?"

"Fantasy. Science fiction. I mostly read those sorts of books, like I said."

"What are you writing now?"

"About you."

She pulled a pack of Players from her purse, offered me one. I refused. Her nails were polished red. I felt very young. She smiled, and I felt more at ease. "You like me?"

"Yes," I said.

"I like you too. Have you made any friends here in London?"

"People change, go away. All I need is Waterloo Sunset."

She nodded. "This is all paradise to you?"

"I'm never bored. It's all very involving. You just forget the confusement—and it all makes sense, I guess. I've adjusted. Like Michael says in 'The Forsyte Saga,' it's all comedy. We get there."

"Don't be afraid of me, Gerald."

I put down my cup of black, unsweetened tea. "How can you tell?"

"I was young."

"But you still are."

She frowned. "Yes. I suppose you're right. But we'd better go. Getting late."

I offered to pay, but she said, "The manager is a friend of mine."

At Festival Hall, I discovered that the seats were quite close to the stage. We sat and talked more while the stagehands finished setting up the group's equipment. We had missed the warm-up act.

Sitting beside her, so close, smelling her perfume, feeling her there, she seemed everything I wanted, but knew I could never have.

The Kinks came on, starting the set with "Victoria." I tapped my feet. I have been known to sing along with Davies on occasion, when I am drunk. He has a friendly face. An expressive face.

The Kinks played a number of their better-known songs—'All Day and All of the Night,' 'Tired of Waiting,' 'Sunny Afternoon,' 'Set Me Free,' 'You Really Got Me.' Eventually they did 'Waterloo Sunset.'

Elizabeth took my hand in hers.

> *Dirty old river*
> *must you keep rolling*
> *flowing into the night.*
> *People so busy,*
> *makes me feel dizzy—*
> *taxi light shines so bright.*
>
> *Everyday I look at the world*
> *through my window*
> *Chilly, chilly in the wintertime*
> *—Waterloo Sunset's fine.*
>
> *And I don't need no friends.*
> *As long as I gaze*
> *at Waterloo Sunset*
> *I am in Paradise**

After the concert, we walked out to the guard rail by the

* © 1968 Reprise Records

Thames. The reflected stars and moon glared up at us from the smooth water. They were like specks of ice, floating. The river lapped at the riverside. Upriver were the Houses of Parliament. Downriver was the original London Bridge.

We said nothing to one another. It was chilly.

I turned away, closed my eyes, and breathed in deeply. I walked to a nearby bench, and sat down. She sat beside me and put an arm around me. I leaned my head against her shoulder and began to weep, softly.

She stroked my hair. I said, "I never told them I loved them."

"Who?"

"My parents. I'll never see them again. I don't understand any of it. I just don't understand."

After a time, she said, "You haven't done this for a while. Have you?"

I said, "No. Not since fourth grade. I used to break out in tears quite often, then. My friends laughed. My teachers sent home notes. I learned to control it. I cut it off."

She kissed my forehead. I put my arms around her. She was warm.

"Gone," I said. "All gone. All that's left is what I remember."

"Then remember. It's all alive inside you, if you let it be. But you have to be alive yourself, Gerald."

I told her a lot of it. She listened and laughed quietly at the funny parts, and squeezed my arm at the sad parts.

It grew very late.

She said, "You've not told most of this to anyone, have you?"

"No."

"Gerald," she said. "You have to trust me."

"Trust?"

"Yes. I can help you."

"You already have."

"No. Help you understand. But you can't keep yourself so tight, so scared."

"What do you mean?"

"You can't be so de—"

I heard a noise behind us. I turned around. Six feet away stood a Watcher. Its big television eye stared hungrily at me. Just behind it were a group of three Visitors, their arms folded, regarding us from the black of their cowls. Their dark robes were still.

I grew stiff, and grabbed up Elizabeth's hand. "Let's get out of here," I said. I felt sick with fear and dread.

"Don't be afraid, Gerald," Elizabeth said. "They've been here all the time. I want you to come with us."

I turned on her, a feeling of betrayal squirming like a snake in my belly. "All this time... You're one of them! I want nothing to do with them. Nothing!"

By the soft lights of riverside lamps I saw the imploring gleam of her eyes. "There's hope for you, Gerald. Hope, yet. You *want* out of here, don't you? Deep down that's what you desire most of all. I can feel that when I hold you. Have faith, please, dear Gerald." She tightened her grasp emphatically. "Have faith, or you'll become a wraith..." She gestured her free hand. "Just like all of this. Insubstantial. Floating, drifting, dissipating... Hold *on* to someone, Gerald. Hold on to me."

I could barely force the words out. "I... I... like... *like* it here! I... I don't want to leave. I've always dreamed of a life like this! I have everything I've ever wanted." My voice choked away. "Everything..." I turned away and crumbled upon the bench, sobs coming up dry as dead leaves. "Can't you see, Elizabeth? I *trust* this, I trust myself. Everything else... everyone has always turned on me... kicked me down... misunderstood me. All this..." I held out my hands. "All this *is* paradise to me!"

She let go, and looked over to one of the Visitors. It nodded its head, just once. "Yes," she said. "Yes, I suppose it is, Gerald." She stared about her silently for a moment. "Pleasant, engrossing, diverting..." She stared down at me. "Detached."

I nodded and could not look into her searching eyes. I said, "Aren't I pathetic?"

"That's what you've always thought, isn't it? And life has always reinforced it," she whispered.

"Yes."

"It's not just your fear that's keeping you back, you know. It's your pride."

"I've precious little of that."

"Enough. You have enough." A breeze fluttered her skirt and her long hair. The Visitors and the Watcher turned and began walking slowly eastward toward Waterloo Bridge. Their footsteps had a metallic sound.

"Goodbye, Gerald." she said. She turned and began following the Watcher and the Visitors. Her footsteps were soft and susurrating.

Her warmth around my heart was fleeing rapidly, retreating, giving way to the insistent cold, hollow sounds of the sweeping Thames below. The early morning air seemed suddenly to own a polar chill that drove down to my very soul where it huddled deep within me like a burrowed, frightened creature. I felt as empty as a bell.

I seemed to toll with my own loneliness a most mournful peal.

Sick with fear, I stood. The figures had disappeared around a jutting corner: the buttressing cement of a building. I felt weak and stiff. Each effort was a strain, but I began to walk, walk faster, run in the direction they had gone.

Suddenly the air seemed to flame in my lungs—I felt terrible pain. I'd not felt physical pain for so long... so long. It hurt... and yet, it felt right. The jolting slap of my sneakers on the pavement, the jolt of bones and muscles in sockets, the smart of salty tears...

In glorious pain, I ran and I ran, the night dissolving around me into an amorphous mass of indistinction. It was London, it was not London—it could have been *anywhere*.

Desperately, I ran for what seemed hours... or were suddenly minutes only minutes again?

She was waiting for me under the bridge, leaning against the railing. There was no sign of anyone else around.

"Hello, Gerald." She took my hand in hers.

I nodded, wonderstruck, out of breath. "You're real!" I said.

"Yes, Gerald. And now so are you."

Hand in hand we walked down the riverside, and she showed me Waterloo sunrise.

TAPESTRY

by Stephen Leigh

One of the first things that attracted us to Leigh's tale was its exceptional vividness—it conveys the feeling of standing in the hot sunlight in Troyes during the Fair, of seeing, hearing, and smelling Medieval France. Beyond that, "Tapestry" is a story of people playing out their lives on the fringes of recorded history. For them, the great events of the time are merely backdrops to their personal concerns.

PRELUDE

Dust settled on the coifs and cloaks of the men-at-arms behind them; ahead, the walls of Troyes glowered above the fields bordering the road. The Baron de Nogent settled himself on the saddle of his mount, grimacing. He turned to his constable, riding beside him, and shook his head.

"My old rump can't stand much more of this pounding, Benoit. My squire's been sparing of the blankets again. I'll be glad to reach the hostel. Renard has promised the most comely of his maids to keep my bones warm. Now that's a comfort not to be missed, eh?" The Baron winked at the man, grinning.

"It's better than we'll find among the Saracens. Louis will travel in comfort, but nothing better than we might find in Champagne. But Troyes..." Benoit shook his head beneath his hood of mail.

"'But Troyes?'" echoed the Baron. "We're two days ahead of Louis, and the Hot Fair beckons us for our amusement. I know the proper burghers to fill our stomachs and pamper our, ahh, more base desires. What could be wrong with Troyes, man?"

"A dream." Benoit shrugged.

The Baron glanced at the man, thin beneath the bulky covering of his chainmail. Benoit had entered the Baron's service only a few scant years before, but the man had shown his prowess as a soldier and an uncanny schooling in the art of warfare; far too much of each for a man of his professed background. The Baron suspected that Benoit was in truth an exiled nobleman—still, the man had shown himself trustworthy and competent, and the rank of constable was not one the Baron bestowed lightly. Second in command, Benoit carried the baton, and his justice had been strict: the Baron was pleased. "A dream?" he said.

"I've had such dreams before, my liege. You've found them accurate, have you not?"

The Baron smiled as memories came to him. He twisted the reins in his hand absently; the charger tossed its head. Ahead of them, the folk of the surrounding countryside, walking purposefully toward Troyes and the Fair, stood aside to let the company of knights pass, their heads respectfully bowed. "I recall how startled de Joinville was when you mentioned that a dream had told you Louis would take the cross. Ah, the look on his face... And you also said that Dame Hersent—my pardon, the Queen Dowager Blanche— would be named Regent."

"As she has become." Benoit smiled at the remembrance. "And this dream was as clear. I saw a sorcerer and much danger for you. He meant to kill you, though he has never met you before, nor does he hold a complaint against your house. I awoke before the end of the tale, but the threat was distinct— and there is, I understand, one in Troyes who might fit those requirements: an alchemist about whose activities much gossip has been expended. A Richarte Taillebois."

"I know him not."

Benoit brushed dust from his scarlet cloak and the cross sewn there. "Yet the dream...Baron, I would be wary and cautious in Troyes, if you must go there at all."

"I wouldn't run from imagined danger, my friend." As Benoit began to speak, the Baron silenced him with a wave of his gloved hand. "Enough, Benoit. I promise you that I will be vigilant—and with you as my guardian, I doubt that I need worry."

The Baron glanced before them. The walls had separated into an alternating series of square and round towers with thick stone between. The spires of Troyes's many churches pricked an adamantine sky, and the mouth of Preize Gate loomed before them.

"You'll enjoy yourself, Benoit. The Fair of St. Jean is a time to forget silly dreams and imagined troubles." He stroked the beribboned mane of his horse, stroking the sweaty neck. "Think of the pleasures that await you."

The Fair of St. Jean.
The Hot Fair.

For most, it was a time of novelty, a break in the daily routine, a celebration. For Richarte, the days of the Fair were shadowed by impending death and an unwanted return.

Troyes moved with sudden crowds. The lanes from the Porte de Paris to the Abbey of Notre Dame Aux Nonnains teemed with revelers and the foreigners who had followed the merchants from the Mai de Provins, forty miles to the west. The tangled and narrow streets about the Church of St. Jean au Marche had been surrendered to the invading tents and stalls of merchants. Here, in lambent brilliance, the congestion found a nexus.

A company of jongleurs performed near the Templar Commandery, the bass drone of a viol scratching below tenor voices. The song was bawdy, frankly sexual; the fairgoers participated with laughing jeers and ribald comments while the viol player fingered his instrument suggestively. A priest robed in Dominican vestments shook his head dutifully, but those close to him saw the smile that battled the obligatory frown.

Where the Rue de Domino emptied its crowds into the Rue

Champeau, an old man dressed in yellow tights and a blue tunic cajoled his tame bear into a lumbering dance. The bear had no teeth and its fur was patchy: oblates of reddish-grey skin scabbed with dark umber were open to the torment of flies. The bear halted once to growl and paw at the nagging insects. The man slapped the beast on the snout with his tabor, muttering a guttural obscenity and grinning gap-toothed at the spectators. The bear moaned in frustration and attempted a stumbling dance. Children screamed in mock terror as the animal careened near them.

A woman in a surcoat of scarlet linen argued loudly with a seller of peppercorns. She held five deniers in her open palm as the monger shook his head sadly. A sergeant of the fair, perhaps slightly bored and indolent in the July heat, altered his ambling course slightly to take him nearer the squabble.

A hundred scenes, altering with movement, a restless gaiety...

Richarte Taillebois, in his robe of black, skirted a pool of brackish water in the unpaved street. He was a mote of drab night against the bolts of new cloth, the gay and strident coloration of the burghers and noblemen, and the intricate belts of silver, gold, and silk on the waists of their wives. Richarte was tall, with a full beard that held the ruddiness of copper and hair that summer had lightened to ripe wheat. To the people of Troyes, he might well have descended from the northern raiders who had plundered the towns of Champagne four hundred years earlier. He had their light eyes, their fabled height, and his speech was tainted with the accents of some barbarian tongue. But Troyes was tolerant of the foreign—it was, after all, the influx of fairgoers twice yearly that brought the town wealth. Richarte had made his niche.

Dabbler in the arcane, alchemist, and (it was rumored) sorcerer.

The burghers came to him for his potions, the priests sought him for his surprising knowledge of scripture (and his orthodoxy—Richarte was in sympathy with the goals of the enquêteurs), the Abbess found his concoctions effective in remedying the transgressions of foolish nuns. It was even whispered that Sire Dore, the Golden, had sent for Richarte and received medications to ease the pain of his aged joints. Richarte was tolerated; he was perhaps even liked.

The bells of St. Pierre tolled Sext, followed by the short-

waisted chimes of St. Etienne. The clamoring laughter of the
fair ebbed momentarily, then swelled anew.

Richarte fingered a silver medallion that hung about his neck
on a fine chain, his long fingers scissoring. He scowled—to
his left, a tradeswoman who had been staring at this apparition
in black made the sign of the cross, though she continued to
stare—and he turned down the Rue Moyenne, pursued by the
many-throated voice of the fair.

He stopped before the sign of the Grey Stallion. Nicholas,
the proprietor of the tavern, had his shop ledge down. A few
books stood there—Nicholas was also one of the town's book-
sellers. Richarte let the flood of people eddy around him; as
he hesitated, the nasal honk of a krumhorn echoed among the
close-set buildings and a troop of inebriated dancers turned into
the street with a clapping of rough hands, performing an energetic but sloppy gavotte. The noise decided him—Richarte
moved to the door of the Stallion, thrust it open, and entered.

The tavern held night. Darkness sighed around dicers near
the back wall of the long and narrow room; twilight shadowed
the tables. A wan light filtered in from the shop ledge but,
discouraged, died quickly. Tapers had been lit; behind the
flambeaux, soot scrabbled up walls. The darkness was alive
with voices: loud grumbling and louder guffaws from the wag-
erers as dice clicked against wood; the strident wheedling of
prostitutes (their forces augmented for the fair's duration by
an army of tradeswomen and serving wenches willing to earn
a few extra deniers); the tidal soughing of conversations over
the clatter of earthenware mugs. Nicholas himself bustled in
from the kitchens and taps, shouting hoarse orders to his help.

It seemed very tiresome.

Richarte shook his head. He had begun to turn and leave
when he heard his name shouted above the din.

"Richarte! You blind fool, come over here!"

A hand waved in turgid dimness. Richarte squinted, nodded,
and made his way to the table. As he approached, the shades
of the Grey Stallion resolved themselves into the figure of
Rutebeuf, seated at an oaken table ringed with the vestiges of
past bottles. The man gestured at a stool, his hand plucking
a loaf from a basket on the table in passing.

"Sit, my good man—I thought you were a thrice-damned
friar in those robes. Have some of the bread and try the wine;
Nicholas claims it traveled from Reims, but I suspect it to be

plain Auxerre, but good enough for the likes of us, no? By sweet Jesus, man, you look a wraith. Have you no clothes with happier colors? Surely there are enough merchants at the fair to convince you to buy a bolt of pretty cloth?"

Richarte, despite himself, smiled into the torrent of words. He had started wandering the streets in a foul mood, but Rutebeuf had dispelled it for the moment.

He did not appear to be waiting for answers to his multiple questions. The man broke off a piece of the loaf and placed it with an affected and nonchalant delicacy in his mouth. He shook his head at Richarte as the dark-clothed sorcerer sat quietly.

"Don't begin again, poet," Richarte said as Rutebeuf swallowed the bread. "You should learn to be more sparing of your words." The bottle of wine shivered as Richarte leaned forward on the table. "And I'm sorry if my dress offends you."

Rutebeuf swallowed again, clearing his throat. "'God has made me a companion for Job/Taking away with a single blow/ All that I had/With my right eyes, once my best/I can't see the street ahead/Or find my way.'" A turn of stubbled cheeks, a rolling of a yellow-shot eye: Rutebeuf waved a hand to Richarte in invitation.

"The meaning of that escapes me. It's a babble to me."

"Are you in mourning? I can hardly see you in that robe, though I must admit that it sets off the medallion well—is that a pagan scene? You court heresy, my friend, since the Dominicans are already suspicious of alchemists and their ilk. Or have you and Jeanne been arguing? This is the Hot Fair, man; you're supposed to be happy, drunk, or some combination of the two."

Richarte found himself shaking his head with helpless bemusement. "You've had too much wine."

"I've not had enough, as I'm still speaking coherently."

"Which question do you wish answered?"

Rutebeuf spread his hands wide, then broke off another mouthful of bread. "It's no matter to me. Any one of them is sufficient to start a conversation." His fingers held the bread up to his regard; he narrowed his eyes, then tucked it into his mouth. Crumbs dusted his tunic.

Richarte knotted his long fingers. The silver about his neck swayed hypnotically; silver flecked the table with lights like shy stars. "Jeanne and I haven't argued—I've not seen her for three days, though since the avoir de pois has begun and the Cloth Market is over, I might have better luck. As for my attire, it seemed to fit my mood." With the last words, Richarte began to feel the melancholia wash over him once more. He shook his head, as if the movement could banish the mood.

Rutebeuf canted his head to the left, an eye laced with blood staring under his lifted eyebrow. Behind the young poet, the dice clicked and a gruff voice shouted dismay.

"Even when touched by wine, I can see your feelings, my friend. The Hot Fair is for revelry, not your dour stupidity. Have your experiments been going wrong? Have you acquired an affliction"—with an overdone leer—"that you wish kept secret?"

Richarte shook his head, caught halfway between irritation and amusement.

"You've confessed your multitude of sins," Rutebeuf continued, "shrived yourself and promised to go crusading like King Louis? Is that what makes you look as if the wine were vinegar?"

A half-smile lifted one corner of Richarte's mouth.

Rutebeuf sighed nasally, subsiding. He leaned back, his eyes closed as he pulled the bottle of wine toward him and drank. "We're to play at riddles, then? Fine. I have a new one: 'Five curious creatures I saw traveling together...'"

"Fingers on a hand." Richarte shook his head. "That's too obvious, poet."

"And you spoke too quickly. I could have been describing the feet of three men, one of whom had but one leg." Rutebeuf scowled, so comically forbidding that Richarte's humor broke the surface of his moodiness for a moment.

He laughed.

"And which is correct, my teller of tales?"

Rutebeuf shrugged. "Well... the fingers of a hand." He smeared moisture across the table with a forefinger. "And you still haven't answered my question: why this foul vapor wrapped around you like that damned cloak? You've been turning this way for weeks, man, growing darker as the Fair approached."

"Aren't you being a bit romantic?" But it's easy to explain, he thought. I simply need to kill a man with whom I have no quarrel, who does not know me and will have no chance to defend himself.

"Romanticism is a fault of mine. But it *has* been that obvious. Even Jeanne spoke to me of it."

Rutebeuf's words plunged Richarte back into reverie, as if a shim had passed between himself and the world. All about Richarte was saturated with a glaze of his own distaste: Rutebeuf's tipsy humor, the gruff camaraderie of the tavern, the distant revelry that could be heard outside the door of the Grey Stallion. The poet had been right, but for the wrong reasons. Richarte knew that his moodiness sprung not from the onset of the Fair, but because the army of Louis had begun their slow march to Aigues-Morte. That procession, those holy soldiers, were the parameters of his personal crisis.

Yes, he had to kill a man. No, he did not want to do so.

"So I've become a matter for discussion among my acquaintances? I'm surprised I've not been handed over to the Dominicans." Richarte could have softened his tone with a smile. He did not smile.

Once again, Rutebeuf shrugged. "Better friends than otherwise." A pause. "Sorcerer."

As Rutebeuf intoned the last word with drunken precision, the Grey Stallion's door groaned and spat light into the room. A figure stood there, girt with a thin sword, limned by sun. Then the door shut behind him. The tavern denizens turned away from the unwelcome intrusion of day to the more important liquor on their tables.

Rutebeuf spoke, watching the newcomer make his way to the back of the room. "That's Benoit d'Orabis, constable of Baron de Nogent's knights. So that erstwhile crusader has stopped by the Fair, eh?" The last few words were pitched upward in a sharp query as Rutebeuf turned back to the table and saw Richarte's face. The sorcerer was glaring at the figure of d'Orabis, his mouth twisted beneath the moustache, the eyes narrowed. Richarte's skin was a white pallor against the dark cloth of his cloak, and one hand clenched the medallion about his neck, straining the chain. As Rutebeuf's voice trailed into silence, Richarte's eyes seemed to snap back into focus. He shook his head, the jaw-length hair moving.

"You know the man?" Rutebeuf's whisper was low. He leaned forward as if expecting a conspiratorial answer.

"No." Curtly.

"You looked daggers at him, my friend. The knave doesn't

know it, but he's pierced through. Nicholas will have to sweep out the bloodied rushes."

Richarte laughed, loud and sudden. "I was admiring his tunic, nothing else."

"And that laughter wouldn't convince a drunkard, and your eyes skitter like a guilty man's before a priest." Rutebeuf stroked the smooth glass of the wine bottle.

Silence. Richarte pulled his cloak tighter about his shoulders.

Rutebeuf contemplated his fingertips. "De Nogent has taken the cross with Louis. And I've heard tales that the French King gave his knights new vestments for the ceremony this New Year—gave them in shadowed darkness. When the knights awoke the next morning, they found that a cross had been sewn into each garment. The fervor is on us again."

"And it will do them no good." Richarte spat out the words. They tasted bitter on his tongue, and an inner voice scolded him for his anger—but the venting of his bitterness felt good. His gaze swept to d'Orabis, then back to the table, where Rutebeuf watched him with a strange contemplation.

"You have foreknowledge, Richarte, or is this another of your fabliaux, like that unbelievable tale of metal birds and fiery battles in the clouds? What will happen with this crusade?"

"Does it matter to you?"

"At the risk of offending his Holiness Innocent, these pious undertakings bleed us dry. Troyes has yet to recover from Count Thibaut's little venture. So . . . what will happen?"

"Louis will not be pleased—I will warrant that much. Leave it be, Rutebeuf; the subject bores me." Richarte's voice held a dangerous edge, but Rutebeuf's perception of such things was not keen at the moment. The poet waved a hand in dismissal.

"Poor Dame Hersent . . ." Rutebeuf scratched the stubble on his chin with a thumb and forefinger. "An ignoble ending, then? And the Baron de Nogent? You might as well continue the tale, Richarte. You can't simply offer a taste and then take the dish away."

Richarte's growing anger was visible in the narrowing of his cerulean eyes, in the erect manner in which he sat, in the whitened skin of his knuckles as his hands lay fisted on the table. "You can find a hundred entertainers on the streets today," he said curtly. "Have them fabricate you a tale."

"But yours is so amusing." Rutebeuf frowned comically, pouting, wiping away imaginary tears with a sleeve.

Richarte's fists struck the table once, then again. The wine bottle clattered in alarm. "Then listen," he said in a harsh whisper. "De Nogent will not go matching swords against the infidels, will not even see Aigues-Morte. Does the knowledge cheer you, Sire Rutebeuf?"

Rutebeuf shook with suppressed laughter. He raised his eyes heavenward. "D'Orabis should know of this—he can relay the information to his lord." The poet staggered to his feet, opening his mouth in the beginning of a bellow.

"Rutebeuf, no!" Richarte clutched Rutebeuf's sleeve with a hand, his command harsh and too loud; the patrons of the Grey Stallion turned to stare at this new entertainment. Rutebeuf, with drunken swiftness, was suddenly contrite.

"I apologize, Richarte," he said, too loudly for Richarte's taste. "The wine speaks for me. But this tale of the Baron . . ."

"What of the Baron?" Benoit d'Orabis called across a suddenly quiet room. Like Richarte, he was tall, but his wiry body was that of a hardened soldier, with muscle tone that Richarte lacked. The hand on his sword hilt was an implicit threat.

"Nothing, good sire." The anger had leached away from Richarte as quickly as it had come, to be replaced by a dull fear: was this the way it would end, everything he'd come to do undone because a man he called a friend could not hold his tongue? Richarte shook his head, forcing his voice to become properly servile. "My friend meant no offense to you or your liege."

"Do I know him?" D'Orabis's voice was that of the nobility, confident that when he spoke, the common rabble would answer.

"He is Rutebeuf, a poet of small reputation and a poor drinker."

"He should learn to speak more softly," the constable replied, then turned back to his conversation with Nicholas. Richarte pulled Rutebeuf, his face drained of color, back to his seat. Gradually the susurrus of conversation swelled and surrounded them again. Dice began clattering against the back wall.

"Richarte—" Rutebeuf shook his head, exhaling loudly. "Forgive me."

Richarte scowled. "You don't know what you've done, man."

"I know I almost involved you in a duel with d'Orabis. I've *seen* you with a sword." Rutebeuf was quickly regaining his humor. He smiled. "My wager would not have gone for you, I'm afraid."

"Poet, you are sometimes only a fool." Richarte rose with a scowl and a curse of disgust. He nodded to Rutebeuf curtly, his eyes unreadable, and walked away. Rutebeuf watched the sorcerer leave, watched him favor d'Orabis with the barest sketch of a bow, watched him wrench open the door with a swirling of his cloak.

Then the clamor of the fair swallowed him.

Jeanne laughed: silver dusting midnight satin. She lay back on the bed, a hand pillowing her head, her unbound hair spread on the sheets like dark, arthritic fingers. Her eyes held the reflection of a flambeau on the wall.

"Richarte, I'm glad we met." She caught her lower lip between her teeth and touched the man beside her with a soft hand. "You do know that, don't you?"

Beyond the open window, the moon spilled creamy light around the stars. Richarte's eyes were flecked with that illumination. He caught Jeanne's hand with his own, squeezing. "Yes. You should know that without asking, trollop."

"My fine despoiler, my stealer of virtue." She rolled towards him with a rustling of cloth, her lips half-open in a questioning smile.

"Not again, m'mselle. Even an incubus must rest sometime."

Burrowing her head into his chest, she nipped him with strong teeth, laughing again as he grunted in surprise.

"You assured me there was nothing supernatural about you," she said. Jeanne sat abruptly, her hair cascading over small breasts. She pouted, eyes downcast, her hands at breast and pubis in false modesty. Her attitude reminded Richarte of Rutebeuf's drunken clowning that afternoon and of what it had nearly cost him. The memory leached away any tolerance he had for play. He caught at Jeanne's hands, but she tugged loose, shaking her head.

"You've probably given me a bastard child, and I'll be

forever tainted. I'll rot in hell because of you."

"The potion I gave you prevents that, vixen. You lie." He forced himself to smile—he had no wish to offend Jeanne with his moods. "Liars are also burned in hell. Don't you listen to your priests?"

"If I listened to the priests, would I have let you in tonight, or would I have put your sleeping draught in my family's wine?"

"Which is another reason I can't stay longer, amie. The draught's power will be gone soon, and neither you nor I would care to be found this way. Your father would have my manhood for having ruined his chances of marrying you to that Parisian banker."

It was a lie, he knew—the draught would last hours yet. Richarte placated his guilt by thinking it a necessary deception. He had yet another task tonight.

"Voillet le Duc? He's a tiresome old man and he hasn't any teeth. He couldn't give me children and father would like a grandson." Jeanne touched Richarte's cheek with a smooth hand. "I would prefer your company."

Richarte half-turned, looking toward the open window and the rooftops of Troyes. "Your father wouldn't permit that. He might profess to like me, but a dabbler in the occult arts—a potential heretic—won't be his idea of a suitable match.

Jeanne shrugged, a gesture Richarte felt more than saw. "You could convince him if you would open suit and declare yourself."

You ask impossibilities and don't know it. Richarte shook his head. "It wouldn't do any good," he temporized. The skin of his back prickled as if she were about to touch him. He waited for the hand's caress, but it never came.

"Would you do it, if I asked you?"

Her frankness startled Richarte. The question had lain, unasked, between them since they had become lovers, but he had always managed to evade, managed to turn the subject so that it drifted to other, safer, topics. He had lied if he felt the need, salving his conscience with the thought that she would not believe the truth. Her sudden directness caught him unprepared and he couldn't think of an answer or how to tread that thin line between truth and lie.

And even as the words, hazy, began to form in his mind,

he knew he'd waited too long and that his silence had spoken
for him.

Jeanne had turned away. The inky wash of her hair trailed
down the thin back and into the curve of her waist. Now it
was Richarte that reached out to touch. His forefinger traced
the valley of her spine from shoulder to buttocks.

"Jeanne, if I could . . ." Richarte licked dry lips.

"You'll burn in hell if you say more." Softly.

He began again. "I told you from the beginning that this
would do neither of us good. But we pursued each other despite
that." *And should I want to—and I do—I can't stay here*. But
he couldn't say that: she wouldn't understand.

Her face still looked away from him. "I do love you," he
said, as if that confession would reach her. "It's a mistake, but
I do."

"Love a mistake?" A whisper from darkness.

He didn't hear her. "What?" Richarte leaned toward her.

Jeanne turned on her elbow, head glancing over shoulder,
her back still toward him. "I can't hide what I feel, Richarte.
I knew what loving you might mean."

"I know." He nodded. "But we both have other duties,
accepted before we met. Ignoring them will only give you more
pain." *And in my case, it would be fruitless. I have no control
over my fate*. The thought did not console him.

"Would you stand by and allow my betrothal to le Duc?"

"Would it avail me to protest?"

She stared at him, saying nothing. Then: "You speak only
of me, Richarte. What are *your* commitments? What are *your*
obligations? For all I know of them, you could be spouting a
falsehood designed to allow yourself a graceful excuse."

"You wouldn't like or understand them, Jeanne." Richarte
shook his head dolefully. He stretched, a hand rubbing his eye.
"It's the truth. No one here could understand."

"Allow me to judge that."

For a moment, he was tempted. The commands of three
years before seemed distant. An interior caution held him back.
She can't believe, he thought. *She'd think me a poor creator
of tales*. There were times—walking through the reality of
Troyes, greeting the friends he had made in his years here,
drinking and laughing with Rutebeuf—when he could scarcely
credit it himself.

And she knew the Baron de Nogent. Her father was a friend. He hated the fact that he had cultivated the acquaintance of her father, and thus Jeanne, simply on that basis—a cold-hearted calculation on his part three winters ago. He had not intended to let his feelings come to this point.

No. He shook his head. "You would hate me, Jeanne. I wouldn't care for that."

"Hatred is better than distrust, Richarte."

Her eyes challenged his.

The bells of St. Pierre rang Matins. Both Jeanne and Richarte glanced toward the window.

"I have to go, Jeanne." Richarte did not look back to her.

From behind him, he heard the whisper of cloth as she moved. "I know," she said. Her voice was as dull as the bells of St. Remi, sounding faint in the west as the echoes of St. Pierre died.

"I love you."

"I know that too." A pause. Richarte did not dare turn around. He waited for her next words. "I wish it weren't so," she said.

He had no answer to that.

The windows of the second floor solar threw light onto the dirt of the street. Looking up at the hostel from his vantage point across the lane, Richarte could see shadows moving against the warm yellow of the oiled parchment—evidently the Baron and his retinue were enjoying a late repast. Richarte nodded in satisfaction. Even if the encounter with Jeanne had been tainted with rancor, perhaps he could still salvage something of the night. The Baron would most likely be wine-befuddled. As Rutebeuf had rightly remarked, Richarte was not greatly skilled in the art of the sword, and he did not care to have the Baron draw his blade.

Richarte glanced down the street. It was emptied of the earlier crowds, though as he looked a few drunken couples crossed the street several houses down, talking loudly among themselves. The stalls of the Fair, just visible in the shadows of the distance, were shuttered and empty.

The sorcerer was again attired in black; dark hose and a tight-fitting shirt devoid of any trappings. His light hair was besmeared with soot, as was his face. He seemed to be a fragment of mobile night. A pouch hung at his waist. Richarte thrust a hand into the leather and brought out an angular instrument of satin metal. He turned it in his hand as if admiring the workmanship, and placed it back in the pouch. Then he slipped from his niche and crossed to the wall bordering the Baron's hostel.

He had not thought there would be guards—not in friendly Troyes, not during the abandoned gaiety of the Fair, not with the Baron under the protection of the cross. He was pleased to find the assumption to be truth: the gate to the hostel was not even latched, nor was there anyone in the small courtyard beyond. Now that he was closer, Richarte could hear the sound of a lute and someone's dissonant baritone singing above loud conversation. The sorcerer smiled—the noise would cover his entrance.

There was warm light showing between the hostel's door and the frame. Richarte leaned against the burnished planking, listening; he heard nothing. If guards had been posted, they were asleep or simply not sharing the relaxed attitude of the revelers upstairs. Richarte reached into the pouch once more, withdrawing a small vial of glass. He stooped, cracking the vial sharply against the doorframe. In the darkness, the glass shattered with a sharp tinkling, followed by a menacing hiss. He shoved the broken vial under the door with the toe of his sandal, his breath held. A few moments later, he was rewarded by a muffled thud from the far side. Richarte smiled.

The door was not secured. Richarte pushed it open cautiously, peering inside. A valet in de Nogent's livery lay crumpled on a stool beside the door, a plate of stew spilled beside him. Richarte moved to the boy—he was young, no more than twelve—and checked the pulse. He shifted the boy to a more comfortable position, smoothing the ruffled hair. After staring at the unconscious form for a moment, he moved toward a flight of stairs down the hall.

Richarte half-ran with clumsy stealth. His steps shivered the rushes that lay on the floor, and the stairs groaned beneath his weight. As a thief, the sorcerer could have used much schooling. But the gaiety of those above made quiet, if not unnecessary, at least less imperative. He raised no alarms—no call shattered the night as he reached the landing to the second floor. He stayed to the moving shadows of an oil lamp suspended from a chain in the ceiling above him. The solar door was to his left, while a hallway leading to the kitchens was directly ahead. Richarte moved down that hall, knowing that the solar would share a hearth with the kitchens. From there, he hoped, he could do his task from hiding.

He didn't find the thought satisfying—Richarte, if he must kill, would have preferred to face his victim, or at least he forced himself to believe that. Yet he wanted the charade to be over, and this method would be the quickest: if he were lucky, no one would hear the click of his weapon, and the Baron would crumple as poison flooded his body—it would be as if the man had been stricken by some swift disease.

But his heart was not one with his logic. Richarte was not at ease with his soul.

He was almost surprised at the relief that mingled with the quick fear as there was a shout from below.

"Treachery! My Lords, there is sorcery afoot!"

The door to the solar was flung open as Richarte slipped into the shadows of the hallway. Benoit d'Orabis stood in the doorway, peering down the stairwell. Behind the man, Richarte could see a tapestried arras and the shadows of men. "Who calls?" d'Orabis shouted, his hand on the hilt of his unbuckled sword.

"It's Guibert, sire. Faucher, the valet . . . he's been ensorceled."

Richarte, crouching, prepared to run.

But d'Orabis had lowered the scabbard and his sword had gone to his side. "More likely he's found the cask of wine, Guibert."

"No, sire. There's no smell about him, and I can't rouse him." A pause. Richarte heard the sound of flesh slapping flesh from below. "He won't awaken. Please come, sire."

D'Orabis didn't answer. He went back into the solar and emerged a moment later with another man. The two went loudly down the stairs, buckling their scabbards to their waists.

Richarte's bowels turned queasily. He began moving toward the kitchens as the sound of voices in contention came from the floor below. The lutist had ceased fingering his strings. Richarte had just reached the door when d'Orabis bounded back up the stairs. The constable paused at the landing, staring down the darkened hallway as Richarte's breath left him. He was sure that the man's eyes would pluck him from the shadows, that at any moment d'Orabis would pull sword from scabbard with a clangor of good steel and come rushing toward him. The sorcerer waited, unable to move, helpless.

D'Orabis, with a curse, flung open the solar door, calling for the Baron. Richarte waited no longer. To his right, another set of stairs led down to a rear entrance. As the sound of boots clattered on the floorboards, Richarte made his retreat. He did not pause until he was again in his own rooms.

They could be private in the midst of crowds—that was a truism Richarte remembered from a hundred tales. The throngs of fairgoers eased around Rutebeuf and the sorcerer and left them in loud solitude. Richarte had dressed in silken blue to-day—a short tunic underneath which he wore scarlet hose. His boots were soft cordovan leather. His attire was that of any wealthy man of Troyes, yet he was still marked as foreign. It was the small things: he was a hand taller than anyone in the crowds about them, his bearing was a shade too erect, and his sun-flamed beard was in sharp contrast to the stubbled jaw of Rutebeuf.

Richarte, who had been told long ago that his safety lay in obscurity and plainness, no longer cared.

The sorcerer and the poet strolled the Rue de l'Epicerie, occasionally stopping to examine a merchant's wares, listen to a jongleur, or laugh at the playlets of the street mummers. And, in the main, talking.

"*I* fail to understand, Richarte?" Rutebeuf shook his dark head, hefting a small loaf of bread in his left hand. "You tell Jeanne that things are fine between you, yet when she asks you to declare yourself, you refuse. I talked with her this morning near the baker's, my friend, and she is wroth. You claim to love her, but . . ." He shook his head once more. "Yes, I fail to understand that, Richarte."

"Does it have to make sense?"

"One *would* expect a smattering of logic from a person dabbling in the sciences."

"One would also expect sense from a king, but Louis goes to play war with the Saracens."

"And back to the crusaders again?" Rutebeuf exhaled noisily. He tossed the loaf from his left hand to his right. "Richarte, you make no sense at all. What does Louis have to do with Jeanne?"

Richarte didn't answer. A juggler passed them in the narrow street, walking slowly in the other direction, his eyes on three balls whirling from hand to hand. Street urchins followed him with awed amusement, laughing and pointing, picking stones from the streets and trying to juggle them themselves. Richarte and the poet passed the stand of a spice-monger—rough planks draped with standards on which strange heraldic creatures were rampant. The fragrance of distant lands lathed the breeze.

"Rutebeuf, do you have the patience for a roundabout tale?"

A shrug, a sigh, a nod. Rutebeuf made an airy and grandiloquent gesture of invitation.

"I'm serious, poet."

A smile ghosted across Rutebeuf's mouth. *"I* never thought you anything but serious." The smile returned, full this time, and the poet's dark eyes glittered with sun. "You have no humor in you at all, Richarte. You're *always* serious. Gloom hangs about you like a fog. In fact, I have a difficult time imagining you making light-hearted love with M'mselle Jeanne. Not with *that* dour face." Rutebeuf screwed his face into an overdone imitation of his friend.

They came near the tangle of streets around the Church of St. Jean Au Marche. Tierce had rung not long before, and the long shadow of the steeple lay over the houses just ahead of them. The belltower was a sharp darkness against the blue sky, dwarfing the buildings below. Richarte had been silent, gathering his thoughts. He knew that he wanted to talk and unburden himself, but he was unsure of the words. "Think of this situation," he ventured at last. "What if you had taken an oath to do a task, yet when the time came to fulfill your oath, all desire to do so had gone?" Richarte shook his head as Rutebeuf started to speak. "No, wait a moment more. Add to that the absolute certainty that whether or not you perform that task, you will be summoned to face your superiors; you cannot escape them. And one thing more: what if you knew—knew beyond any doubt your skepticism can raise—that you are simply performing a deed that would occur despite you a few days later, that you are simply anticipating the reality?"

"It seems clear enough. You've given your word—that is sacred. You'll be punished for failing—and no man wishes punishment: look at the poor idiots pretending to be devout during Mass. And it will happen in any case. What makes you loath to do as you said you would do?" Rutebeuf glanced toward the taller man, shielding his eyes against the sun.

Richarte stood just in the shadow of St. Jean's, his face

haloed by sun, the remainder of his body in cool shade. Fair-goers passed the two on either side. "What if that task is to kill a man, a person who has never done you harm?"

Rutebeuf cocked his head to one side, staring at Richarte sidewise. "Louis? Is *that* the connection? Surely . . ."

Richarte was shaking his head vigorously. "Not Louis. But Louis gathers men to him—there are those that will join him. Here in Troyes there are those that are following his cross. One of those."

"Who?"

Richarte waved the question aside. "Rutebeuf, my masters have a long reach. They're farther removed from Troyes than you could imagine, but I'll be snatched from here soon. In that I have no choice, no choice at all. Can you see my dilemma? I was sent here to do their task, but I've been here too long. Troyes is more real to me than their land. I don't want to kill, and I don't wish to leave Jeanne or you or Troyes. That's why I've been muttering about Louis—his march to Aigues-Morte signals the end of my time here."

"Perhaps a priest . . ."

"If I told a priest even as much as I've told you, he would natter about devils and sin and sorcery and call for the Do-minicans. There's nothing supernatural about this."

"Then I don't know how to counsel you, Richarte." Rute-beuf scowled, brushing hair back from his forehead and glanc-ing from the steeple of St. Jean to the bustling of the Fair. His right hand, clutching the loaf, beat a slow rhythm on his thigh.

Richarte smiled sadly. "I knew that."

"The priests tell us that only God ordains when a man dies—but you say that you can foretell when this"—a brief hesitation: Rutebeuf kicked dust in the street—"man of yours will die. Can you be sure?" Rutebeuf's stubbled jaw worked once. He scratched his cheek with a thumb and forefinger.

"I'm sure," he said, but the sorcerer avoided Rutebeuf's gaze. No, you're not entirely certain, he thought, there's no way I can be sure. Who is to say how many pasts there are for each of us?

Rutebeuf inhaled deeply, wrinkled his nose as if the air offended him. "Why do you tell me all this?" he asked finally. "I can't help you—*won't* help you. And I can't advise you because what you say makes no sense—unless your masters are of the infidels." He raised an eyebrow in question.

Despite himself, Richarte laughed with soft amusement. Rutebeuf let his frown relax into a grin. "It's that humorous?" the poet asked.

"No." Richarte still smiled. The sun threw his shadow at his feet as he moved from the shade of St. Jean's. "I think the sun's affected my head, or I've sniffed too many of my own potions. I know none of the Saracens; it makes much less sense than that. I wanted to talk to someone else and see if it made more sense when related to another." A beat. Nearby, a fiddler began a motet. "It didn't."

"Good." Rutebeuf sighed with mock relief. "I would have been worried if you thought it had." The poet squinted at their surroundings as if seeing them for the first time, then glanced at the sun with one eye shut, the other half-open. "The Stallion has opened by now if Nicholas has kicked his wife from the bed. A glass of wine might clear your head of all these distant ghosts." He looked at Richarte.

The sorcerer began to shake his head.

"Wine is better than a priest for fortifying one's soul," said the poet.

Richarte laughed once more. "Then let's drink." He put a burly arm around Rutebeuf's shoulder.

In the afternoon warmth, Richarte's rooms lay somnolent. The summer heat seemed to have taken residence within his walls, a palpable and unfriendly presence. Outside the shutters, the noise of the Fair was muffled by the houses across the Ruelle des Chats. Even those houses seemed tired; they leaned ponderously toward their neighbors like slumbering giants. Richarte opened the shutters to whatever vestige of a breeze could be found. He cursed, wiping sweat from his brow.

Turning from the window, the sorcerer flung his dark cloak over a high-backed chair, the linen folding over the oaken anger of lion-headed arms. The rest of his room was an esoteric clutter—books, Greek translations in tortuous Latin, were stacked haphazardly on tables. To the rear were the glass vials and stoneware utensils of an alchemist: jars of labeled herbs straggled along a shelf over equipment whose functions daily stretched the limited imagination of the cleaning drudge Richarte employed.

The man inhabited an unkempt den of his own devising.

It was comfortable, and he could move in it easily. That

was all that mattered. He went once more to the window, wrinkling his lean face in disgust—someone had emptied their chamberpot into the gutter again. The foulness of the city was something to which he had never acclimated himself. The years in Troyes had not softened the omnipresent stench, the houses leaning with overfamiliarity, the constant noise now augmented by the Fair—all were minor irritations he bore with little good grace.

"Abominable mess," he muttered under his breath.

"The street or your rooms?"

Richarte started in surprise, nearly striking his head against a shutter. As he peered into the murk of his rooms, he was greeted by bright laughter. "Truly, Richarte, the abomination is of your own doing?" Plaited dark hair, white wimple, large eyes, and a bandeau of blue satin: Jeanne laughed again. Behind her, an elderly woman in drab skirts smiled at him tentatively.

"Haven't you learned manners befitting a lady? To enter a man's rooms without so much as a knock, even when accompanied by your servant..."

"You, featherbrain, left your door standing open," Jeanne interrupted. She put her hands on her hips, a mock scowl lifting one corner of her full mouth. A foot, clad in cordwain, tapped impatiently against the floor. "Well, will you bid me enter?"

"It seems I have no choice."

"Good." Jeanne smiled. Turning to the woman behind her, she nodded her head. "Blanche, you may wait in the outer rooms." Then, to the look of reproach: "I won't be long enough to get into any mischief. Go, now."

They waited until the old woman had left them, closing the heavy door behind her. As the thud of wood against wood sounded in the heavy air, Jeanne spoke. "Aren't you going to kiss me, Richarte?"

"A proper woman..."

"Would never have quarrelled with her lover, especially when he is a sorcerer. Come here."

They embraced, but Richarte's kiss was but a quick meeting of lips. He moved away from her again, going to the table laden with retorts and glassware. He toyed with the equipment there absently.

"Rutebeuf was not wrong, then."

Richarte glanced up. "Hmmm?"

"He said I would find you in a foul humor. He was right."

Richarte nodded. "You can leave if my company is unbearable."

"What's wrong, Richarte?" Concern twisted her face into a frown, and that vulnerable caring hurt him more than he'd thought possible. He lifted a flask from the table and held it to the light from the window, swirling the amber liquid inside. He pursed his lips in distaste.

"Nothing," he said at last. He set the flask down again and met her eyes.

"I'm not blind, Richarte. I thought last night was simply my fault. But you're still distressed, and I'm beginning to think I was wrong. Something else bothers you, something deeper."

A long pause: Richarte went to his bookcase, running his hand over tooled leather bindings. He could feel Jeanne's gaze on him, waiting for him to speak. He went through a dozen sentences in his mind and rejected them all.

"Louis has camped not far from Troyes," she said. "The Fair has been swelled by those who've taken the cross and everyone is jolly. Why not you?"

"The crusaders," Richarte muttered, his head still bent over his volumes.

"What?"

Richarte turned, shaking his head. He started to speak, stopped—glancing toward the window, sunlight limned his face with gold—then began again. "I wanted to tell you this long before now, Jeanne, before it would hurt us both this much. But I'm a coward. I waited, thinking I might find a way to change it. I didn't want to hurt *myself,* didn't want things to change. I thought..."

He shook his head again, looking at her. "I'm leaving soon, Jeanne. I won't return to Troyes afterward."

"You've taken the cross?" Relief swept the bemused concern from her face. She laughed. "Richarte, King Louis will protect his men. You'll send the infidels—"

"No!" Richarte's bellow was loud in the afternoon stillness. His own vehemence startled him. The sorcerer wiped a forearm across his sweat-dampened forehead, crushing back the banged hair. His gaze skittered around Jeanne's frightened eyes. "No," he repeated softly. "I've not taken the cross. I simply ... have to leave Troyes. I have no choice."

"You said you loved me." Quiet accusation—her voice was

full of a crystalline fragility.

"That wasn't supposed to happen," he said, more to himself than to Jeanne. "I wasn't to be involved with anyone here, but somehow friends happened: you, Rutebeuf . . . I'm sorry."

She nodded, too calmly. Richarte moved as if to embrace her, but stopped when he saw her expression. She stared at him with a curious antipathy, a sudden reserve that made him halt in mid-stride.

"My father had wanted me to ask you to dinner tomorrow. Some of those who have taken the cross will be leaving Troyes to join Louis in a few days. The Baron de Nogent will be there, and his constable d'Orabis asked of you." Her voice was stripped of emotion, flat and colorless. It made Richarte duck his head in pain, caused him to reach out a hand in sympathy.

"Jeanne," he began.

Her eyes stabbed the proffered hand. She waited as he slowly pulled his arm back and shifted his weight uncomfortably. "Will you be there?" she asked.

"Do you want me there?"

She lifted her chin. "It's not my concern. My *father* is the host, and he may invite whom he will. *He* would like you to come." Her stance was a challenge—one arm on her hip, her weight canted to her right foot, her gaze unblinking on his face. Richarte didn't know whether to accept or refuse, didn't know how to ease that accusation.

"I'll be there." He didn't know if that was the answer she desired. He only knew it might give him a chance to atone.

Jeanne nodded, her face carefully stoic. She glanced around the room once more, as if taking it in for a final time. Then, with an abrupt nod of her head, she turned and strode quickly away before Richarte could move or speak. The door to the outer room opened and closed.

With its soft thud, the room seemed suddenly more hot and oppressive.

Richarte was writing. His quill scratched across parchment, a rasp that was loud in the night stillness. Light from a candle set in its polished reflector threw a yellow diagonal across the paper.

"THE TALE OF KING JORDIM AND THE KNAVE CHI-TARIER:

"King Jordim was not loved by his subjects. He had taken

the power he held by cruel strength and he maintained his hold with brutal reprisals against those that opposed him. His kingdom was one of greatness unparalleled in history—his magicians were capable of sorceries beyond any dreamed in earlier times, his coffers overflowed with the bounty of a rich and fertile world, the entire known world bowed to his sceptre. Yet he kept a heavy hand on the throats of his people. 'For thy own good' was his answer to any questions raised by his timorous councilors.

"It was a lie. Jordim's tactics benefited his own self first. Always.

"King Jordim had in his Keep a hall of magnificent proportions. This immense corridor ran the entire length of the huge palace; it took some hours to walk. On the arras of this hall, Jordim had made a tapestry that depicted the full history of his kingdom through the past centuries, designed with an eye to the interplay of people, events, and their balance. The tapestry—crafted with great detail—held all important events of the past through to Jordim's reign. And it was not yet finished, for Jordim kept his master weaver, Kyim, at his task, adding each day to the tapestry so that it always reflected the current state.

"The Weaver Kyim is important to the tale. He was a minor sorcerer himself, not greatly gifted in talent, but one who had channeled his gifts: all his study had gone into weaving. While the most common sorcerer could out-conjure Kyim in the art of levitation and in causing dairy cows to deliver sour milk, in weaving Kyim had no peer. It was gossiped that King Jordim's fortunes were connected with the tapestry; by affecting the events of the tapestry, one could alter the King's fate. Such gossip gave birth to much talk and speculation concerning the manner in which Kyim had woven his masterwork. The Guild of Mages buzzed with theory. Some contended that the tapestry was woven so delicately that to snip one small thread from its beginning would cause ever-widening changes through the later work, a rippling of chaos that would alter the very face of the tapestry. Others believed that the threads were so dense and complicated that nothing could totally destroy the fabric—even if an early event could be altered (and there was no surety that it could), snipping that early threadwork would do nothing to the events depicted at the far end where Kyim still labored. Still others insisted that Kyim had extended his work into the

ethereal planes and that there existed an infinite multitude of
tapestries; to damage the Keep Tapestry would affect only one
of those copies—it would be nearly impossible to alter the
events of the work in Jordim's palace.

"But some of the sorcerers felt that an attempt must be
made. No, they could not predict results, but an experiment
could be made, a very small alteration on a small event.

"There was also a common knave, whose sympathies lay
with the rebel mages. His name was Chitarier..."

Richarte let the quill fall from his fingers, tracking ink across
the parchment. It wouldn't work, he thought dolefully. The
attempt was as clumsy as all the others. All the ways to explain
to Jeanne and Rutebeuf, to apologize: it still didn't seem real,
didn't seem right—allegory was no better than truth. He'd
been here too long. Troyes was now more real than shadowed
memory, dreams. If they'd been more precise in placing
him...

It was the night of Jeanne's supper. He knew now that he
wouldn't go. Not with the Baron and his suspicious constable
there. Not with the silent accusations he'd see in Jeanne's face.

It was far easier to sit in his room and watch the candle's
light shudder against the desk.

Torches flared in the satin night, guttering noisily and throwing mad shadows on the houses bordering the Porte de Paris.
The men and horses gathering there were lit fitfully—a flashing
of burnished helms, a fluttering gonfalon with a rampant
dragon, the glinting of fine-meshed mail. The noise of horses,
riders, and iron echoed through slumbering Troyes: low talk,
the blowing of nervous steeds, the jingle of bridle and bit.

The Baron de Nogent and his retinue prepared to ride to join
King Louis.

"You see, Benoit? All your nightmares came to naught. No
arcane sorcery, no treachery; simply an enjoyable time watching tumblers and jongleurs and pursuing the tavern wenches.
We'll have joined the King tomorrow or the next day, and
we'll be in Aigues-Morte within a fortnight." The deep baritone
of de Nogent carried well in the night stillness.

D'Orabis, riding beside him, shook his head once, smiling.
"Begging your lordship's pardon—it was evidently some silly
premonition. Though that evening when Faucher fell asleep at
his post..."

"You found nothing when you searched the house."

Benoit shifted his weight in the saddle. "Nothing. I apologize again, and did Faucher give you sufficient saddle blankets this time?"

"Yes. I think I can stand this night's ride." The Baron laughed, deep and rich despite his years. He sat forward in his saddle, the leather creaking. "Ho, watchman! Open yon gates!"

In the torchlight, a man could be seen coming sleepily from the gatehouse door, a knuckle rubbing sleep-rimmed eyes. "Who bellows at this hour of night?" he said, petulantly.

"The Baron de Nogent desires to rejoin his King," called Benoit. "Move yourself, man. The Saracens await. If you won't take the cross yourself, at least don't hinder good Christians from pursuing their own honor."

The man looked up, startled, then bowed to the riders. "Begging your pardons, good sires. A moment, a moment." He stumbled back into the tower and in a few moments they could hear the drawbridge being lowered over the dry moat. The iron gates were thrown open, and the Baron and his knights began to ride forward.

And at the same moment: from the long shadow of the Viscount's Tower to the rider's left, a cowled figure ran, a long cloak trailing behind. He shouted, and the Baron reined in his horse, watching the figure approach. Benoit leaned toward the Baron, his hand lightly on the hilt of his sword. "Baron—" he began.

At that instant, the apparition stopped and flung something toward the Baron. There was immediate reaction—Benoit moved to urge his mount forward, but one of the other knights was quicker; sword drawn, the man rode in front of the Baron, striking the thrown object with the flat of his sword.

An explosion of orange fury thundered like a thousand storms against the walls of the city. Men and horses alike screamed in agony, throwing their hands up against the searing light and concussion. The Baron and d'Orabis were thrown from their chargers. Seeing the Baron move, Benoit struggled to his feet and aided his Lord to his feet, shouting.

"Bring a torch! You—Guibert, Renard—bring that man here!" He gestured to the Viscount's Tower, where a figure could be seen standing as if in disbelief, making no effort to flee.

For the man who had ridden to shield the Baron, it was too

late. The Baron and d'Orabis could see that without a torch. The constable breathed shakily—he had never seen death so violent before. He sketched the sign of the cross over the mangled and torn body.

Near the Tower, the intruder had been seized and roughly bound. He was brought forward, one large fist in his hair. Benoit thrust a torch at the man's face.

"I know him, Baron. I saw him when we first entered Troyes, though I didn't know his name then. It is the Sorcerer Richarte." D'Orabis struck the sorcerer with a mailed fist. Blood ran from the mouth of the dazed man.

The Baron held back his constable as he brought his arm back for another blow. "Nay, Benoit. Let the Provost deal with him. We must not delay ourselves much longer." Then, to Richarte: "May God have mercy on your soul, man. That was a coward's blow, and my knight's spirit will testify against you." The Baron turned away. Around the courtyard, men tended their mounts and checked equipment. The curious awakened by the quick storm began to gather.

Richarte licked blood from his torn mouth. He stared at the hostile face of d'Orabis. "It didn't matter," he said. "I could not have harmed him."

D'Orabis stared at the sorcerer with narrowed eyes. He spat at Richarte's feet. "Take him away from me," he said.

As the sorcerer was roughly hauled toward the growing crowd, d'Orabis called out to Richarte once more. "You will suffer more than him, sorcerer. Remember that as they burn you."

Jeanne came to his cell the next day, in company with Dame Blanche. The older woman scowled at the damp stones of the donjon and stood to one side, radiating her distaste for the environment.

Jeanne stared at Richard through the barred window. His face was puffed and bruised, discolored; a tracery of dried blood ran from nose and mouth into the matted beard. His hair was dark with sweat and tangled. Chains held his hands close to the wall, tethered by iron bands. The cell stank of human waste and damp straw.

"Why, Richarte?"

She spoke softly; he looked up, his eyes widening with surprise as he saw the face at the window, ruddy with torchlight.

His swollen lips moved as if undecided between smile and frown, but his eyes were moist.

"Jeanne, you shouldn't have come. Your father..."

"He doesn't need to know as yet. Richarte, listen to me: you once told me that your sorcery wasn't malevolent, that you believed in God and his commands. I believed you then; I *still* want to believe you. Yet you tried to slay the Baron, a good and innocent man." Her voice trembled, and she shook her head, regaining control. "Tell me why, Richarte," she said, more steadily. "Make me believe again."

"My lady, you couldn't trust me, not after all I've done to you." He bowed his head, he would not look at her.

"Do you tell me now that it was all a lie—all the words of affection, all that we shared?"

"Don't say that." Her mute, angered confusion brought his head up. His eyes reflected an inner pain. "I meant those words. All of them."

"And the Baron?"

"I tried a hundred times to explain to you. I could never find the words. Remember, I spoke of a commitment I had to fulfill."

"Such as this?" She laughed, a short bark devoid of amusement. "You can't expect my understanding of that, Richarte; that you were just performing a humble duty. Given the choices, I find it easier to believe that you've been ensnared by some demon conjured up by your rites. You never indicated to me that you even knew the Baron."

Richarte struggled to sit up, to stand: the fetters held him back. He coughed, deep and liquid, consumptive. "Believe me, my love—"

Her eyes were suddenly bright with tears. She shook her head. "Don't presume so much on our affection, Richarte. I don't know what I feel for you at the moment."

Richarte sank back onto the stone flags of his cell. He brought his hands up in supplication, the chains clanking dully. "Jeanne, men are killed every day. Your precious Louis is going to kill more than I ever could—some will be your countrymen. Baron de Nogent will not make Aigues-Morte, will die in Champagne: I know that. And his early death might have done more good. I wouldn't have attempted this if I hadn't believed that."

"His early death would have meant that he would have died

without a chance to face his enemy with sword in hand, slain by . . ." Her voice broke off and she turned away from him. He could not see her, but her words came from the darkness beyond his cell. ". . . slain by a man that would give the Baron's death no honor, striking from a distance. And no one but the Deity knows when a man is to die."

He said nothing. There were no words for his feelings.

Jeanne peered through the bars once more. Her face was settled now, somewhat hardened, though the eyes were moist and the damp trail of her pain fell from the corner of one eye down her cheek. "It doesn't matter what you've done or why. I can get you released, Richarte. I'll tell my father that you were a foreign soldier—"

"Jeanne . . ."

She would not listen to him. Her eyes widened, willing him to be silent, as if by talking she could convince him. ". . . and that you were simply doing your duty, as you say. The Provost would understand that, I know. They'll hold you for a proper ransom, and when it's paid . . ."

"There can be no ransom."

"Surely your lord cares for you. He would pay."

"I won't die here." His voice was very soft. "And your father would disown you."

"He would be angry for a while . . ."

"Jeanne, I appreciate what your offer means. I can't let you do it." Despite himself, he smiled.

"At least you would live, Richarte. Our . . . *relationship* would have to end, but you'd live."

He shook his head. "No, they told me that I wouldn't die here."

"More sorcery?" She bit her lip, looking away for a moment. "I've shrived myself with my confessor and promised to do penance for my sins, Richarte." She swallowed, hard—in the quiet of the prison, he could hear it. "Sometimes you must renounce what you don't wish to give up. You should do the same before your soul meets the Creator."

"Jeanne, believe me once more. If I thought I might be able to stay here, to see you—I'd do anything. But I can't."

"Or won't."

"It would not make any difference."

She did not reply. Richarte heard the rustling of cloth as Jeanne turned to leave. He spoke quietly then, as darkness filled the cell's window. "Lady Jeanne, I never once lied to you about love, about my feelings for you."

From the emptiness beyond the door, he heard her reply, faint among the stones. "I want to believe that, Richarte. I truly do."

Silence. He thought she had gone until he heard her voice again.

"I will pray for you, Richarte, and I'll remember. If you change your mind, if there's something you want me to do . . . I'll send Dame Blanche here tomorrow. Tell her."

And she left him.

"M'mselle Jeanne!"

The shout came from behind her, down the crowded stretch of the Rue de Croisettes. Jeanne turned to see Rutebeuf, waving at her from beneath the gilded spheres of an apothecary. She waited, bracing a basket of bread rolls against her waist with one arm, as he wove his passage toward her through the maze of shoppers and street vendors.

Rutebeuf grinned, slightly out of breath, nodding his head in salutation and rubbing his stubbled chin with one hand. "A good morn to you, m'lady. I thought it might be you—no other woman in Troyes has your graceful walk."

Not wanting to, still she could not hold back her smile—Rutebeuf's foolish manner momentarily pierced her moodiness. The poet glanced at the slate-grey clouds massing above the shops. "Ah, small wonder that the sun chooses to cloak himself rather than be shamed by Lady Jeanne's smile," he said with far too much emphasis. He clapped his fist against his forehead in mock wonderment.

"Do you wish to become a jester to entertain the fairgoers, poet? Or have you found the Stallion already open this morning?" The smile held for a moment, then wavered and died.

"If nothing else, it's a poor day for a fire."

Jeanne drew back as if slapped. The hand on the basket clenched harder, the knuckles white. "That's in poor taste. Richarte is your friend, and I—you know my feelings for him."

The gaiety did not leave him. He grinned back at her, gap-toothed. "My pardon. I was just musing—you've evidently not heard the news I bear." Rutebeuf rubbed his hands together, gleefully. "Then I may bring yet another smile back to your face."

"Indeed?" She stood poised between anger and curiosity.

"Indeed," he answered. He shifted his weight from one leg to another as the noisy crowds flowed around them, bright with multi-hued clothing, loud with the calls of vendors. "It seems that there was an odd occurrence in the crypt under the Count's castle last night—there is gossip of witchcraft and sorcery." Rutebeuf shook his head, coyly gazing at the people walking past them. "I, of course, condemn all such doings as any good Christian—"

"Rutebeuf," Jeanne said dangerously.

He raised his eyebrows, but he stopped, lowering his voice and inclining closer toward her. "I was talking—well, drinking—with one of the Sergeants of the Fair." He plucked a roll of bread from her basket, taking a quick bite. "He told me"— he chewed and swallowed—"a tale of a strange disappearance in the night, of a chain-locked prisoner gone from his cell, of manacles still fastened in place and holding only air. There are stories of a strange light being seen during the night, and a wailing sound like the keening of a lost soul. All very peculiar—and the Provost is most upset, for there is now no one to burn at his pile of sticks."

"Richarte? Is that what you're saying, Rutebeuf? Richarte is gone?" Jeanne's voice was hurried, pitched high. Her eyes burned him.

Rutebeuf stepped back from the intensity of her stare. A tentative smile. A shrug. "So it would seem."

Emotions warred on her face, passing like the shadows of quick-moving clouds. She started to speak, stopped, and glanced at the spire of St. Jean, just visible beyond the gables of the houses, grey stone set against a wan and colorless sky. She seemed to relax suddenly, as if some inner tension had broken; she seemed to relax, to let her shoulders slump imperceptibly. "That's it, then." Her voice was very distant.

Eyebrows sought new heights on Rutebeuf's forehead. "You say no more than that? I thought you'd be pleased..."

Jeanne shook her head as if ridding herself of an unpleasant thought. She smiled at Rutebeuf. "I loved him, you know. I was always afraid that his experiments would lead him into devilry and demonic vices, and it didn't bother me that what he did was against God. No, I was afraid for *him*." She glanced at Rutebeuf, still holding the remainder of the bread roll, and transferred the basket to her other hip. "I wish I could understand him, Rutebeuf. I wish he could have explained." She glanced away from him, staring down the length of the street to where the first stalls of the Fair stood, deluged with townspeople and visitors. Her face averted, she spoke to the poet. "I wonder what they'll say of him?"

"I don't care what is said, m'mselle. He was a good man, a fair man: I know that. I liked him, and I refuse to be shamed by those feelings. Nor should you be. If he did wrong, I believe it to be unintentional, or something he could not prevent. I'm sure of that."

Jeanne gazed at the shopfronts, not looking back at Rutebeuf. When the silence had stretched for a minute, the poet began to walk away, back down the Rue de Croisettes toward the Rue de l'Épicerie.

"Rutebeuf," Jeanne called. "Thank you for your tale."

He glanced back, but she was not looking at him. "Good day, m'mselle." Taking a bite of the bread, he strode away.

The crowds moving to the nexus of the Fair eased around her like a river skirting a boulder unmoving in midstream. To her unfixed gaze, they were a blur of shouting color. The warm breeze of summer wafted the folds of her surcoat. The air was heavy with the promise of rain to come. "I believe you, love," she murmured, a soft whisper only she could hear. "I'll pray for you."

She pulled herself from her reverie with a start. She shifted the weight of the basket once more, ran the sleeve of her blouse across her eyes.

A lopsided smile on her face, she moved toward the sounds of gaiety that marked the Fair.

BIOGRAPHICAL NOTES

GREGORY BENFORD received his Ph.D. in theoretical physics from the University of California in 1967, and is now Professor of Physics at Irvine. He has published over sixty scientific papers and has an impressive string of professional credits. He is also an extremely successful science fiction writer, having won the Nebula Award in 1975 for a work of short fiction, and again in 1981 for his novel, TIMESCAPE. He is the author of five other novels as well as dozens of short stories. He lives with his wife in Laguna Beach, California.

DAVID BISCHOFF wants to write serious science fiction. He also wishes to write less-than-totally-serious science fiction. He has written many novels to date, including NIGHT-WORLD, TIN WOODMAN (with Dennis Bailey), and STAR FALL and its sequel, STAR SPRING. His most recent book is a collaboration with Charles Sheffield, THE SELKIE, a horror/suspense novel. In another collaboration, Bischoff and Tom Monteleone have created DRAGONSTAR, which was serialized in *Analog*. A *Doctor Who* fan, he currently lives in Arlington, Virginia.

MIKE CONNER is the author of I AM NOT THE OTHER HOUDINI and has had stories published in *Orbit, New Dimensions* and *The Magazine of Fantasy and Science Fiction*. He lives with his wife and children in northern California.

RONALD ANTHONY CROSS has sold stories to *Orbit, Future Pastimes, New Worlds, Other Worlds* and *The Berkley Showcase*. He writes music and is a practicing lacto-vegetarian. He believes that the real facts of his life are to be found in his stories. He lives in Santa Monica, California, with his wife and son.

GEORGE ALEC EFFINGER is the author of six science fiction novels, the most recent being THE WOLVES OF MEMORY. Others include WHAT ENTROPY MEANS TO ME and HEROICS. He has also written scores of short stories that have appeared in all the major anthologies and magazines. He is considered a knowledgeable, witty master of the sly tone and unusual subject matter. He loves baseball, and lives in New Orleans.

FREFF is redheaded by choice, a Japanese food freak, and the product of an eclectic experiential education (including the Ringling Brothers Clown College and press passes to four space launches and a recovery cruise). His talents lie in writing, art, performing, music and self-deprecation. Along with his wife, Amelia Sefton, several cats, about fifty musical instruments, an Apple II computer, and other beings, he resides in the Frog Palace in Brooklyn, New York. His most recent band is Weird Load, his most recent comedy group Zen Vaudeville.

KARL HANSEN recently finished a stint with the Indian Health Service in Colorado. His short fiction has appeared in CHRYSALIS and OTHER WORLDS. His first novel, WAR GAMES, was released last year, with a sequel to follow, and he's sold *The Hybrid Trilogy*, which is in progress. His other interests include motorcycles and his family.

STEPHEN LEIGH has, like many writers, held a number of jobs, such as camera salesman, art teacher, waiter, and rock vocalist. Since 1976 or so he's been writing and selling science fiction, notably to *Analog, Isaac Asimov's Science Fiction Magazine*, and Bantam Books, which has published his first two novels, SLOW FALL TO DAWN and DANCE OF THE HAG. Recently he has been appearing at science fiction conventions as half of the juggling team "Cosmos and Chaos." He lives in Cincinnati, Ohio, with his wife, Denise Parsley.

KEVIN O'DONNELL, Jr. is the author of WAR OF OMISSION, MAYFLIES and the so-far three-book series, THE JOURNEYS OF McGILL FEIGHAN: CAVERNS, REEFS and LAVA. His stories have appeared in all the magazines from *Analog* to *Omni*. He is the publisher of EMPIRE: *For the SF Writer*, a little magazine aimed at anyone interested in writing, editing or publishing SF (for information: P.O. Box 967, New Haven, CT 06504). He and his wife live in Connecticut.

JESSICA AMANDA SALMONSON has had three novels published within the past year: THE TOMOE GOZEN SAGA, THE GOLDEN NAGINATA and THE SWORDSWOMAN. She is also the editor of the acclaimed anthology AMAZONS, with AMAZONS II and HEROIC VISIONS in the works. She is a samurai film buff, a student of swordplay and a vegetarian. She describes herself, with some surprise, as a woman who finds "bus fumes and city violence much more fun than the unsophisticated world outside the city limits." And so, she will be moving back into Seattle, Washington, from the suburbs as soon as she can.

LOIS WICKSTROM is the founder and editor of *Pandora*, a small press magazine. She and her husband and two daughters live in Tampa, Florida, where she is a Poet in the Schools.

Most of her published work to date has been non-fiction, which she has sold to *Mother Earth News, OMNI, Christian Science Monitor*, and gobs of other places. In addition, she has written the FOOD CONSPIRACY COOKBOOK and two children's picture books.